01

*

WITHDRAWN

Lost
and
Found

*Also by Jayne Ann Krentz
in Large Print:*

Eclipse Bay
Grand Passion
Wildest Hearts
Family Man
Perfect Partners
Sweet Fortune
The Adventurer
A Coral Kiss
Midnight Jewels
Shield's Lady
Crystal Flame
Sweet Starfire
Witchcraft

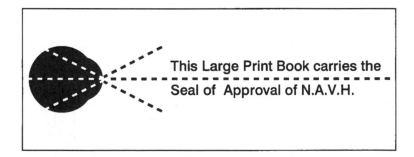

This Large Print Book carries the
Seal of Approval of N.A.V.H.

Jayne Ann Krentz

Lost
and
Found

Thorndike Press • Thorndike, Maine

Copyright © 2001 by Jayne Ann Krentz.

Published in 2001 by arrangement with G.P. Putnam's Sons, a member of Penguin Putnam, Inc.

Thorndike Press Large Print Basic Series.

The tree indicium is a trademark of Thorndike Press.

The text of this Large Print edition is unabridged.
Other aspects of the book may vary from the original edition.

Set in 16 pt. Plantin by Christina S. Huff.

Printed in the United States on permanent paper.

Library of Congress Cataloging-in-Publication Data

Krentz, Jayne Ann.
    Lost and found / Jayne Ann Krentz.
      p. cm.
    ISBN 0-7862-3099-1 (lg. print : hc : alk. paper)
    ISBN 0-7862-3100-9 (lg. print : sc : alk. paper)
  1. Art consultants — Fiction. 2. Art galleries,
    Commercial — Fiction. 3. Family-owned business
    enterprises — Fiction. 4. Large type books. I. Title.
  PS3561.R44 L6   2001b
    813'.54—dc21   00-051211

To Leslie Gelbman

What a joy it is to work with an
editor who shares a vision.

1

"It is never wise to become emotionally involved with a client," Vesta Briggs said.

"I'm not involved with Mack Easton." Cady cradled the phone against her shoulder and tugged off first one high heel and then the other. "Not in the way you mean. I'm just consulting for him. I thought I made that clear."

There was a short, terse silence on the other end of the line. Cady sighed silently and sank down onto the sofa. The phone had been ringing a moment ago when she had come through the door. She had lunged for it on the off chance that it was Fantasy Man.

It had not been Mack Easton. It had been her great-aunt.

"There's something in your voice when you talk about him," Vesta said. Icicles of disapproval hung on each word. "I get the impression that you are interested in him in a personal way."

"He's just a voice on the phone."

But what a voice. Every time she heard it,

7

a thrill of awareness zinged through each nerve ending. Her vivid imagination did the rest, conjuring blatantly erotic fantasies out of thin air.

It was a voice that had begun to whisper in her dreams but she saw no reason to mention that to her rigid great-aunt. Vesta Briggs was not a romantic.

Cady slipped off one silver earring and set it down on the glass-topped coffee table. Probably not a good idea to tell Vesta that in addition to being a voice on the phone, Easton had also become a frequent e-mail correspondent, she thought. He seemed to enjoy locating arcane bits and pieces of information relating to the art world on-line and forwarding them on to her. Lately, she could have sworn that he had begun to flirt with her via computer.

She saved all of his on-line correspondence in a special folder labeled "Fantasy Man." She had gotten into the habit of checking her computer first thing each morning to see if he had paid her an on-line visit during the night. She didn't want to use the word "obsessive" to describe her new routine, but she was aware that some people might view it as a tad compulsive.

Of course, if there was anyone who would understand obsession, it was Vesta, she thought. She glanced at the row of family photographs arranged on one wall. Her gaze fell on the woman with dark hair and enigmatic eyes. It had been taken some fifty years ago when her great-aunt was in her thirties, shortly after she had founded Gallery Chatelaine. There was a withdrawn, remote quality about the image. Vesta looked as if she was listening to a conversation that only she could hear, one that had taken place in the distant past.

As far as anyone knew, the only thing Vesta had ever cared about was Chatelaine's. There had been no room in her life for love or marriage or children. For five decades she had single-handedly controlled the fate of the business she had created. With unflinching determination, skill and vision she had brought her gallery to its current respected position in the art world. But her lifelong preference for privacy could no longer conceal her growing eccentricities.

A lot of people were convinced that Cady took after Vesta. Lately Cady had begun to worry about that possibility herself.

It was true that, in spite of Vesta's austere personality, she had always felt a deep attachment to her. It wasn't just because her great-aunt had taught her everything she knew about the art and antiques business.

The feeling of unspoken understanding between the two women went deeper. Even as a child Cady had sensed some deep, long-buried pain beneath the layers of protective frost that Vesta wore like an invisible shroud.

"Easton is a good client," Cady said, trying hard to inject reassurance into her words. "What's more, I'm really enjoying this end of the business."

"Tracing lost and stolen art and antiques?" Vesta paused. "I can see why that might appeal to you. You always were more adventurous than Sylvia."

"Which is why Sylvia makes a much better CEO for Gallery Chatelaine than I ever could," Cady said quickly. "She thrives on that corporate stuff."

"And you don't." Vesta sounded resigned.

"No." Cady settled deeper into the sofa. "I'm happy with my little art consulting business. I wasn't cut out to run a large operation like Chatelaine's. We both know that."

"You may change your mind someday."

"No." This was old territory. It had been well covered after Cady's divorce three years ago.

There was more silence on the line.

"Be careful," Vesta said after a while.

"Don't allow yourself to be seduced by this new client of yours."

"*Seduced?*" Cady repeated in a strangled voice, unable to believe what she had heard. Vesta never discussed sex. "I told you, I haven't even met him."

"There is often a great deal of money at stake when it comes to art. You know that as well as I do. A man who requires your expertise to get his hands on that cash cannot be trusted. It sounds like your Mr. Easton finds you useful."

"That's the whole point of my art consulting business. To make myself useful."

"It's all well and good for a client to find you useful. But don't let yourself be used. There's a difference."

"Good grief, Aunt Vesta, it's not like I'm having a red-hot affair with the man." *Unfortunately,* she added to herself.

"Yes, well, that's enough on the subject of Mack Easton. I didn't call just to discuss him," Vesta said.

"Good."

"I also wanted you to know that I'm having second thoughts about the wisdom of a merger with Austrey-Post."

Deeply relieved by the change of topic, Cady swung her legs up onto the sofa and leaned back in the corner. "Sylvia told me

11

that you had mentioned you might postpone the vote on the proposal."

"I haven't made a final decision yet but I will soon." Vesta paused. "I just thought you should know."

"I'm no longer a member of the board," Cady reminded her. "I won't be voting."

"I'm aware of that. Nevertheless, I think you should stay informed."

"Sylvia is not a happy camper," Cady said carefully.

"I know. She wants the merger to go through."

"She's got a vision for the gallery, Aunt Vesta."

"Yes."

"It's a great vision, one that will make Gallery Chatelaine even more important in the art world than it is already."

"Yes."

There was something in Vesta's voice that told Cady there was more to the story, but she knew her aunt well enough to know that there was no point pushing for an explanation. Besides, this was Sylvia's problem.

"Did you go out tonight?" Vesta asked.

Another change of subject. Interesting.

"I went to the preview of the Kenner collection," Cady said.

"Oh, yes, that's right. I remember that you

12

mentioned it. I expect that it was well attended. The sharks of the art world have been circling for years, waiting for Anna Kenner to expire. Her collection of eighteenth- and nineteenth-century decorative arts is one of the finest in the country."

"Well, the good news is that Mrs. Kenner managed to outlive several of the sharks. She was ninety-seven when she died."

"Good for her. I always did like Anna. She bought some of her best pieces from me several years ago."

"Yes, I know. She hired me to consult after I moved here to Santa Barbara. I liked her."

Tonight Anna Kenner's Santa Barbara mansion had been filled with scavengers dressed in formal attire. They had come to view the lady's personal possessions in preparation for tomorrow night's auction. Anna's heirs had little interest in the lovely English porcelains, Georgian silver, Chinoiserie panels and exquisite furniture she had accumulated in her lifetime. They were anxious to convert her worldly goods into cash as quickly and profitably as possible. The denizens of the art world had been equally eager to help them accomplish that goal.

Cady had spent most of the evening standing in an alcove, an untouched flute of champagne in one hand. She had watched the dealers, consultants, museum curators and private collectors prowl through the fine rooms. People had paused here and there to examine carefully arranged groupings of art and antiques and to make inquiries about provenance and value. The auction house representatives, also garbed in somber black and white, had stood discreetly nearby to supply answers and advice.

It had all been very civilized and quite elegant with a proper air of hushed solemnity, Cady thought; but she could not suppress the sense of melancholia that swirled up out of the depths. She ought to know better. The ritual was a familiar one. She had grown up in the art world. She was well aware that there was little place for sentiment when it came to the business of auctioning off a valuable collection.

But tonight the process of preparing for what was essentially a high-end garage sale had been tinged with sadness. She had a right to brood, she thought. Anna Kenner had been more than a client. She had become a friend.

"The good news is that Anna was wined and dined in style during the last few years," Cady said. "I think she rather enjoyed it."

"I certainly hope so," Vesta said dryly. "I doubt if there was any expense spared to secure that consignment."

"None. The big auction houses sent people out from New York. The locals also spent a fortune on her. She told me that the courtship began while she was still in her early eighties. Who could know she would live so long?"

Like other wealthy collectors in her position, Anna Kenner had received the royal treatment from dealers, consultants and curators during the last years of her life. Her birthdays had been celebrated with elaborate floral arrangements from auction houses. Her evenings had been filled with invitations to lavish gallery openings and museum receptions. As she had once told Cady, her dance card was always full.

It was ambulance chasing with class, Cady thought, but it was, nevertheless, ambulance chasing.

"Well, it's getting late," Vesta said. "I'm going to take my swim and then go to bed. Good night, Cady."

There was something not quite right here, Cady thought. This was not a typical Vesta phone call.

"Aunt Vesta?"

"Yes?"

"Is anything wrong?"

"What makes you think there's something

15

wrong?" Vesta asked crisply.

Cady winced. "It's not like you to call without a very specific reason."

"I explained my reasons for calling. I wanted to warn you about getting too cozy with Easton and to let you know that I was reconsidering the merger."

"I see."

Mack Easton and the merger didn't seem to warrant a late-night phone call, Cady thought. But with Vesta you could never be sure of what was going on beneath the surface. She wondered if her aunt was simply lonely.

"Aunt Vesta?"

"What is it now?"

"I love you."

There was a short, startled pause on the other end of the line. Cady braced herself. Vesta was not given to sentiment.

"I love you too, Cady," Vesta said. The words sounded stiff and rusty as if she'd dredged them up from deep underground.

Cady was so stunned she nearly fell off the sofa.

"We are so much alike, you and I," Vesta continued. "But I hope things will turn out differently for you."

Cady tried to collect her thoughts. "Differently?"

"I hope you will be happy," Vesta said with stark simplicity. "Good night, Cady."

The line went dead.

Cady sat with the phone in her hand until it started to make strange sounds. She hung up the receiver, got to her feet, collected her shoes and went slowly down the hall to her bedroom. There she unzipped the subdued, cowl-necked dress she had worn to the preview. She pulled on a pair of black tights and a leotard and went barefooted down the hall into the living room. She switched on some Mozart and stood quietly for a moment.

When she was ready she went slowly through the yoga exercises that she had practiced faithfully since college. It had been suggested by more than one acquaintance that she was a little obsessive about her daily workout. But she was convinced that it was the flowing, stretching movements combined with the deep-breathing techniques that allowed her to control her body's predisposition toward panic attacks.

A predisposition she had inherited from Vesta's side of the family.

She was careful about her routine, but just to be on the safe side, she kept a tiny pill wrapped in tissue inside the small case attached to her key ring. She had not had to resort to the little tablet in years, but there was a certain sense of security in knowing that it was available if she ever got over-whelmed by the terrible jitters. She thought about it during that significant pause that occurs between the closing of an elevator's doors and the first movement of the cab. She visualized it whenever she found herself sitting in an airplane that had been delayed on the ground for an extended period of time. Most of all, she contemplated it when-ever someone tried to coax her into going swimming in a lake or the ocean or any other body of water where she could not see beneath the surface.

The problem with panic attacks was just one more trait that she shared with Vesta, she thought as she curved into a slow, arching movement that released the tension in her shoulder. She had heard the comments for years. *You're just like your aunt. . . . You take after your aunt. . . . You have your aunt's eye for art and antiques.* But she and Vesta were at opposite poles when it came to the subject of deep water.

To the best of Cady's knowledge, her eighty-six-year-old aunt had swum almost every day of her adult life. Vesta loved the water. She'd had a large pool installed on the terrace of her home near Sausalito in Marin County, California. She was especially fond of swimming alone at night in the dark.

It occurred to Cady that she was as compulsive about her yoga as Vesta was about her nightly swim.

Something else they had in common.

Sometimes she wanted to scream in frustration. But there was no denying that the comparisons between herself and her aunt were growing more acute as each year passed. The parallels were getting a little scary. After her infamous nine-day marriage blew up in her face, she'd heard murmurs to the effect that she had also inherited Vesta's inability to deal with the male of the species. The words "You're going to end up just like Aunt Vesta" had taken on new meaning during the past three years.

Lately even her parents, usually serenely absorbed in their academic careers, had started to become concerned. After the divorce they had developed an irritating habit of making polite but increasingly pointed inquiries into Cady's social life.

She unfolded herself from the last exercise and sat cross-legged, gazing out into the night. The strains of a concerto spilled over her and through her, veiling the shadowy spaces that she knew from long experience were better off left unexplored.

Genetic inheritances were tough, but nature wasn't everything, she reminded herself. Self-determination played a role, too. She was not a Vesta Briggs clone. If she worked hard, she could avoid developing Vesta's less appealing characteristics. She would not become a self-absorbed loner who surrounded herself with the visible evidence of the past.

Damn, she was still brooding, in spite of the Mozart and yoga. Maybe a frozen pizza and a glass of wine would do the trick.

What she really needed tonight was a distraction, she thought. Preferably another one of the fascinating, out-of-the-ordinary consulting assignments she had started accepting from Fantasy Man. There had been three jobs in the past two months, each one more interesting and more intriguing than the last.

Mack Easton had tracked her down via the internet. The only thing she knew for certain about him was that he operated a very low-profile on-line business he called Lost and Found. Driven by curiosity, she had tried to research him and his business on-line but the usual search engines had come up empty-handed. You didn't find Mack Easton, apparently. He found you.

Easton brokered information related to

lost, strayed and stolen art. As far as she could discern, his clients included a wide variety of private collectors, museums and galleries. They all had two things in common: They wanted help tracing and recovering art, antiques or antiquities; and, for various reasons, they did not want to take their problems to the police.

Easton worked by referral only. In his initial phone call, he had explained that he frequently required consulting assistance from experts who had specialized knowledge. That was where Cady came in. She knew the world of the so-called decorative arts, the realm where exquisite design and functionality intersected. She loved the objects and artifacts of the past that had been crafted with an eye toward both beauty and practicality: Glorious Baroque salt cellars, gleaming seventeenth-century inkwells created by master silversmiths, glowing French tapestries, brilliantly illustrated wall panels and handmade furniture — those were the things that called to her across the centuries. Purists could have their fine art, their paintings and sculpture and the like. She was drawn to art that had been shaped to a useful purpose, art that satisfied the needs of daily life as well as the senses.

She closed her eyes and summoned up

the mental image she had constructed to go with Easton's voice. As always, the picture refused to gel. Probably because no man could live up to that fantastic voice, she thought.

"It's all well and good for a client to find you useful. But don't let yourself be used."

If she hadn't known better, Cady thought, she would have suspected that her aunt was speaking from personal experience. But that was impossible. No one used Aunt Vesta.

The phone rang, jarring her out of her reverie. She hesitated briefly and then uncoiled to her feet and crossed the crimson carpet. She paused, her hand hovering over the instrument, and listened to the second and third ring.

Her parents were in England at the moment, doing research for their next papers in art history. But the fact that they were several thousand miles away did not mean that they weren't calling to ask about her boring love life.

She really did not need that conversation tonight. Not after Vesta's call.

The phone rang a fourth time. She could let it go into voice mail.

But what if it was Fantasy Man?

The odds were staggeringly not in favor of that possibility, but the slim chance that it was Easton calling with another consulting assignment was sufficient incentive to make her scoop up the phone.

"Hello?"

"What do you know about sixteenth-century armor?" Fantasy Man asked.

Oh, boy. The voice cued every nerve ending in her body. *Get a grip, woman. He's probably married. Voices like this one do not stay single for long.*

Or maybe he's twenty or thirty years older than you are.

So what? Maturity was a good quality in a man.

"Funny you should ask . . . ," she said, striving for a businesslike tone. Mentally she crossed her fingers behind her back.

Okay, so arms and armor weren't her favorite examples of the decorative arts. Nevertheless, she knew the basics. More importantly, she knew whom to call to bring her up to speed in a hurry. She had connections at some of the best museums and galleries in the country.

"I think we should meet to talk about the assignment," Fantasy Man said. "There are some complications involved."

This was the first time he had ever suggested that they should get together face-to-face. *Don't get too excited, here. It's just a job.*

23

"Yes, of course," she said. "Where do you want to meet?"

"At the clients' place of business."

She seized a pen. "Where is it?"

"Las Vegas," Fantasy Man said. "Place called Military World. A small museum that features reproductions of arms and armor from the medieval period to the present. Does a big gift shop business."

"Reproductions?" she repeated carefully. Her initial enthusiasm evaporated instantly. Reality returned with a dull thud. Military World sounded like a tacky, low-rent souvenir operation. She had professional standards. She did not work for people who collected and sold reproductions.

On the other hand, this was Fantasy Man. In spite of Vesta's warning, she was determined to encourage future assignments with Lost and Found.

Sometimes you had to lower your standards a notch. Business was business.

"When do you want me in Vegas?" she asked, pen poised above the pad.

"As soon as possible. How about tomorrow morning?"

Yes.

"I'll have to check my schedule," she said smoothly. "But I seem to recall that I'm free tomorrow."

And if she wasn't free, she would cancel whatever appointments stood in the way of meeting Fantasy Man in person.

2

The ranks of medieval warriors, forever frozen in their steel carapaces, loomed behind him in the shadows. Mack Easton's face was as unreadable as that of any of the helmeted figures standing guard on the other side of the office window. There was something about Easton that made him appear locked in time too, Cady thought. A quality of stillness perhaps. You had to look twice to see him there in the shadows. If it hadn't been for the glow of the computer screen reflecting off the strong, fierce planes of his face and glinting on the lenses of his glasses, he would have been invisible.

Not a youthful face, she thought. Definitely mature. But not *too* mature. Thirty-nine or possibly forty, a good age. An interesting age. At least it looked interesting on Mack Easton.

The weird thing was that, even though she had never been able to imagine an exact image of him with only the telephone connection to go on, now that she was actually face-to-face with him she could see that he fit the voice perfectly. Take the serious, dark-rimmed glasses, for example. Never in a million years would she have thought to add that touch if she had been asked to draw a picture of him based on their long-distance conversations. But when he had removed them from his pocket a few minutes ago and put them on, she had decided they looked absolutely right on him.

"We have a photograph," he said. "It was found in the museum's archives."

"Museum" was not the word she would have used to dignify Military World, she thought. What was she doing here? She must have been temporarily out of her mind last night when she took Easton's call. She was at home in hushed galleries, art research libraries and the cluttered back rooms of prestigious auction salons. She mingled with connoisseurs and educated collectors.

Military World, with its low-budget reproductions of arms and armor from various wars, was very much as she had envisioned it: tacky. Then again, maybe that was just her personal bias showing. She had never been overly fond of armor. To her it symbolized all that was brutish and primitive in human nature. The fact that the artisans of the past had devoted enormous talent and craftsmanship to its design and decoration struck her as bizarre.

The office in which they sat belonged to the two owners of Military World, a pair that went by the names of Notch and Dewey. They hovered anxiously in the shadows, having surrendered the single desk to Easton and his laptop computer.

Mack occupied the space behind the desk as if he owned it. She got the impression that was the way it was with any place he happened to inhabit at any particular moment. Something that just sort of happened to him; something he took for granted.

She wished that she could get a better look at his eyes, but the reflection on his glasses concealed them as effectively as the steel helmets hid the features of the armored figures beyond the windows.

He pushed the photograph toward her across the battered desk and reached out to switch on the small desk lamp. She watched, unwillingly fascinated, as the beam fell on one large powerful-looking hand. No wedding ring, she noticed. Not that you could be sure a man was unmarried just because he didn't happen to wear a ring.

With an effort, she tore her gaze away from his hand and focused on the photo. It featured a horse and rider garbed in flamboyantly styled armor that looked as if it had been designed for a video game or dreamed up by an artist for the cover of a science fiction fantasy novel. She recognized it as a fairly accurate reproduction of the elaborately embellished armor crafted during the Renaissance. Such impractical styles had never been intended for the battlefield. They had been created for the sole purpose of making the wearer look good in ceremonies, festivals and parades.

The photo itself was an amateurish shot. Poorly lit. The kind of picture that a tourist might have snapped with a throw-away camera.

She looked up and peered into the shadows where Easton's face was supposed to be. All she could see was the hard angle of a grim jaw and the hollows beneath high, ascetic cheekbones. There was nothing soft or open about him. She had the feeling that Easton had learned long ago not to expect too much from the world other than what he could seize for himself.

"Fifteenth century, judging from the helmet and breastplate," she said. "Italian in style." "In style" was a polite way of saying "reproduction."

"I'm aware of that, Miss Briggs," Easton said with icy patience. "But if you look closely, you can see a portion of another display behind the horse's, uh, rear."

She took a closer look. Sure enough, if she looked past the tail of the fake horse, she could just make out the dimly lit image of a standing figure garbed in heavily decorated steel.

"Half-armor," she murmured. It was always good policy to impress the client, even if you weren't particularly interested in the job. Word of mouth was important. "In the style of the northern Italian armorers of the sixteenth century. Looks like part of a garniture meant for jousting at the barriers. Suits of armor from this era often consisted of dozens of supplementary and interchangeable pieces that allowed the set to be modified for specific uses. Sort of like a modern all-in-one tool kit."

"It's the helmet that we're interested in here," Mack said.

She peered at it. The bad lighting made it difficult to see much detail. "What about it?"

"It's the only piece that was stolen."

She looked up. "Is there a better photo around?"

One of the two men who hovered near the far end of the desk, the individual who went by the name Dewey, edged closer with a crablike movement.

"Lucky to have that one," he said, sounding apologetic.

She could only guess at Dewey's age. His face was a worn and weathered map that could have belonged to a man of fifty or seventy. He was dressed in military surplus complete with camouflage fatigues, battered boots and a wide leather belt. His graying hair was caught in a scruffy ponytail secured with a rubber band. She would not have been surprised to learn that he commuted to and from work on a very large motorcycle.

It was hard to imagine that he was representative of Lost and Found's typical clientele. How in the world had he and his partner managed to find the very-hard-to-find Mack Easton? More to the point, why had Mack agreed to help them? Surely he was too expensive for this pair. If he wasn't, she certainly was.

"I was going for a shot of the fifteenth-century display," Dewey explained. "We had just finished setting it up, you see. This was maybe two years back, right, Notch?"

The other man nodded vigorously. "Right."

Notch wore a fringed leather vest over a faded denim shirt. At some point in the shirt's obviously colorful history, the sleeves

31

had been ripped off high on the shoulders, no doubt to better show off the tattoos that decorated both beefy arms. A heavy steel key chain dangled from his belt. It looked as if it could double as a handy weapon in a bar fight. A red bandanna wrapped around his head secured Notch's thinning locks.

There was an indefinable air of connection between the two men that told Cady that Notch and Dewey were more than business associates. They were partners for life.

Dewey returned his attention to Cady. "I wanted to get a picture for our album. Lucked out and accidentally got a bit of the other exhibit in the shot."

"Never would have guessed that the helmet on the sixteenth-century suit was the real thing." Notch spread his hands. "Like, who knew, man?"

Cady cleared her throat. "How did it come into the, uh, museum's collection?"

"I found it right after we bought Military World from old man Belford. He had it stashed away in the back room. I polished it up and added it to the rest of the outfit. Seemed to match, y'know?"

"I see." She tapped one finger against the photo while she considered her options. As much as she wanted to take on another assignment for Lost and Found, she had a reputation to maintain. One had to draw the line somewhere. She did not trace reproductions.

Surreptitiously she glanced at her watch. She might be able to catch the one o'clock flight if she left Military World within the next forty-five minutes. She could be home in time for dinner.

She turned back to Easton. Something in the way he was watching her told her that he had noticed her checking the time. She summoned up what she hoped was an expression of professional interest. "What did the insurance people say when you notified them about the theft?"

Notch and Dewey exchanged uneasy looks.

Mack did not move. "There's a slight problem with the insurance situation."

She sighed. "In other words, the helmet was uninsured?"

Notch made an awkward sound deep in his throat. "Things have been a little rough lately, financially speaking. Dewey and me had to economize and make some cutbacks, y'know? Sort of let some of the insurance go."

"Not that the insurance company would have covered the helmet for anything like its true value, anyway," Dewey said quickly. "If we'd had coverage, it would have been for a reproduction, not the real thing on account of we didn't know it was genuine, if you see what I mean."

"I don't want to be rude," Cady said gently, "but what makes you think the helmet is a genuine sixteenth-century piece?"

Dewey and Notch stared at her, open-mouthed.

"You're supposed to be an expert," Dewey said. "Can't you tell from looking at it?"

She made a bid for patience. "This is only a photograph. There is no way I or anyone else can use it to determine whether or not the helmet is genuine."

Notch looked stricken. "But Mack here said that you knew your stuff."

"Old armor is very popular right now," she explained. "A lot of the well-heeled early retirees in the software industry are collecting it like mad. Guess it reminds them of all those sword-and-sorcery video and computer games they love to play. Prices are going through the roof. Unfortunately, antique armor is fairly easy to fake. Bury a piece of steel in the ground with some acidic substance for a while and, presto, you get aged armor."

Notch bristled. "Are you sayin' our helmet is a forgery?"

"I'm saying that is an extremely likely possibility." Cady spread her hands. "Even the experts get burned a lot when it comes to armor. And the business of creating counterfeits isn't exactly new. A lot of the best reproductions of antique armor were made in the nineteenth century. By now, the steel has taken on the patina of genuine age and can easily pass for the real thing."

"I still say our helmet is the real thing," Notch declared.

Cady slanted a quick, searching glance at Mack. He moved his head in the smallest of negatives. He was staying out of the argument, letting her handle the clients.

Summoning up her best professional expression, she turned back to Notch and Dewey. "Why are you convinced that the helmet is genuine when every other piece in your collection is a reproduction?"

"Simple." Dewey rocked triumphantly on his heels and looked shrewd. "Someone stole it."

"I beg your pardon?"

"Someone ripped it off," he elaborated. "Why would anyone take the risk of stealing the damn thing if it weren't real?"

She drummed her fingers on the photo. "People frequently steal stuff that has very little value. Good grief, a shoplifter is only too happy to grab a tube of toothpaste. Whoever took the helmet might have wanted it for his desk. Or perhaps a teenager swiped it to show to his buddies."

"Why take only the helmet?" Dewey retorted. "Why not take the whole damn suit?"

"Might have been a little awkward getting it out the front door," Cady said dryly.

"Not that hard to do," Notch said. "People think that a full suit of armor is real heavy because it looks like it weighs a ton and because they've seen pictures of knights having to be hoisted up onto their horses. But that ain't the way it was."

"He's right," Dewey added. "Heck, a modern soldier, fully equipped, carries about the same amount of weight as a fifteenth-century knight."

"I understand," she said. "I didn't mean that your thief couldn't have managed to lift the whole suit; I meant that someone probably would have noticed him walking out the door with it."

Dewey snorted. "The guy didn't walk out the front door with it during regular hours. He broke in at night. Could have helped himself to a dozen pieces of armor. Taken his time about it and cleaned us out. But all he ripped off was that helmet."

Mack finally moved. He sat forward; not far, but enough to get everyone's attention. He met Cady's eyes across the expanse of the desk.

"This wasn't a casual smash-and-grab," he said. "It was a professional job. Very smooth. Almost invisible."

"Invisible? How?"

"Hell," Notch said gruffly. "We couldn't even convince the cops that there had been a burglary. The bastard didn't leave any tracks, that's for sure. Pardon my language, ma'am."

In spite of her growing reservations about getting involved in the affair, Cady felt the first faint stirrings of professional interest. "What do you mean?"

Mack propped his elbows on the arms of his chair and steepled his fingers. "Dewey and Notch do have some security here at Military World." His voice was dry. "Maybe not state-of-the-art, casino-style security like they've got out on the Strip, but, trust me, it amounts to more than a couple of locks on the doors. Notch is right. Whoever broke in last week knew what he was doing. He was good enough to disarm the sensors while he was inside and reset them again when he left. And all he took was that one piece."

The lines around Dewey's eyes deepened into ruts. "If I hadn't noticed the helmet missing the other day, we still wouldn't know we'd been robbed."

"You might be better off letting the police handle this," she said, striving for a practical, diplomatic approach.

"Not if the helmet is genuine." Mack met her eyes over the tips of his fingers. "We both know that if it's the real thing, it will disappear into a private collection or turn up in some museum complete with papers and provenance. We'll never be able to prove that it's the property of Military World."

"In my professional opinion," Cady said, "I don't think the chances are great that the helmet is genuine."

"But what if it is?" Dewey broke in eagerly. "What would it be worth?"

"Well, that's hard to say," she temporized.

"You must have some idea," Notch insisted. "You're an expert. That's why Mack called you in to consult."

She looked at Easton and was almost sure she caught a flicker of laconic amusement in his eyes. She sat back in her chair and put her fingertips together in imitation of his own enigmatic pose.

"If the helmet is actually the work of one of the great sixteenth-century Italian armorers," she said judiciously, "it could be worth a considerable amount of money. As I said, armor is highly collectible at the moment."

"How much is 'a considerable amount'?" Notch breathed. Excitement glinted in his eyes. "Couple thousand, maybe?"

Dewey sidled closer to hear her reply.

She hesitated, studying their eager faces. It was probably not a good idea to feed their fantasies of sudden wealth. On the other hand, she was here in the capacity of expert consultant. She was going to get paid for wasting her time today. The client deserved something for his money.

"It's not unusual for good, uncommon pieces such as that helmet, assuming it's genuine, to go for several hundred thousand dollars at auction."

"Several hundred thousand?" Dewey repeated. "Holy shit. Excuse me, ma'am."

Notch stared at her. He looked dazzled. "We could pay off the mortgage on Military World. Own it free and clear. Expand the place. Go big time."

"I stress that such a price would be for a genuine piece of antique armor that was in excellent condition with a good provenance," she said quickly. "Speaking of which, have you got any?"

Notch blinked, bewildered. "Any what?"

Easton answered for her. "Provenance. A paper trail that spells out the helmet's history of ownership and identifies the experts who have authenticated it in the past. It's used as evidence to help prove that a work of art or an antique is genuine."

"Huh." Dewey switched his attention back to Cady. "You mean like a receipt or something?"

"Yes, that's exactly what I mean," she said. "Documentation is crucial. Do you know who owned the piece before it came to Military World, for instance? Was it ever exhibited in a museum? Was it part of a private collection?"

Notch exchanged an uncertain glance with Dewey. "I s'pose I could look through some of old man Belford's records, but I wouldn't count on finding much. He wasn't big on bookkeeping. You remember him sayin' anything about how he got ahold of that helmet, Dew?"

"No," Dewey said sadly. "The old man was one or two bricks shy of a load toward the end."

Easton touched the photo. "That picture counts as provenance. It's concrete proof that the helmet belongs to Military World."

"It could be helpful," Cady agreed. "But

first we've got to find the helmet and determine whether or not it's genuine."

"That's where you come in," Easton said softly. "You've got the contacts. If a quality piece like this was stolen for the underground market, there will be rumors."

"Tracking down rumors requires a great deal of time," she reminded him. "And I'm not exactly cheap, Mr. Easton."

For the first time he smiled. "I'm aware of that, Miss Briggs."

The smile produced a fizzy feeling in her stomach. Was he flirting with her?

Nah. What were the odds?

She cleared her throat. "I might not turn up any useful leads."

"I'll take the risk. We'll work this the same way we did the last three jobs. I'll use my computer program to keep track of whatever is going on in the on-line markets and auction sites. You will check your sources in the other markets. Agreed?"

"Well —"

Dewey shifted, reaching into his back pocket. "If it's cash up front you want, I've got some." He hauled out a worn wallet, opened it and seized two twenties with a twitching movement. "Here you go. How much of your time will that buy?"

She gazed helplessly at the two twenties.

She had no idea how to tell him that forty dollars wouldn't purchase even half an hour of her time.

"Well —" she said again.

"Hold on, I've got a little too," Notch said eagerly. He started unbuttoning his shirt, revealing a money belt strapped around his hairy stomach. "Couple hundred bucks in here that I've been savin' up to pay for the repairs on my truck. But they can wait. How much do you need, Miss Briggs? A hundred maybe? All of it?"

Mack Easton was to blame for this, she thought. He had sold a dream to two men who probably hadn't seen anything resembling the real thing in years. She looked into Notch's and Dewey's eyes and knew that neither of them had ever had a major break in their lives. The possibility that the helmet was genuine sixteenth-century armor had brought forth a crop of hope and excitement in ground that had long lain barren.

She knew when she was trapped.

"I can make some phone calls," she said reluctantly. "And check some sources. I'll see if anyone has heard of any exceptional pieces moving in the private collector market in the past week."

Dewey and Notch glowed.

She was doomed. Well, it wasn't as if she

had a whole lot of other things going on in her own life right now, she thought. She could spare a few days to research the lost helm. She would have to be extremely cautious in making her inquiries. If any of her colleagues discovered that she was working for an outfit called Military World, it would be years before people stopped laughing.

"I'll tell you what, I'll give it a week," she said, surrendering to the inevitable. "If I don't turn up any leads by next Thursday, we'll call it quits, okay?"

"*All right,*" Dewey crowed. "Thanks, Miss Briggs. I knew the minute I saw you that you were a real lady." He tried to shove the two twenties into her fingers.

She did not know how to explain to him that where she came from, nice women did not accept twenties from strange men.

"You won't be sorry," Notch said, happily thrusting some mangled bills toward her. "Mack here says he's got a feeling about that helmet and he's almost never wrong. Me and Dewey are gonna get rich. I know it in my bones."

"We'll see." Gently she pushed the cash back at them. "Keep your money." She glared into the shadows where Mack sat. "Mr. Easton and I will work out the details of my fee."

"You sure?" Dewey asked. "Because Notch and I don't mind stakin' you."

"I'm sure."

Mack smiled slightly. There was cool satisfaction in his eyes. "Notch, you and Dewey had better get back out there on the floor. You've got customers. Miss Briggs and I will settle the details of her consulting fees."

"Right you are, Mack." Notch grinned at Cady. "Nice meetin' you, ma'am. Be lookin' forward to hearin' from you real soon."

Dewey bobbed his head. "Have a good trip back to Santa Barbara, Miss Briggs."

"Thank you," Cady murmured.

She waited until the two men had disappeared through the door of the office. Then she turned back to Mack. "You do realize that when this is finished, it will be your job to inform Notch and Dewey that they aren't going to get rich off that helmet? I'm certainly not going to be the one to deliver the bad news that it's a genuine fake."

"You take care of your end of this deal, Miss Briggs. I'll handle my clients."

"One more thing."

"What?" he asked.

"I want your personal guarantee that you will not tell anyone else in the business about this job."

He was clearly amused now. "Worried about what your colleagues will say if they find out you're chasing reproductions?"

"To be absolutely blunt about it, yes."

He lowered his voice to a tone that vibrated with mocking sincerity. "Don't worry, Miss Briggs. Your reputation is safe with me."

Either he had deliberately infused the words with all sorts of sexual implications, or her fantasies were getting out of control. It was time to change the subject.

"Mind if I ask you a question?" she asked.

"What is it?"

"Why did you take this job? You can't tell me that Military World is a typical Lost and Found client."

"Dewey and Notch are old friends of the family. They served under my father's command a long time ago. We've kept in touch with them over the years. When the helmet went missing, they called me to ask if there was anything I could do about it."

"I see." It was the first tiny glimpse she'd had of his past. It made her hungry for more, but she could see that it wasn't going to be forthcoming at the moment. "You know as well as I do that this is probably a wild goose chase. Why are you acting as if you think the helmet is genuine? Why raise their hopes?"

He shrugged. "When Notch called me and told me what had happened, my first assumption was that the piece was a reproduction and not worth trying to trace. But I agreed to come here and take a look around. Now I'm inclined to think someone may have known what he was doing when he grabbed the thing. If he had just wanted a nice souvenir, why not take the fifteenth-century parade helmet? It's a lot flashier."

She thought for a moment. "I assume you called the company that crafted the rest of the garniture to see if it had made the missing helmet?"

"Yes. It's an old-line firm that specializes in museum-quality reproduction pieces. I was told that they had made a helm to go with the rest of the suit, but not the one in that picture."

She pondered the dimly lit photo. There was no denying that there was something about the shape of the helmet that did not match the lines of the breastplate and the other pieces.

"There are a lot of other companies that specialize in reproductions," she reminded him. "This could be a mix-and-match suit that has been assembled from several different sources."

"I called all of the usual firms. None of

them had any patterns that duplicated the design of that helmet. None of them knew of any competitors who were producing any similar designs."

"I've got some books I can check. And I'll talk to some people. I've got a couple of friends who curate arms and armor collections at two of the big museums. I'll see what I can do." She got to her feet and picked up her purse. "I suppose there's no point telling Dewey and Notch not to pin their hopes on recovering this piece."

"Afraid not. They're psyched, as you can see."

"This is Vegas. It's obvious where they're coming from. But I would have thought you'd be a bit more pragmatic, Mr. Easton."

He rose in an easy, deceptively languid movement that took his face back into deep shadow. "I'm following a hunch, Miss Briggs."

She paused at the door and turned back to study him for a moment. "The same kind of hunch you followed when you asked me to trace that Spanish ewer last month?"

"Yes."

His instincts had been right in that case. They had been right in the other two jobs she'd done for him, too. In the art world, you learned to respect good instincts.

"I'll see what I can do," she repeated. "But no guarantees. Understood?"

"Understood, Miss Briggs." He came around the end of the desk. "You know how to reach me. Call me as soon as you've got anything solid."

Something in his voice, an edge of warning perhaps, made her glance quickly at his face. He was standing in a narrow shaft of light. She got a good look at his eyes for the first time. They were fog gray.

Another of the odd little thrills of awareness shot through her, raising the fine hairs at the nape of her neck.

She nodded once, turned and continued briskly out of the office. Mack followed and fell into step beside her.

"I'll have Dewey call you a cab to take you to the airport," he said.

"Do you live here in Vegas?" She tried to make the question eminently casual.

"No. But my flight doesn't leave until this evening. Thought I'd use the time to go through Military World's old records and files. You never know what might turn up."

And that, she thought, was all she was going to get out of him. He didn't live in Las Vegas. So what? The information told her nothing useful.

Together they walked through the gloom-

48

shrouded ranks of still and silent soldiers, through the history of a thousand years of war technology. Twelfth-century mail gave way to the heavy metal of the sixteenth century that, in turn, evolved into the familiar camouflage-clad figures of the modern era. Swords and lances gave way to guns. The shapes of the helmets changed slightly. The lethal, high-tech gear that constituted the new version of knightly armor appeared.

Only the technology changed, she thought. The goals remained the same.

Armor was not her favorite among the decorative arts.

3

When she got home that night she poured herself a glass of wine, sat down at the computer and opened the "Fantasy Man" file. She browsed through some of the more recent correspondence she had received from Mack Easton and paused to read one piece in particular.

Dear Miss Briggs:

You're the expert, but as far as I'm concerned you're wrong when you say that the essential element of Regency style is an intellectual approach to design. It's sophisticated on the surface, of course, but underneath there is a lush, seething sensuality. The pieces make you want to stroke them. Then again, what do I know? I just trace old antiques, I don't study them . . .

Maybe the references to seething sensuality and stroking had not been intended as anything other than descriptive, Cady thought.

Dear Miss Briggs:

You were right about that restaurant in San Francisco. I tried it last week when business took me to the city. Great pasta. What is it about good food that makes a man think of fine art and great sex?

It would certainly be fascinating to know what kind of sex Mack Easton classified as great.

She took a deep breath and reached out to shut down the computer. She had not misread the signals today. Mack had been flirting with her.

On the plane back to San Francisco he resorted to doing what he often did late at night when he could not sleep. He cranked up his laptop and opened the file in which he stored the on-line correspondence she had e-mailed to him during the past two months. He started with the most recent messages, pausing at one of his favorites.

Dear Mr. Easton:

I am pleased to hear that you were satisfied with my work on the Spanish ewer project. Let me know if I can be of fur-

51

ther service. I have enjoyed the consulting that I have done for Lost and Found and hope to do more of it in the future.

By the way, I still feel that the Neoclassical design elements of the Regency period are fundamentally intellectual in nature, not a cover for "lush, seething sensuality" . . .

It only went to show that even the experts could be wrong, he thought. He knew lush, seething sensuality when he saw it. And he had certainly seen it today when he had looked into the eyes of Cady Briggs.

All those late-night fantasies that had been keeping him awake lately had a strong basis in reality. The lady was everything the voice on the phone had promised, and more.

4

Jonathan Arden gave his tiny silver-haired client a reassuring smile as he placed his palm on the surface of the old pedestal table. Hattie Woods watched anxiously.

Silly old fool, he thought. He closed his eyes for effect and held himself very still for a few seconds. Then he shuddered, drew a deep breath and raised his lashes.

"*Yes.*" He sucked in a small, sharp breath and snatched his hand off the top of the table as if it had been burned.

"Oh, dear." Alarm flashed briefly across Hattie's soft features. "Are you all right, Mr. Arden?"

"Yes, thank you. I'm afraid it goes with the territory, so to speak. Especially with the older pieces." He managed a weary smile. It was important to give the appearance of having expended an enormous amount of energy.

"The table is genuine, then?" Hattie asked eagerly. "Old furniture can be so tricky, you know. I realize the Austrey-Post experts have authenticated it, but mistakes

53

get made in the best galleries. I can't bear the thought of having a fake in my collection. I'm going to leave everything to a museum, you see. They've promised to name a wing after me. It's vital that every piece be an original."

"I understand, Ms. Woods."

"That's why I asked you to take a look at it for me. I wanted to be sure."

"There is no reason to be concerned about this table." He glanced quickly around the gallery showroom. It was only lightly crowded this afternoon. No members of the dignified staff stood close enough to overhear his conversation with Hattie. "Early nineteenth century. English Regency period. It really is a lovely old piece."

"And the history?" Hattie pressed in a lower tone. She was practically bubbling with excitement now. "Did you feel anything curious or especially interesting?"

Clients liked their antiques with lots of drama attached. A table that had been used to sign a famous treaty or to write a king's letter of abdication was far more valuable than the same piece of furniture that had simply stood gathering dust in a private home. Jonathan studied the table, considering possibilities.

"It has seen its share of excitement, I can tell you that," he said. "There is an aura of old violence surrounding it. I could feel intense anger and some fear when I touched the surface. Also . . ."

"Yes? What is it, Mr. Arden?"

"Pain, I believe." Jonathan kept his voice subdued, almost meditative. "I would not be surprised if a duel took place in the vicinity of this table. A few drops of blood must have fallen on it to have left such strong emotional traces."

"Blood." Hattie regarded the table with awe. "Imagine that."

Jonathan leaned closer and lowered his voice another notch to close the deal. "In my opinion it's an exceptional value. In fact, it's a bargain. The experts here at the gallery obviously did not recognize the true excellence of the piece."

Hattie clutched her purse and gave Jonathan a look that glittered with the feverish obsession of the true collector. "Now that I know for certain that it's genuine and that there's some interesting history attached to it, I have no problem with the price. Worth every penny."

"I think you'll be very pleased."

"Thank you so much, Mr. Arden." Hattie tightened her grip on her elegantly carved cane and started toward the glass doors at the front of the gallery. She moved with a careful air that spoke of delicate bones and a frail sense of balance. "You have been most helpful. I must admit that when you were first recommended to me, I had some serious reservations. When it comes to investing in art and antiques, I have always relied on my long-term relationships with dealers and friends in the business for professional opinions. It never occurred to me to consult a psychic."

"You certainly aren't alone." Jonathan fell into step beside her. "Very few people are sufficiently open-minded to take advantage of information that can be obtained from the metaphysical realm."

Hattie chuckled. "Well, I like to think that I am a bit more open-minded than most in that regard. I have had a lifelong interest in metaphysics, you know. I read a great deal in the field. But your particular talent was new to me."

Jonathan held the glass door open for her. "Psychometry is an uncommon psychic talent."

"Well, I'm not so sure about that." Hattie pursed her lips and tilted her head in a dainty, considering fashion as she stepped out onto the busy San Francisco sidewalk.

"When you think about it, there are many occasions in life when we look at an old object or walk into a strange room and are suddenly aware of some sort of sensation."

"An aura?" he suggested.

"Yes, indeed." She brightened. "An aura. A sense of something having happened in the vicinity. An unmistakable feeling of an emotional connection with the past. I expect that in your case, that ability is simply more acutely developed than it is in the rest of us."

"Perhaps. Whatever, I am delighted to have been of service, Ms. Woods."

"I shall be in touch the next time I am considering an acquisition."

Hattie inclined her head in a birdlike nod of dismissal and walked gingerly toward a black Lincoln that was parked in front of the gallery. A short, square man in an ill-fitting suit and tie straightened quickly from the fender to open the rear door for her. She gave him a vague smile as she got into the back of the big car. Then she glanced at Jonathan and lifted a thin-boned hand laden with a fortune in gold and gems in farewell.

Silly old fool. The elderly made such easy targets, he thought. Loneliness did ninety percent of his work for him. Medications, chronic illness and the mind-clogging tendrils of dementia did the rest. Talk about shooting fish in a barrel.

The short, square driver got behind the wheel, started the engine and eased the heavy Lincoln away from the curb. Jonathan smiled with satisfaction.

When the Lincoln was out of sight, he walked to where his Jaguar was parked, opened the door and got inside. He glanced in the rearview mirror and grinned again as he calculated his cut on the table. All in all, it had been a good day's work.

The table was counterfeit, of course; an excellent fraud manufactured sometime during the past few months in a small European factory that employed some extraordinarily skilled forgers. The workmanship and the phony provenance had been good enough to fool the gallery staff. At least for a short time.

His job was to lead the right client to the right piece before its authenticity could be questioned. Timing was everything. The scam was a slick one, but to be on the safe side it was important that none of the fakes fell into the wrong hands. There were experts, although very few according to his sources, who could detect the fine nuances that marked even the most brilliant reproductions.

He saw to it that the furniture moved

quickly once it arrived at the gallery. None of the items could be allowed to stand around long on the showroom floor, where it might attract unwanted attention. For that same reason, none of the pieces was designed to appear so unique or so magnificent as to warrant excessive interest.

He had definitely moved into the big time with this latest venture. It certainly beat the phony investment schemes he had marketed for so many years. He was moving in much higher, much wealthier social circles, too. The money was rolling in quite nicely. He would have to look into the possibility of opening one of those off-shore accounts that the real pros used.

5

Vesta Briggs stood alone in the two-story chamber and absorbed the soothing ambience of the past. If it were not for the heavy steel door with its computerized lock and the total absence of windows, one would never know that the richly paneled walls and the gleaming granite floor of this room covered what was, in fact, an elegant vault.

The display cases extended from floor to ceiling. The shelves held her collection of precious antique boxes, hundreds of them, perhaps over a thousand now. She had begun collecting them years ago when she had finally accepted that, for her, there would be nothing to live for except Chatelaine's.

She turned slowly, breathing deeply of the atmosphere of the chamber. There was comfort to be found in the immutable past: a realm that remained frozen and locked in time, a world that could be visited again and again in memory and in dreams. She savored the cold fire of the glittering, polished works of art arrayed before her. Beautiful damascene chests from the sixteenth century; elegant seventeenth-century jewelry cases; gilded toilet sets that had once decorated the boudoirs of eighteenth-century ladies and courtesans; exquisitely carved writing cabinets from the early eighteen hundreds. Each had been crafted to hold secrets and precious objects. All were fitted with locks.

She walked slowly across the room and stopped at the little spiral staircase. It led to a narrow balcony that encircled the chamber at the midway point. She put her hand on the polished rail and thought about the quarrel with Sylvia. It had not been pleasant. Perhaps she should have explained her decision to postpone the merger vote to her niece. Sylvia was the CEO of Gallery Chatelaine, after all.

But she wanted to be certain, Vesta thought. There was so much at stake. And in the end, the simple fact was that she did not have to explain anything. Not yet. Sylvia had assumed the day-to-day operations of Chatelaine's, but they both knew that even though she had been forced to retreat into semiretirement, the founder of Chatelaine's still controlled the shares that determined the fate of the gallery.

She knew what the rest of the family was

saying behind her back. The business with the psychic had been the last straw for Sylvia. Vesta smiled grimly. Long ago she had been labeled eccentric. Now they would wonder if dementia had set in.

The expression on her niece's face when she had confronted her about her appointments with Jonathan Arden had been almost amusing. The rest of the family would soon be buzzing with the news that Greataunt Vesta had finally lost it completely. But they would keep quiet about it, she thought. Oh, yes, they would go to great lengths to conceal the information. None of them would want to risk having the news leaked to the art world. That sort of gossip would not only be professionally embarrassing, it would be bad for business.

She gazed at a beautiful ornamental gold box on a nearby shelf and wondered what Cady would say when they told her about the visits to the psychic.

Cady was not like the others. Cady understood her. That was because they were so much alike in so many ways. Cady wouldn't leap to the conclusion that she had lost her grip on reality. Cady would ask questions first. Cady would look beneath the surface. It was her nature.

Vesta put a hand to her waist and removed

the magnificent piece of ancient jewelry known as the Nun's Chatelaine. She had worn it to the Carnival Night committee meeting earlier that evening. Eleanor Middleton's boundless enthusiasm for her duties as chair of the annual Phantom Point community event was admirable but tiresome. Still, it was important for Gallery Chatelaine to be represented on the committee. And given her *semiretirement* status, Vesta thought, she had no excuse for sticking someone else in the family with the task of volunteering for the committee work. She had never shirked her responsibility to Chatelaine's.

For a moment she studied the old chatelaine in the light of a nearby lamp. The heavily carved medallion in the center glowed with the rich luster of very old gold. The stones that encircled it still shimmered with ancient radiance. The five gold-link chains spilled through her fingers. Small gold keys set with gemstones were attached to four of the chains. No key dangled from the fifth chain.

She had discovered the Nun's Chatelaine shortly before she had opened the gallery. It had turned up in a heap of costume jewelry in an estate sale she had attended; a masterpiece concealed by a mound of worthless plastic, glass stones and cheap metal. She had known at once that it would become the symbol of her new business venture.

The Gallery Chatelaine logo was based on the design of the antique device. An image of the chatelaine appeared on everything from business cards to the engraved announcements sent out whenever a special collection went up for sale. A large, sculpted reproduction of the beautiful object hung over the front door of the main gallery in San Francisco and also above the door of the small art boutique here in Phantom Point.

She studied the heavy chatelaine, aware of the warmth of the metal against her skin. It was only a key ring, but what a fabulous key ring, she thought. Her fingers tightened around it. She could feel the history trapped inside. She knew the details because she had spent years researching the object's origins.

In the beginning it had been fashioned for a twelfth-century bride. An extravagant gift from her husband on her wedding day, it had been a symbol of his faith and trust in her. The keys that had dangled at the ends of the chains had been emblems of the power she wielded in her new role as the lady of the castle.

Those first keys had been forged of iron.

They had unlocked the chambers that contained the lord's treasures: expensive spices from the East; precious manuscripts containing magic and mystery that had been carried all the way from Spain; jewelry and fine woolen robes that were donned for special occasions.

Many years and several children later, the lady had been widowed. Following the fashion of the day, she had retired to a convent where her talent for organization had assured her a rapid rise through the ranks of the nuns.

Within a short time she had found herself supervising the convent's business and financial affairs. Once again the keys that hung from her chatelaine unlocked doors that protected secrets and mysteries: the illuminated manuscripts in the library; the chapel with its rare and expensive wall tiles detailing the lives of the saints; the boxes in which the property charters and account rolls were stored.

The Nun's Chatelaine had floated down through the centuries, sometimes disappearing for years at a time before reappearing in the hands of a collector or a woman who was simply attracted to its unique beauty. Sometime during the eighteenth century, when decorative chatelaines had been all the fashion rage, the iron keys had been replaced with new ones fashioned of gold and set with gems. But the spectacular medallion had been left untouched. Perhaps the jeweler who had replaced the keys for his client had recognized that such fine craftsmanship should not be altered for the sake of fashion.

With the chatelaine in her hand, she climbed the spiral staircase to the narrow balcony. She went to a display case and took down one of the exquisite boxes, a very fine eighteenth-century creation decorated with beautifully painted enamels and gleaming gilt. A plain metal duplicate of the fifth key, the one that she had removed earlier from the Nun's Chatelaine, was in the lock.

She braced herself for the torrent of emotions that poured through her whenever she opened the box. When she was ready, she raised the lid and carefully placed the Nun's Chatelaine inside, beneath the other secrets she kept there. For a moment she stood remembering the past.

After a while she closed and locked the box and pocketed the plain duplicate key. She set the gilded and enameled treasure chest back on the shelf and shut the glass door. Just one more beautiful little chest among hundreds.

She descended the ladder, left the vault where the past was safely confined and locked the heavy door.

The all-too-familiar jittery sensation was plaguing her again tonight. The twinges of anxiety had grown increasingly bothersome during the past few weeks. A glass of whiskey was no longer enough to quell them. She might have to resort to one of the pills the doctor had given her. She dreaded using the tablets. They worked, but they left her with an unpleasant hangover. It would be a full twenty-four hours before she felt in control again. Much better to beat back the panic attack before it took hold, if possible.

She climbed the stairs to her bedroom, changed into a swimsuit and a terry-cloth robe and went back down to the first floor of the hillside villa.

Outside on the terrace she switched off the household lights and stood looking across the night-darkened bay to where the city of San Francisco glittered and sparkled in the distance. She removed her robe, dropped it on a lounger and walked across the tile to the pool steps.

She did not turn on the underwater lights. The dark water greeted her with the quietly exhilarating embrace of an old, familiar lover, one who knew the past and shared the memories.

She swam three laps before she sensed that something was wrong. She paused, treading water, and peered into the shadows of the garden that surrounded the pool.

"Is anyone there?"

No response.

It was the anxiety, she thought. She would not allow it to win tonight. She would do battle with it and defeat the panic attack before it took hold.

With grim determination she struck out for the opposite end of the pool. She would not give in to the nameless fear.

6

"She's trying to screw us." Mack did not take his eyes off the computer screen as he spoke into the phone. "My fault. I'm the one who picked her as a consultant."

Why was he so surprised? he wondered. It wasn't like this was the first time he'd made a mistake of this magnitude. There was always some risk involved in using a freelancer who was well connected in the business. The temptations were great.

Still, he had been so sure of Cady Briggs. She really had caught him off guard with this maneuver. Hell, off guard didn't cover it. He felt as if he'd been kicked in the gut.

It occurred to him that for some reason he was taking this bit of treachery a little too personally. This is business, he thought. Act like a businessman. Cady Briggs was just another consultant gone bad. It happened. No point sitting here staring at the evidence. Get over it and do something businesslike about the situation.

"You okay, Mack?" Dewey asked uneasily on the other end of the line. "You sound like you just ate something that don't agree with you."

"What's wrong?" Notch demanded from the extension he was using in the office of Military World. "We got a problem?"

Mack roused himself from his morose contemplation of the data on the glowing computer screen.

"Yeah, we've got a problem. Cady Briggs just bought a ticket to San Jose." He studied the data arrayed before him. "She's made arrangements to pick up a car there. When I talked to her assistant a few minutes ago, I was told that Miss Briggs would be out of town for a couple of days. She's on her way to see a client who lives in the Santa Cruz Mountains."

"Who?" Notch sounded bewildered.

"Ambrose Vandyke. Retired computer mogul. Made his fortune designing software that sends robotic programs out onto the internet to retrieve data."

"Well, shit," Dewey muttered. "You mean she's workin' on another job when she's supposed to be tryin' to find our helmet?"

"I don't think this is an unrelated job," Mack said. "I believe the lady has located your missing armor."

"Hey," Dewey said, sounding far more cheerful. "You really think so?"

Mack stared at the screen. "Almost positive."

"*All right*," Notch chortled. "You hear that, Dew? She found the damned thing. We're gonna be rich."

"In that case," Dewey said, "why the hell does Mack sound like he's getting ready to attend a funeral?"

"If I sound somewhat less than enthusiastic," Mack said, "it's because I think Miss Briggs has plans of her own for your helmet. Plans that don't include either of you."

"Huh?" Notch asked. "What's he talkin' about, Dew?"

"Don't know yet but it don't sound good," Dewey growled. "Fill us in here, Mack. This ain't no time to get secretive on us. We're your clients, remember?"

"The problem," Mack said, "is that, contrary to standard Lost and Found procedure, Cady Briggs did not notify me that she had a lead on the helmet."

"So what? Maybe she just wants to check out her information first," Dewey offered. "You know, make sure of things before she tells you she's onto somethin'."

"There was no need to go this far out of her way just to verify some piece of information. She could have done that on the phone. That's what I pay her to do. I made it clear to her that if she picked up anything solid in the way of a lead, she was to notify me immediately. I handle all recovery work."

A heavy silence greeted that information. Dewey and Notch breathed for a while.

Notch finally cleared his throat. "You think maybe she's found the helmet and she's goin' after it herself?"

"That's the logical conclusion here," Mack said.

"But why would she do that?" Dewey asked. "Why wouldn't she call you first?"

"One good reason is that she has come up with something far more profitable to do with your helmet than return it to you. She told us that old armor was very, very hot in the antiques market, remember? Prices for the good pieces are going through the roof."

"Uh-oh," Notch said. "I think I'm beginning to get the picture here."

"You sayin' what I think you're sayin'?" Dewey asked uneasily.

"She grew up in the art business," Mack said. "She knows the players. If she has located your helmet, she could just as easily have located a new buyer for it, too. I have a hunch that she's on her way to see the current owner to try to broker her own deal on the underground market."

"You mean she's gonna sell our helmet to someone else instead of returning it to us?" Notch's voice rose. "Like she's supposed to?"

"I think that is a very real possibility," Mack said.

"Got to hand it to her," Dewey's voice was laced with resignation and a tinge of reluctant admiration. "If she gets her hands on our helmet and sets up a deal that doesn't include us or you, Mack, she could make herself a bundle. A lot more than you were gonna pay her, I bet."

"Yes." Mack tapped a key to bring up a new flight schedule. "A lot more. And she won't have to deal with any middlemen or pay any auction house commissions and fees."

"Guess I knew right from the start it was all too good to be true," Notch said. "Dewey, you and me weren't born to get rich quick, and that's a fact."

"It was sort of nice thinkin' about what we could have done with the money, though," Dewey said wistfully. "We had us some great plans for Military World."

"Easy come, easy go," Notch said philosophically.

"It hasn't gone yet." Mack took off his glasses and set them down on the table beside the keyboard. "Cady Briggs seems to have overlooked the fact that she's still under contract with me."

There was a short beat of startled silence on the other end.

"What are you gonna do, Mack?" Dewey asked.

"What do you think I'm going to do? I'm going after her." Mack got to his feet. "I plan to remind her that she's working for me and that Lost and Found is really big on the concept of employee loyalty."

7

Her hands were shaking. Cady stood in the night-darkened shadows of the dripping redwoods and tried to breathe from the bottom of her stomach. She could not take the pill she kept in the little case on the end of her key chain. It would dull her senses, and she needed all of them badly. The tendrils of fog that swirled around her were already doing a great job of blurring the situation.

It was the fog that had saved her a few minutes ago. The mist and the night had shielded her when the two men had walked past her hiding place.

So close. It had been so horrifyingly close. If she hadn't heard them coming toward her, hadn't followed her instincts and moved into the trees . . .

Don't go there. You can dwell on the near miss later when you have your panic attack. Right now you have to think.

She studied the illuminated windows of the small A-frame cabin. The two men had walked out of the front door a few minutes ago carrying bulky objects swathed in waterproof tarps. The lights inside the small structure had revealed the ski masks that covered their faces. They had moved swiftly, depositing their burdens in the nondescript van parked in the drive. She had overheard their conversation when they returned to the house because they had passed within a few feet of where she stood.

They had been discussing the timing of the burglary.

". . . *It's taking too long to load this stuff. We've gotta get out of here.*"

"*Take it easy. Another couple of trips and it's over.*"

"*I don't like this. I've got a bad feeling about this job.*"

"*You like the money, don't you?*"

Cady had called Ambrose Vandyke from the airport in San Jose. He had given her precise directions to the cabin. He had been cheerful and eager. There had been no hint of fear in his voice. The two men must have arrived sometime after he had hung up the phone, she thought.

She had walked into the middle of a burglary in progress. The only reason she had not *driven* into it was because she had found the gate at the foot of the narrow, twisted drive locked. She had tried calling

76

Vandyke's number on her cell phone, but there had been no answer. Unwilling to turn back after having come so far, she had pulled on her raincoat, gotten out of the car and made her way around the gate. She had noticed the van when she had emerged from the trees. The shrouded shapes in the back of the vehicle and the open door of the cabin had sent a chill of warning through her.

The logical thing to do was to retreat to a place where she could safely put in a call to 911 without risk of being overheard. But heaven only knew how long it would take for help to arrive in this remote location. Meanwhile, Ambrose Vandyke was in grave danger. She could not stand here and do nothing.

She wondered if creating a distraction would serve a useful purpose. Eyeing the van, she tried to think through the suffocating tide of fear.

The vehicle was parked at the top of the very steep drive. If she could get to it without being seen, release the parking brake and put the van in neutral . . .

She sensed the presence of someone coming up behind her a beat before he moved, but by then it was too late. One large hand closed around her mouth, silencing the scream before she could utter a sound.

An arm wrapped around her waist, pinning her hard against a large, masculine body.

"Quiet." Mack spoke directly into her ear as he hauled her deeper into the fog-bound redwoods. "Not a sound."

She nodded frantically to show that she understood. Relief crashed through her, coming so swiftly on the heels of the heart-stopping fear that it was almost too much to bear.

Mack took his hand away from her mouth. She clutched his arm to maintain her balance, turned and stood on tiptoe to whisper her warning.

"Burglary. Two men, I think."

"I saw them," he said, just as softly.

"How did you — ?"

"Never mind. Got to get you out of here."

She shook her head quickly. "We can't leave Vandyke alone with them. Who knows what they'll do to him?"

"I'll see what I can do. In the meantime, go back to the car. Call 911 and get the hell away from here. Understood?"

"I was about to release the brake in the van so that it would roll down the hill with all of the stolen things. I thought that would bring them out of the house long enough for me to get inside, bolt the door and call the cops."

"You're assuming there's a bolt on the door."

"Everyone has a bolt. Mack, we've got to do something. They could be getting ready to murder Mr. Vandyke, even as we —"

"Okay, okay. Let me think."

Mack studied the front door of the cabin and then switched his gaze to the van. She could almost see him mentally calculating distances and odds.

"Well?" she prodded.

"I think we'll go with your idea to release the parking brake. But I'll handle it. You stay here. Whatever you do, don't show yourself. Got it?"

"Sure. Got it."

"If anything goes wrong, run for it. Don't think twice, just do it."

She said nothing.

"Understood?" he asked with an edge.

"Right. Sure. Understood."

The decision made, Mack did not hesitate any longer. He left her in the dripping darkness, gliding swiftly out into the open. She watched, her heart in her throat, as he circled around the van, keeping the vehicle between himself and the front door of the cabin. She prayed the fog would thicken to give him more cover.

When he disappeared on the far side of

the van, she almost stopped breathing altogether. A few seconds later the vehicle started to move.

In eerie silence it lumbered slowly backward. A fresh wave of fear engulfed her. This wasn't going to work if the two men didn't realize that something had gone wrong outside the cabin.

The vehicle continued its strangely silent retreat down the incline into the fog. She looked for Mack in the empty space near the front of the cabin. There was no sign of him.

In desperation, she reached down to find a rock she could hurl through a window to get the burglars' attention. Before she could toss it, however, one of the men appeared in the doorway. He stopped abruptly.

"Sonofabitch, Sandler. The *van*. You stupid bastard, you didn't set the brake."

The furious burglar burst through the doorway. He crossed the small deck and jumped the three steps to the ground. An instant later, he lurched violently as if he had tripped over an invisible object in his path. He stumbled and went down without making a sound. His body flopped out of sight in the darkness below the deck.

The second man loomed in the doorway. "What the hell — ?"

He took a step forward and came to an

abrupt halt. Unlike his partner, he did not drop like a stunned steer. He froze.

In the glow of the doorway, light glinted malevolently on the steel poised at his throat. Not a small pocketknife.

Cady sucked in her breath at the sight of the ancient sword. She realized that Mack must have found it in the back of the van.

Sandler was paralyzed by the blade. "What?"

"Drop the gun," Mack said from behind him. "Do it now."

"What?" The burglar said again, sounding bewildered.

"You've got three seconds."

Sandler did not say "what" again. Apparently having grasped the enormity of the change that had taken place in the situation, he gingerly removed the weapon from his belt and stooped to set it down on the deck.

Mack shifted slightly, gliding around Sandler. He did not take the tip of the blade away from the man's throat. When he got near the gun, he used the toe of one running shoe to nudge it out of reach.

"Cady," he said loudly into the darkness. "Come here."

She needed no second urging. She hurried out of the cover of the trees and rushed toward the open door.

"Pick up the gun." Mack did not take his attention off Sandler. "Hand it to me."

She scooped up the weapon without a word and gave it to him. He checked it swiftly with obvious expertise before he lowered the sword point. Then he took a step back to the open door and glanced briefly into the interior of the cabin.

"You'd better see to your friend," he said to Cady.

"Oh, lord, Mr. Vandyke." She went to the doorway and peered inside. "Are you okay, Mr. Vandyke?"

"Over here."

She whirled and saw a young angular man with dark brown hair sitting in the corner. He was bound hand and foot with duct tape. A colorful surfboard hung on the wall beside him. His brown eyes welled with relief at the sight of her.

"Scissors on the table," he said. "Next to the computer."

She dashed across the wooden floor, seized the scissors and rushed back to free Ambrose from the tape.

"I've been so worried about you, Mr. Vandyke," she said as she gently cut the tape. "Are you all right?"

"Yeah." Ambrose groaned and rubbed his reddened wrists. "Thanks to you and your

82

friend. I assume you're Cady Briggs?"

"Yes, and I was scared to death."

"You and me both," Ambrose said. "I was afraid you would walk into the middle of this and they'd get you, too."

"They almost did get her," Mack said in a very even voice.

Ambrose blinked owlishly. "Who are you?"

"The name is Easton. Mack Easton."

Ambrose nodded. "Good thing she brought you along."

"You want to give me a hand here?" Mack said. "The guy on the ground is still unconscious. We need to get this one secured first."

"You bet." Ambrose grimaced and caught his breath as he scrambled awkwardly to his feet. "Don't worry, there's plenty of duct tape."

Outside there was a dull, clanging thud. Cady realized the van had finally come to rest.

"Good grief," she whispered. "The armor."

"Relax," Ambrose said, "that stuff was built to withstand a lot of impact, remember?"

She went to the door and looked out at the vehicle. It was scrunched at an angle against a large boulder.

"I don't think that being bounced around in the back of a van is quite what the original designers had in mind for that armor," she said.

"Yeah, well, I'm not nearly as worried about the condition of that steel right now as I might have been before these two bastards showed up." Ambrose finished his task and stood back to examine Mack. "Who exactly are you, besides being Cady's friend?"

"I'm her boss," Mack said.

8

She hadn't tried to screw him, after all.

Two hours later, after the cops had left with the two burglars in custody, Mack stood in front of the blazing fire. He listened to Cady and Ambrose Vandyke discuss the old armor that had been dragged out of the van and piled in the corner. He did not trust himself to join in the conversation. It was all he could do to just stand there and look civilized.

At least he hoped he looked civilized. He'd been running on adrenaline for several hours now. Large doses of the stuff had unpredictable effects.

"A friend of mine named Tim Masters specializes in arms and armor. He told me about your collection, Ambrose," Cady said. She looked up from where she sat cross-legged, with the missing helmet in her lap. "He said that he had done some consulting for you and that you were focusing on rare pieces produced by the best northern Italian armorers. He mentioned that you were trying to acquire a complete garniture . . ."

Mack tuned out the discussion and swallowed some tea Ambrose had made for his guests. The taste of the stuff irritated him. He had never been a fan of tea. He liked coffee. Strong coffee.

Okay, so he had made a miscalculation based on the evidence he'd had in hand. He had leaped to what had seemed a logical conclusion. But he had been wrong. She had simply been doing her job as she'd understood it, tracing the missing helmet. The fact that she hadn't followed procedure and had taken a terrible risk that could have gotten her killed was a major problem, but he would deal with that later.

Right now he just wanted to savor the enormous relief that came with knowing she was safe and that she hadn't tried to cross him.

The satisfaction he felt was out of all proportion to the situation. It was not the professional relief that should have accompanied the realization that he hadn't made a major business miscalculation. Once again, he was reacting as if the whole damn thing had been personal. Hell, you'd think he'd just discovered that his lover hadn't been cheating on him with another man. *That* kind of personal.

Definitely over the top, given that until tonight he'd spent less than an hour and a half in her company. That had been the meeting in Vegas, and it had been one-hundred-percent business.

An hour and a half spent together discussing a job hardly qualified as a personal relationship. Of course, there had been the phone calls during the past two months. But you couldn't really count those.

All right, so I'm counting the phone calls. So sue me.

Somewhere inside he was poised on the fine line between control and a testosterone-driven euphoria. On an intellectual level, he knew what was happening to him. The threat of danger and violence left a chemical aftermath as potent as sexual desire. Took a while to work it off. But he could deal with that angle. It was Cady who complicated the mess. Every time he looked at her, the intellectual thing went out the window.

He had arrived here tonight in the grip of an icy rage that had been directed as much at himself as it was at Cady. The sight of her rental car parked outside the gate at the foot of the fog-bound drive had changed everything in an instant. Some part of him had known immediately that something was terribly wrong. That was when the fear kicked in.

"Incredible." Ambrose studied the helmet

Cady held. "Absolutely incredible. Hard to believe that all these years it was just stashed in a box in the back room of that little museum in Vegas."

"Ignorance was bliss in this case." Cady examined the engraved steel piece with an expression of reluctant appreciation. "Just look at the workmanship on this helmet. The shape is so elegant. The gilding on the tracery motifs is exquisite. See how it makes the design stand out against the background? Imagine spending so much time and artistic vision on an object made for the practice of warfare."

"Cool, huh?" Ambrose said cheerfully. "Wonder how it ended up in the Military World collection."

"I found a record of it in an early twentieth-century military museum catalog. There was a note that it had been removed to be sold at auction in New York in 1925. No record of the buyer, however. It simply disappeared."

"Maybe that guy Belford, the one you said opened Military World, bought it and just kept it in storage all those years."

Cady shrugged. "Possible. We'll probably never know for sure. How did it get into your collection, Ambrose?"

The inquiry attracted Mack's attention.

He roused himself from his reverie long enough to look at Ambrose. "Good question. How did you get it, Vandyke? I've got a program that, among other things, tracks on-line auctions and sales, public and private, legal and not-so-legal. I didn't see any trace of that helmet."

"Which is why he called me in to consult," Cady explained. "I specialize in the rumor mills of the art world, the kind his program can't track. Given your background in the software business, I'd expect you to be an on-line kind of collector, Ambrose."

"I didn't locate the helmet through an on-line contact," he said. "I was approached by a private dealer who told me he knew someone who wanted to broker a very quiet sale. I told him I was interested. He brought the helmet here and I paid for it in cash."

"You didn't question the provenance?" Mack asked.

Ambrose looked abashed. "I admit that I didn't ask too many questions."

"Right," Mack said. "And now we know where that gets you."

Ambrose turned red. "Okay, okay. But as it happened, the paperwork that I did see actually looked clean."

"Aside from the fact that the auction receipts were phony," Cady murmured.

"Yeah." Ambrose made a face. "Aside from that. But how was I to know the papers were fake?"

"You should have checked with Tim or someone else who knows arms and armor before you acquired the piece," Cady said.

"You're right." He gazed sadly at the helmet. "But I wanted it really bad and I didn't want there to be a problem, if you know what I mean."

Mack was surprised to feel a pang of genuine sympathy for Ambrose. Vandyke might be a retired software multimillionaire, but he was only twenty-three years old.

"Speaking of problems," Mack said, "how did you meet that pair that you ended up entertaining here tonight?"

"They just appeared on my doorstep. I don't know how they found out that I had the helmet."

"You were probably set up the day you bought the piece," Mack said. "I think it's a safe bet that those two were working with the so-called art consultant who arranged for the theft of the helmet and then sold it to you. When I get back to my computer, I may be able to pull up some names for the cops."

"I don't get it. Why sell the helmet to me and then steal it?"

90

Mack smiled humorlessly. "So that they can resell it to another collector. And steal it from him and sell it again. And again."

"You've got to hand it to them," Cady said. "It's certainly a creative way to ensure repeat business."

Mack flexed the fingers of one hand, remembering the feel of the old sword in his palm. "Like you said, collectors are paying sky-high prices for armor at the moment. Whenever one area of the art market gets hot, there's a rise in art theft in that area. The old law of supply and demand."

"Yeah, I know all about that law." Ambrose studied the helmet for a long moment. Then he raised earnest, remorseful eyes to Cady. "I'm really sorry about all this."

"I figure it's sort of like a plane crash," Cady said. "Could have been worse. We got lucky and walked away from it, thanks to Mack."

She smiled at him with serious, intent eyes. He realized that she considered him a hero for the moment. He wondered how long that would last.

"She's right," Ambrose said. "Man, I really owe you. If there's ever anything I can do to repay you —"

"I'll let you know," Mack said.

"I mean it," Ambrose insisted.

Mack raised a brow. "So do I."

Ambrose got to his feet. "What's this program you use? The one you said allows you to follow private art auctions on-line?"

"A friend designed it for me a couple of years ago." Mack turned back to the fire. "It allows me to retrieve information related to the movement of art and antiquities in the underground markets. Sales, thefts, private auctions. I'm building a specialized database that tracks a lot of the regular players who do business in those markets, good guys and bad guys. It stores the names of known forgers, dealer habits, methods of operation. Trends and patterns."

Ambrose frowned with professional concern. "Must take constant updating."

"Yes." Mack moved his shoulders slightly to loosen the prowling tension. "Unfortunately, the friend who designed it for me has set up his own on-line business and no longer has time to work on my program. There are still a lot of holes in my database."

"What kind of holes?"

Mack regarded him thoughtfully. "Do you really want to talk about this or are you just curious?"

"Are you kidding? I've got a very personal interest here. I am now officially the victim of attempted art theft. Tell me about the holes in your program, Mack."

Mack glanced at Cady. The strain of the evening showed in her eyes. "It's a little late to go into detail, but maybe we can discuss it some other time."

"Anytime, man. Anytime. After what you did for me, I am like totally at your service. Besides, this art tracing stuff sounds kind of intriguing."

"I'll call you." He made a mental note to give the idea some serious consideration. It wasn't often that he got the opportunity to pick up a free-lance consultant with Ambrose Vandyke's unique skills. He glanced at his watch. "Cady, we'd better get out of here. We need to find a motel. Neither one of us is in any shape to drive far tonight."

"You're welcome to stay here," Ambrose said quickly. "I know it's a little grotty, but I think I can find some clean towels."

"Thanks," Cady said. "But I think a motel would simplify everyone's life. Where's the nearest one? Santa Cruz?"

"Nah, you don't have to go that far. There's a little lodge less than a mile from here. Dude who runs it is a friend of mine." Ambrose reached for the phone. "I'll give him a call and set things up for you."

"That sounds great." Cady picked up the helmet and got to her feet. "By the way —"

Ambrose slanted her a speculative gaze as he held the phone to his ear. "Yeah?"

"I know you've already paid once for this piece and there's a good chance you'll never recover the money. But if you decide that you really do want it, I believe Mack's clients would be interested in talking to you. Right, Mack?"

He smiled wryly. "I don't think there's much doubt about it. My clients view that helmet as the equivalent of a winning lottery ticket. They can't wait to cash in on it."

"It's a deal," Ambrose said immediately.

"You haven't heard the price yet," Mack said.

Ambrose grinned good-naturedly. "I think I can afford it."

"In addition to buying the helmet, you may want to invest in a good security system for your expanding collection."

"You know, that thought crossed my mind more than once tonight while I watched those two dudes load my stuff into that van."

He turned back to his phone call and spoke rapidly to someone on the other end.

Mack glanced at Cady and saw that she was watching him. He could almost read the words "My Hero" scrawled in glowing neon letters in her eyes. It was getting harder and harder to ignore the deep, heavy tug of desire. He wondered if nature had arranged things so that the male stopped thinking clearly when the female smiled the way Cady was smiling now. As a method of ensuring the reproduction and continuation of the species, it had a lot going for it.

He reminded himself that he had already reproduced once in this lifetime. He had the college tuition bills to prove it. At his age a man was supposed to start thinking of long-range retirement plans.

9

An hour later Cady turned onto her back, folded her arms behind her head and stared up at the low-beamed ceiling. She was exhausted, but sleep was proving impossible. She was on edge and overstimulated. Not surprising given the events of the evening, she decided.

She concentrated, trying to sort out impressions. She had every reason to be teetering on the precipice of a panic attack, but this didn't feel like the onset of one. She knew what that felt like and this wasn't it.

Nevertheless, her nerve endings were pulsing with enough bio-electricity to power a small town.

She turned her head on the pillow to look at the clock. Three in the morning. Unfortunately, it would be quite a while yet before she could legitimately abandon the attempt to sleep and go out for breakfast.

She shoved aside the covers, got to her feet and went to the sliding glass door that opened onto the narrow balcony that wrapped around the second story of the small lodge. The darkness outside was absolute. The trees loomed over the peaked roof. It had started to rain in a serious fashion an hour ago. The overhanging eaves dripped steadily.

The need for fresh air, even if it was damp and chilly, was suddenly overwhelming. She turned and scooped up the light dressing gown she had left on the foot of the bed. It was a good thing that she had taken the precaution of packing for an overnight stay, she mused. The thought of facing Mack tomorrow morning with unbrushed teeth was not to be borne. She cinched the sash of the dressing gown, slid her bare feet into the loafers she had worn earlier and unlocked the glass slider.

Damp, bracing night air heavy with the scent of the woods enveloped her. She stepped outside and went to stand at the balcony railing. Shoulder-high wooden partitions separated her from the rooms on either side, but she could see that no light came from either of them. Apparently Mack was not having any trouble sleeping.

Lucky Mack.

Or was he lying awake in bed, staring at the ceiling as she had been doing until a short time ago?

Don't think about Fantasy Man in bed. Your

nerves can't take the additional stimulation.

She touched the wet railing with the tip of one finger. It was so quiet here in the rain-drenched redwoods. Hard to believe that the high-tech commercial wonderland that was Silicon Valley lay within commuting distance, assuming that one was prepared to commute on narrow mountain roads.

A shiver of awareness went through her. She sensed Mack's presence just before he spoke out of the darkness to her left.

"What's the matter?" he said. "Couldn't sleep?"

His question settled one issue — Mack was not in bed. He was standing in the dense shadow on the other side of the partition. She wondered how long he had been out here gazing into the wet night.

His hands were thrust deep into the pockets of a black windbreaker. He was a compelling if enigmatic figure, his expression unreadable in the darkness. Awareness went through her in a flash of invisible lightning that left her strangely breathless. It was as if she found herself poised at the top of a very high Ferris wheel.

She clutched the robe more securely at her throat and tried not to think in terms of fantasy and gender. They were business associates. He was her employer. There were rules of engagement to be observed, especially in view of the fact that she wanted to work for him again in the future. As often as possible.

"You okay?" he asked.

She could hear the genuine concern in his voice. She realized she had not answered his question.

"Fine. Great. No problem," she said quickly, trying to sound casual. What was a little danger, mayhem and a near-death experience on the job? All in a day's work in the art consulting business. She was a professional. "Just having a little trouble getting to sleep. Thought some night air might help."

"I'm not surprised. I thought you were handling things a little too coolly earlier this evening. Wondered when it would hit you."

Irritation surged through her. She *was* cool, damn it. She wasn't even having a panic attack although she had every right to one under the circumstances.

"Okay, so walking into a burglary-in-progress is not how I spend most of my evenings," she said brusquely. "But I hear that a change of pace now and then is good for you." She remembered the image of light glinting on a very old sword, and shuddered.

"Besides, you did all the heavy lifting."

"You gave me a hell of a scare tonight."

She froze, uncomprehending, at the tone. She could have sworn that he was quietly furious. But that made no sense. Why should he be mad at her? She was the one who had reason to be annoyed.

Her consulting instincts took over. This was a client, she reminded herself. She was going for repeat business here. Besides, they had both been under a lot of stress this evening. Allowances had to be made.

"I got a pretty good scare myself," she said, deliberately choosing a more diplomatic note. "And it got even worse when I realized you were going to do a lot more than just send the van rolling backward down the drive. I couldn't believe it when I saw you holding the point of that blade to that man's throat."

"Creating a distraction with the van wasn't going to solve the problem."

His voice was the temperature of ice now. It occurred to her for the first time that maybe he was the one in danger of having a panic attack. She took a step closer to the partition and peered at his face, trying to catch a glimpse of his expression.

"Are you okay?" she asked gently.

"Depends how you define okay."

"We've both had a difficult evening."

"You think?"

She did not like the cold amusement in his voice. It sounded as though he were exerting enormous self-control. She knew the feeling. She hesitated a second and then decided to take the plunge. This was Fantasy Man, after all. He had quite possibly saved her life tonight. He had certainly prevented the theft of a fortune in old armor. Mack deserved a reward. She braced herself for the supreme sacrifice.

"I have a pill in my key chain case," she said. "I keep it handy for emergencies. It's for acute anxiety attacks. You can have it if you need it." She tried not to think about the long trip home tomorrow without her small security blanket in her purse.

There was a short pause.

"Thanks," he said finally. "Very generous of you. But I found one of those little miniature bottles of whiskey in the mini-bar. I think it will do the trick."

"Oh, good." She tried to conceal her relief.

There was a beat of silence.

"Do you have to use the pills frequently?" he asked.

"No. But I have a tendency toward panic attacks. Everyone says I inherited it from my aunt's side of the family, but as far as I know she and I are the only ones who suffer from them."

"Have you always had trouble with the attacks?"

"They started when I was in college." She gripped her lapels more tightly. "But I think they stem from something that happened when I was fourteen. There was an . . . accident. I nearly drowned. Later, when I started getting the panic attacks, the feeling reminded me of how I felt when it happened."

"You use the pills often?"

"No. Not anymore. Not for ages." She listened to her own words with mounting horror. The conversation had taken a bad turn. By now Mack had probably concluded that she was nothing but a twitchy bundle of nerves — unstable, unsteady and unreliable. Not a terrific professional image. Visions of future consulting jobs began to fade rapidly. "I haven't had a serious problem for a long time. Years, in fact."

"How many years?"

If she didn't get the topic changed in a hurry, she was going to get a real panic attack tonight after all.

"At least two," she said, trying to sound casual and unconcerned. "Three, actually."

102

Three was pushing it a bit but in another couple of months it would be a full three years since the last severe attack. "Actually, it's been so long, I can hardly recall the last time I had a problem." Mentally, she crossed her fingers behind her back. "Regular yoga and deep breathing do the trick. I just keep the pill handy for an extreme emergency."

"I see."

Definitely time to redirect the focus of this conversation, she decided.

"What you did at Ambrose's cabin tonight," she said. "That was amazing. I assume from the way you dealt with those two thugs that this is not the first time you've been in that sort of situation?"

There was a small pause. She got the impression that Mack was considering his words carefully. Apparently the fact that they had shared a major bonding experience tonight did not mean that he suddenly wanted her to know his life history.

"My father was career military," he said finally. "I got married in college and needed a job in a hurry so I followed in his footsteps for a few years. When I got out I went to work for a company that did security consulting for corporations. One way or another I've spent a fair amount of time around guns or people who carried them."

"I see."

She digested that news cautiously. It certainly cast a whole new light on Mack Easton. She came from the world of art and until tonight she had assumed that he also came from that same realm. She had understood from their first telephone conversation that he was different from the other men she had known well in her life, but she had not fully comprehended just how different.

"How did you end up in the business of tracing lost and stolen art?" she asked.

"After my wife died, I decided to get into a line of work that involved fewer guns."

"I see. I'm sorry, I hadn't realized. When did you lose your wife?"

"Six years ago."

The quiet acceptance of loss in his voice told her everything she might have wanted to know about his marriage. He had loved his wife. He had come to terms with grief.

"I'm sorry," she said again, very gently this time.

Silence dripped as steadily as the rain for a time.

"You know," Mack said after a while, "I can't even remember the last time a recovery job went south the way this one did tonight."

He sounded thoroughly disgusted. She sighed inwardly. So much for the prospects of future work for Lost and Found. Without any real hope of altering his opinion of her performance, she sought some mitigating circumstances.

"It was a highly unusual situation," she pointed out. "Not exactly a routine assignment."

"You failed to follow procedure. You should have called me as soon as you traced the helmet to Vandyke."

"Wait a minute, that's not fair. I admit things went bad, but it wasn't my fault. I just flew in to examine the helmet. Ambrose had described it to me over the phone, but with old armor, you have to take a close look. How was I to know those two had planned a robbery?"

"You should have kept me in the loop."

"Give me a break, I didn't even know if it was the missing piece. I was just doing my job as a consultant, following up a lead."

"That's no excuse. I don't pay you to take risks. I expect my free-lance consultants to exercise good judgment and common sense and to stay within the boundaries of their expertise. I thought I made it clear when I hired you the first time that your job is to trace rumors and leads. I arrange for recovery."

He really was annoyed. A cold sensation settled over her.

"Are you telling me that I'm fired?" she asked.

"I'm thinking about it."

Not a certainty yet. She took a deep breath. It wasn't much, but she would cling to the tiny glimmer of hope.

"The situation that developed tonight is highly unlikely to ever occur again," she said briskly.

"Yeah?"

"In fact, I can practically guarantee that it won't."

"Is that so?"

"Next time, I'll keep you fully apprised," she vowed. "There won't be any more screw-ups."

Mack did not respond.

"I'll send you daily progress reports," she assured him. "Via e-mail so you'll get them in a timely fashion."

"Hmm."

He was weakening. She was almost sure of it.

"I'll institute my own internal procedures," she continued earnestly.

"Procedures?"

"I'll make sure you know the exact status of any trace job I'm working on, twenty-four hours a day. That way you can ask questions or give instructions at any point."

More silence. She held her breath.

"I take it you like working for Lost and Found?" he finally asked neutrally.

"Very much," she said quickly. "I realized after that first job that I did for you, the one involving the ewer from that Spanish monastery, that I wanted to do more trace work. Don't get me wrong, I enjoy consulting for my clients who want to acquire good pieces. But when you think about it, the Lost and Found work is a natural extension of my business. It takes advantage of my skills in a way that is extremely interesting. Fascinating, in fact."

"I see. You're in it for the thrill, is that it?"

"The challenge," she said. "I'm in it for the challenge."

"Uh-huh."

She waited, hardly daring to move.

"I don't want any more incidents like the one tonight," he warned.

He *was* weakening.

"As I said, I'll institute my own additional procedures to keep you fully informed."

He brooded on that. Mentally she drew up and designed a variety of professional-looking forms that she could use to transmit reports.

"All right," Mack said, finally. "We'll try it again. I'll give you a call the next time I get something in the decorative arts."

She allowed herself to relax. "Thanks. I really appreciate this. You won't regret it."

"You're sure of that?"

"Absolutely. Come on, Mack, you have to admit that I'm good at what I do. I've turned up all three of the missing objects you sent me after. Four, counting the helmet."

"Can't argue with that."

"I've got good instincts for this kind of work."

"Good instincts," he agreed dryly. "And good contacts."

She shrugged. "The art world is a small one and I was raised in it from the cradle. I can pull in information from a variety of sources that you can't reach with your computer program."

"You don't have to sell me on your ability to do the job. I already know you've got a flair for it."

She gazed steadily at the shadowed outline of his face. Best to change the subject again, she decided. "Well, now that we've settled my employment status, there's something else we should discuss."

"What's that?"

"I haven't thanked you for what you did

108

tonight," she said quietly. "I'm not sure how to do it. In fact, I don't even know how to begin."

"Forget it," he growled. "It's company policy at Lost and Found to keep an eye on employees."

"I see." She thought about that. "How *did* you know where I was tonight?"

"Called your assistant."

"Oh." Caddy nodded. "Smart. Well, would you mind if I gushed with gratitude just a little? Real live knights, with or without the armor, are rare these days."

"I said forget it."

Exasperated, she moved to stand next to the partition. She went still when she realized how close he was. Right there. Mere inches away. Close enough for her to feel the heat of his body. Close enough to see that he wasn't wearing his glasses. Close enough to make her catch her breath.

"Thanks anyway," she whispered.

He looked at her for what seemed like an eternity. With a flash of womanly intuition, she knew that he was going to kiss her.

All she had to do was step back and let the thin partition do its job. But why should she? she wondered. This was Fantasy Man and they were both single. And he had saved her life, probably.

My hero, she thought. The genuine article.

She did not retreat. He took his hands out of the pockets of his windbreaker very slowly, giving her plenty of time to change her mind. But she knew that she was not going to change it. She would not change anything about this moment, not for the world.

He reached over the top of the partition, caught her head between his palms and kissed her.

Fantasy Man.

His hands were big. She could feel the strength in them. It sent a delicious shock wave through her. Yet he cradled her face as if she were a piece of eighteenth-century Sevres porcelain. His mouth closed over hers, deliberate, persuasive — hungry. His fingers tightened ever so slightly. She could feel the power and the desire in him.

The rush took her completely by surprise, overwhelming her. It was as if her previous experience in this department had consisted of a few encounters with some attractive fakes and a handful of nice forgeries, but at long last she was dealing with an original creation.

So maybe this wasn't the smartest thing in the world. Still, where was the harm? She could handle it. True, she hadn't had much practice in a while because her social life had been in cold storage lately, but she wasn't going to lose her grip on reality just because Mack was kissing her. She was in full control here.

Mack slanted his mouth more heavily across hers, deepening the kiss. Heat pooled heavily in her lower body. It was probably a good thing that the partition was complicating matters, she thought. Otherwise, she would have been sorely tempted to wrap herself around him. Might have made a complete fool out of herself.

A kiss was one thing. Sleeping with a client was something else again. Definitely not good business policy.

Mack groaned softly. His hands fell away from her face. He raised his head.

It was all ending too soon.

She opened her eyes and saw that Mack was in motion. He had one foot on the lower crosspiece of the railing and was reaching for the top of the partition with his hand. In the next second he was over the top, vaulting lightly down onto her side of the balcony.

He caught her by the shoulders, pulled her into his arms and kissed her again. This time there was no partition between them.

Rules were made to be broken.

She put her arms around his neck. The moisture in the air had dampened his hair and his windbreaker, but that hardly mattered. He was hot enough to dry the rain off both of them. He was holding her so snugly against him that she could hardly breathe. That didn't matter either. Nothing mattered except getting as close as possible.

The intensity of her excitement blindsided her. Desire, fierce and relentless and thrilling, flooded her senses. She gripped his shoulders hard.

"Mack."

He slid one hand down her back to her upper leg, gripped and lifted her up against him. Her robe fell open. She gasped at the sudden deepening of the intimate physical contact and clung to him more fiercely.

"I've been thinking about doing this for hours," he muttered.

"Me too."

"No wonder neither of us could sleep."

He picked her up in his arms and shifted his mouth to her throat. She felt the night whirl around her. She realized that he was crossing the balcony to the sliding glass door.

"Open it," he breathed when he reached the barrier.

She groped for the handle and managed to haul the door aside. He carried her into the deeper shadows of the room.

By the time he fell with her in his arms down onto the rumpled sheets, she was wild and breathless and more excited than she had ever been in her life. A great, glorious urgency consumed her.

She rolled with him across the broad bed, frantic and eager and a little delirious. He fought her for the embrace, using his weight to pin her down at last. When she came to rest he was on top of her, one leg between her thighs. The robe had come undone completely in the passionate scuffle, leaving her sheathed only in the thin nightgown.

Mack already had a hand beneath the edge of the garment. She felt his warm, strong palm on the inside of her thigh and then he was cupping her, probing her, stroking her. She felt the moisture between her legs and knew that he could feel it too.

She kissed him with growing desperation. Every place she could reach with her mouth was fair game — the curve of his shoulder, the lobe of his ear, the inside of his wrist. Somewhere in the back of her mind a tiny warning bell sounded. This was not her love life. Wild flings with virtual strangers was not her style.

But the pealing of the small bell was too distant and too weak to be anything more than a minor distraction.

Mack lifted himself away from her long enough to strip off his windbreaker, the black T-shirt underneath and his trousers.

When he came back down on top of her a moment later, she was more than ready for him. He did not hesitate. He used one hand to guide himself slowly, heavily, deeply into her.

His low, husky groan held both anticipation and satisfaction.

She was wet and ready for him when he entered, but she had never experienced such a full sensation. There was too much of him. Her first thought was that he would never fit. Her second thought was that he was perfect, just what she needed to give her relief from this driving tension.

He stroked slowly, once, twice, and then the too-tight feel of him inside her swamped her overstimulated senses. Her whole lower body clenched.

Mack sucked in his breath.

The release that followed stunned her with its intensity. Mack covered her mouth and swallowed the shriek.

In the next instant, his body stiffened, every muscle taut. She dug her nails into his back. He wrenched his mouth away from hers and buried his face in the bedding beside her.

His own exultant shout was only partially muffled by the plump, fluffy down pillow.

She had been right, she thought. Some rules were made to be broken.

She rose languidly from the depths of the pleasant exhaustion that had settled on her immediately after the climax. Outside on the balcony the rain continued to fall in a steady patter.

She opened her eyes and saw the large dark silhouette that was Mack lying beside her. He was on his stomach, his face turned away toward the night. The quilt covered him to his waist, leaving bare the sleek contours of his back. She thought of how he had lifted her so easily and carried her into the bedroom. Fantasy Man.

She smiled to herself, savoring the delicious sensation that was flowing through her. She wondered if this feeling was common after truly great sex.

"Mack?"

No response.

"Mack?" Louder this time.

"Mmm?" He did not raise his head from the pillow.

She levered herself up on one elbow. "I was just wondering about something."

"Could you wonder about it in the morning?" he mumbled into the pillow.

"I've been thinking. Earlier you told me how you managed to find me at Vandyke's house, but you weren't clear on *why* you followed me there."

There was a short, distinct pause.

"A hunch."

"It must have been more than a hunch." She frowned, thinking back on the events of the evening. "I know you said something about keeping an eye on your outside consultants, but I doubt if you go chasing after each one every time he or she makes a trip while under contract to Lost and Found."

Mack did not respond to that observation. She wondered if he had gone back to sleep.

"Mack?"

"Do you always do this?"

"Do what?"

"Get chatty after sex?"

The irritation in his voice hurt. She told herself that he was just grouchy because she had pulled him out of a sound sleep. Heroes needed their rest. But she had to know.

"Was it your intuition?" she asked gently. "I know men don't like to admit that they pay attention to stuff like that, but you can tell me."

He did not move for a few seconds. Then, very deliberately, he pushed the pillow up against the headboard, punched it a couple of times and turned onto his back.

"I guess you could call it intuition," he said finally.

A light, happy sensation fizzled through her. Obviously a bond of some sort had been established between them during the past few months. What had happened tonight was more than just a one-night stand.

"You sensed that I might be in danger?" she asked. "That's amazing."

There was a short pause from his side of the bed.

"I don't think you can say that I sensed it," he said.

"Well? What made you decide to ride to the rescue?"

"This is important to you, isn't it?"

"Yes." She wasn't sure why, but she understood that she needed to know the answer.

"All right, I didn't know that you might be in physical danger until I arrived at the cabin and realized that things didn't look right."

"So why did you follow me there?"

He scrubbed his face with his hand. "Because I figured that you had brokered your own deal with Vandyke. Thought you'd dug up a buyer for the helmet."

"*A buyer?*" It took an effort to wrap her mind around the enormity of her misunderstanding. But when she finally grasped the significance of what he had said, she went first cold and then hot with rage. "Wait a second. You thought I'd arranged a deal for the helmet?"

"Yeah."

"One that did not include your clients?"

"Yeah."

"How could you possibly think that?"

He shrugged, either unaware or uncaring of her rising fury. "When I realized you'd suddenly hopped a plane to see the guy who had the helmet, I did the logic."

"You did the logic?" It was all she could do to keep her voice relatively even. "*What* logic?"

"If you recovered the helmet and returned it to Dewey and Notch, you would receive your usual fee from Lost and Found. But you would get that fee regardless of whether or not you located the piece, right?"

"Right," she said very tightly.

"On the other hand, if you talked Vandyke

into selling the helmet to another collector or a dealer on the underground market, someone who wouldn't ask too many questions, you could pick up a hefty commission in addition to whatever I paid you. All you had to do was report back to me that you couldn't trace the helmet. You see where I'm going here?"

"Yes, I certainly do, Mr. Easton." She pushed herself up onto her knees and wrapped the quilt around her. "Where you're going is an insult to my professional integrity and my reputation."

It must have finally dawned on him that she was furious.

"I was just being cautious," he said carefully.

"Cautious, nothing. You thought I was planning to cheat you." Her voice climbed in spite of her best efforts. "You assumed that I was going to double-cross you. You just leaped to the conclusion that I was a crook."

"I was going with the probabilities. You have to see how it looked from my point of view."

"No, I do not have to see how it looked from your point of view." She scrambled off the bed, taking the quilt with her. "I can see from my point of view that your point of view is nothing less than an insult. How dare you accuse me of trying to con you?"

"I didn't accuse you of anything." He sat up slowly. "I wasn't taking any chances, that's all. Lost and Found is a business. I have to run it like one."

"Is that right? Well, I happen to be in business, too. This is my professional reputation you're trashing here. How am I supposed to respond to that kind of thing? How would you act if the shoe was on the other foot?"

"I'm trying to explain —"

"I think you've done enough explaining. I don't want to hear any more of your stupid explanations." She drew herself up in the quilt. "You followed me because you thought I was betraying you, not because you were concerned about my safety."

"I'm sorry." He rolled to his feet and faced her across the width of the bed. "I made a mistake."

"Yes, you certainly did."

"It wouldn't have happened if you had kept me in the loop."

"It's called taking the initiative. And don't you dare blame this on me. I didn't even know if it was the right helmet, for crying out loud. I knew how excited Dewey and Notch were. I didn't want them to get their hopes up and then disappoint them."

"I apologize." Mack shoved his fingers through his hair. "That's all I can do. We've already agreed that next time you'll follow procedures so that this kind of misunderstanding doesn't happen again."

"Don't worry, Mr. Easton, there's not a chance in hell that there will be any future misunderstandings between us." She smiled coldly across the rumpled sheets. "Because there isn't going to be a next time. When you get back to your office, you can remove me from your roster of consultants because I won't be taking any more assignments from Lost and Found."

"Calm down." He reached for his trousers. "You're a little wired right now. Probably more delayed stress. We'll discuss this after we've had some sleep."

"No, we will not discuss this in the morning. You and I have nothing more to talk about, Mack."

"Take it easy." He drew up his zipper with a quick, efficient motion. "You told me earlier that you liked the work you do for Lost and Found. And you're good at it. Why would you want to give it up just because you're a little pissed at me right now?"

"You're right. I do like the work." Cold triumph blazed through her. "But it occurs to me that I don't need to take any more

121

consulting contracts from Lost and Found. I can find my own clients."

He stilled. "What the hell are you talking about?"

"I've had some experience in the field now. I've got the hang of this business and I've got plenty of connections in the art world. Once the word gets out that I'm available to trace lost and stolen art, clients will be beating down my door."

"You think it's that easy?" Disbelief mingled with outrage in his voice. "I've got news for you. It's one thing to trace missing art through the underground markets. Recovering it is something else altogether. You saw what happened tonight. There are some nasty players in this end of the business."

"So? If I need muscle, I'm sure I can hire it."

"You don't know what you're talking about." He started around the bed. "You're upset. Maybe you're having one of your panic attacks."

"I'm not panicked, I'm pissed. Believe me, I can tell the difference."

"Cady —"

She leveled a finger at the sliding glass door behind him. "Get out of here."

He stopped at the foot of the bed, watching her in the shadows. "Don't you think you're overreacting?"

"No. Leave. Right now. You're right about one thing; I have been under a lot of stress tonight. I need some sleep."

He hesitated. Then he bent down, jerked his windbreaker off the floor and went to the door. "We'll discuss this after breakfast."

"No, we will not. I wouldn't take another job with Lost and Found if I was starving. Is that clear?"

"We need to talk."

"We have nothing more to say to each other. I'm about to become your competition."

"I've got nothing against cooperating with the competition on occasion."

She gave him a steely smile. "Your new competition has a lot against cooperating with Lost and Found. Leave, Mack."

He opened the slider and stepped out onto the balcony. There he halted once more and glanced back over his shoulder.

"Does this mean that I'm not a hero anymore?" he asked.

She did not deign to respond to that. Instead she rushed around the foot of the bed, seized the handle of the slider and slammed it closed.

She watched through the heavy plate glass as he vanished back over the partition.

The trouble with a good fantasy was that it never stood up to a reality check.

She was still seething when she stalked into her condominium the following afternoon. It was good to be home, she told herself. So what if the place felt a little empty? She was used to it, wasn't she?

Besides, now that she was expanding into the business of tracing lost art, she would probably be doing more traveling. That would mean spending a lot less time here alone.

She dropped the handle of the small, rolling suitcase and picked up the phone to check for messages. There were three of them. She had a fleeting vision of one being from Mack. Maybe he had called to grovel. Not that she would change her mind about working for Lost and Found, of course. But she wouldn't mind listening to a little groveling.

Talk about a fantasy.

None of the three calls was from Mack. The first was unimportant. But the second, the one from her cousin Sylvia, stunned her.

". . . calling to let you know that Aunt Vesta is dead. She drowned in her pool while swimming last night. They think she had one of

her anxiety attacks, became disoriented and couldn't make it to the steps. The funeral is scheduled for Tuesday here in Phantom Point . . ."

The third call was from her parents.

". . . We're on our way back for the funeral. Can't stay long . . ."

Vesta Briggs was dead. The indomitable head of Chatelaine's was gone. It was hard to grasp the sudden change in the world.

Cady hung up the phone and gazed unseeingly out into the night. Her eyes burned. In another minute she would be crying.

Vesta had become difficult and increasingly eccentric toward the end of her life. Nevertheless, she had been a presence in the art world. The funeral would be well attended, but Cady doubted that there would be many tears shed.

10

"So, what went wrong on the last job, Dad?" Gabriella asked.

Mack sighed inwardly and kept his attention on the early seventeenth-century tapestry hanging on the museum wall. It was one of several on display. Each showed vibrant scenes from a unicorn hunt and in the process depicted a past that was part reality and part myth. The colors, especially the rich reds and blues, were extraordinary, given the age of the wool and silk. The tapestries teemed with life and energy. Each of the faces of the literally dozens of human figures had been endowed with individualized features. The myriad animals ranged from hunting hounds to griffins. Plants bloomed in glorious detail.

The tapestries were on loan from a private collection. The special exhibition had given Mack an excuse to meet his daughter for lunch in San Francisco and an afternoon of wandering through a museum.

Museum-going was a family passion. He had met his wife, Rachel, at an exhibition of

Impressionists during his sophomore year in college. Many of their dates had taken place in museums and galleries. When Gabriella had arrived, they had continued the practice. Gabriella had toured her first museum in a carrier attached to Mack's back.

After Rachel's death, he had taken his daughter back into museums, endless numbers of them. Together they sought solace in the art and artifacts that were the tangible proof of the universal nature of the human experience.

When the natural vicissitudes of parenting a teenager had struck, he had discovered that museums could transcend, for short periods at least, a host of thorny issues involved in single-fatherhood. Other dads attended ball games with their kids. Mack and Gabriella toured museums. He learned that the two of them could talk in quiet galleries surrounded by art even when communication had become impossible everywhere else.

On summer vacations they had hit foreign institutions — the Hermitage, the Ashmolean, the Louvre and countless more of the great treasure-houses of Europe. On school breaks they had crisscrossed the country, touring everything from the New York Met and the Art Institute of Chicago to the Seattle Art Museum and the Getty.

"What makes you think something went wrong?" he asked.

"Dad, this is me, your one-and-only heir apparent. I can tell when things go wrong on a job. Just like you know when I've got a new boyfriend."

He did turn at that and gave his self-proclaimed heir a considering look. She had always been Gabriella, never Gabby. Rachel had insisted on it right from the beginning. On the first day of kindergarten Gabriella had announced to the teacher that she would only answer to her full name. The edict had been enforced all through elementary and high school. She had just turned nineteen, in the midst of her freshman year in college, and she showed no signs of softening her stance.

"You've got a new boyfriend?" he asked with grave interest. "What happened to Eric? I kind of liked the guy." He raised a hand before she could answer. "Wait, I'll bet that's what went wrong, isn't it? I read somewhere that the quickest way to get rid of your daughter's boyfriend is to tell her that you approve of him."

Gabriella rolled her eyes. They were gray-blue, the same shade as his own. Her fair hair, fine-boned features and lovely smile, however, had come from her mother's gene pool. It had been six years since Rachel had been killed by a drunk driver. The initial razor-sharp pain of loss had eventually worn down to a quiet memory. But sometimes when he looked into his daughter's face like this, he could feel whispers of the old rage and bitterness that he had experienced when he had been forced to accept the brutal fact that Rachel would never see Gabriella grow up into a beautiful, intelligent young woman.

"Dad, I told you, Eric is just a friend."

"You're sure?"

"He's gay, okay? Stop trying to change the subject. You told me that you recovered that old piece of armor and that Dewey and Notch made a deal to sell it to that software genius up in the mountains."

"Ambrose Vandyke."

"Whatever. It looks to me like it was a win-win situation for everyone. But you're acting as if things went wrong. What happened?"

"I miscalculated," he said. In ways he hadn't even realized until too late, he added silently.

He moved on to the next tapestry, a scene of seventeenth-century French court life in all its elegance, charm and stunning decadence.

Gabriella hurried after him. "You never miscalculate."

"Everyone makes mistakes."

"Does this have something to do with that new free-lancer you've been using lately? The one you said had a special expertise in European decorative arts?"

That question gave him serious pause. He still wasn't accustomed to the occasional flashes of adult insight that were starting to come with increasing frequency from his daughter.

"What makes you think it has anything to do with her?" he asked.

"Give me some credit here, Dad. You've used a lot of consultants over the years, but I knew there was something different about this one the first time you mentioned her."

"Yeah? How did you come to that conclusion?" He was stalling. Sometimes it worked with teenagers. They were so focused on themselves and their own problems, so preoccupied with the business of becoming an adult, that they didn't always pick up on the fact that other people were not supplying full answers.

"I don't know." Gabriella's brows came together in an uneasy frown. "It's the way you talk about her, I guess. You get sort of quiet whenever her name comes up in the

130

conversation. If I ask you about her, you just tell me how good she is. What a great eye she has."

"She is good. I'd swear she's got a sixth sense where fakes are concerned. Terrific instincts when it comes to tracing missing art, too."

Hell, Cady was good enough to follow through on her threat, he thought. She *could* become his competition. She certainly had the skills and the contacts to handle a lot of the trace work. The thought of her doing recovery, however, was nothing short of appalling. Granted, nine times out of ten there was little physical danger involved. But occasionally, as the Vandyke job had so graphically illustrated, matters got complicated. Cady knew nothing about that end of the business. The first time things went wrong, she would be in big trouble.

He winced, thinking of her parting shot. *"If I need muscle, I'm sure I can hire it."*

"You've used other free-lancers who were good, but you never got that tone in your voice when you told me about them."

"Gabriella —"

"Come off it, Dad, this case was the first time you met Cady Briggs in person, and you come back acting weird. Something happened, I know it."

Gabriella wasn't going to allow herself to be distracted, he realized as he moved on to the next tapestry. He studied the unicorn in the scene in front of him.

"Miss Briggs went outside normal procedures," he said carefully. "There were some problems in the recovery. Everything turned out all right in the end, but we had to get the police involved."

Gabriella brightened visibly. "You mean Miss Briggs screwed up?"

"I wouldn't put it quite like that."

"She *did* screw up. I can tell. She screwed up royally, didn't she?" Gabriella looked very satisfied now. "So, did you fire her?"

"Not exactly."

"Why not? You just said that she didn't follow procedures and that you had to call in the cops. You've always told me that, whenever possible, you try to recover objects for your clients without involving the authorities. That's the reason people come to Lost and Found in the first place. They don't want publicity and attention."

"Sometimes you can't avoid it. This was one of those situations."

"You just said that things went wrong because Miss Briggs failed to follow procedures. Why defend her?" Gabriella asked stubbornly.

"I'm not defending her. Free-lance consultants have a certain degree of latitude. That's why they're free-lance rather than full-time employees." Damn. Now he was making excuses for Cady. "She's new at the business. She'll learn." Probably the hard way, he thought, when she tries to hire that muscle.

"What did you mean when you said that you didn't exactly fire Miss Briggs?"

"I decided to give her a second chance because she's good at what she does. But she said that she wasn't interested in doing any more consulting work for Lost and Found."

"You mean she got mad and quit?"

"That's pretty much how we left it."

"Why didn't you say so? Guess that takes care of the problem, doesn't it?" Gabriella was clearly relieved. "You won't have to worry about her screwing up any more jobs in the future, will you?"

"Apparently not. Mind telling me what you've got against Miss Briggs? You've never even met her."

Gabriella looked away, concentrating very hard on the tapestry. "I don't think she's good for you."

He did a double take. "What the heck is that supposed to mean?"

"It's hard to explain." Gabriella flushed.

"You get a sort of brooding note in your voice whenever you talk about her. It's like she makes you depressed or something."

This was what came of sending young people to college, he told himself. He was not about to attempt to explain the difference between frustrated sexual desire and clinical depression to a nineteen-year-old. He wasn't sure he understood the technical nuances involved, himself.

"I'm not depressed."

"Are you sure?"

"Positive."

"Maybe you should talk to Dr. Jenny, Dad."

The thought of talking to the grandmotherly therapist who had helped guide Gabriella and himself through the grieving process after Rachel's death and later gave him advice on parenting a sensitive teen was daunting. He could just picture himself trying to explain the differences between sexual frustration and clinical depression to the good doctor.

"I'm fine, Gabriella." It was past time to change the subject. "The good news is that Dewey and Notch are in clover, thanks to Vandyke."

That comment successfully sidetracked her. She brightened. "Did he give them a ton of money for that old helmet?"

"He did, indeed. Vandyke is very casual about money. I think he's more interested in surfing and collecting old armor than he is in good bargains. With what he gave them, Dewey and Notch can pay off the loan on their business and expand their exhibits. They're happy as clams."

Gabriella smiled. "Hey, that's great. Bet Granddad was pleased when you told him that you had been able to help."

"I gave him a call last night. He was glad to know that Notch and Dewey are now set, financially speaking." He moved on to the next exhibit, mentally bracing himself. "Since we're on the subject of finances, there's something I want to talk to you about."

"Don't tell me you've changed your mind about getting me a car this year? I don't have to wait until I'm a sophomore?"

"No, I haven't changed my mind about a car, honey. I'm going to sell the house."

That stopped her cold, just as he had feared it would. She whirled away from the tapestry to gaze at him with a shocked expression.

"Are you serious?" she demanded.

"I'm still in the planning stages," he said gently. "I haven't listed it yet. But, yes, I'm serious."

"Dad, you can't mean it." Her voice rose. "You can't do it."

"Gabriella, it's too big for me now that I'm mostly there on my own. I don't have time for such a large garden. You know that I'm doing more traveling these days. It would be convenient to live closer to a major airport. It's a long drive in to San Francisco from Sebastopol."

"But what about when I come home at breaks and during summer vacation?"

He smiled slightly. "Don't worry, I'll make sure the new place has a second bedroom."

"That's not the point." Gabriella moved her hand in a troubled gesture. "You've got Mrs. Thompson coming in once a week to clean the house. If you need a gardener, you can hire one. I realize that it's a long trip to the San Francisco airport, but you can take a shuttle if you don't feel like driving, can't you?"

He had known this would be difficult. "Honey, I realize that this is coming as a shock to you."

"It's our house. We've always lived there."

"You're an adult now. We both know that you won't ever be coming back there to live permanently."

"Don't count on it." She made a face. "I

136

hear that it's real common for unemployed offspring to return to the nest to take advantage of free room and board until they find a job."

"No sweat. If you need to freeload for a while after college, we'll work something out. I'll have my lawyer draw up a contract for indentured servitude for you to sign. Nothing fancy. Shouldn't be any problem."

Her mouth tightened. "This isn't a joke. I can't believe you'd actually sell our house."

"Like I said, I haven't listed it yet."

"But you're going to list it, aren't you?"

He hesitated. "Yes."

Her hand tightened around the strap of her purse. "This has something to do with what went wrong on the job you did for Dewey and Notch, doesn't it?"

It was his turn to be stunned. "No, nothing at all. I've been thinking about this for some time now."

"I don't believe it." She searched his face. "Dad, please don't tell me that Cady Briggs is involved in this."

"Cady has nothing at all to do with it."

"Are you sure?"

He shook his head, exasperated. "What makes you think Cady Briggs has got something to do with my decision to sell the house?"

"I don't know. All I know is that you never mentioned the idea until today." She made a face. "Jeez, Dad, I can't believe you're acting like this because of a woman. Aren't you a little old for that kind of thing?"

"What kind of thing?" he asked neutrally.

Her cheeks turned a bright pink. "You know what I mean."

"No, I don't think I do."

"Stop teasing me, Dad. This is too important. This is our home you're talking about."

The sheen of moisture he thought he saw in her eyes worried him. He draped an arm around her shoulders.

"Take it easy, sweetheart. I'm not going to rush into anything. I'll take my time. There are a lot of decisions to be made. Come on, let's go get some lunch."

Later that afternoon he made the ninety-minute drive south with a very quiet Gabriella beside him. He deposited her safely at her dorm on the wooded campus of the University of California at Santa Cruz and got back into the car for the long trip home.

It took him north again to San Francisco and across the Golden Gate Bridge, through the rolling hills of Marin County and beyond, into the green and gold of the Sonoma County landscape.

He followed Highway 101 to the turnoff that led to the comfortable old house that, at some point during the past year, had become too big and too empty. He brought the car to a halt in the tree-lined drive and switched off the ignition.

For a time he stayed where he was, hands resting on the steering wheel, and studied the home where he had watched his very smart, very lovely little girl grow up into a very smart, very lovely young woman.

He was grateful to the old house. It had helped him raise Gabriella. It had sheltered them both after Rachel's death, and it had provided stability and a sense of security for a motherless girl. But it had done its job and now it held only old memories. As hard as he tried, he could not see himself going on much longer inside those high-ceilinged rooms. The door to the past was waiting for him to close it.

Gabriella had guessed right. Something *had* happened on the last job. He had partially opened another door and caught a tantalizing glimpse of his own future.

11

It took him ten days of heavy-duty thinking, the sort of somber, serious contemplation that Gabriella would probably have mistaken for brooding — or, worse, depression — to concoct a plan.

Granted, as plans went, it was pretty half-assed, he decided as he came to a halt in front of Cady's front door. But he was stuck with it, primarily because he had been unable to come up with anything more promising.

Cady opened the door after he'd leaned on the bell for nearly a full minute. She was barefoot. Her dark hair was pulled back into a strict knot that emphasized her interesting features. She was dressed in tights and a leotard, and she had a sexy, stretchy little skirtlike thing tied around her waist. All the clothing was stark black. He wondered if that was a bad omen.

She stared at him for a few seconds with the expression of a woman who has just discovered an extraterrestrial on her front step.

"I had to come down to Santa Barbara on

business," he said into the awkward silence. "Happened to be in the neighborhood. Had your address in my files. Thought I'd take a chance and see if you were home."

Thought I'd leap off this cliff because I had nothing better to do and I was going nuts trying to think of an excuse to see you again, he added silently.

She blinked a couple of times, looking startled and somewhat confused. But not annoyed, he thought. That was a positive sign. He became aware of the music that was flowing down the hall behind her. Mozart.

"You caught me by surprise," she said. "I was just finishing my yoga exercises."

"Didn't mean to interrupt."

"No, no, it's okay," she said quickly. "I just wasn't expecting you to show up in person."

"Is there any other way to show up?"

"I thought you'd call first to discuss the situation." She sounded disgruntled now, maybe even flustered. "I take it the fact that you're here means that you're interested?"

She had expected him to call? And here he'd been thinking that he would be lucky to get a foot in the door. His spirits rose. Obviously he had missed some significant signals somewhere along the line. Wouldn't have been the first time.

"I'm interested," he said, feeling his way through the verbal minefield. "Definitely interested."

"Good." Something that might have been relief flashed in her eyes. "I realize that I probably wasn't very clear in the message that I left on your voice mail last night."

"Uh-huh." He kept his voice noncommittal and made a mental note to call for his messages as soon as he got back to the hotel. He hadn't checked them since yesterday afternoon. He'd been too busy obsessing on how to make this little drop-in scene appear casual and off the cuff.

"I don't blame you if you're confused."

"I've been confused before," he assured her. "You get used to it."

She gave him a slightly quizzical smile. "I would have called sooner but I was out of town and there was a lot going on."

"I've been a little out of touch, myself," he said. "Didn't know you'd been gone." He suddenly recalled her plans to set herself up in competition to Lost and Found. His stomach clenched. "A consulting job?"

"No, a funeral. My great-aunt died while I was helping you recover that armor for your friends."

"Great-aunt?" That got his full attention.

"You mean Vesta Briggs? The head of Chatelaine's?"

"Yes."

"I'm sorry." He couldn't believe he had missed the news. He made it a point to keep up with events in the art world. For the death of Vesta Briggs to have escaped his notice, he must have been more than just a little out of touch during the past ten days. He must have been in a complete fog. "I didn't know."

"They think that she had an unusually bad panic episode while she was swimming alone. She may have assumed that it was a heart attack. The symptoms can be very similar. At any rate, the doctor told my cousins, Sylvia and Leandra, that in her extreme anxiety, Vesta probably grew exhausted and disoriented very quickly and went under."

"I'm sorry," he said again. He couldn't think of anything else to say, under the circumstances. "Must have been a shock."

"Everyone told her that she shouldn't swim alone, especially at night when she was the only one in the house. But my aunt was always very strong-willed."

He nodded. "The trait obviously runs in the family."

Cady's jaw tightened briefly. Then she

143

sighed. "I won't argue with you on that point." She stepped back. "I suppose you'd better come inside. I need to fill you in on the situation and I don't want to do it here in the doorway. Would you like some iced tea?"

He did not like cold tea any better than he liked hot tea, but he was nothing if not adaptable.

"The tea sounds good," he said as he moved through the front door into the hall.

She led the way into an airy living room defined by stark white walls and minimalist furnishings.

"Have a seat." She motioned to a sleek black chair.

The condominium was on the second floor. The sliding glass doors opened onto an expansive tiled balcony. He glanced out and down at the stylishly landscaped grounds. A small fountain gurgled amid a selection of lush plants arranged in an artful grouping. Expensive, tasteful and not unlike a lot of other upscale condo developments in the area.

It was the interior of Cady's home, with its sculptural spaces and contemporary décor that surprised him. He chose the black, Italian-modern chair positioned on a crimson area rug and watched Cady go behind a glass-block counter set with black and turquoise tiles. She opened the stainless-steel refrigerator and removed a pitcher. The tea inside was the color of amber.

"This isn't quite what I expected," he said, watching her pour the tea into two glasses.

She glanced up from her task. "What do you mean?"

He moved a hand slightly to indicate her interior décor. "Given your professional expertise and your background, I expected to find you living with a lot of really good antiques."

"I spend a great deal of my working time with old pieces." She picked up the glasses and carried them into the living area. "I find that the contemporary style at home suits me. It gives me a break that allows me to think in ways that I can't when I'm immersed in the past."

"Makes sense." He took one of the glasses and tried to look like he had half a clue about what was going on here. "Since, as you say, your message was a little vague, why don't you start at the beginning and fill me in?"

"All right."

She walked to a low-backed leather sofa

and curled into the corner, one sleek leg bent at the knee. He noticed a sheet of creamy notepaper filled with elegant, feminine handwriting lying on the glass table in front of the sofa. Next to the note was an open envelope. A small, elaborately carved gold key set with a blue gemstone rested on top of it.

"Long story short," Cady said, "is that Aunt Vesta, in addition to leaving me her house, an important piece of jewelry and her collection of antique boxes, bequeathed me a controlling block of shares in Chatelaine's. The entire family is still in shock."

"Why is it so strange that she would leave you the shares?"

"She knew that I had no interest in the day-to-day operation of the business. It was understood in the family that she would leave her voting shares to my cousin Sylvia, who is currently the CEO."

"And now?"

Cady sipped tea thoughtfully and then lowered the glass. "Now, for all intents and purposes, I hold the future of Chatelaine's in my hands. And I have no idea why Vesta arranged for that to happen."

"I take it congratulations are not in order?"

"I told you, I never wanted to be a part of

Chatelaine's. Corporate operations, five-year plans and retirement benefit programs bore the socks off me. Aunt Vesta knew that."

"Yet she stuck you with those shares."

"Yes." Cady tapped one elegantly manicured fingernail against the glass. "At a time when, as fate would have it, Chatelaine's is facing a major crossroads."

"What kind of crossroads?"

"Next month the board was scheduled to vote on whether or not to merge with the Austrey-Post galleries. The proposal has been in the works for months."

Mack felt he was on firmer footing now. He knew something about the long-standing friendly rivalry between the two privately held firms.

"That would be a major move, all right," he said.

"It has a lot of possibilities. Combining the resources of Chatelaine's and Austrey-Post would catapult the new company into the big leagues as far as the art world is concerned. Sylvia is already talking about expanding to the East Coast and possibly opening a branch in London. Randall and Stanford want to establish a presence on the internet."

"Who are Randall and Stanford?"

"Randall is Randall Post," she said. "His grandfather, Randall Austrey, founded the Austrey Gallery. Austrey's daughter eventually married John Post. Austrey made his son-in-law a partner in the firm and the gallery became Austrey-Post."

The name clicked. "Randall Post is your ex-husband, isn't he?"

Her jaw tightened. "Yes."

He had done his research before contacting her the first time. Post was the man she had divorced after a nine-day marriage. Morbid curiosity pulsed through him, but he could see that Cady was not inclined to elaborate on her relationship with her ex.

"Stanford would be Stanford Felgrove, then?" he asked. "The current president and CEO of Austrey-Post?"

"Right. John Post died when his son, Randall, was thirteen. Randall's mother remarried Stanford Felgrove." Cady's mouth was a grim line. "Jocelyn Post died of alcoholism and left fifty-one percent of Austrey-Post to her second husband. Stanford Felgrove took over control of the gallery. Today, Randall is only a junior partner in the firm his grandfather founded and which his mother inherited."

"That's got to be a little hard for your ex to swallow."

"Yes." Cady paused. "Randall and Stanford have handled the situation by dividing the business into two different spheres. Stanford manages corporate operations. In fairness, he's good at it. He has certainly kept Austrey-Post profitable. Sylvia tells me it has just completed a record-breaking year. Randall is the one with the background in art and antiques, though, and the connections. He courts clients and brings in the major consignments. Both of them are pressing for the merger."

"Am I missing something? Is there a problem with the merger?"

"That's the sixty-four-dollar question." Cady tapped the glass again. "Until shortly before my aunt's death, things were on track for the board vote next month. There shouldn't have been any glitches. Both boards wanted the merger to happen. The families on both sides are enthusiastic about the prospects for the future."

She stopped talking abruptly.

"But?" he prompted.

"But a few days before she drowned, Aunt Vesta postponed the vote. At about the same time, she changed her will to leave me the shares in Chatelaine's."

"And you don't know why?"

"She just said that she was having some

last-minute doubts about the wisdom of the merger."

He considered that for a moment and then shrugged. "If that was true, why wouldn't she have discussed them in detail with your cousin Sylvia and the other members of the board?"

"I don't know. Probably because she was uncertain of her information." Cady's hand tightened visibly around the glass. "My aunt was secretive by nature and the tendency got more pronounced as she got older. She rarely confided in anyone. But I do know that she was in favor of the merger, at least until quite recently."

"I believe you. Vesta Briggs controlled Chatelaine's. Something as big as a merger couldn't have gotten to the voting stage without her approval."

Cady wrapped one arm around an upraised knee and regarded him with a steady, troubled expression. "I think something must have happened very recently. Something that put some doubts in her mind."

Leaning back in the chair, he thrust out his legs and regarded the tips of his shoes. "When did she change her will in order to leave you the shares?"

"The lawyer said the change was made about a week before she died."

He looked up. "If you're right, then whatever happened to give her some doubts about the merger must have occurred at about the same time."

"That's my theory."

He swallowed some tea, managed not to make a face and put the glass down on a black coaster. "You want to find out what it was that gave her the reservations about the merger, right?"

"Yes."

He looked at her. "Where do I come into this?"

"Isn't it obvious? I want to hire you to help me find out what's going on."

"*Hire* me?" He was so stunned by her casual announcement that for a few seconds he couldn't get past the impact. "*You* want to hire *me?*"

"What's so weird about that? As I said in the message I left on your voice mail, I need an investigator and you know the art business."

"Cady, I trace and recover missing works of art. I don't investigate murky financial situations. That's an entirely different line of work. It sounds like you need a good accounting firm."

"Perhaps. But Sylvia told me that the Chatelaine accountants had gone over the

Austrey-Post books with a fine-toothed comb. As an added precaution, she and Vesta asked Sylvia's husband, Gardner, to take a look at them, too."

"Gardner's an accountant, I take it?"

"Yes. A CPA. He owns his own business in Phantom Point. He confirmed the accountants' verdict. Financially, things look great at Austrey-Post."

"Financial problems can be concealed by someone who knows what he's doing."

"Yes, but my aunt didn't back away from the merger after she looked at the books. Her decision to postpone the vote occurred at about the same time that she made some appointments with a man named Jonathan Arden."

"Who is Arden?"

Cady sighed. "Promise you won't laugh."

"Trust me, I'm not in a laughing mood."

"Arden is a psychic."

It took him a few seconds to absorb and process that information.

"As in someone who, uh, claims to have paranormal talents?" he asked cautiously.

"Yes."

"You're not joking, are you?"

"No," she said wearily. "I am not joking."

"It's a little hard to imagine the head of Chatelaine's consulting a psychic. Are you sure your aunt was in full possession of her faculties there at the end?"

"Several members of the family have their doubts," Cady admitted. "But I spoke to her on the phone a number of times during the past few months. She seemed as lucid and clearheaded as ever to me."

"Did she have a history of being interested in this kind of stuff?"

"Metaphysics? No."

"Any idea why she would suddenly develop an interest?"

"No." Cady put down her glass. "Seeing a psychic was completely out of character for her. She had no patience with fortune-tellers and psychics and the like. As far as she was concerned, they were all con artists."

"Mmm."

"What I'm trying to explain here is that the timing of those appointments with Arden and the decision to change her will is too coincidental to be ignored. Jonathan Arden is involved in this. I can feel it."

"You can feel it?"

"Yes."

"And you expect me to figure out just how he's involved?"

"Yes. Furthermore, we need to keep your investigation absolutely quiet."

"Quiet?"

"Only the members of my family know about the psychic thing. We have to keep it that way. The merger proposal has been postponed, but it is still very much on the table. It's vitally important that we don't stir up any wild speculation about my aunt's state of mind during the past few months. That kind of gossip would not be good for Chatelaine's or Austrey-Post. Is that clear?"

"Trust me, my lips are sealed." She was sinking deeper and deeper into some bizarre conspiracy plot, he thought. "Look, maybe you're coming at this from the wrong angle."

"What other angle is there?"

"Have you considered the possibility that your aunt left you those shares because she wanted to force you back into the family business?"

Cady shook her head once, emphatically. "She understood that I wanted no part of Chatelaine's. She accepted my decision."

"Are you sure of that?"

Cady hesitated. "Yes."

He saw the flicker of uncertainty and pursued it ruthlessly. "Maybe she hadn't accepted it. Not deep down where it counts. Founders of family-owned businesses often have very strong feelings about whom they want to inherit. If your aunt was convinced that you should return to the firm, she might have seen the shares as a way of accomplishing her goal."

Cady glanced at the single sheet of notepaper and the key on the table. "I hadn't thought of that possibility," she admitted reluctantly.

"It makes a lot of sense," he said persuasively. "If that's the case, there shouldn't be any big problem dumping your shares back on the family. There's got to be some legal way for you to transfer them to your cousin or the other members of the board."

"Probably."

He exhaled deeply. "You're not buying my logic, are you?"

She wrapped her arms around both knees and looked at him across the expanse of the minimalist room. "No. I think there's something wrong and I intend to find out what it is before I make any decisions about the shares and the merger."

"I was afraid of that."

"The only question here is whether or not you want to take the job I'm offering."

One of these days, he would have to learn to be careful what he asked for, he thought. He had come here today hoping to restart a prickly relationship with an unpredictable woman. He had achieved his goal, assuming you could count a job as a relationship.

"What will you do if I turn it down?" he asked.

"I'm not sure." She pursed her lips in a meditative expression. "Find another investigator to help me check out Jonathan Arden, I suppose. I would much prefer to work with you because you're very low profile. It's highly unlikely that anyone in either Austrey-Post or Chatelaine's has ever even heard of you. That kind of anonymity would be extremely useful in this case."

"Always knew there was some advantage to being low profile."

She said nothing, waiting.

"Why do I have the feeling," he asked after a while, "that I'm not getting the whole picture here?"

"What do you mean?" she asked with an expression of offended innocence.

He groaned silently. She really was holding out on him. If he had an ounce of common sense he would not touch this situation with a ten-foot pole.

"Never mind," he said. "I'll take the job."

"Excellent." She gave him a brilliant smile, unclasped her knees and swung her bare feet to the floor. "Now that's settled, we can talk about the details of my plan."

Premonition tightened his insides. "Are

there a lot of them? Details, that is?"

"As I told you, I can't just go charging into Phantom Point with my own personal investigator in tow. Not only would it start nasty rumors about the financial status of both galleries, it would offend a lot of folks. Also, you're going to be asking questions. Subtly, of course."

"Hey, subtle is my middle name." This was a mistake. He could sense the potential for disaster looming on the horizon. But he could not seem to work up the willpower to turn aside before it was too late.

"You'll have to go in as an insider."

"Okay. What do you intend to do? Bring me in as an employee of Chatelaine's?"

"I considered that." She waved the idea aside with a whisking motion. "But that wouldn't put you into the right circles. You'll need to be able to move in my aunt's world. That means mingling with the people she came in contact with in the course of her daily life. Family, friends, clients."

He watched her face, unwillingly fascinated. "You've given this a lot of thought, haven't you?"

"I've been pretty focused on it since the funeral."

"So, how do you intend to insert me into the right circles in Phantom Point?"

157

"Simple. I'm going to introduce you as my future fiancé."

He stared at her for what must have been at least five seconds. He was dimly aware that it took him that long to recover sufficiently from the shock to be able to speak coherently.

"Are you serious?" he asked without any inflection whatsoever.

"Dead serious. It will put you in the eye of the storm."

"That is not a reassuring sort of metaphor."

"Relax, this is perfect. Just about everyone has despaired of my ever getting married again. The assumption is that I'll end up like Aunt Vesta, you see."

"What, exactly, is a *future* fiancé?"

"We haven't officially announced our engagement but intend to do so soon."

He nodded. "In the future."

"Right."

"In other words, we're sort of semi-engaged?"

"Sort of."

"Well, that certainly clears that up nicely. Thanks for the explanation."

"Believe me, when I show up in Phantom Point with a potential fiancé, the curiosity factor will be huge. After all, I've just inherited a controlling interest in Chatelaine's. People will stand in line to get a chance to check you out."

"Wonderful," he muttered. "They'll assume that I'm marrying you in order to cash in on Chatelaine's."

"Precisely. You see how this will work?"

"Sure do. Everyone will think I'm marrying you for your money. Your family and friends will conclude that I'm an opportunist. A fortune hunter."

"Okay, so it's not great for your ego. But it's perfect for our purposes."

"Perfect."

"Well?" she prompted impatiently.

"Well, what?"

"Now that you've heard the details, are you still interested in the job?"

He hadn't heard all the details, not by a long shot. What was she keeping back?

"Sure." He could be cool, too. "Not like I'm doing anything else at the moment."

She looked relieved. "Good. That's settled then."

"I'll want a contract, of course."

"I beg your pardon?"

"I never work without a contract."

"Oh, right. A contract."

"Just the standard one will do," he said.

"Like the ones I signed with you when I

worked for Lost and Found?"

"Yes."

She cleared her throat. "I'll, uh, draw something up."

"Have you got a basic contract?"

"Well, no. I haven't had a chance to ask a lawyer to draft one that I can use for this kind of job."

"Swell." He said smugly. "Why don't you dig out the last one you signed with Lost and Found? You can borrow the basic boilerplate from it."

"Good idea," she said, a little too brightly.

"About my fee," he continued smoothly.

She sat very still. "It's negotiable."

"No, it's not negotiable. I'll give it some thought on the way home tonight. I'll have a figure for you by morning. It will be up to you whether or not to accept or reject."

"And if I reject?"

"You can always shop around for another low-profile investigator who doesn't mind masquerading as a sleazy opportunist."

Some of the enthusiasm in her eyes vanished. A steely expression replaced it. "You're going to make this difficult, aren't you?"

"The way I see it, it's already difficult. I'm just trying to make sure I get fairly compensated for all the *difficulty* involved."

"And also for having to put up with knowing that everyone will think you're a fortune hunter, right?"

"Yeah, that, too. A man's got his pride."

"Hard to put a price on pride," she said.

"Don't worry, I'll come up with one." He got to his feet and started toward the door. "I'd better be on my way. I've got a few things to take care of at home before I start my new job with you."

She jumped up and hurried after him down the hall. "Thanks, Mack. I really appreciate this."

"Uh-huh." You appreciate me so much you aren't telling me the whole truth, he added silently.

"Do you have any other questions?"

He paused, a hand on the doorknob. "One small issue does come to mind."

"What is it?"

"How far are we going to take this cover story of ours?"

She stopped abruptly a short distance away. "I beg your pardon?"

"This phony engaged-to-be-engaged thing. How far does it go?"

"How far?"

"Are we sleeping together?"

Her jaw did not exactly drop, but her lips parted slightly. She recovered with as-

161

tounding speed, however.

"I'm sure most people will assume that we are, uh, intimate. We'll be staying together at Aunt Vesta's place, after all."

"But we are not going to be sharing a bed?"

She flushed but her gaze did not waver. "Of course not. I would never sleep with one of my employees. It's against company policy."

12

"What the hell is this about Cady getting engaged?" Stanford Felgrove demanded.

Randall Post watched his stepfather tee up the ball on the sixth hole. There were two reasons why he hated playing golf with him. The first was that Stanford was a slick, smooth-talking opportunist.

Some days it took everything Randall had to pretend that he had little interest in the company that Stanford had stolen from him.

"Sylvia said that Cady and this Mack Easton haven't officially announced the engagement yet," Randall said evenly. "Probably waiting until Cady's parents return from England."

"Any idea how long she's known him?"

"According to Sylvia, Cady says she met Easton sometime during the past couple of months but she never mentioned that she was serious about him until a few days ago."

Stanford grunted. "Like right after the old bitch drowned, you mean."

Randall shrugged. "Apparently."

"Well, well, well. Isn't that interesting?"

Stanford adjusted his grip and widened his stance slightly. He swung the club, hard and fast. Randall watched the trajectory of the ball with morose satisfaction. The small sphere traveled in an arc that veered sharply to the right. It landed, bounced and rolled into some high grass at the edge of the manicured fairway. Stanford had a pronounced tendency to slice the ball.

"What's interesting about it?" Randall asked.

"The timing of it all." Stanford walked to the back of the cart and thrust the driver into his bag. "Obviously this Mack Easton knows an opportunity when he sees it."

Randall moved forward to address his own ball. "You're implying that he asked her to marry him *after* he discovered that she had inherited those shares in Chatelaine's?"

"That sure as hell is what it looks like to me. Damn. Just like that old bitch Vesta to complicate things by leaving those shares to Cady. What the hell was she thinking?"

Randall tuned out the conversation long enough to take his swing. He felt the sweet, solid sensation on impact that signaled a good drive. He straightened and watched the ball fly down the middle of the fairway.

Satisfied, he turned and went back to the cart.

Stanford did not congratulate him on the drive. He sat in the cart and stared straight ahead stone-faced toward the distant green, as if he hadn't even noticed the near-perfect shot. Randall smiled coldly to himself and dropped his club in the bag. Stanford hated the fact that his stepson was the better player. Randall was pretty sure that the bastard would rather do anything than play with him.

But it was Stanford who insisted on the occasional rounds of golf together because he felt it cemented the image of unity at the top of Austrey-Post. And that was crucial because they both knew that Austrey-Post needed Randall.

It was Randall's social connections, inherited from his grandparents and his mother, that allowed him to secure the important consignments. It was the prestigious collections of art and antiques from the right clients, sold in turn to the right collectors, that maintained Austrey-Post's status in the world of art.

"Vesta always hoped that Cady would one day change her mind and decide to join Sylvia at the helm of Chatelaine's." Randall climbed behind the wheel of the golf cart.

"Everyone in the business knows that." *That's why you were so keen on me marrying Cady three years ago, you bastard. Don't you remember?* he added silently.

"If you hadn't screwed up on your honeymoon, we'd be looking at an entirely different situation now," Stanford muttered. "I still can't believe you were so lousy in bed that Cady filed for divorce nine days after the wedding. You must have been as limp as spaghetti."

Randall said nothing. He knew that Stanford despised him. The feeling was mutual.

For some time now, Randall had been quietly grateful that his grandfather had taken steps to ensure that if anything ever happened to his grandson, his shares in the galleries would go to distant relatives, not to Stanford Felgrove. Randall sometimes wondered if he might not have suffered a convenient accident years ago if Stanford had seen his way clear to get his hands on the shares his stepson controlled.

But shortly before he died, the old man had finally understood that Jocelyn was probably going to kill herself with the booze. He had been too late to prevent control of the company from slipping into Felgrove's clutches, but with the help of a good lawyer, he had been able to save forty-nine percent of the business for his grandson. Unfortunately, that left fifty-one percent in Stanford Felgrove's hands.

But not for long, Randall thought, piloting the small cart along the narrow path with one hand. Not if the merger with Chatelaine's went through. There would be justice in the universe at last if the deal came together. He was so close now. Nothing could be allowed to get in the way. Surely Cady could be convinced of the importance of voting for the merger proposal. She would understand. She was like a sister to him. Which, of course, had been part of the problem in their short-lived marriage.

Three years ago everyone had agreed that a wedding between Randall and Cady made great sense. They had so much in common, after all. They had grown up together. Vesta had certainly been pleased. In all the time he had known her, Randall had never seen her closer to appearing genuinely happy than she had on the day he and Cady had taken their vows.

Stanford had been damn near ecstatic. Randall knew that it was because the bastard had seen the marriage as a way to get a toehold on Chatelaine's.

The abrupt ending to the nine-day disaster had shocked everyone. He and Cady had put on a united front, explaining simply that they had realized they had made a huge mistake. Neither of them had ever told anyone the truth. As always, Cady had been a good friend to him in that regard, just as she had in every other way.

"This Easton is obviously a guy with his eye on the main chance," Stanford said. "We should be able to do business with him. Make him understand that a merger will be profitable for all concerned."

Randall brought the cart to a halt near the point where Stanford's ball had vanished into the tall grass. "Has it occurred to you that Easton may have his own agenda? Or maybe he doesn't even give a damn about the business angle. Maybe he wants to marry Cady because he's in love with her."

"Bullshit. No man in his right mind would fall for a woman like Cady Briggs. She gets more like her aunt every day." Stanford climbed out of the cart and selected a club. "The only reason Easton is nosing around Cady is because he's got his eye on Chatelaine's. Count on it."

Randall watched him walk to the edge of the fairway. "You always assume that everyone is motivated by the same things that motivate you. That could be a mistake."

Stanford poked about in the grass with

the head of the club, searching for his ball. "I guarantee you that it's no coincidence that this Easton is suddenly interested in marrying Cady. I know his kind."

Because he reminds you of yourself, you s.o.b.? Randall mused. Does Easton make you think of how you took advantage of my mother when she was so deep into the bottle that she couldn't understand what she was signing?

He turned his head, pretending not to notice when Stanford unobtrusively maneuvered the ball into a better position before he took his swing. This was the second reason why he hated playing golf with his stepfather, he thought. Stanford cheated.

"By the way," Stanford said when he got back into the cart. "I hear George Langworth probably won't live out the month. Word is getting out to the big galleries and auction houses that his collection will soon be up for grabs."

Everyone in Phantom Point knew that George Langworth had been fighting cancer for three years. He was in his late seventies. Randall was not surprised that the information that George had very little time left had leaked beyond the boundaries of the small community. The Langworth collection of nineteenth-century art and antiques was world-class. It wasn't just the auction houses and dealers who would be interested, Randall thought. Some of the major museums would also be hovering hopefully in the wings.

"I heard that one of the big houses sent a representative to talk to Brooke about her husband's collection a couple of days ago," Stanford continued. "If you're not already on top of that situation, you'd sure as hell better get there fast."

Randall ignored that. He stopped the cart near the point where his own ball had landed and got out to select a club.

"Did you hear me?" Stanford said sharply. "There's no excuse for losing the Langworth consignment. I don't want one of the ambulance chasers from the other galleries talking Brooke Langworth out of that collection. You've got an in with her. You've worked with her on the Carnival Night committee for the past three years."

Randall walked to where the ball lay on the sleekly mown grass. "I haven't seen much of her lately. She had to resign from this year's committee because of George's poor health."

"But you *know* her, damn it. Hell, for a while there, the two of you were an item."

"That was four years ago, Stanford."

Stanford grunted. "Before she dumped you to marry George and his money. I know. If you ask me, you got lucky. She had some good connections, I'll grant you that, but at the time she didn't have a dime to her name. The only reason she was interested in you was so that she could get herself a nice chunk of Austrey-Post. Be glad George came along and offered her an even better setup."

Randall smiled grimly. Stanford didn't have a clue, he thought. It was his interest in Austrey-Post that had made Brooke break off the relationship four years ago. *Obsessive,* she had called it.

"Point is," Stanford continued, "George is not going to be around much longer. The way I hear it, his son and daughter will get most of the money through a trust. But Brooke gets that big house, the yacht and the antiques. She's probably going to have to sell the collection to raise the cash to pay the death taxes. You know the drill. Tell her we'll take care of everything for her."

Randall pretended not to hear the orders. He took the shot instead. It landed on the edge of the green. Perfect.

A short time later he dropped the ball into the cup with a single putt. He smiled slightly as he replaced the flag. He always won, in spite of Stanford's cheating, and he knew it irritated the hell out of the bastard.

But the big win was still to come. He had been stunned by Stanford's decision to approach Chatelaine's about a merger, but he had immediately understood the incredible potential it represented. A glorious opportunity had fallen into his lap and he intended to take full advantage of it.

It was supremely gratifying to know that Stanford would be the architect of his own downfall. Felgrove was so fixated on the financial benefits of a link with Chatelaine's that he had no clue to the fact that the deal contained the seeds of his own destruction.

He had been a long time avenging his mother and himself, Randall thought as he got back into the golf cart. But the chance had come at last. Nothing could be allowed to stand in the way of the merger.

A sense of quiet pleasure went through Gardner Holgate as he watched his wife walk into the restaurant. They had been married for nearly a decade and had shared the joys and tribulations of raising their twin sons; but every time he saw her, he was struck anew by the wonder of it all. He had been a dull, boring nerd all through high school and college, the kind of guy girls teased and sometimes wanted as a friend, but not the sort they saw as romantic or exciting. Nothing had changed as far as he could see. He was an accountant — a CPA, after all. He spent his days burrowing through state and federal tax codes and filling out arcane forms on a computer. He counseled clients who had been traumatized by letters from the IRS.

Sylvia, on the other hand, was polished and elegant, a tall, willowy blonde with serious, intelligent eyes and a natural flair for business. Her cousin Cady could discuss the rinceau motifs used in the decoration of sixteenth-century majolica dishes for hours on end, but Sylvia could design long-term corporate strategy. Cady could talk to clients about the influence of Renaissance theories of proportion on Regency craftsmen. Sylvia could chart five-year plans. What had he ever done to deserve a woman like this?

Sylvia spotted him and started toward him, tension in every step. She had been like this since the reading of Vesta's will. It worried him. Discovering that Cady had inherited a controlling interest in Chatelaine's had come as a shock to everyone, but most especially to Sylvia. Over the course of the past several years Vesta had groomed her to take over the firm. His wife had the instincts of a true business leader. Sharing power, even with a close cousin, was not going to be easy.

Vesta had been unpredictable right to the bitter end. Now her nieces were left to sort out the thorny question of who would control Chatelaine's.

Sylvia gave him a wan smile as she approached the table. He rose, kissed her lightly on the cheek and held her chair for her.

"She's bringing Mack Easton with her," Sylvia announced as she took her seat. "He's going to be staying at the villa. I think we have to assume that this relationship is serious."

Gardner sat down across from her. "We are talking about Cady, I assume?"

"Of course we're talking about Cady." Sylvia snapped her napkin across her lap. "Who else? Aunt Vesta must be having a fit wherever she is."

"Because Cady intends to install her fiancé in the villa? I know your aunt was a little old-fashioned about that kind of thing, but —"

"Not because Cady will be sleeping with Easton in the villa," Sylvia interrupted impatiently. "Although you're right, Vesta wouldn't have approved. I'm talking about the fact that this man is obviously trying to take advantage of Cady."

"You're sure of that?"

"Nothing else explains this sudden announcement of an impending engagement."

He thought about it. "Wouldn't be easy to take advantage of Cady. She's a lot like you. Sharp and smart. Too sharp and too smart to get conned by a fast-talking gigolo."

"Being sharp and smart doesn't always protect you from falling for the wrong man. Just look at Leandra."

"No offense, dear, but sometimes I have serious doubts that your cousin Leandra came from the Briggs family gene pool."

"Leandra's smart enough," Sylvia said with instant family loyalty. "It's just that she's not an ambitious overachiever like Cady and me. Also, she's a few years younger than us, remember. That makes a world of difference. She'll mature one of these days. I think the fact that she's dating Parker is a good sign, don't you?"

"Probably."

"I know that he's a little old for her, but maybe that's what she needs after Dillon. Someone settled and calm and thoughtful."

"Everyone knew that she was making a big mistake with Dillon Spooner. It just took Leandra two years to figure it out for herself."

It had also required several thousand dollars of Vesta's money to buy Leandra out of the foolish marriage to the self-proclaimed artist, but he decided not to mention that small fact. It wasn't as if Sylvia wasn't well aware of it. If he brought it up, however, she would become defensive on her cousin's behalf. The Briggs family stuck together. For the most part he considered it an endearing trait. The only time it became irritating was when the clan extended their definition of family to include Randall Post.

"Getting back to this situation with Cady," Sylvia said, "the thing is, her biological clock is ticking. That kind of loud noise can be extremely distracting to a woman, regardless of how smart she happens to be. It makes her vulnerable."

"I'll take your word for it."

Sylvia opened her menu. "Also, don't forget that she can be impulsive. Remember how she walked away from Chatelaine's a few years ago? And then there was that farce of a marriage to Randall."

"Okay, I'll grant you that she's got a bit of a wild streak. I still don't think you should leap to any conclusions about Easton until you've got more information."

Sylvia tapped the corner of the menu against the table and looked thoughtful.

"You're right. We need to find out more about him."

"Cady and her Mr. Easton are due to arrive tomorrow. You'll meet him soon enough."

"This is such a mess." Sylvia sighed in frustration. "What on earth did Vesta think she was doing? Why did she change her mind about those shares?"

"We'll probably never know the answer to that." Gardner smiled humorlessly. "Unless, of course, you can persuade that psychic she was seeing to hold a séance, or whatever they call those sessions with the dearly departed."

"And that's another thing," Sylvia muttered. "Why was Vesta seeing that phony, Arden? She hated charlatans and frauds. She must have been losing it there at the end. Some sort of subtle dementia, probably."

"Had to be pretty subtle. She seemed her usual self to me."

In his private opinion, the old tyrant had remained true to form right to the end. It was just like Vesta to throw the family into an uproar one last time before departing for the next world. Little wonder that there had been few tears shed at the funeral, he thought.

"I've talked to Stanford and Randall,"

Sylvia said. "Told them both what was going on. Explained that we now have to get Cady's approval for the merger to take place."

"There's no reason why she shouldn't be in favor of it."

"Don't count on it. A merger would mean some big changes for us. Overnight the company would start operating on a much larger scale. The board of directors would be expanded. There would be several new partners added. Cady doesn't like big business. She prefers to run her own show single-handedly."

"So do you," he said before he stopped to think.

Sylvia's gaze sharpened and then, to his chagrin, something that might have been uncertainty flickered in the depths of her blue eyes. He put out his hand and touched her fingers.

"That's what makes you a natural for the CEO's chair in the new Chatelaine-Post," he said quickly.

"Being able to run a business is fine as far as it goes. But Cady's the one with the eye. Remember how she picked out that genuine Riesener cabinet from the pile of reproductions in the Guthrie consignment? And those French clock cases she found at an es-

178

tate sale? Those English panels that turned up at auction?"

"Having a good eye for art and antiques does not make her a terrific choice for running a business. You know that, and I think Vesta did too. It takes sound management skills and a corporate vision to make the gallery turn a profit. Hell, you can *buy* all the expert eyes you need on your staff. Cady couldn't possibly replace you in the CEO's office."

"Well, that is no longer a sure thing, is it?" Sylvia said quietly. "Cady inherited enough shares not only to block the merger but to determine who becomes the next CEO."

"Maybe she'll decide that she doesn't want to return to an active role in Chatelaine's," Gardner said.

"If that was the case, she would have turned her shares over to me or someone else in the family. No, she's coming back for a reason. I think Mack Easton may be it."

"You believe that he's the one who convinced her to hang onto those shares she inherited from Vesta?"

"Yes," Sylvia said. "Think about it. His presence in her life is the only thing that has altered since she decided she did not want to be a part of Chatelaine's. There's no other explanation for her decision to come back. Easton is angling for a piece of the action, trust me."

"Are you seriously suggesting that some man has a hold on Cady that is strong enough to allow him to manipulate her? This is your cousin we're talking about."

Sylvia hesitated. "It does sound a little far-fetched, doesn't it?"

"Very."

"You think I'm overreacting?"

"Let's just say that I think you're heavily into a worst-case scenario here. Then again, that's what CEOs are paid to assess."

"What do you believe is going on?" she shot back in obvious exasperation. "Your instincts are very good when it comes to judging people. Where do you think Easton fits into this picture?"

"Maybe it's all very simple." Gardner put down his menu and picked up his coffee cup. "Maybe the guy's in love with her."

Sylvia looked briefly startled by that possibility. Then she frowned and shook her head. "I don't buy it. The timing of this announcement about an impending engagement is just too coincidental."

"If you're right," Gardner said slowly, "you've got a big problem."

She gripped the menu. "Not as big a problem as Cady will have if she marries an opportunist thinking that he's the man she's been waiting for all of her life."

The phone rang just as Leandra was finishing chapter five of *Breaking the Bad-Boy Habit: The Thinking Woman's Guide to Finding and Appreciating Nice Guys*. She put the book down on top of the large pile of similarly titled self-help books that cluttered her coffee table and scooped up the phone.

"Hello, Parker," she said without preamble. "I was hoping you would get home early. I was thinking about drinks and dinner at one of the marina restaurants. How does that sound?"

There was a short, terse silence on the other end of the line.

"It's me," Dillon said.

Oh, damn. At the sound of her ex-husband's voice, she tightened her grip on the phone. "What do you want, Dillon?"

"I was just calling to see if you might be interested in spending the weekend here in the city."

"With you?"

"That was the plan."

"The answer is no. Dillon, listen to me. I want you to stop calling, do you understand? This is the third time since the funeral."

"Damn it, you won't even give me a chance."

"I gave you a lot of chances while we were married and you blew off all of them, remember?"

"That was a long time ago."

"The last incident was eighteen months ago, as I recall."

"Things have changed. *I've* changed. I tried to tell you that when I saw you at your great-aunt's funeral."

Her gaze fell on the cover of the book she had been reading. She recalled the advice in chapter five. . . . *Falling for bad boys is a bad habit. As with all bad habits, it takes willpower and practice to break the pattern. Remember: the key word in the phrase* bad boy *is* boy. *When he calls and tries to whine his way back into your life say to yourself, "I am a mature woman. I don't date immature boys.". . .*

"Why did you bother to come to the funeral, anyway?" she asked aloud. "You never cared for Aunt Vesta."

"Give me a break, you can't hold that against me," he muttered. "A lot of people didn't care for your aunt. Hell, most folks didn't even like her very much. But I noticed that a whole lot of them showed up at the funeral."

She could not deny that. The church had

been filled to overflowing. Vesta had wielded power and influence in her corner of the art world. She had also been a pillar of the community here in Phantom Point. Still, it had been a shock to see Dillon in the large crowd pretending to mourn the passing of Vesta Briggs.

"Dillon —"

"You want to know why I came to the funeral?" His voice took on that earnest, husky tone that had always sent shivers down her spine. "I wanted to see you, that's why. I wanted to talk to you. Explain things."

"I don't know where you're going with this, Dillon."

"I want to try again."

"Try what?"

"Our marriage."

I am a mature woman. I don't date immature boys.

"I'm sorry, Dillon," she said. "But I don't think this is good for either of us. We both need to get on with our lives."

"I have gotten on with my life. Leandra, listen, a major gallery has taken an interest in my work. I'm going to have my first big show in a few months. I'm on my way."

"I've heard that before, Dillon. Please, I really can't talk to you. I'm dating a very nice man these days."

"That guy I saw you with at the funeral?" Dillon's voice rose on a scathing note. "He's old enough to be your father."

"That's not true. Parker's only forty-two."

"Probably needs medication to get it up in bed."

"Stop it. Stop it right now, do you hear me? Parker is a wonderful, thoughtful man. He takes me to nice places. We went to Hawaii a couple of months ago."

"I still say he's too old for you."

"So what? You're too *young* for me."

"What are you talking about?" Dillon demanded. "You and I are the same age."

"Chronologically speaking, yes," she said primly. "But not in terms of emotional development. I am a mature woman. I don't date immature boys."

"Where in hell did you learn to talk like that? You reading those dumb self-help books again?"

She did not respond. Instead, very gently she replaced the receiver. When the phone rang again she did not answer. She sat for a while thinking about past mistakes and how hard it was to break bad habits.

13

Cady stood in the center of the two-story vault, the small gold key in her hand, and turned slowly on her heel. She surveyed the tiers of exquisite boxes, chests and small cabinets that lined every shelf of every wall.

There were hundreds of them, large and small, each one a work of art and an example of brilliant craftsmanship. They spanned the centuries and the millennia. One shelf held a selection of elaborately decorated medieval boxes, some designed as reliquaries, others made to hold the simple necessities of daily life such as needles and thread. Another case displayed gleaming sixteenth-century boxes made of chiseled steel damascened with gold. They had been produced by the same master craftsmen who had forged swords and armor. Jewelry boxes etched and nielloed in impossibly convoluted motifs and studded with semiprecious stones were arranged on the shelves above the balcony level.

Renaissance-era boxes that had been gilded and enameled until they glowed with a light of their own stood behind glass panels on the rear wall. Breathtaking little boxes fashioned out of rock crystal and jaspar and onyx in the seventeenth century filled another section of shelving. Ancient boxes crafted of carved alabaster and jade occupied a case near the steel door that secured the vault room.

Mack halted in the opening and glanced around the windowless vault. "So this is where you disappeared while I was unpacking."

"Yes."

He studied the heavy steel door. "I assume there is a way out if this thing were to accidentally swing shut."

"The lock is computer coded on the outside but there's a manual latch inside."

"That's good to know." He studied a small ebony and gold box in the case that was nearest to him. "Quite a collection."

"Aunt Vesta collected boxes for five decades. She used to say that there was something about them that reflected the most fundamental aspects of human nature."

Mack took his attention off the ebony box and looked at her. "That would be?"

"Our need to keep secrets." She glanced at an early seventeenth-century enameled box. The lid and sides of the delicately gilded chest were decorated with scenes of an obviously illicit love affair. "The wish to bury our mistakes. The urge to hide the unpleasant parts of ourselves and our pasts. Our desire for privacy."

"Could be." He did not move from the doorway. "Or maybe these fancy boxes just symbolized those things for your aunt."

"Maybe."

"Did Vesta Briggs have a lot of secrets?"

She stroked the lid of the gilded chest. "She was eighty-six years old when she died. I have a hunch that by that age most people have acquired a lot of secrets. I think they're entitled to keep them."

"I won't argue with that."

She opened her fingers. Gold glinted in the palm of her hand. "The lawyer gave me a sealed envelope after the funeral. Inside was a note and this key."

He nodded as if he already knew about both. Then she recalled that Vesta's letter and the key had been on the coffee table in her condo the day he had arrived, unannounced, at her door. So the man was observant. So what? Wasn't that why she had hired him?

"What was in the note?" he asked.

Without a word she removed it from the pocket of her trousers and handed it to him.

Mack took the single sheet of paper from her hand. He searched her face briefly and then read the note aloud. She knew the words by heart.

Dear Cady,

I have come to the conclusion that after I am gone I want someone else to know the whole truth about the past. I feel that you are the only one in the family who could possibly understand. We have so much in common, you and I. Isn't DNA amazing?

I am not sure why it has suddenly become so vitally important to me to tell you what happened all those years ago. Perhaps it is because I feel I owe you an apology. Perhaps, in the end, it is simply that I can't bear to take this particular secret alone to my grave. I need to know that someone else understands at last.

Love,
Vesta

Mack refolded the letter and handed it back to her. "Do you recognize the key?"

"Oh, yes." She glanced down at the gleaming object in her palm. "It used to be attached to the Nun's Chatelaine."

He took a step forward, clearly intrigued. "The original? As in the one on all the cards and business letterheads used by Chatelaine's?"

"Yes. I think I mentioned that one of the things she left to me in her will was an important piece of jewelry. It was the Nun's Chatelaine."

"Where's the rest of it? You've only got a single key."

"I think," she said slowly, "that when I find the box that this key opens, I'll find the chatelaine."

"How old is the piece, anyway?"

"The gold medallion dates from the thirteenth century. The chains and the keys were replaced in the seventeen hundreds."

Mack whistled softly. "An impressive key ring."

"It was designed to secure keys right from the beginning but the term 'chatelaine' didn't come into use until much later. By the sixteenth century, the word referred to the lady of the castle. By the early nineteenth century, it had come to mean both the lady and the keys that were the symbol of her office."

"Collectors use it pretty loosely today, don't they?"

She nodded absently. "Today the word refers to a wide variety of waist-hung devices designed to hold keys or implements or watches and ornaments."

"You think your aunt deliberately hid the Nun's Chatelaine in one of these little chests?"

"Looks that way."

"Sonofagun." He shook his head. "Why would she do that?"

"Because she wanted to conceal it, of course." Cady smiled wryly. "We're talking about Aunt Vesta here. She was always a very private, very secretive woman. She became extremely obsessive toward the end of her life. Just ask anyone."

"Strange way to leave an inheritance behind."

"In her note she says something about wanting me to know the whole truth." She surveyed the hundreds of boxes. "I wonder what she meant by that?"

"No telling until you open the right box, I guess." He contemplated the tiers of glittering objects. "It's going to take a while to work your way through this vault."

"I certainly don't have the time to do it now. We've got other, more pressing problems. These boxes are safe enough for the moment here in this vault and so is the

Nun's Chatelaine."

"This collection must be worth a fortune," he said thoughtfully.

"Mmm, yes. Generally speaking, Vesta was not the sentimental type when it came to art and antiques. She was businesslike to the point of ruthlessness. If the price was right, she was willing to deal. But as far as I know, she never sold a single item from this vault. She never exhibited any of the boxes publicly. Never loaned any of them out to museums for display. I was one of the few people who was ever allowed inside this room."

"And now they're all yours."

"Yes."

"What will you do with them?"

"It occurred to me," she said slowly, "that it would be nice to give them to a good museum, one that will display them properly and give Aunt Vesta credit as the original collector."

"The Vesta Briggs Collection," he said. "Sounds like a hell of a memorial."

"I kind of like it. I think Vesta would have liked it, too." She dropped the key back into the envelope together with Vesta's note and stuffed both into her pocket. "Well, as I said, the boxes will have to wait."

"If you're finished in here, I've got some questions for you."

"Sure." She shook off the melancholy sensation that had settled around her when she had walked into the vault a few minutes ago. Time to get down to business, she thought. She had hired Mack to conduct a discreet investigation. The sooner he got started, the better. "Why don't we go into my aunt's study? We can talk there."

"All right." He moved out of the doorway, making room for her to get past him. "Are you okay?"

"Of course I'm okay. Why shouldn't I be okay?"

He winced. "No need to snap. Idle curiosity, that's all." He paused a beat. "Just trying to do a job here, boss."

She shot him a quelling look as she closed the heavy steel door. "Is your room all right?"

"Dandy. Great view. I can see the bay, Angel Island, and the city. I expected the basement, you know. Hired muscle doesn't usually get such spiffy accommodations."

"You are *not* hired muscle," she muttered.

"No?"

"Not on this job. I did some checking around after we signed that contract. You can imagine my surprise when I found out that hired muscle comes a lot cheaper than you do."

"Really?"

192

"Yes, really." She touched the red button to lock the vault. "For what I'm paying you, I expect brains as well as brawn."

"If it's strategic thinking you want here —"

"It is."

"Then I should point out that you'd better hope none of your friends or relatives sneaks upstairs to the second floor and notices that we're using separate bedrooms. It would ruin the image of semi-engaged passion."

"Don't worry, there's not much risk of damaging my image in that department."

"No?"

She made a face. "Since my divorce it has generally been assumed that I'm as frigid as everyone thinks Aunt Vesta was."

"Is that a fact?" A laconic gleam lit his eyes. "Well, we know differently, don't we?"

"Let's change the subject, shall we?"

"You started it. If you're not worried about your image, how about having a little concern for mine?"

"You don't have an image," she assured him as she started down the hall. "No one here in Phantom Point knows anything about you except that you're semi-engaged to me."

"That's just what I meant." He sounded aggrieved. "I told you, as a semi-engaged

193

man I've got my pride."

"I thought we agreed that for the price I'm paying you, you would forget your pride."

"Not sure that's going to work. I'm starting to think that the male pride thing is hardwired into the genes."

She gave him her most withering look. Was he teasing her? There was no telling from his blandly innocent expression. "I wouldn't worry about it if I were you. People will assume that in the romance department you're probably a lot like me."

"Ice water in our veins?"

"You got it."

"Just one problem with that picture," he said, following her around a corner.

"What?"

"We both know it's false. We practically set fire to the sheets that night at the lodge."

For an instant the breath caught in her throat. Sizzling memories of their hot, damp bodies coming together in the darkness whirled through her head, rattling her composure. Not for the first time, she reflected. Fantasy Man had been invading her dreams on a regular basis since that night in the mountains.

It occurred to her that she had better make the ground rules clear.

"Hold it right there." She jerked to a halt and spun around to face him. "One of the conditions of this job is that neither of us makes any further reference to what happened at the lodge. Understood?"

"No, it is not understood," he said calmly. "We've signed a consulting agreement stipulating my services and fees. You can't go changing the conditions of employment at this stage. If you had any issues, you should have mentioned them before you hired me."

She planted her hands on her hips. "You know, Mack, it's not too late to fire you."

"There's a serious financial penalty clause for early termination without cause."

"Don't worry. I can afford it."

"Don't bet on it. There are also legal penalties. You want to fire me? It'll cost you."

He *was* teasing her. She took her hand off her hips and threw them up into the air instead. "This is ridiculous."

"Yeah, it is. You don't have time to find a replacement for me and you know it. I'm all you've got to work with."

"A truly sobering thought."

"Hey, it was your idea to hire me, remember?" He took her arm and steered her forward down the hall. "Come on, let's get to work."

He did have a point. Resigned to the inevitable, she allowed herself to be hauled off down the broad, tiled hall.

The upscale community of Phantom Point had been designed from the ground up as a California version of an Italian hillside resort town. The developers had maintained strict architectural controls. All of the residences, with their faux-Mediterranean façades, artfully faded pink, yellow and white stucco walls, gleaming tile roofs and elaborate wrought-iron gates, had been marketed as either villas or palazzos, depending on the size.

Vesta's villa was two stories high, with a pool terrace and garden. It was perched on a hillside overlooking the bay and the city of San Francisco. The graciously proportioned rooms were crammed with museum-quality antiques. This was one way, at least, in which she definitely differed from her aunt, Cady thought as she walked into the study. Vesta had chosen to live amid the relics of the past. Her aunt had literally immersed herself in the artifacts of eras that were now frozen in time.

The study, with its antique French carpets, nineteenth-century bookcases and heavy mahogany desk, reeked of old-world atmosphere. The interior had a shadowy feel, even when it was fully illuminated. The only outside light came through the French doors that opened onto the terrace.

Mack surveyed the book-crowded room with a thoughtful expression. Then he went to stand behind the large desk. Very deliberately he removed his glasses from his pocket. He put them on and examined the few items positioned on the polished wooden surface as if they were pieces of a puzzle.

Cady followed his gaze to the antique copper-and-crystal inkwell, plump Art Deco fountain pen, green-glass reading lamp, worn leather blotter and a pad of notepaper. The notepad bore the familiar Nun's Chatelaine logo.

"Looks like your aunt was the organized type," Mack said.

"Vesta was obsessive about order and neatness, just as she was about everything else. I think clutter made her feel out of control."

He nodded, just a small inclination of his head to acknowledge the comment. He went back to studying the desk as if information of vital importance had been etched into the wood.

"You said you had some questions," she prompted.

"Yes."

He was starting to make her more than a

little uneasy. Annoyed, she folded her arms. "Well?"

"Let's take a look at the pool," he said.

She froze. "Why?"

"Just curious." His smile was enigmatic.

He crossed the beautifully faded carpet, opened the French doors and walked out onto the tiled terrace.

Cady followed slowly. The late winter day was cool and crisp. A snapping breeze created whitecaps on the bay. In the distance the city sparkled in the sunlight.

She trailed after Mack and finally came to a halt beside him at the edge of the pool. She looked down into the turquoise depths, trying hard not to imagine the scene the morning the housekeeper had found Vesta's body.

"Okay," Mack said. "We've played enough games. Why don't you level with me?"

She looked up swiftly. "I don't understand."

"Sure you do. You didn't hire me just to find out whether or not your aunt had some last-minute doubts about the financial wisdom of the merger. You brought me here because you believe that Vesta Briggs was murdered."

"Mack, I —"

"You want me to help you find her killer, don't you?"

She took a deep breath. This was the first time she had heard her own private fears voiced aloud. They sounded wild and fanciful, just as she had known they would.

"How did you guess?"

"I'm not as slow as I look. It's been obvious from the start of this thing that you were holding out on me."

"I read somewhere that drowning deaths are among the easiest murders to pass off as accidental," she said cautiously.

"Sure. Just ask any insurance fraud investigator. No marks on the body and the water washes away evidence. But I checked before I left to meet you here. There was a report filed by the local authorities. It said that there was no evidence of foul play. No sign of forced entry. Nothing was stolen, even though just one or two of those French vases in the hall would probably fetch a few hundred thousand from a collector."

She flexed her fingers, trying to ease the tension that made her feel suddenly brittle. "I know that her death was ruled accidental. Everyone believes that she had a panic attack and drowned."

"But you aren't buying that scenario, are you?"

She folded her arms and stared down into the pool. "I don't know what to think. But I do know that a lot of things feel very wrong."

"Let's take this from the top," he said a little too patiently. "What's the motive?"

"The merger."

He looked dubious. "Are you serious?"

"Doesn't it strike you that her death is just a little too convenient?"

"For whom?" Skepticism laced his question.

"I don't know yet. Someone who had a lot to gain by the merger, I suppose."

"You suppose?" he repeated dryly.

"Think about it." She turned, aware that she had to convince him with her logic, weak as it was in several places. "Everyone wanted it to go through. But it's clear, given the fact that Vesta left those shares to me, that she had developed some last-minute doubts."

"I still think it's very probable that she left those shares to you because she wanted to force you back into the business."

"I disagree. She wouldn't have done that to me. She knew I wanted no part of Chatelaine's. But she also knew that I would suspect something was wrong if I inherited those shares. She knew I'd ask questions."

"You're sure of that?"

"I knew her. I knew how her mind worked." She hesitated, listening to her own words, and winced. "At least, I understood her thinking processes better than anyone else in the family. You never even met her."

"I can't argue that point. But have you considered the possibility that you may be thinking a little too much like your great-aunt in this instance?"

She ground her teeth together in silent frustration. "What are you saying? That I'm getting a little obsessive here?"

"Maybe. And maybe you're letting your imagination run wild."

"Great. Now I'm not only obsessive, I'm also the victim of an over-active imagination. Maybe I hired the wrong consultant."

There was a short, hard silence.

"Could be," Mack said evenly.

This was not going well. It was his fault. He had sprung this tricky conversation on her without any warning. She had hoped to work up to it more slowly.

"Hear me out," she said quietly. "As an exceedingly high-priced free-lance consultant, your job is to satisfy the client. You asked for a motive and I gave you one. I'm telling you that I think that someone who had a lot to gain from the merger may have discovered that Vesta was on the verge of killing it."

"And killed her, instead?"

"Yes. It could have looked like an efficient way to make certain that she didn't call off the deal," she insisted. "The killer assumed that with her out of the picture, the proposal would ultimately be accepted by the boards of both galleries because everyone else was in favor of it."

"As your exceedingly high-priced free-lance consultant, I'm telling you that murder to ensure a merger is a real stretch."

"But not a complete impossibility."

"No." He removed his glasses very slowly, folded them and dropped them into the chest pocket of his shirt. "Not a complete impossibility. When it comes to murder, any cop will tell you that nothing is beyond the realm of possibility."

"I know it sounds thin to you."

"Transparent." He shook his head. "Cady, a murder investigation is even farther outside my field of expertise than rummaging through the financial details of a proposed merger. If you're serious about this, you need an experienced private eye."

"Aside from the fact that I've got absolutely no evidence that points to murder, I told you, for a variety of reasons, I don't want to bring in a stranger to ask questions. It won't work. Not here in Phantom Point."

He looked down into the clear, gem-blue water for a long moment and then raised his head to meet her eyes. "Tell me, why do you feel you have to find out the truth? Why is it your responsibility?"

She shrugged. "No one else will look beneath the surface. No one else even thinks there's a problem. I'm the one who got the shares so I'm the one who has to do something."

"Try again."

She frowned. "What do you mean?"

"This is going to be hard enough as it is with both of us cooperating. It won't stand a snowball's chance in hell if you don't start dealing straight with me."

Maybe bringing him here had been a mistake after all. She had hired him because he was shrewd and perceptive and because he knew the murky side of the art world, a rare mix. But he was also demonstrating far too much insight into the workings of her own mind.

It was too late to make other plans. She was committed to this project and she needed him. If the price of his assistance was an honest answer to his question, she had no choice but to pay it.

"My aunt was not a very lovable woman, Mack. She was very smart, very difficult, very imperious. A real control freak. She may have had lovers at various times in the past, but everyone who knew her will tell you that she never fell in love. The assumption is that she was incapable of loving anything except Chatelaine's. She lived for the business. In the end the only tears shed at her funeral were mine."

"You haven't answered my question. Why do you have to look beneath the surface, as you put it?"

She looked out across the bay. "I think it's because I have been told so many times over the years that I have a great deal in common with Vesta. A lot of people are convinced that I will end up just as she did. Cold and alone, with only my work."

He watched her for a moment.

"I get it," he said finally. "You want to know the truth about how and why she died because, deep down, you're afraid that she represented your own future."

"I think so. Yes." She turned away from the view to meet his eyes. "Well? Is that enough straightforward honesty for you?"

"It'll do. For now."

She was afraid to relax. "Does that mean

you'll stay on the job?"

"I'll stay."

She took a step toward him. "Do you really think I'm crazy to suspect that my aunt might have been murdered because of the merger?"

"Whatever else you are, you aren't crazy. Like I said, when it comes to murder, nothing is impossible." He watched her with bleak intensity, as if he was willing her to accept what he had to say. "I'll do what I can, but I can't promise anything. You may never get the answers you want."

"Life's like that sometimes," she sighed. "Doesn't mean that you don't go looking for the answers, though, does it?"

He was very quiet for a long time.

"No," he said eventually. "It doesn't mean that you don't go looking for them."

14

Mack came to a halt on the sidewalk. He looked down the length of Via Appia, the colorful boutique-and-restaurant-crowded street that ran along the waterfront of Phantom Point.

"What's with all the banners and flags?" he asked.

"Carnival Night," Cady said. "It takes place next week. Big annual fund-raiser for the arts here in Phantom Point. It's supposed to be a sort of Venetian carnival with everyone in masks and costumes. They close the streets to traffic here in the shopping district. All the galleries and restaurants stay open late."

He nodded and walked on down the pavement beside her to the entrance of a small gallery in the middle of the block. An oversized sculpture of the Nun's Chatelaine hung over the front door.

Cady stopped. "This is the little branch gallery Aunt Vesta opened a couple of years ago when Sylvia finally talked her into semiretirement. Vesta kept an office here.

My cousin Leandra runs the showroom. It specializes in late-nineteenth-century art. Not the important pictures. Those go to the San Francisco gallery."

He surveyed the doorway. "Think this is going to work?"

"Why shouldn't it? I've got the perfect excuse for spending the day going through Vesta's office files. I'm trying to bring myself up to speed on Chatelaine's financial situation before I decide what to do with my shares."

"If you say so."

She gave him an impatient look. "You said you wanted to go through her private files at the house. Swell. Great idea. I have no objection. But this was her office. We need to see if she left anything behind here that will tell us why she was backing away from the merger. I'm the only one who can do that without risking a lot of questions."

"Fine. Go for it."

Cady made a face. "You think it's going to be a waste of time, don't you?"

"Uh-huh. I've got a hunch your cousin Sylvia has already gone through your aunt's desk. Be the logical thing for the CEO to do. It's what I would have done if I'd been in her position."

"Maybe."

He started to feel a little guilty for being so negative. "But then again, it might be worth a shot. After all, your cousin apparently isn't asking the kind of questions you're asking, so she wouldn't have looked for answers."

Cady brightened. "Right. My point exactly."

She opened the gallery door before Mack could offer any further advice.

He followed her through the opening into a small showroom filled with atmospheric paintings of the Victorian era. Dark portraits, brooding landscapes and a selection of highly romanticized Arthurian themes dominated the offerings. Most of the frames were heavily carved and gilded.

An attractive, pleasantly rounded young woman with dark hair and vivacious features put down the book she had been reading. She rose from behind a small desk.

"Cady. Heard you were in town. Good to see you again."

Cady hurried forward to exchange hugs and air kisses.

"Leandra, I'd like you to meet Mack Easton. Mack, this is my cousin, Leandra Briggs. She was Aunt Vesta's personal assistant. Vesta always said that she'd be lost without her."

"Fat chance," Leandra said cheerfully. "Aunt Vesta could have run both branches of Chatelaine's single-handedly and would have done so right up until the end if Sylvia hadn't managed to talk her into semiretirement. Our great-aunt was amazing."

"So I've been told." Mack glanced at the title of the book on the desk. He wondered how hard it was to break the bad-boy habit, whatever the hell that was. "How long have you been with Chatelaine's?"

"Since my divorce eighteen months ago." She grimaced good-naturedly. "Things were a little rough financially for a while. My ex wasn't what you'd call real great with money. He racked up a lot of bills during our marriage and I got stuck with most of them. Aunt Vesta bailed me out and then created this job for me."

"Nice of her."

Leandra laughed. "I would have said that she did it out of the kindness of her heart, but everyone will tell you that she didn't have a heart."

"I've heard that theory," Mack said.

"It's not true," Cady said with instant loyalty. "Vesta loved Chatelaine's."

Mack and Leandra both looked at her. Neither said a word.

Cady sighed. "Okay, maybe that's not

much of a tribute. But I think she had a heart. She just didn't show it to the world."

"Hard to believe that she's gone," Leandra said wistfully. "It was so sudden, you know? Can't imagine this place without her. Every morning when I arrive to open up, I expect to see her in her office. She was always here before me. Always the last one to leave."

"She certainly made Chatelaine's a respected institution," Mack said.

"That's for sure," Leandra responded. "So, how long will you be staying here in Phantom Point, Mack?"

"I'm not sure yet." He looked at Cady. "Maybe indefinitely."

"Indefinitely?"

"Depends on Cady. I'm a business consultant," he said smoothly. "I can set up shop anywhere."

"Business consultant, huh?" Leandra tipped her head to the side. "What kind of business?"

"On-line," he said. It was amazing how any reference to an internet-based business cut off a lot of potentially awkward questions.

"Cool," Leandra replied. "Hey, are you one of those super-rich software types who made a killing when you took your company public?"

"No. Unfortunately, the kind of information I broker doesn't lend itself to an IPO."

Leandra blinked. "IPO?"

"Initial public offering," he clarified. "The kind that sometimes makes people very rich, very fast."

"Oh. Too bad."

He grinned. "Yeah. I've been saying that a lot lately myself. Too bad."

"Randall wants to take the new Chatelaine-Post Galleries on-line," Leandra said. "He says there's a lot of room for growth there, especially when it comes to art and antiques."

"He's right," Mack said neutrally.

Cady moved to the doorway of a small office. "If you'll excuse me, Mack, I'd better get to work. I want to take a look at some of the quarterly reports and files before I sit down with Sylvia to go over the merger proposal."

"Sure," Mack said. "Don't worry about me, I've got plenty to keep me occupied. Thought I'd do a little sight-seeing in town."

"There are several great little cafés and bistros and shops here on Via Appia," Leandra offered helpfully.

"Thanks." Mack looked at Cady. "I'll pick you up here after work and walk back to the villa with you. Don't worry about dinner. I'll get something today while I'm out."

She looked first surprised and then grateful. "Thanks."

"No problem."

He crossed to where she stood, bent his head and kissed her before she realized what he intended. He felt her stiffen when his mouth closed over hers.

He raised his head before she could figure out how to react.

"See you after work, sweetheart," he murmured, amused by her disgruntled glare and icy smile.

They both knew she could not complain about the kiss. It was all part of the act. A part she had not anticipated and for which she had obviously not made allowances.

Feeling a good deal more positive about the world in general than he had a few minutes ago, he walked out of the little gallery without a backward glance.

"So that's your Mr. Easton." Leandra dropped into a small chair on the opposite side of the desk from Cady. "He looks . . . interesting."

Cady picked up her mug of tea. It was strange to find herself sitting here behind Vesta's old desk. It was also weird to think of Mack as her Mr. Easton.

"Interesting?" she repeated carefully.

"You know, not flashy or slick. But interesting."

"He's definitely interesting," Cady agreed. Also exasperating. And aggravating. And irritating.

"Solid," Leandra continued reflectively. "There's a real solid feel to him. Know what I mean?"

Solid was certainly one way to describe Mack, Cady mused. But she did not think she wanted to pursue the nuances of that particular definition with her cousin.

"I think so," she said instead.

Leandra drummed a set of cherry-red acrylic nails on the desk top. "So, when's the big day?"

"What big day?"

"Come on, Cady. The wedding, of course."

Cady felt her cheeks grow hot. Better get used to the question, she thought. "We haven't officially announced our engagement. Can't think about a firm date for the wedding until we're actually engaged."

"You know, that sort of surprises me," Leandra said with a disconcertingly thoughtful mien. "I always figured that if you ever got married again, you'd do it the same way you did with Randall. Just jump right in, you know?"

"Jumping right in with Randall did not

213

turn out to be a smart way to go," Cady reminded her. "I had to turn around and jump right back out. I'd rather not go through that routine a second time."

"I know what you mean. I feel the same way about Parker. He's started hinting that he'd like to set a date but I guess I'm a little gun-shy after the huge mistake I made with Dillon."

Cady sat back in her chair and regarded her cousin more closely. "Are you and Parker Turner that serious?"

"It's serious, all right. He's perfect for me. But before I make a commitment to him, I feel it's only fair to make sure that I've broken this habit I've got of falling for the wrong kind of men. Guys like Dillon. You know, bad boys."

"I see."

"I'm making a lot of progress. I found a great book called *Breaking the Bad-Boy Habit: The Thinking Woman's Guide to Finding and Appreciating Nice Guys.* It's really helped me get a handle on my problem." Her voice trailed off. "But it's hard to break a bad habit and Dillon's not making it any easier, that's for sure."

"What do you mean?"

"He started calling me right after the funeral. I heard from him again yesterday.

Says he wants us to get back together."

"Does he know about Parker?"

"Sure. I told him."

"What did he say?"

Leandra hesitated. "He got mad. Said Parker was too old for me."

Cady picked up a pen and toyed with it. "Is Dillon pressuring you?"

"He sure is."

"Do you think he's likely to become a real problem?"

"Dillon was a problem from the word go. I don't know what I ever saw in him."

"I mean, as in a stalker," Cady said slowly.

Leandra stared at her, mouth open.

The front door of the gallery opened. Sylvia, garbed in an expensively tailored business suit, came through the doorway.

"Dillon?" Leandra said. "A stalker? I don't . . . I mean, I never —"

"Stalker?" Sylvia glanced from Cady to Leandra and back again. "What's going on here?"

Cady looked at her. "Leandra tells me that Dillon has started calling her since Aunt Vesta's funeral. He's pressuring her to get back together."

"I didn't know that." Sylvia frowned at Leandra with grave concern. "Is he making himself difficult?"

"I've told him to leave me alone, but he —" Leandra broke off abruptly and burst into tears. "Oh, damn." She leaped to her feet and fled down the short hall that led to the small restroom. The door closed sharply behind her.

There was a short silence. Cady and Sylvia both studied the closed door of the restroom.

"What do you think?" Sylvia asked finally.

"I think," Cady said slowly, "that Dillon may be a problem."

"I think you're right," Sylvia agreed. "Wouldn't be the first time. Remember how angry he got when it became clear that Leandra was going to go through with the divorce?"

"I think he had been operating on the assumption that no matter what he did, Leandra would never dump him. But he failed to take Aunt Vesta's influence into account."

"That he did." Sylvia turned back to her. "I'm on my way into the city but you said you would be spending the day here. Thought I'd drop by before I left. I wanted to mention a couple of things. You might want to make some notes."

Warily, Cady reached for a pen and a notepad. "Okay, shoot."

"First, Gardner and I would like to invite you and your Mr. Easton to dinner at the club tomorrow night. It will give us a chance to meet him."

Interrogation time for her Mr. Easton. She hoped Mack could deal with it.

"Thank you," she said very politely. "We'll be there."

"Chatelaine's is hosting a reception to preview the Breston collection the following evening. Eight o'clock in the city. I'd like you and your Mr. Easton to attend, if possible. It will be the first big event the gallery has put on since Vesta died. It would be good public relations for you to be there. A show of respect, if you see what I mean."

Sylvia's crisp tone triggered a sense of deep regret in Cady. This thread of tension between herself and her cousin was new, and it was Vesta's fault.

"All right. I think we can manage that."

"Finally, since you're in town, you wouldn't want to miss the twins' birthday party the following day," Sylvia concluded.

"Not for the world," Cady said, glad to be able to generate some genuine enthusiasm.

Sylvia's expression softened. She smiled for the first time. "Good. I think that's it for now. I'd better be off. If I miss the ferry, I'll have to drive into the city."

For a few seconds Cady hovered on the brink of telling Sylvia about her fear that Vesta had been murdered. But intuition warned her to keep silent. She knew her cousin well enough to be fairly sure that Sylvia would react to the information the same way Mack had last night: with disbelief, incredulity and more than a little concern about Cady's new obsession.

The big difference was that Mack was being paid to tolerate her wild whims and conspiracy theories, Cady reflected. Sylvia was not. Sylvia was, in fact, very likely to conclude that it was her responsibility to start phoning other members of the family to warn them that Cady was having *problems*.

Cady shuddered at the thought of her relatives being informed that she was showing more signs of Vesta-like eccentricities.

" 'Bye, Syl. See you at dinner tomorrow night."

Two hours later in Vesta's private study, Mack closed the last desk drawer and sat back to think. He had rifled through every folder, the address file and a stack of recent correspondence. The search had not brought enlightenment. Probably because there was none to be had.

He was wasting his time. Cady's theory of

a murder plot motivated by financial considerations connected with the merger between Chatelaine's and Austrey-Post was a fantasy. He knew it, even if she did not. He wondered absently if there were any ethical questions involved in taking her money as a paid consultant when it was pretty clear that there was nothing on which to consult.

Screw the ethics. He wasn't here because he needed the job. He had signed that damn contract because it was the easiest way to stay close to Cady.

He swiveled the chair around and contemplated the view of the terrace garden and pool through the French doors. He wondered what his next step would be if he were to start acting like a real investigator. What would he do if he decided to grant his client the benefit of a doubt and take her concerns seriously?

It wasn't as if she was a complete nut case, he reminded himself, trying once again to take a positive angle. He knew that better than most. Over the course of the past couple of months, he had developed a great deal of respect for her intuition and her instincts in one area, at least. When it came to tracing rumors and leads on lost and stolen art, she was one of the best free-lancers he had ever used.

Maybe he shouldn't be so quick to dismiss her conclusions about her aunt's death.

Deliberately he switched gears, shifting away from gloomy analysis of the strange workings of Cady's mind to the puzzle that had presented itself. He wasn't a licensed private investigator, but he did know something about information gathering. He had specialized in it during his stint in the military and later he had built a business based on the skills involved. And it wasn't like he had anything better to do today until Cady came home this evening.

The trick was to look first for the pattern and then search for the places where it had been broken.

Cady, who claimed to have understood Vesta Briggs better than anyone else, had been adamant about one observation. Her aunt's appointments with a psychic had been very much out of character. The consultations with Jonathan Arden, therefore, fell under the heading of a break in the pattern.

He swiveled the chair back around so that he faced the big desk again and reached for the card file. Flipping through it quickly, he found Arden's name and address in San Francisco.

The possibility that Arden was a legitimate psychic, assuming that was not an oxy-moron, had to be considered. Maybe Vesta Briggs had developed a genuine interest in metaphysics. She certainly would not have been the first to do so. A glance through any phone book in any city in the country proved that there was no shortage of folks who claimed psychic abilities and no lack of people who longed to believe in them.

One thing was certain, he thought, getting to his feet. He needed more raw data and he wasn't going to find it here in Vesta's study.

Two hours later he put down the news-paper, rested both hands on the steering wheel and pondered the less exciting as-pects of real-life stakeout work. From where he was parked, half a block down the street from Jonathan Arden's address, he had an excellent view of the garage and the six apartment doors. Thus far, nothing of note had occurred. He glanced at his watch and thought about calling it a day. He still had to drive back across the Golden Gate Bridge and pick up something for dinner before he met Cady at the little gallery on Via Appia.

A consultant's work was never done.

He had his hand on the key in the ignition when he saw the door of the apartment on the far end of the second floor open. A slender man in his late thirties emerged and walked down the outside corridor. His hair was expensively styled. So were the trousers and designer knit sportshirt that he wore. He carried a tennis racket in one hand. As Mack watched, he opened a door and disappeared into a stairwell.

Mack got out of his car and crossed the street. When the grilled gate of the garage door opened a short time later, he was ready.

Arden piloted a green Jaguar out onto the pavement. He drove away quickly, not waiting until the security gate had clanged shut behind him.

Careless, Mack thought. Very careless.

He drove back across the Golden Gate an hour later and managed to take a wrong turn when he entered Phantom Point. He found himself in a peaceful hillside neighborhood with views of the bay that included Belvedere and Tiburon as well as Angel Island and the city. He continued along the winding street for a time, searching for a convenient place to turn around.

The villa with the gracefully arched doors and windows was in a quiet cul-de-sac. It was clearly new construction. There was a For Sale sign out front.

He brought the car to a halt and sat looking at the house for a while.

Mack had been right. Going through Vesta's office files had been a complete waste of time. The only good thing she could say about the day, Cady decided, was that she'd had a chance to catch up on family news and gossip with Leandra.

"Going to come back tomorrow?" Leandra asked as she switched off the gallery lights.

"No, I've seen enough financial reports to last me awhile."

"Learn anything useful?"

"Nope." Cady hitched the strap of her bag over one shoulder. "Just that Chatelaine's is in great shape."

"Even I could have told you that. Sylvia knows what she's doing."

"Yes. She's got a real head for business."

Leandra hesitated near the door. "You're serious about this, aren't you?"

"About what?"

"About getting a handle on Chatelaine's current financial status. You spent the whole day behind that desk going through files. I didn't think you were interested in the business."

"I feel that I have a responsibility to vote

my shares in the way that will be in the best interests of the firm," Cady mumbled.

Leandra shrugged. "Sylvia says the merger is in the best interests of everyone concerned."

"I'm sure she's right. But I think Vesta would have wanted me to make up my own mind."

"I guess so. She obviously wanted you to get more involved in Chatelaine's, or she wouldn't have left you those shares."

Cady lounged on a corner of the desk. "Leandra?"

"Mmm?"

"You worked with Aunt Vesta more closely than anyone else except Sylvia during the past year and a half. You saw her every day. You must have known about this thing with the psychic."

"Jonathan Arden? Sure. I knew that she went to see him a couple of times. I thought it sounded sort of interesting. But Sylvia said to keep quiet about it. She said it would be embarrassing if the news got out."

"What's your take on it? Do you think Aunt Vesta was really losing it there at the end?"

"That's what Syl says, but I'm not so sure. Looked to me like she still had all of her marbles."

A large, dark shadow appeared silhouetted against the glass door of the gallery. Mack twisted the doorknob and walked into the showroom.

"Well, well, well," Leandra said with a cheeky grin. "Aren't you the punctual type."

"I try." Mack met Cady's eyes. "Ready to call it quits for the day?"

"Yes." She straightened away from the desk and started forward. "I'm starving and I could use a medicinal glass of wine."

"What a coincidence. I'm in the mood for the same therapy."

15

They walked back to the villa, following one of the pleasant residential streets that wound up the hillside above the marina. The lights were on in most of the homes they passed. On the far side of the bay, fog had enveloped the city, but the night promised to remain clear here in Phantom Point.

"How did your day go?" Mack asked as he opened the front door of Vesta's house.

"A complete waste of time, just as you predicted." Cady walked into the hall and dropped her purse on the nineteenth-century neoclassical bench. "I don't know what I expected to find, but whatever it was, it wasn't there."

Mack closed the front door and locked it. "No clues, huh?"

"None. Just heaps of letters to clients and business associates. The usual stuff. Advance notes regarding important collections that would be on display in the main gallery in San Francisco. Consulting advice on various acquisitions. That kind of thing."

"What about computer files?"

"My aunt was never keen on computers." Cady headed for the kitchen. "They made her uncomfortable because of the privacy issues."

"She used them in her business, didn't she?"

"Of course. It would be difficult to run a modern firm of any size without computers. But she didn't trust them. Believe me, if Aunt Vesta had had a secret to hide, the last place she would have chosen to conceal it would be a computer."

Mack followed her into the kitchen. "That fits with what you've told me about her. By the way, I picked up some sourdough bread and cracked crab for dinner."

"Sounds great. That reminds me, we've been invited to an ambush tomorrow night at the yacht club."

"Ambush?"

"My cousin Sylvia and her husband, Gardner. They want to meet you. I'm pretty sure they intend to grill you to see if they're right in suspecting that you want to marry me because of my shares in Chatelaine's."

"Got it." He opened the door of the wine closet and removed a bottle. "An ambush."

"What about your day?" she asked as she took a box of crackers out of the cupboard.

He laughed very softly.

She frowned over her shoulder. "Did I say something amusing?"

"Not really. It's just that for a minute there we sounded like an old married couple. 'How did your day go, dear?' 'Not so great, how was yours?' "

She winced. "Well, we are supposed to be semi-engaged."

"I'm not sure that semi-engaged is an officially recognized category in the etiquette books."

"Do you read etiquette books, Mack?"

"No," he admitted. "I don't read much fiction."

"That's what I thought. Let me worry about the technicalities of our situation." She opened the refrigerator to take out some feta cheese. "Find anything interesting in my aunt's personal files in the study?"

"Nothing in her files. But I may get lucky with some other data that I came across."

She turned to reach for a plate and bumped lightly, accidentally, against Mack. A twinge of awareness went through her. This little remains-of-the-day scene was getting downright cozy.

"What data?" she asked.

"Some info I collected this afternoon."

She paused, one hand in the cracker box.

He sounded a little too vague, she thought. "How did you go about collecting this new data?"

"The old-fashioned way. Spent some time sitting in a car outside Jonathan Arden's apartment."

She yanked her hand out of the box and spun around. "Are you telling me you staked out his apartment in the city?"

"For a while."

"Like a real private investigator, do you mean?"

"I keep telling you, I'm a consultant, not a PI."

"Hmm." She pondered an image of him watching Arden's apartment from some shadowy doorway. "See anything interesting?"

"Saw Arden leave his place with a tennis racket and drive off in an expensive Jag." He helped himself to one of the crackers. "Got the license number."

"Can you do anything with that?"

He shrugged. "Not much. I know someone who can tell me whether or not the Jag is registered to Arden. But it probably is and so what?"

"If he's a known con artist —"

"Again, so what? Being a professional psychic is not an illegal activity." He paused to bite down on the cracker. "However —"

She jumped at the bait. "Yes?"

"Interestingly enough, Arden is not listed in the phone book." Mack polished off the cracker and swallowed. "Or any other directory that I could find."

"What do you think that means?"

"Don't know." He opened a drawer, rummaged around in it for a moment and plucked out a corkscrew. "Probably just that he's so exclusive he only works by referral. Or —"

"Or?"

"Could mean he's new to the area. Hasn't had a chance to get into the directory."

She drummed her nails on the counter. "Doesn't sound like you got much out of that stakeout. Maybe you should have followed him or something."

"To the tennis courts to watch him lob balls over a net? I think that would have been a little obvious, don't you? Be tough to fade into the background."

The cork came out of the bottle with a soft whoosh.

Morosely she watched Mack pour the red wine. "Arden's the only lead we've got. I refuse to believe that he's an honest psychic."

"If he's a con artist, he's probably got a history of running scams. Also, chances are his previous operations involved the psychic bit."

"You think so?"

He finished filling the glasses and put the bottle down on the counter. "Most cons develop a unique style of doing business and stick to it. If that's true in Arden's case, we may get lucky with some of the info I found in his trash."

"His trash?" Shock lanced through her. "I thought you just watched his apartment. Mack, what did you *do* today?"

"I told you, I collected some information. That's what you hired me to do."

"Good grief." She crossed the kitchen and gripped two handfuls of his shirt. "Tell me you didn't break into Jonathan Arden's apartment."

"I didn't break into Jonathan Arden's apartment," he said obediently.

"I don't believe you. You must have broken into it. How else could you get into his trash?" She tried to shake him but there was no discernible motion. He just stood there, rock steady, and looked at her with laconic amusement. "Are you crazy? What if Arden had returned and found you inside? What if he's the person who murdered Aunt Vesta? You could have been killed."

"I'm touched by your concern."

231

"Don't you dare laugh at me. It was one thing for you to come to the rescue that night at Ambrose's cabin. That was your case and a man's life may have been at stake. But I do not want you risking your neck to help me prove that someone murdered my aunt. Do you understand? You're supposed to investigate, not play hero."

"Does this mean that you still think of me as having hero potential?" He looked interested. "I was under the impression that I'd been demoted after what happened between us at the lodge that night."

"I've already warned you once about bringing up that subject."

"You know, all of these restrictions are going to make it hard for me to do my job, boss." Ignoring her hands on his shirt front, he reached around her to pick up another cracker. "But if it makes you feel any better, I seriously doubt that Arden is a killer."

"How can you possibly know that?"

"Well, for one thing, there's no obvious motive. What would he have to gain from the merger? Also, as a group, professional con artists prefer to avoid violence. In addition to not being a very profitable way of doing business, it unnecessarily complicates things."

"What do you mean, 'it unnecessarily

complicates things'?" she demanded.

"Most people who get conned are reluctant to go to the cops. They feel foolish and embarrassed because they allowed themselves to be sucked into a scam. The elderly, especially, tend to keep quiet because they're afraid their kids and heirs will find out and assume that they've lost it. Gives the little ingrates a good excuse to go after a power-of-attorney on the grounds that grandpa can no longer manage his own finances. The kids get their hands on the money. Grandpa gets warehoused in a nursing home."

"Yes, I've heard that, but —"

Mack reached over one of her clutching hands to pick up a glass of wine. "But all that changes if someone gets murdered," he said gently.

Slowly, she released his shirt front and took a step back. "Because murder means the cops have to get involved?"

"Yes. And a murder investigation brings with it a lot more attention than any pro wants."

She frowned at the wrinkles she had made in the fabric of his shirt. "I get your point but I still don't want you taking chances. Having you arrested for breaking and entering isn't going to get us anywhere." Impulsively she reached out to brush the crumpled cloth, trying ineffectually to smooth it.

He looked down at where she was fussing with the fabric. "Would you fire me if I got arrested?"

The amusement in his voice was infuriating. She snatched her hand away from his shirt and turned on her heel to pick up her wineglass. "I'd have grounds. After all, you wouldn't do me a heck of a lot of good in jail."

"No, I guess not. Probably bad for your business image, too."

"Very bad." She realized that he was not going to give credence to her very real fears. She was not sure she herself understood the depths of her own reaction. All she could do was try to conceal the cold chill he had given her behind the legitimate annoyance of an irate employer. "Mack, I mean it, I don't want you taking any chances on this job."

He nodded. "I know exactly how you feel. Sort of the way I felt when I found you in the middle of a burglary-in-progress at Vandyke's cabin."

She spun back around, heat rising in her face. "You were extremely annoyed."

"I was pissed, all right."

"Fine." She smiled coolly. "So you do understand. Stick to collecting information.

Feed data into that whiz-bang database of yours. See what pops out. That's all I'm paying you to do."

"Well, no, it isn't. Not quite."

"I hired you to consult. Stick to the job description." She took a swallow of wine to settle her nerves.

"The job description includes acting the role of your current besotted lover and soon-to-be official fiancé, remember?"

She sputtered on the mouthful of wine and groped wildly for a napkin. Mack handed her a paper towel instead. He watched with polite concern as she regained her self-possession.

"There's no risk involved in that part," she got out with an effort.

"I'm not so sure."

She would not allow him to provoke her anymore tonight. He had done enough damage to her nerves for one day. "I can't see that playing the part of my possible potential future fiancé puts you in danger of getting shot or arrested."

"You never know."

"Damn it, Mack —"

"Take it easy." His mouth quirked slightly at one corner. "I told you I didn't break into Jonathan Arden's house. It was the truth."

She tried to read his expression and failed

miserably. "I'm not sure I believe you."

"I noticed. Does that make us even?"

"For what?"

"For the fact that I thought you had ulterior motives when you went traipsing off to see Ambrose Vandyke about a certain chunk of heavy metal. You know, the trust thing."

She groaned and waved one hand in disgust. "Yes. Sure. We're even."

"How nice. A fresh start for us." He took a long swallow of wine.

She eyed him closely. "If you *didn't* break into Arden's apartment, how did you get that information you said you found?"

"Went through the apartment building trash container in the garage."

She stared at him for a few seconds before she became aware of the fact that her jaw had dropped. "Yuck."

"In a word, yes. Luckily I had some gloves with me. Had to change clothes when I got back here, though. There were only six apartments in that building but I swear, every single tenant ordered in pizza last night."

"What if someone had seen you?"

"I had a back-up story ready, just in case. If anyone had asked questions, I planned to tell them that I was a guest of one of the tenants and that I had accidentally dropped my watch in the trash that morning while getting dressed."

"Heck of a plan. Lost your watch in the trash. Yes, of course. Now, why didn't I think of that?"

"You'd be amazed at the kind of stuff people throw away without stopping to think. Garbage, especially a whole apartment building's worth, seems so anonymous, doesn't it?"

She thought about all the stuff she had casually discarded into various trash containers over the years. "Yes, it does. What exactly did you find?"

"Some junk mail. A lot of credit card applications. Empty envelopes. That kind of stuff."

"Do you really think we'll learn anything useful?"

"Probably not. I doubt that Arden is the careless type."

"My, you're certainly Mr. Optimistic."

Mack shrugged. "Let's just hope we don't prove the old gigo theory right."

"The gigo theory?"

"Garbage in, garbage out."

At ten forty-five that night he sprawled in the chair in front of the computer, propped his elbows on the arms and put the tips of his fingers together. He regarded the data on the screen.

"Not much," he said. "According to this, Jonathan Arden has no history of running his psychic scams for fun and profit in the art world. At least, my database has no information on any con artist who matches his description or operating style."

"Sheesh." Cady stopped pacing the study and came to lean over his shoulder. She glared at the glowing screen. "You mean he's for real?"

"A real psychic?" He smiled faintly. "I doubt it."

"You know what I mean," she said impatiently.

He spread his fingertips apart briefly and then put them back together. "All I can say with any assurance at this point is that Arden has no record of scams involving claims of psychic talents in our neck of the woods."

"Doesn't mean he might not have a record elsewhere."

"No, but as I warned you, this program is very specialized. It's limited to tracking activity in the art world. I'm not the FBI or Interpol here."

"Hmm." She did not move. Instead, she

continued to lean over his shoulder, glaring balefully at the screen.

He took the opportunity to inhale the scent of her, trying hard to be subtle about it. She smelled good. Faint traces of some flowery body cream or maybe that was soap, he thought. But mostly there was the warm, delightfully female fragrance that was unique to her. It stirred memories of the night at the lodge, making him feel edgy and restless.

"But the question still remains," she continued, obviously heedless of the effect she was having on him, "why was Aunt Vesta seeing Arden? I just can't bring myself to believe that she thought he was for real."

She did not know what woke her later that night. She lay quietly for a while, listening to the small sounds of the large house. She heard no alarming noises, no footstep in the dark or muffled thuds. After a while she pushed aside the covers and got to her feet beside the bed.

Grabbing her robe off the hook on the back of the door, she wrapped herself in its folds and went out into the hall. Barefooted, she padded along the interior balcony that overlooked the two-story living room. When she reached the staircase, she descended to the first floor.

She came to a halt in front of the French doors and gazed out onto the night-darkened terrace. The underwater lights were on in the pool. A dark, sleek, unmistakably masculine shadow moved beneath the surface, gliding toward the far end with powerful, efficient strokes.

Mack was doing laps.

She watched him for a while, aware of an increasing sense of unease. When he reached the tiled pool wall, he whipped around with a supple twist of his body and shot back in the opposite direction. Every time he broke the surface for air, his strong shoulders gleamed wetly.

Deep inside her, the uneasy sensation grew until it began to resemble full-blown anxiety. She told herself that she should go back to bed, maybe do some yoga breathing. Instead her fingers closed around the doorknob.

Outside in the pool, Mack reached a wall, flexed and glided back through the water.

She opened the door and stepped out onto the terrace. The cool night air made her pull the robe more snugly around herself.

Slowly she made her way to the edge of the pool. Mack must have sensed her presence. He came to a halt in the water and surfaced, flinging drops from his hair and face with a single, quick movement of his head. He found her in the shadows immediately.

"Something wrong?" he asked, treading water.

She hesitated. "No."

"Couldn't sleep?"

"Mack, how can you swim in that pool?"

For a few seconds he studied her. Then he swam slowly toward the edge where she stood. When he got close, he put one hand on the tiled rim.

"Does it bother you to think of anyone swimming here because this is where your aunt died?"

"Well, yes." She wrapped her arms around herself. "Yes, it does."

"You told me that the pool was drained and refilled after Vesta drowned."

"Yes, but —" She broke off, unable to explain her feelings. Instead she looked around at the looming vegetation. "It's like a jungle out here. Aunt Vesta planted all the shrubs and hedges to ensure her privacy. But they give me the creeps."

"You're thinking that someone hid here in the garden and waited until she was in the water before he attacked her?"

"Are you going to tell me again that I have an overly active imagination?"

241

"No." He studied her for a long moment. The other-worldly, up-from-under lighting cast hard, cryptic shadows below his cheekbones and under his eyes. "Like I said, murder by drowning happens."

He planted both hands on the edge of the pool and hauled himself out of the water in a single, easy movement. He got to his feet in front of her.

She was intensely conscious of him standing there big and wet and naked except for a ridiculously small bathing suit that did nothing to hide the bold outlines of his maleness.

"You're dripping," she muttered.

"Yeah. I am." He turned and walked to where a towel lay across a white lounger. "Sorry about that."

She winced. "I didn't mean to snap at you. It's just that everything about this pool terrace sets my nerves on edge. I don't like the idea of you swimming alone out here."

"What do you suggest I do?" He used the towel to wipe the water off his chest. "Hire a lifeguard?"

"Think I'm a little over the top here?"

"A little. But that's okay. I'm willing to make allowances, given the circumstances."

"What circumstances?"

"What with all the excitement at Vandyke's

cabin and your fears that your aunt may have been murdered, you've been under a lot of stress lately."

"So have you," she shot back. Then she sighed. "Thanks to me. Mack, I've been thinking. I had no right to involve you in this situation. I know it's outside the boundaries of your usual kind of work."

He propped a bare foot on the lounger and applied the towel to his leg. "You know, you're cute when you go on these small guilt trips."

She could not look away from where the dark hair streaked his upper thigh. A heated tension pooled in her lower body.

"You're right. I am a little tense."

He took his foot down off the lounger and walked toward her, knotting the towel around his waist as he moved. He halted directly in front of her, caught her chin on the heel of his hand and tilted her face slightly so that she was obliged to meet his eyes.

"Stop fretting about it," he said. "You're paying my full fee, remember? For that you get full service, whether you want it or not."

She could not move; awareness of him was so keen now it was painful. "What exactly does full service include?"

"Whatever it takes to get the job done."

She braced herself. "About what happened that night at the lodge —"

His eyes gleamed. "Thought you said you didn't want to talk about it."

"I don't." She swallowed. "But I think it's necessary to clarify one point."

"What point would that be?"

She drew a deep breath. "Regardless of what occurred between us personally, I want you to know that I'm very grateful for what you did for Ambrose and me that night."

"Does this mean that you still think I'm a hero?"

"You're not going to take this seriously, are you?"

"I am one-hundred-percent serious about my heroic status. The male pride thing, remember?"

"For heaven's sake," she muttered. "It's not like you fell off a pedestal. You don't need to be restored to hero status. You are one. Nothing can alter that."

He moved a fraction of an inch closer. "Even though I took advantage of the situation to get you into bed that night?"

"Don't push it, Easton."

He smiled. "Just wanted to see how far your gratitude went."

"You just hit the limit." Why did she let

him do this to her, she wondered. "Look, since you seem determined to bring up the subject of what happened between us at the lodge, I might as well tell you that I've been thinking about it and I'm prepared to admit that I might have overreacted. A little."

"Go slow. I may hyperventilate."

She refused to let him sidetrack her. She had come this far, she would see it through to the end. "I was angry at the time. But looking back, I can see that there were extenuating circumstances."

"You think so?"

"It's not your fault that we wound up in bed together."

"You don't think that I took advantage of you?"

"I think," she said carefully, "that it was very much a mutual thing. We were both stressed out from the aftereffects of danger. We weren't ourselves, if you know what I mean."

"Can't say that I do." A reflective expression came and went across his hard face. "I'm pretty sure that I was myself. And you looked a lot like yourself. You think maybe our bodies were temporarily taken over by alien entities that night?"

"Work with me here, Easton. I'm trying to help us both get past some issues, okay?"

"You know, I've got nothing against the grand old tradition of the rescued damsel throwing herself into the arms of the knight in shining armor, but —"

Outrage flashed through her. "I did not throw myself into your arms just because I thought it was a nice way to thank you for saving my life, do you hear me? *That's not why I did it.*"

"As I was saying, I've got no problem with tradition, but there's a lot of pressure on the heroic knight in those situations," he continued, just as though she had not interrupted. "I'm not sure people appreciate that."

"Pressure? What pressure, for crying out loud?" She was completely exasperated now. "You weren't exactly dragging your feet, as I recall. You came over that partition the way Superman jumps tall buildings. In a single bound."

"It's like this: even while he's enjoying the experience, the hero knows that sooner or later the fair damsel will realize that the armor is a bit tarnished. Worse yet, there's some rust in places. He knows that when things cool down she probably won't see him through the same set of rose-colored glasses —"

"Stop it, Mack." She put her fingers on

246

his mouth to silence him. "That's not how it was for me."

"No?" he asked against her fingers.

"You insult me when you imply that I would have gone to bed with whoever rode to the rescue that night." She took her hand away from his mouth. "Let's get one thing clear, Easton. I went to bed with you because you were you."

"Yeah?" He sounded interested but not yet entirely convinced. Skeptical.

"I don't know why I'm bothering to have this argument," she said. "It's hopeless."

"Not at all. Personally, I'm prepared to let bygones be bygones."

"Decent of you."

"I thought so. What do you say we kiss and make up?"

He bent his head and crushed her mouth beneath his own before she could register the question in her mind.

Fantasy Man. Not again, she thought wildly. This was not smart.

His kiss was a slow, demanding caress. Not the instantaneous conflagration that had ignited her senses at the lodge. This was a building fire that would leave smoldering embers for a long time to come.

He was still damp in places, stirring unsettling memories. His hair had been wet from the rain that night at the lodge, she recalled. There was something slightly primeval about all this moisture.

He was also hard, just as he had been that night. She could feel his erection through the layers of towel and swim briefs. Excitement warmed her blood. She inched closer.

His mouth moved on hers, seducing and persuasive. The hunger she had been trying to deny was suddenly howling at the windows and breathing down the chimney, threatening to demolish all the tightly locked doors. She heard herself make a small sound that she knew Mack could only interpret as evidence of her desire. Probably because that was exactly what it was.

Drawn by a reckless compulsion, she spread the fingers of one hand across his bare chest. Big mistake. Should have known better than to touch him with all this energy crackling in the air. Like standing out in an open field in the middle of a lightning storm.

A shiver went through her.

He broke off the kiss, lifting his head just as she was thinking about putting her other hand on him. He was breathing a little harder than he had been a moment ago.

"If," he said in a sexy-rough voice that sent a couple of jagged bolts of electricity through her, "you ever decide to change your company policy about sleeping with your employees, be sure to let me know."

She stared at him, unable to think of a single coherent sentence.

He gave her an intimate, very knowing smile that made her set her back teeth together. She felt the flutter of nerves in her stomach. Not an incipient panic attack, she assured herself as he walked around her and disappeared into the house.

Something even more disturbing.

She had a nasty feeling that she was falling in love with Fantasy Man.

16

In keeping with what appeared to be the uni-
lateral architectural design motif of Phantom Point, the yacht club had been decorated in faux Mediterranean palazzo style.
The walls were covered in plaster that had
been applied in thick daubs and swirls to
give the impression of crumbling age. Soft
lighting illuminated sea scenes from antiq-
uity. The chairs were covered in Renaissance
hues.

Nice place for an ambush, Mack thought.
Then again, maybe it didn't actually count
as an ambush if you had been warned ahead
of time. He could feel the invisible vibes that
told him Cady was tense, even though she
was trying not to show it. Her brittle mood
was probably the result of the not-so-subtle
grilling he was undergoing. She was poised
on the brink of anticipation, just waiting for
him to screw up.

The good news was that the ex-husband
hadn't shown up.

Sylvia looked at him across the low cocktail table. She had a chilly gleam in her eyes.

He had no trouble envisioning her in a CEO's chair.

"What sort of business are you in, Mack?" she asked. "Cady said something about consulting work?"

"Right." He reached for an olive. "Consulting."

"What sort of consulting do you do?" Gardner asked.

"Business consulting." Wonderful word, *"consulting."* It covered a multitude of sins, Mack reflected. So did *"business,"* for that matter. He was getting a lot of mileage out of both this evening.

"Start-ups?" Sylvia pressed. "Venture capital? Acquisitions?"

"Some acquisition work," Mack said, thinking of the art and antiques he had recovered for various clients. Recovering stuff was a form of acquiring, he assured himself.

Gardner gave him a look of polite curiosity that did not quite manage to conceal the thoughtful assessment in his serious dark eyes. "Mid-cap? Small-cap?"

"Small-cap. I work a lot with private investors."

Gardner nodded. "Where's your office?"

"I work out of my house these days."

"Really . . . So do I. After it became clear that Vesta was grooming Sylvia to take the helm at Chatelaine's, we decided to switch places. Kids, you know. Couple of boys. Twins. Someone has to be there when they get home. Make sure they get to soccer games and don't spend too much time watching television."

"I know what you mean. After my wife died, I made the decision to work at home until my daughter left for college. Same reasons."

"You have a daughter in college?" Sylvia asked swiftly.

"Yes. Gabriella. She's at Santa Cruz."

"Good school," Gardner said. "Excellent academic reputation. But a little eccentric in some ways, I hear."

"What can you expect from a campus that picked the banana slug as a mascot?"

"Any other children?" Sylvia demanded.

"No," Mack said.

"Going to be interesting starting all over again with a new bunch of rug rats, isn't it?" Gardner asked. "At least this time around you'll know what to expect."

In her chair, Cady went so still you would have thought she had been flash-frozen. Mack pretended not to notice.

"Mmm," he said noncommittally. "How old are your twins?"

"Eight as of the day after tomorrow,"

Gardner said proudly. "You're invited to the party."

"Thanks, I look forward to it."

"How did you and Cady meet?" Sylvia asked.

"On the internet," Mack said.

Predictably, that statement brought an appalled silence that lasted nearly thirty seconds. Mack glanced at Cady and saw that she was concentrating very hard on fishing a bit of cork out of her wineglass. He got the feeling that she was trying hard not to laugh.

"You're joking," Sylvia said eventually. "It was an internet connection?"

"Beats the bar scene," Mack said. "At least it does when you're my age."

Cady finally managed to ease the invisible shard of cork out of the wine.

Gardner frowned slightly. "Bit risky meeting on-line, isn't it?"

Mack thought about the events at the Vandyke cabin. "Yes, it is. We got lucky, though."

Sylvia gave Cady a troubled look. "I've heard some horrifying stories about people assuming false identities on-line to stalk unsuspecting people. Mack could have been a serial killer, for all you knew."

"Fortunately, he turned out to be a consultant instead." Cady took a quick swallow of wine and then licked a tiny drop off her finger.

Sylvia's expression tightened. Mack realized that he was starting to feel a little sorry for her.

"It wasn't a chat-room meeting," he said gently. "It started out as a business connection. I needed an expert in European decorative arts and came across Cady's web page."

That was close enough to the truth, he thought. So what if he had done a thorough background check on her before contacting her? No point going into the gritty details.

"I see."

The uneasiness in Sylvia's gaze diminished fractionally. But it was clear that she was not yet convinced that he was not a serial killer. Or at the very least, a modern-day fortune hunter.

"Why did you need an art consultant?" Gardner asked with genuine curiosity. "Do you collect?"

"I was interested in a Spanish piece at the time," Mack said. "For an acquaintance."

Cady apparently decided that the interrogation had gone far enough. "Any idea why Aunt Vesta started seeing a psychic?"

As a diversion strategy, it worked brilliantly. Sylvia flinched and cast a quick glance around the lightly crowded lounge.

"Not so loud, Cady. As far as we know, no one is aware of the visits. For the sake of Chatelaine's image, I'd like to keep it that way."

"We think she only saw him a couple of times," Gardner offered helpfully.

"But why?" Cady asked again in a lower tone. "I mean, you've got to admit that it was completely out of character for her. She scoffed at that kind of stuff."

"No offense," Gardner said dryly, "but your aunt was always a little on the weird side. I wouldn't put it past her to have suddenly developed an interest in the paranormal."

Sylvia turned back to Cady. "We don't know what was going on between Aunt Vesta and Jonathan Arden. She refused to discuss it. We can only assume that some form of dementia or mental illness was setting in. No one outside the family knows about this." She paused to give Mack a meaningful nod. "Except for your Mr. Easton, of course."

"It's okay." Mack put an olive pit into the tiny dish on the table. "Her Mr. Easton is starting to feel like a real member of the family."

Sylvia's hand tightened around her glass.

"We would appreciate it if you would refrain from discussing Vesta's eccentricities outside the family circle."

"Mack wouldn't think of mentioning the subject to outsiders," Cady remarked. "Isn't that right, Mack?"

"Right," Mack said.

Suddenly his attention was drawn to two men who were approaching their table. One appeared to be in his early sixties, polished and genial. He paused here and there to greet other polished people scattered about the lounge. Wherever he stopped, there was friendly chatter and good cheer. A natural salesman, Mack thought.

The man with him was much younger; early thirties maybe, athletically built and well dressed in tailored trousers and a linen jacket. He, too, seemed quite at ease, but Mack noticed that his congenial expression did not quite reach his eyes.

Gardner followed Mack's gaze. "Well, well, well, if it isn't good old Uncle Randall."

Something told Mack his luck had run out for the evening. The ex-husband had arrived.

Sylvia turned quickly, smiled warmly at the newcomer and gave him her cheek to kiss. "Hello, Randall. This is a pleasant surprise."

It was the barely veiled irritation in Gardner's eyes that interested Mack. Sylvia's mild-mannered husband had not liked that friendly little peck on the cheek, he thought.

"Cady, honey." Randall put a hand on Cady's shoulder in a too-familiar manner and bent down to kiss her. "Good to see you again. I heard you were in Phantom Point."

Mack felt something inside him clench. Hard. He suddenly understood exactly how Gardner felt. It was clear that Randall Post was one hell of a close friend of the family.

The older man arrived in a small cloud of sophisticated bonhomie. Somewhere along the line he had collected a martini from the bar.

"Evening, everyone. Cady, heard you were in town. Nice to see you."

"Hello, Stanford," she said.

Her tone was polite, Mack noticed, but there were no pecks on the cheek between Stanford Felgrove and Cady. It was the same with Sylvia and Stanford. Friendly but not intimate.

"Won't you join us for a drink?" Sylvia waved a gracious hand at two vacant chairs. "We were just chatting with Cady and her *friend,* Mack Easton. Have you met him?"

"Don't believe we've had the pleasure." Stanford stuck out a hand. "Stanford Felgrove. I run Austrey-Post."

Mack got to his feet and went through the hand-shaking ritual with Stanford. He turned to Randall. As long as he was up, he might as well get this over and done, he decided.

Randall extended a firm hand. "Easton, was it? So you're Cady's new friend?"

"Yes. And it will soon be fiancé, not friend. Cady and I are planning to announce our engagement in the near future."

Cady stiffened.

"Heard about the upcoming engagement." Randall's grin was ice cold. "Congratulations. You're getting yourself a terrific wife."

"Randall ought to know." Stanford chuckled and tossed back a lot of the martini. "He was married to her himself for a while. I'm sure you've heard all about that nine-day wonder, eh, Easton?"

Cady tensed. They all looked uncomfortable.

Mack took note of the cooling temperature in the vicinity, but it didn't affect him. He was too busy dealing with the white-hot wave of possessiveness that was crashing through him. It had been so long since he had experienced this sense of primitive male territoriality that it took him a few seconds to recognize and catalog it. He wondered if Cady would fire him on the spot if he succumbed to the almost over-powering urge to smash his fist into Stanford Felgrove's face.

"I heard about her marriage," he said. He looked at Randall. "Everyone makes mistakes."

A long time later Cady came to a halt and leaned on the steel railing that guarded the waterfront path. She looked out over the moonlit surface of the bay to where the lights of the city glittered in the night. She was exhausted and keyed up at the same time. It had not been a comfortable evening.

She turned toward Mack. "All right, go ahead and say it."

He came to a halt beside her and leaned back against the railing, looking at the homes that marched up the hillside. "Okay, I'll say it. You and Randall Post seem pretty friendly for a couple that was divorced three years go."

"It was a friendly divorce."

He nodded. "I've heard about those. Never actually seen one, though."

"Well, now you have."

"Why'd you two get married in the first place?"

"You don't think he's my type?"

"No."

"You think you know what my type is?"

"I'm not going there." He sounded slightly amused. "I just know that Randall Post wasn't for you."

"How do you know that?"

"Male intuition."

"So, there is such a thing?"

"Sure. Real men don't talk about it much, that's all."

"I can see where it might be a little awkward to discuss in mixed company."

"Sort of like telling off-color jokes." He contemplated the hillside lights for a moment. "So, why'd you marry him?"

"For a long time I assumed the experience of falling in love would be a lot like looking at a really fine work of art. I'd know the real thing when I saw it."

"Sometimes it is like that."

"Maybe. But I have a hunch that most cases of falling in love at first sight are actually cases of falling in *lust*. Sometimes you get lucky and the relationship works on other levels. But you can't count on that happening. The thing is, if you're one of the lucky ones, you don't go back and question your good fortune. You just assume your intuition was right on target."

"And if you're one of the unlucky ones?"

"You obsess on what went wrong and you ask yourself how you could have been so dumb."

"I take it you obsessed for a while?"

"Sure. I'm good at that." She hesitated. "What was it like for you when you decided to get married?"

"I was one of the lucky ones. Love at first sight. Rachel and I met during our sophomore year at college. I took one look at her and never looked twice at anyone else. We got pregnant in our junior year. Ran off to Vegas to get married. Everyone in both families had a fit. Dewey and Notch were the only ones who sent gifts."

"Your families were probably afraid that you wouldn't finish college."

"Marriage did delay things for us. I joined the army and we went into debt and in the end we managed to work things out. When Gabriella came along the following year, all was forgiven."

"How did you lose your wife?"

"Drunk driver."

"Dear heaven."

"Yeah. You feel so much rage for a time

261

and there's nowhere to go with it. You want to talk obsession? I can tell you all about obsession."

She shivered. "I can imagine."

"Knowing I had to be there for Gabriella kept me hanging on by my fingernails. Sometimes it was the only thing that kept me hanging on. I managed to stay just this side of sane for the most part, but there were days when I wasn't sure I would make it."

"You were fortunate to have your daughter."

"I can't even think about what it would have been like if I hadn't had her. We just kept moving forward through the nightmare together because we didn't have any choice. And then one day we looked around and realized that we had gotten past the worst of it. The light at the end of the tunnel wasn't an oncoming train after all."

"I am so sorry for both of you."

"It's been six years. Gabriella and I are okay. You don't forget nightmares, but when they've been exposed to enough sunlight, they fade."

She leaned on her forearms and loosely linked her fingers. "I've always heard that men who were happily married generally remarry after the loss of their wives. But you didn't."

"No."

"Because you never again fell in love again at first sight?" She turned her head to look at him. "Because you never found another woman as wonderful as Rachel?"

"I'll let you in on a little secret, Cady. You don't fall in love at first sight unless you're actively looking."

"And you haven't been looking?"

"Rachel was taken from us just as Gabriella was heading into the teenage years. She got very anxious when I started seeing women socially again. Her therapist told me that the idea of having to cope with a stepmother disturbed her deeply."

"Not surprising."

"We probably could have worked things out if the right woman had come along. But as I said, I wasn't really looking. I had my hands full raising Gabriella and getting Lost and Found up and running. I didn't have time to work on a marriage too."

"I can understand that."

Silence fell. Cady listened to the slap of the dark water below the path. She did not look down at it.

"You haven't answered my question," Mack said after a while.

"Why did I marry Randall?" She drew a breath. "Well, let's see. I was twenty-nine years old and it had become very clear that I had been, in my mother's words, much too picky when it came to men."

"Picky, huh?"

"I told myself it was time to stop looking for a fantasy and get real. I decided to go for friendship and shared interests." She paused. "Everyone knows friendship and shared interests make a really solid foundation for marriage."

"I've heard that." He folded his arms. "So you married a friend who shared your interests, is that it?"

"The pressure was on. I could hear my biological clock ticking."

"You wanted a family."

"Is that so wrong?"

"Hell no. Sounds perfectly normal to me." He looked at her. "Go on."

"It wasn't like Randall and I didn't have lot of strong connections. We've known each other all of our lives. He took me to the senior prom when my date dumped me for a cheerleader at the last minute. He gave me my first kiss."

"First kiss. That's a big deal, all right."

"Well, it was actually more of an experiment. Neither of us had ever been kissed and we decided to find out what the big deal was. We were both seriously disappointed. Which, in hindsight, should have been a clue."

"Yeah."

"It was Randall who raised the subject of marriage. He had just ended a relationship with another woman. She married someone else. Someone much older and wealthier. Randall and I started spending time together. Somehow the idea of marrying him just seemed very sensible. Everyone, especially Aunt Vesta, thought it was a terrific idea."

"When did you and Randall decide you'd made a mistake?"

"On our wedding night." She paused. "When Randall started sobbing at about the time I figured he should have been inflamed with passion."

Mack winced. "He actually cried? Are we talking real tears?"

"Yes. We spent the night sitting side by side on the edge of the bed, discussing the fact that he was deeply in love with another woman."

"Who?"

"The woman he had been seeing before our marriage. Her name is Brooke Langworth now. She married George Langworth immediately after she broke up with Randall. They have a home here in Phantom Point."

"Tough way to spend your wedding night."

"Yes, but at least I finally understood why Randall had been such a gentleman during our engagement. I thought he had been holding back because he found it awkward to make the transition from friend to lover. And that was true, but not for the reasons I had assumed."

Mack turned his head to look at her. "Do I take it that you two never, uh —"

"Consummated our marriage? Nope. We reverted to being friends. It was a lot more comfortable for both of us. We spent our honeymoon discussing how we were going to fix the mistake we had made. Unfortunately, we couldn't stay in Hawaii forever. When we got home I filed for divorce."

"Do you know this Brooke Langworth?"

"I've met her on one or two occasions, but that's about it. Brooke didn't grow up here in Phantom Point. She lived in the city until she married Langworth."

"How did she and Randall meet?" Mack asked.

"She worked for Austrey-Post for a while. They started dating at that time." Cady hesitated. "Sylvia told me that Brooke's husband, George, is in the last stages of terminal cancer."

"Interesting."

She was startled by the thoughtful tone of his voice. "Why? Aside from the soap-opera elements of the story, I fail to see anything really interesting about it."

"Probably because you were in the middle of it." He straightened, draped an arm around her shoulders and urged her gently along the path. "Congratulations on getting yourself out of that mess, by the way."

"It wasn't like I had much choice. I couldn't stay married to Randall. Not after I realized that he was still passionately in love with Brooke. Randall and I are friends, but friendship has its limits."

"I'm with you on that. The guy should have leveled with you going into the marriage."

She sighed. "Randall's intentions were good. He did his best to try to put Brooke behind him and get on with his life. The problem was that he didn't give himself enough time to heal from the pain of the breakup of their relationship."

"You and Sylvia do this a lot?" Mack asked.

"Do what?"

"Make excuses for good old Randall?"

She glared at him. "I'm not making excuses. I'm explaining."

"Sounds to me like you're making excuses."

"Randall is a friend."

"Let him make his own excuses," Mack said.

17

Mack contemplated the artistically arranged pile of elegant old snuffboxes.

"Magnificent, aren't they?" asked a voice. "I believe we can let you have the lot for somewhere in the neighborhood of six thousand."

"An interesting neighborhood." Mack picked up the discreetly folded card that sat next to the boxes. There was a number written in a fine hand inside. "Price tag says ten thousand."

"According to what I hear, you'll soon be entitled to the family discount."

"Forget it. I don't do a lot of snuff."

The stranger chuckled and put out a hand. "Mack Easton, right? I'm Parker Turner. Leandra pointed you out. Thought I'd introduce myself. I believe we have something in common."

"That would be — ?"

"Honorable intentions toward certain female members of the Briggs clan. I'm hoping that Leandra and I will also be announcing an engagement soon."

Mack shook hands. Parker's grasp was firm and strong. A small gold signet ring gleamed on one of his fingers. He wore a tux, as did the other men on Chatelaine's staff tonight. The female employees were dressed in discreetly cut black evening gowns. Cady, Sylvia and Leandra also wore black. They circulated among the clients and guests who had been invited to the reception.

No expense had been spared tonight as far as Mack could see. The champagne and hors d'oeuvres alone must have cost as much as one or two of the better pieces of old furniture. The event had the sophisticated ambience of a museum or symphony fund-raiser, but he knew that most of the cash raised here tonight would go directly into the coffers of Chatelaine's. The trick was to make the clients feel that they had been invited to an elite event in the world of the arts, not to a rummage sale.

"I've heard your name mentioned," Mack said. "You're on the staff here at Chatelaine's, aren't you?"

Parker nodded easily. "Been with the firm for over twenty years. Started in shipping and receiving."

Mack surveyed Parker's excellently tailored tux. "Looks like you've moved out of shipping and receiving."

Parker laughed and glanced self-deprecatingly down at the expensive attire he wore. "Between you and me, everything you see standing here in front of you, I owe to Vesta Briggs."

"How's that?"

"The day I went to work for her, I was dressed in jeans, a T-shirt and a cheap leather jacket. I wore a headband, if you can believe it. At the time I thought I was cool. Miss Briggs took me in hand and re-defined the word for me. The lady changed my life and I will be forever grateful to her memory." Parker raised his champagne flute in a small, respectful gesture.

"Did Vesta take such a personal interest in all of her employees?"

"No." Parker looked amused. "Only in the ones she thought would be useful to Chatelaine's."

"I get your point."

"Don't mistake me, I admired Miss Briggs enormously. She was utterly devoted to the company. Everything she did was for the good of Chatelaine's. Never met a more single-minded human being in my life. She was really quite amazing and, as I said, she had a profound effect on my life. If it hadn't been for her, I'd probably be driving a truck today instead of drinking champagne and wearing a tux."

"When do you and Leandra plan to make the big announcement?"

"As soon as I can convince her to take another chance on marriage. She got hurt in a very nasty divorce about eighteen months ago. Takes a while to recover from something like that."

"So I've heard."

Parker looked across the crowded showroom to where Leandra stood chatting with two men who were examining an antique microscope. His expression tightened. "It was hard watching her marry that sonofabitch, Spooner. Everyone, especially Vesta, knew that it would end in disaster."

On the other side of the room, Leandra gestured toward the old microscope. Mack watched one of the pair shake his head. He got the impression that the instrument did not fit into whatever budget the two had established for investing in art and antiques.

"Were you in love with her when she married Dillon Spooner?" Mack asked.

Parker grimaced. "I think it was seeing her marry him that made me realize the depth of my own feelings. I'd known Leandra for years, of course, and liked her. But she's several years younger, as you can see. We didn't move in the same circles. I thought of her as just one of the kids in the Briggs family."

"What happened?"

"I was invited to the wedding along with the rest of the staff here at Chatelaine's. Danced with Leandra at the reception and suddenly realized that she was no longer a kid. But by then it was too late, of course. Besides, she was wild about Spooner. She wouldn't have looked twice at me. All I could do was stand by, together with her family, and wait for the marriage to fall apart."

"What made everyone so sure this Spooner guy was a loser?"

"It was obvious that he thought he'd found a meal ticket by marrying into the family that controlled Chatelaine's." Parker's mouth quirked slightly. "Vesta Briggs soon set him straight on that point. The marriage fell apart when it became clear that she wasn't going to finance his painting. She expected him to get a day job and keep it. That came as a serious shock to Spooner."

On the far side of the room, Leandra laughed at something one of the two men said. She caught sight of Mack and Parker and raised her glass to acknowledge them.

"After the divorce you moved in to pick

up the pieces, is that it?" Mack asked.

"That's how it started. I was divorced myself several years ago, so I knew the ropes. What about you? How did you meet Cady?"

"Business connection."

"Do you collect art or antiques?"

"Neither." That was the simple truth. "But a friend of mine was looking for a piece for his collection and he needed some help. I asked around on his behalf and Cady's name came up." Close enough. "One thing led to another."

"I see." Parker nodded. "Well, I wish you the best of luck."

"Same to you."

Parker smiled wryly. "Don't know about you, but personally I find it a little scary to be contemplating starting a family at my age. Always thought of fatherhood as one of those things you stumbled into when you were young and impulsive."

"Family?" For some reason the word seemed to get stuck in Mack's brain. "As in kids?"

"Leandra tells me she wants two. How many is Cady talking?"

"We, uh, haven't discussed the subject."

Something in his voice must have given him away. A knowing look gleamed in Parker's eyes.

"Glad I'm not the only one who's nervous about becoming a midlife father," he said dryly. "But if its any consolation, Leandra assures me that there are a lot of self-help books published for expectant parents these days."

"I'd call that a major success for Sylvia," Cady said an hour later on the way back to the car. "She really knows how to create that special air of excitement that it takes to bring in the clients."

"I could see that," Mack said.

He took in the street scene outside the gallery, automatically registering the lightly crowded sidewalks and the good street lighting. Chatelaine's shared the upscale commercial neighborhood with a couple of trendy restaurants, an art gallery and a small hotel.

The sidewalks were still damp from the recent rain. The crisp, cold breeze carried a damp chill off the bay.

Beside him, Cady walked with her hands thrust deep into the pockets of a black raincoat.

"Were you bored?" she asked.

"No," he said. "Spent some time talking to Parker Turner."

"He's a nice guy. Not like Dillon, that's

for sure. Everyone says he's very serious about Leandra."

"He's serious, all right. Talked about the joys of midlife fatherhood."

He winced at his own words. What the hell was he doing here? Did he really want to bring up the subject of babies?

"Midlife fatherhood, hmm?" Cady pursed her lips. "That's definitely serious."

"Yeah."

In silence they walked the remaining few steps to where the car was parked at the curb. Mack opened the passenger door. Cady slid into the seat. She looked up at him just as he was about to close the door.

"Must be a relief to be finished with fatherhood," she said very casually.

"Relief?"

"You know what I mean. You're finished with your parenting responsibilities. The trials and tribulations are behind you. Now that Gabriella is off to college, you've got your freedom back. You can set your own hours. Travel. Do what you want. That must be very gratifying for you."

He considered that. "I don't think you ever really finish with the parenting thing."

He shut the door quickly and turned to walk around the front of the car.

The skinny man in the battered leather

jacket came out of the shadows of a darkened doorway, moving with the quick, jerky
speed of an insect. Light glinted on the
barrel of the small, cheap gun in his hand.

"Don't move. Not one fucking inch."

The voice was a hoarse, rasping whisper.
Mack figured that in addition to adrenaline,
there were probably some other drugs in the
night crawler's bloodstream.

"Gimme the wallet." The insect twitched
the gun. "Do it now."

"Sure. No problem." Mack reached inside his jacket. "Any chance we can do a
deal here?"

Behind him, the car door opened. Cady
had evidently just realized that something
was happening.

"Don't get out," he said to her, making it
an order.

"Do what he says," the insect rasped.
"Get back inside."

Cady closed the car door very quietly.

"About this deal," Mack said, wanting to
distract him from Cady. "How about I give
you all the cash in the wallet. You let me
keep the cards and license. It's a nuisance
having to replace them."

"No, man. No deal. No way. I need the
cards. Gimme the damned wallet."

"Take it easy." Mack slid the wallet out of

his jacket and held it up. "Here it is."

"Drop it on the ground." The insect flicked anxious glances to either side, checking the sidewalk. "Hurry."

Mack tossed the wallet to the ground. The insect scuttled toward it. He bent down, trying to keep an eye on his target and at the same time pick up the object of the exercise. His movements were awkward. Apparently he had not thought this part out ahead of the mugging.

Two men came around the corner and stopped short several yards away.

"Hey, what's going on there?" one of them yelled in a loud, attention-grabbing voice.

"I'm on the line with 911," the other one shouted, phone to his ear.

"Oh, shit, oh, shit, oh, shit." The insect panicked. He started to turn to face the new threat. He was off-balance and rattled.

Mack launched himself forward, colliding heavily with the scrawny creature. The force of the impact carried them both to the sidewalk with a jolt that he knew he would feel in the morning. Metal clanged loudly as the gun landed on the pavement.

Footsteps thudded in the shadows. The two men were racing to the rescue. He heard the car door open again. Cady was out of the vehicle.

"Mack, I've got his gun. Get away from him, he's not worth it."

"Cops are on the way," one of the two men shouted.

Mack could tell from the way the insect clawed and scrabbled to get free that the creature had lost all interest in the wallet. Its primitive survival instincts had kicked in. Fleeing into the night was its only goal.

Mack found some space and some leverage and managed to deliver a short, chopping blow. The insect jerked spasmodically and then slumped.

The two men pounded to a halt.

"It's okay," one of them said. "We've got him. You all right?"

"Yeah." Mack rolled slowly to his feet, gingerly feeling the place on his rib cage that had absorbed most of the jolt from the encounter with the sidewalk. "Thanks to you two."

Cady was suddenly all over him. "Are you hurt? I don't see any blood. Did that creep do any damage?"

"I'm all right," he said, breathing carefully, testing the ribs. No deep twinges. That was probably a good sign.

A siren sounded in the distance.

The insect moaned. "The bastard set me up."

Mack crouched down beside him. "Who set you up?"

"My dealer. I owe him some money. Fucking bastard said he'd call it even if I got your cards."

"Why did he want my cards?"

"How the hell should I know? Probably wanted to sell them." The insect moaned again. "He set me up, I tell you. This is all his fault."

Mack raised his gaze to the two men who were holding the insect. "You were at the gallery reception, weren't you? I noticed you looking at that old microscope."

The one on the left nodded. "I'm Dave O'Donnell. This is my partner, Brian Meagers. We collect antique scientific instruments."

"Mack Easton. Thanks for showing up at the ideal moment. Great timing."

"We pride ourselves on our timing," Dave replied.

Cady smiled gratefully at the pair. "I'm Cady Briggs. I can't thank you enough for what you did."

"No problem." Brian Meagers took a closer look at her. "Hey, you're one of the Chatelaine Briggses, aren't you?"

"Yes."

"Met Leandra, earlier. Nice person."

"She's my cousin. I saw her trying to sell you that nineteenth-century Powell and Lealand microscope. A lovely old instrument."

Dave chuckled. "It's gorgeous but it's a little out of our range."

Cady gripped Mack's hand very tightly. "I think that under the circumstances, I can arrange for you to get the family discount."

"Are you sure you're all right?" Cady thrust a glass of brandy into his hands. "You're awfully quiet."

"I'm all right." Mack leaned back in the big chair and sipped brandy. "He wasn't fighting me, he was just fighting to get away."

She sat down on the sofa. "What is it? You haven't said more than ten words since you spoke with the cops."

"I've been thinking."

"I sort of figured that."

He looked at her. "About something the mugger said."

"What was that?"

"I asked him if we could do a deal. I'd give him all my cash, he'd let me keep the cards. He said he had to have the cards."

"So? You don't really think that a juiced-up street mugger is going to bargain with

281

you in a situation like that, do you?"

"No. But I did think it was interesting that he insisted that he had to have the plastic."

Cady shuddered visibly. "What's so unusual about it? You heard him say that his dealer had told him to get them. Probably wanted to sell them to one of those identity thieves who steal your credit cards and then trash your credit rating."

"Maybe." Mack swallowed more brandy. "But it occurred to me that there is something else you can do with someone's plastic besides assume an identity and run up a lot of bills."

"What's that?"

"Research. If you have a person's credit cards and driver's license, you can find out a lot about him. If you know where to look on the internet, that is."

She watched him for a long time.

"Are you saying that you think the mugging was planned?" she finally asked very carefully. "Not a random street incident?"

"You have to admit that it was a poor choice of venue for a low-end mugger. The neighborhood was definitely out of his league. Too upscale. Too many people around."

"People who are feeding a habit can get desperate. Maybe he was just following the old rule of thumb bank robbers use. Go where the money is."

"Maybe."

"What's happening here? This doesn't sound like the skeptical, logical Mack Easton I hired."

"Forget that guy. He was kind of boring." Mack pushed himself up out of the chair. "Come with me. There's something I want to show you."

18

"Aunt Vesta's phone records?" Cady scooted her chair closer to Mack's so that she could get a better view of the list of numbers and names that he had written on a sheet of paper. "Why are you interested in them?"

"These are the numbers that she had entered into the speed dial feature. I figure they're the ones that she called the most often."

"Makes sense."

"Most are members of the family. Your number is on here." He tapped it with the tip of a pen. "So is her lawyer's and her doctor's. There is also a number for a woman named Hattie Woods in San Francisco."

Cady smiled. "Hattie?"

"Know her?"

"Sure. I remember her very well, although I haven't seen her since last year's Carnival Night. She's been a client of Chatelaine's since forever. One of the first major accounts. Vesta always handled her personally, even after she retired."

"What does Hattie Woods collect?"

"Eighteenth- and nineteenth-century clocks. I used to love to visit her when I was a kid. I couldn't wait for all the clocks to strike the hour at the same time. A total madhouse."

He sat back in his chair and regarded her over the tops of his steepled fingers. "She's the only client I could identify on your aunt's speed dial program. Was she also a close friend of Vesta's?"

"Not really. She and Aunt Vesta certainly had a solid business and professional relationship. I think that they liked and respected each other. But the truth is, my aunt didn't have what most people would call close friends."

"What do you know about Hattie Woods?"

"You mean aside from her clock collection?"

"Yes."

She thought for a moment. "Well, I suppose that the second most interesting thing about Hattie Woods is that, until she retired several years ago, she was a working actress. Never a famous star, you understand. But she must have done hundreds of character roles during the course of her career."

"Did she show up at the funeral?"

"I didn't see her there, come to think of it.

Although I might have missed her in the crowd."

"If she wasn't a close friend of your aunt's, can you think of any reason why her number would have been programmed into the speed dialer?"

"Nope. Want me to call her and ask if she and Vesta had been chatting a lot about anything in particular recently?"

"Yes," Mack said slowly. "Yes. I think that might be a good idea."

"No problem. Hattie won't mind. But what's this all about?"

"I'm not sure yet. Maybe nothing at all. But finding Hattie Woods's number programmed into the speed dialer bothers me."

"Why?"

"Because it fits into the same category as your aunt's visits to a psychic."

"How?"

"It breaks a pattern," Mack said.

At eight the next morning, Cady poured a cup of tea from the pot she had just finished brewing and used the speed dial feature to call Hattie.

"Woods residence." Not Hattie's firm, well-modulated tones.

"I'm calling for Miss Woods." Cady was aware of Mack watching her intently from the opposite side of the table. "Please tell her that Cady Briggs of the Gallery Chatelaine would very much like to speak with her."

"One moment, please."

Another voice came on the line a short time later. It was elegant, charming and edged with a distinct note of urgency and relief. "Cady, is that you, dear?"

"Hi, Hattie. It's been a while. How are you?"

"Extremely happy to hear from you, dear, I must say. I've been waiting for your call. In fact, I was wondering if perhaps I should take the initiative. But Vesta gave very clear instructions and I didn't want to go against her wishes."

Cady nearly fell off her chair. "You were *expecting* my call?"

"Well, yes, of course, dear. Your aunt said that if anything happened to her, you would be in touch. I realize you've been occupied with the sad business of the funeral and all. I told myself to allow you some time. But I didn't want to wait too long."

"I'm not sure I understand what this is all about, Hattie."

"It's about that phony, Jonathan Arden, of course. Isn't that why you called me, dear?"

Cady's mouth went dry. "Well, yes, as a

matter of fact, that is why I called."

On the opposite side of the table, Mack watched her with near-predatory anticipation.

"I don't think we should discuss this over the phone, do you?" Hattie's voice went down to a conspiratorial level. "Vesta was very concerned with secrecy. It was one of the reasons why I didn't attend the funeral. I was afraid of blowing my cover. I knew your aunt would not have wanted that. There is too much at stake."

"Your cover?" Cady repeated weakly.

"Yes, dear. As in *undercover*. I'm sure you're familiar with the term."

"Oh, right. Cover." Adrenaline shot through her. "You did some undercover work for my aunt?"

"Indeed. I believe I did some of my best acting work since my wedding night."

"Hattie, what is going on here?"

"I think we should discuss that after you've had a look at the table."

"What table?"

"The one I allowed Jonathan Arden to persuade me to acquire." Hattie uttered a genteel snort. "Early nineteenth century, he said. And you would not believe the silly story he spun to go with the piece. I suggest we meet as soon as possible. Are you free to come into the city for dinner this evening?"

"Dinner will be fine, Hattie. I'm going to spend the morning helping Sylvia prepare for my nephews' birthday bash. It takes place this afternoon. We can leave right after the party."

"We?"

"I'm sorry, I forgot to mention my, uh, friend." Cady clutched the phone very snugly and let her gaze slide away from Mack's coolly amused eyes. "His name is Mack Easton. He's very much involved in this situation. May I bring him with me tonight?"

"By all means. Whatever you think best, dear."

Cady hung up the phone, hardly daring to breathe. "You were right, Mack. Something was going on between Hattie and Vesta, and it did involve Jonathan Arden. Hattie called him a phony. Something about conning her into buying an antique table. I got the impression that she and Aunt Vesta tried to set a trap for Arden. We're going to get the whole story this evening."

"Hang on. Are you saying that Arden used the psychic gimmick to sell Hattie a forgery?"

"That's what it sounds like. Apparently Aunt Vesta and Hattie were aware that

Arden is a fraud. It sounds like they were trying to prove it. Aunt Vesta hated frauds. I can see her exposing Arden, just for the hell of it."

"Huh."

"What now?" she demanded. "This is our big break. We're onto something here."

"Maybe."

"This was your idea," she reminded him. "Why aren't you demonstrating a little enthusiasm? Is it because Arden's name didn't pop up when you searched your database? Are you annoyed because it isn't perfect?"

"No database is perfect. The fact that mine didn't have any info on Arden just means that until now he's worked his scam outside the art world or else he's been too clever to leave fingerprints."

"Fine. So if it's not the database, why the negativity here?"

"We're supposed to be investigating your theory that your aunt may have been murdered. It looks like we might end up discovering that Arden is a con artist instead. That's not exactly a connection."

"But there could be," she insisted. "What if he murdered her because he realized that she was trying to expose him?"

"I told you, a good con artist avoids complicating his career with murder."

"Maybe he's not such a good con artist." She was growing more irritated by the second. "Maybe he's a really stupid, mean, violent con artist."

"Maybe."

A thought struck her. "You know, after we find out what's going on with Hattie's table, maybe I should pay a call on Jonathan Arden."

"No."

"I could pose as a client." She warmed to her plan. "Tell him that I was referred by Hattie Woods."

"No."

"I might learn something if I talk to him."

"What the hell do you think that will accomplish? Arden's not going to cough up his secrets or make any slips. The guy's a pro."

"You're probably right, but it's worth a try."

"No," Mack said again, very flatly this time. "It is not worth a try."

"You know what your problem is, Easton?"

"Which one? I've got a lot of them at the moment."

"Your big problem," she said, "is that you're having difficulty accepting the change of status in our relationship."

"You call this a relationship?"

She opted to ignore that. "You've always

291

been the employer in the past and I've always been the employee. You're accustomed to giving the orders. But now the situation is reversed. I'm the one in charge and you're having difficulty dealing with that."

He leaned back in the chair, rested one arm along the edge of the desk and regarded her as if she was showing signs of losing it. "You think so?"

"Yes, I do. You've got a bad attitude."

"Can't think of any reason why I'd have an attitude problem."

"I can."

"Yeah?"

"Sure." She shrugged. "I'm assertive by nature and I happen to be in charge at the moment. A lot of men have problems with strong, self-confident, assertive women in positions of authority."

"Who told you that?"

"Common knowledge. A female authority figure pushes a lot of hot-button issues left over from childhood. Reminds men of their mothers or something."

"No shit?"

"Yes." She glared. "I mean, no. The point I'm trying to make is that your reaction to my being the boss is not unexpected or unusual."

"Interesting theory."

"It's not a theory," she said through her teeth. "It's a psychological fact. Get over it."

"Yeah? Well, here's another fact for you. The only kind of assertive women who make me nervous are those who take idiotic risks." He flashed her a sudden, sexy grin. "And for the record, you definitely do not remind me of my mother."

Mack held the wobbly paper plate in one hand and carefully wielded the plastic fork. The trick was not to stab too hard, he reminded himself. If you didn't get it right, the whole thing flipped into the air and landed on the ground. Invariably some frosting splashed your pants leg on the way down. The rest could be expected to hit the toe of your shoe. Such was the nature of birthday cakes and paper plates.

It was an attractive cake. His slice was decorated with mounds of yellow and blue frosting that tasted remarkably like sweetened vegetable shortening. Had about the same consistency, too, he reflected.

The birthday party was being staged on the garden terrace behind Sylvia and Gardner's home. From where he stood, he could look down the hillside toward Phantom Point's boutique waterfront with its pocket-sized park and small marina. The Carnival Night stage was nearly completed, he noticed. In the distance the Golden Gate arced against a gray sky.

The garden was alive with kids and the two family dogs. The noise level was high. On the far side of the lawn, Cady, dressed in jeans and a white open-neck shirt, assisted Sylvia and Leandra in serving cake and neon-colored punch. Even from here he could see how much she was enjoying herself. Her face was bright with laughter as she handed a paper cup to a young boy.

Gardner came to stand beside him. He glanced at the unfinished birthday cake on the plate. "You don't have to eat it, you know. There's a big trash can right around the corner of the house. Be easy to make the whole thing disappear with no one the wiser."

"I can do birthday cake." Mack watched a group of youngsters playing with one of the gifts that the twins had unwrapped earlier. "I've had some practice."

Gardner nodded. "Right. Your daughter. You said she was at Santa Cruz?"

"Finishing up her first year." Mack forked up a bite of cake, wondering if he was in for another round of interrogation. "Wants a career in art history."

Gardner glanced toward the dark-haired twin boys on the opposite side of the garden. His mouth curved slightly with rueful pride. "Lucky you. We who are still dealing with eight-year-olds can only dream about our future freedom."

"Got news for you," Mack said around a mouthful of cake, "college isn't free."

"Heard that." Gardner chuckled. "I've already informed Luke and Thomas that it would be a really smart idea for them to put together a nice little on-line start-up company before they graduate from high school. I'll handle the technical details of the initial public offering for them. No charge. Take my commission in stock options, of course. When they're nineteen-year-old multizillionaires, they can put themselves through college."

"Sounds like a plan. Good luck."

"Thanks. Unfortunately, Luke is convinced he was cut out to be an archeologist and Thomas says he wants to become an accountant like his old man. Neither profession is known for turning out a lot of multizillionaires."

"Looks like you've got your work cut out for you. But they're only eight, right? You've still got time to make them see the light."

Gardner munched cake and watched one

of the twins charge off in pursuit of a ball. "Doing my best."

Mack thought about past birthday parties he had attended. "In the end, all you really want is for them to be happy."

Gardner nodded. "Yeah. In the end, that's what you want for them."

Mack was about to respond when he noticed a familiar figure walk out of the house onto the terrace. "Looks like you've got a late arrival."

"Well, well. Good old Uncle Randall. Wondered when he'd show up."

Mack studied the towering stack of gaily wrapped presents that Randall carried. Shouts of excitement echoed across the terrace garden. The twins and their party guests changed course and dashed toward the newcomer.

"Uncle Randall, Uncle Randall."

Randall dropped the mountain of gifts on a table and stood back grinning as Luke and Thomas tore into the stack. The other youngsters gathered eagerly around to view the goodies.

"Whatever is in those packages, you can bet it will include the must-have games, toys and books of the moment," Gardner said. "Good old Uncle Randall always knows what's hot and what's not."

"You don't like Post very much, I take it?"

"What irritates me," Gardner said, "is the way he acts as if he's a member of the family. Stick around a while, you'll see what I mean. He thinks he's got a special relationship with Sylvia and Cady because the three of them grew up together."

Across the garden, Randall had left the kids to the pile of presents. He was making his way to the table where Sylvia, Cady and Leandra were dispensing cake and punch.

Mack watched him give each of the women a familiar hug and a kiss. Cady was the last one in line. It looked to Mack as though Randall gave her a little extra squeeze.

"You're right," Mack said. "It is damn irritating."

"Better get used to it. If you intend to marry into this family, you get Post as part of the package, whether you like him or not."

"I'll keep that in mind. You said he grew up with Cady and Sylvia?"

"His mother was an alcoholic. Father died when he was in his teens. Jocelyn Post married Felgrove. It was not a good situation. The Briggs family, especially Vesta, felt sorry for Randall. Sort of adopted him." Gardner grimaced. "Now we're all stuck with him."

"I guess that will be even more true if the merger goes through," Mack said evenly.

"Afraid so. Try to think of him as the brother-in-law you wish you never had. Everyone has one of those. Randall Post is ours."

"I'm not sure I can take the philosophical approach here. The guy was married to Cady for a while, after all."

Gardner gave him a look of mild surprise. "I wouldn't worry about that too much, if I were you."

"No?"

"Sylvia says they never even made it into bed. Apparently they decided on their wedding night that the marriage was a mistake. Hell, I could have told them it wouldn't work. If it hadn't been for Vesta and the rest of the family pushing so hard, I think they would have come to their senses before they went through with the ceremony."

Two could play the interrogation game, Mack decided. "Cady mentioned that her aunt was very much in favor of the marriage."

"Vesta always took a special interest in Randall. I could never figure it out, to tell you the truth. Knowing her though, it probably had something to do with her long-term goal of merging the two galleries. That woman lived for Chatelaine's."

"People say that Cady takes after her," Mack said neutrally.

"Bullshit."

"Succinctly put."

Gardner shrugged. "There is a certain physical resemblance. If you look at old photos of Vesta, you can see that. But as far as I could tell, the only thing Cady and Vesta really had in common was an incredible eye for art and antiques. Sylvia told me once that it wasn't until after Cady was diagnosed with a tendency toward panic attacks that people started talking about how she took after her aunt."

"Cady said something about the panic attacks stemming from an accident in which she nearly drowned."

"To this day, Cady hates to swim. She rarely puts on a suit, and if she does, it's only to dangle her feet in a pool. She won't go into a lake or the ocean or any body of water where she can't see the bottom. Panic city."

"But she does know how to swim?"

"Well, she did when she was a kid, and they say you never forget. But as far as I know, she hasn't done any swimming since the incident at the lake that summer. Sylvia says she's got a real phobia. Sort of like a fear of flying, I guess. Gets very anxious even if she goes into a swimming pool. Has full-blown panic attacks if she gets beyond knee-deep water in a lake or the ocean."

"What happened at the lake?"

"Cady's folks took Cady, Sylvia and Randall camping. The three kids went swimming in a secluded cove one afternoon. What no one knew was that two nights earlier a car had gone off the road that ran along a cliff above the lake. It was a very sparsely populated area. No one had witnessed the crash."

"In other words, no one knew the vehicle was in the lake?"

Gardner nodded. "The car wound up on the bottom in fairly shallow water. Sylvia told me that you couldn't see it from the surface because the lake was so murky and there was a lot of vegetation growing in it that year."

Mack winced. "Don't tell me the kids found a body in the car?"

"Actually Cady was the one who discovered it. She was diving with a mask and snorkel. The dead guy was still in the front seat. Must have looked pretty bad."

"After two days in the water?" Mack felt a cold chill go through him. "Must have looked like something out of a nightmare."

"You bet. Traumatizing, to say the least.

Unfortunately, that wasn't the worst of it. Sylvia said that when Cady saw the body, she freaked and tried to get back to the surface. But one of her swim fins got tangled in a seat belt that was floating out the front window of the vehicle. She had to get herself out of the fin before she could escape. When she did, she came in contact with the body. It was pretty gruesome and she almost didn't make it."

"Good God almighty."

"She had nightmares for a long time. Sylvia says Cady used to wake up gasping for breath. The panic attacks were diagnosed a few years later when she was in college."

"Not surprising."

Gardner looked at the table where the three women were laughing at something Randall had just said to them. "Cady once told Sylvia that it was as if the dead man had reached out to grab her and pull her down into the car with him."

At seven thirty that evening Mack stood with Cady in the window of Hattie Woods's Nob Hill apartment and watched the fog swallow the lights of the city.

"I never grow tired of the view," Hattie said behind them.

"I can understand why," Mack said.

"I left L.A. the day I retired. Never could stand the place, to tell you the truth. Couldn't wait to escape. Still, I can't complain. The film business was good to me. Not all actresses can say that. Living in L.A. for all those years was the price I had to pay for a rewarding career."

Mack studied her. "Were you by any chance in a film called *Dead End Street*?"

Hattie gave a soft ripple of laughter. "Don't tell me you actually saw that disaster?"

"I watch late-night television when I have trouble sleeping."

"I'll bet *Dead End Street* put you out like a light."

He smiled. "It wasn't that bad."

"It was ghastly." Hattie sparkled up at him from the depths of a wingback chair.

He liked Hattie Woods, he decided. It was easy to see why she had gotten the character parts. Hattie was petite and vibrant but she lacked the facial bones that usually went with star-power beauty. She did, however, exude a certain charm that drew attention.

Her collection was also intriguing. The wall behind her was covered in floor-to-ceiling glass cases that contained an array of splendid timepieces. The clocks glowed and gleamed in all their unabashed Baroque and Neoclassical glory.

There were sumptuous eighteenth-century creations embellished with sweeping curves, finely detailed figures and enough gilt and gleaming bronze to light up a room. Nearby were ornate nineteenth-century devices that had been designed according to strict Palladian themes, miniature architectural masterpieces.

The clocks had been crafted in an age when they had been viewed as emblems of the perfect melding of art and science. Exquisitely made movements had been showcased in the finest cabinetry and metalwork. In addition to telling the time, many of the clocks also played music or delighted the eye with intricate scenes that appeared and disappeared when the hour was struck.

He could understand why, when she was younger, Cady had enjoyed visiting Hattie. He checked the time on one of the clocks, anticipating the cacophony that would ensue at eight o'clock.

"I was so sorry to hear of Vesta's passing," Hattie said to Cady. "When it came to art and antiques, I trusted her judgment completely. I shall miss her advice and counsel."

Cady left the window and walked across the room to sit down on the edge of the sofa.

"Aunt Vesta was one of a kind."

"Perhaps not." Hattie winked. "She told me that you take after her in many ways. I think it gave her great satisfaction."

Mack saw Cady's hand tighten around her sherry glass.

"I've been told that my aunt and I did have some things in common," she said. "But we were actually quite different in many ways."

"Well, no two people are exactly alike, are they?" Hattie responded.

"No," Cady said crisply. "They are not."

"Shall we get down to business?" Hattie took a dainty sip from her glass of sherry. "You must have a number of questions, my dear."

"Yes, I do." Cady sounded grateful for the change of subject. "For starters, please tell us what in the world is going on. What made Aunt Vesta take an interest in Jonathan Arden?"

"She suspected he was a charlatan, of course. All that ridiculous nonsense about his gift for psychometry. She wanted to prove that he was a fraud."

"But what brought him to her attention?"

"Arden made the mistake of conning one of your aunt's oldest clients, a gentleman who, I'm sorry to say, has fallen victim to

Alzheimer's. Arden suckered him into purchasing a chair that was supposedly late eighteenth century."

"How did Vesta find out what had happened?"

"One of the gentleman's money-grubbing heirs approached her. Asked her how much she thought the chair would fetch at auction." Hattie sniffed. "The wretch didn't even have the decency to wait until the nearly departed had become the dearly departed."

"Aunt Vesta examined the chair and realized it was a fraud?"

"Exactly. She made a few discreet inquiries and discovered that Arden had pulled the same scam on three or four other wealthy seniors in recent months. It infuriated her."

"So she set out to expose him?" Cady asked.

"Yes. At first she tried to do it on her own. She made an appointment, using a different name. She claimed that she had been referred to Arden by the gentleman who had bought the chair. But her acting wasn't up to the task. Vesta Briggs did not do dithery very convincingly, I'm afraid."

"Arden was suspicious of her?"

"Apparently. She took one of her lovely

little boxes to him. Claimed that she had found it in the attic and wanted to know if it was valuable. He refused to give an opinion. Blathered on about how he couldn't get a reading on the thing. She made a second appointment, intending to ask for his opinion of a cabinet she was considering. When she arrived at his apartment, he told her that he had to cancel and that he was not accepting any more clients at that time."

Mack stirred slightly. "Think Arden knew who she was?"

"Perhaps." Hattie moved one shoulder in a graceful little shrug. "If he did know that she was the head of Chatelaine's, however, he never let on. He may have simply been suspicious that she was with the police because her acting was so bad. In any event, she called me in to get the goods on him."

Cady frowned. "Wonder why she went to all that trouble? If she knew that Arden was running a scam, why didn't she just report him to the authorities?"

"Good question," Mack said.

"She hated frauds," Cady continued, "but, even so, it wasn't like Aunt Vesta to get involved in any project that was not directly connected to Chatelaine's. In the past few years she became almost reclusive. Any work that involved travel was turned over to

Sylvia a long time ago. Vesta didn't like to go anywhere except to her office in Phantom Point."

"Oh, my," Hattie said very softly. "I see you don't understand the real problem here."

"The real problem?" Cady repeated cautiously.

"I'm so sorry," Hattie murmured. "My fault. Please forgive me. When you called, I naturally assumed that Vesta had apprised you of the situation before she died."

"No," Cady said. "She didn't tell me anything."

"How typical." Hattie made a tut-tutting sound. "No offense, my dear, I have nothing but respect and admiration for your late aunt, but she did tend to be somewhat obsessive when it came to keeping secrets."

"That's true."

"Well, then, I see that it is up to me to explain the matter to you." Hattie put her sherry glass down, grasped her cane and pushed herself up out of the wingback chair. "Come with me, please. I'd better show you the table first. Then we can all make a good deal more sense out of this conversation."

She led them down a long hall to another room at the back of the apartment. A gleaming table was positioned beneath a crystal chandelier. Mack recognized the early-nineteenth-century style and the glow of old hardwood that had been lovingly polished over the years.

"This is the piece that I acquired on Jonathan Arden's advice," Hattie announced with a theatrical flourish. "It was delivered shortly after Vesta died. I never got the chance to show it to her so that she could confirm her suspicions."

Cady stopped a few feet away from the table. Mack watched her face as she contemplated the piece for a few minutes. Her concentration was so intense, he could almost feel the invisible energy humming through her. After a while, she went forward and drew her finger lightly across the wood and metal inlays that decorated the table.

"It looks like a Thomas Hope design." She went down on her knees and examined the gilt bronze mounts. "There's a very similar example in his *Household Furniture and Interior Decoration*. That would date it to the Regency period — 1810 or thereabouts."

"That's what Jonathan Arden told me." Hattie gave another small sniff of disdain. "He claimed that he could feel the emanations of violence in the vicinity of the table.

Something about a duel and drops of blood having fallen on the surface, if you can believe it."

Mack walked closer to the table. "How did the deal work? I assume Arden charged you a fee for giving you his so-called professional opinion?"

"Yes, indeed," Hattie said. "Quite a hefty fee, I might add. But not any more than I would have paid any outside consultant."

Cady crawled under the table. "Just one problem. This piece is a forgery. Beautifully done, I admit, but definitely late twentieth century, not Regency."

"No, no, no, my dear," Hattie said. "You still don't understand. The problem is not that it is a very fine forgery, just as Vesta anticipated. The problem is that I purchased it at the Austrey-Post gallery."

Cady froze under the table. Then, very slowly, she scrambled out from beneath it and got to her feet. She gazed at Hattie with an expression of fixed intensity. "Austrey-Post?"

"Yes, dear. The same place where Arden took the gentleman who suffered from dementia to buy his chair. Your aunt was convinced that Stanford Felgrove and Randall Post are running fakes through their galleries."

★ ★ ★

Two hours later Mack followed Cady through the front door of the villa. By silent, mutual assent they headed straight for the kitchen. Mack opened a cupboard and took down a bottle of cognac. Cady started pacing. He poured the contents into two snifters and handed one of the glasses to her.

She did not pause. She simply snapped the snifter out of his hand as she went past on her way to the far end of the kitchen.

"You do realize what this means?" she asked. "If Aunt Vesta believed that Austrey-Post was engaging in deliberate fraud, she would have called off the merger in a heartbeat. She would never have allowed Chatelaine's to be tainted."

He leaned back against the counter and tasted the cognac before he responded.

"You're sure the table was phony?" he asked.

"Positive." She waved one hand impatiently. "The veneer work was a little off for the period."

"Could have been a mistake. Old furniture is like armor. A lot of reproductions are good enough to fool the experts. You know that as well as I do. Even the big auction houses and galleries get burned. Austrey-

Post may be an innocent victim here, just like Arden's clients. You said yourself, the craftsmanship on that table was world-class. Maybe it was good enough to fool the Austrey-Post experts."

Cady shook her head swiftly. "Jonathan Arden's involvement makes it look like a deliberate scam. He must have had cooperation inside Austrey-Post. You heard Hattie. Once he thought he had her hooked, he directed her toward that particular piece of furniture."

"I heard." Mack swirled the cognac in his glass while he ran through the implications. "I wrote down every detail you listed when you examined the table. I'll feed the data to the computer tonight. This is the kind of job it does very well. Given what we have, it shouldn't be hard to identify the source of the forgeries. Probably one of the little European operations. They've got some unbelievably skilled people working in them right now. Nothing like old-world craftsmanship, you know."

"Why bother tracking down the source?" She halted at the far end of the kitchen, swung around and started back toward the stove. "We already know that the pieces Arden is pushing are frauds. What's the point in identifying the producer?"

"We can use all the information we can get."

"Forget it. Tracing the source is a waste of time. If it's one of the little Euro operations, we probably won't even be able to get it closed down. It will just claim that it's a legitimate business creating high-end reproductions. Not its fault someone in the U.S. is selling their products as originals. Come on, Mack, you know how it works."

"I know," he said calmly. "But I also know that you can't have too much information. The bigger the picture, the easier it is to detect a pattern. And the easier it is to see the shifts in that pattern."

She halted in the middle of the kitchen and gave him a wryly apologetic look. "Sorry. Didn't mean to growl at you. I'm a little tense tonight."

"You've got a right, given the circumstances."

"Poor Aunt Vesta." Cady swallowed the last of the cognac and turned the glass between her palms. "She must have been beside herself when she first began to suspect that she was within a hair's breadth of linking Chatelaine's with a gallery that was deliberately selling fakes. And the fact that it was Austrey-Post, of all places, would really have hurt. She had a history with that firm. We all do."

"A history named Randall Post."

Her eyes widened. "Are you crazy? Randall's not involved in this. He can't possibly know anything about the frauds."

"You can't know that for certain, Cady."

"I *do* know it for certain. I refuse to believe that Randall is aware of what's going on with those bad pieces of furniture. He doesn't even spend a lot of time at Austrey-Post headquarters . . . His work is in the field. He maintains connections with important people in the art world. He brings in the major consignments. Handles the high-end clients. He certainly doesn't keep tabs on the day-to-day backroom operations of the firm."

"Take it easy. I'm just mentioning obvious possibilities."

Her shoulders stiffened. "Randall is not one of them."

He felt his temper start to fray. "Look, just because he's your ex-husband doesn't mean he isn't capable of fraud."

"He's not just my ex, he's my friend. Damn it, Mack, trust me. Randall would not sell fakes and forgeries."

"You can't be absolutely sure of that."

"I've known him all of my life."

"Sure. In fact, you know Randall Post so well that you married him without being aware of the fact that he was harboring a grand passion for another woman."

Outrage flared. Her fingers were wrapped so tightly around the snifter, he was afraid the fragile glass would shatter. When she opened her mouth, he braced himself for the storm.

But instead of escalating the quarrel another notch, she abruptly spun around and walked to the nearest counter. She set down her glass with extreme care. When she turned back to look at him, he saw that she was still angry but she had herself under tight control.

"As long as we are examining possibilities," she said evenly, "let's start with Stanford Felgrove. I have never liked that man and Aunt Vesta didn't care much for him, either."

He shrugged. "I've got no problem with putting Stanford Felgrove on our list of people who might be working with Arden."

A short silence descended on the kitchen.

After a while, Cady resumed her pacing.

"My aunt went to a lot of trouble to keep her little sting operation very quiet, didn't she?" she said reflectively. "As far as we know, she confided only in Hattie and that was because she needed Hattie's skills as an actress."

"Vesta had several good reasons for keeping things under wraps," he pointed out. "She was considering a merger with Austrey-Post. She had to find out exactly what was going on inside the firm before she made a move."

Cady hugged herself tightly. "Yes. Given her long-term association with Austrey-Post, she would not have wanted to start a lot of nasty rumors about the firm. Even when she was sure of her facts she would have tried to handle things quietly. Gossip about fraud and forgery does no one in the business any good."

"True."

She stopped again and looked at him. "I've been on the wrong track here, haven't I?"

"Maybe."

"There's no maybe about it. I was convinced that Vesta's murder was somehow connected to the merger. But this fraud thing puts a new light on it. I know you keep saying that con artists are not big on homicide, but we are talking a lot of money here. Do you have any idea how much old furniture is worth in today's market? It's not uncommon for good pieces to go for half a

315

million to a million. And the market is getting stronger. Demand has been growing steadily in recent years."

"I'm aware of that," he reminded her dryly. "I'm in the business, if you will recall."

She flushed and then rushed ahead with the remainder of her lecture. "Apparently, Arden has already moved several very expensive pieces through Austrey-Post. We don't know what his cut was, but I suspect that he stood to lose hundreds of thousands of dollars, maybe a lot more, if he was exposed."

He hesitated, then nodded reluctantly. "All right, you've made your point. When it comes to murder, money is one of the big three motives."

"I think Jonathan Arden murdered my aunt so that she couldn't expose his scam."

He looked at her for a long time.

"You may be right," he said at last.

19

At two thirty in the morning, Cady abandoned the effort to sleep. Forcing herself to lie in bed and stare at the ceiling was only making her more jittery.

She shoved aside the covers, got to her feet and found her robe. Padding barefoot across the antique carpet to the window, she looked out over the bay toward the city. The fog had thickened noticeably since she and Mack had driven back across the Golden Gate Bridge. All she could see now was an otherworldly glow emanating from San Francisco.

She gazed into the fathomless mist and thought about her enigmatic, difficult, self-contained aunt.

You're so like her, my dear.

You've got your aunt's eye for art and antiques.

You're the living image of Vesta.

Vesta was never very good with men, either.

And now Vesta was dead.

She was brooding again. This was not helpful. She wondered if Mack was in bed asleep or if he was still working with the computer. It would be easy enough to find out if he was awake. All she had to do was go downstairs to the study and look.

She turned away from the window, went to the door and stepped out into the hall. She stood for a moment, listening. The silence was as thick as the San Francisco fog.

She hurried downstairs. When she turned the corner in the lower hall she saw the blue-green light of the computer screen spilling through the open doorway. Mack was awake and working.

She moved quietly to the doorway and came to a halt. Mack was seated at the desk, staring into the depths of the computer screen. He was dressed in a black crew-neck T-shirt and a pair of khakis. Not the trousers he had worn to dinner at Hattie's, she noticed. Somewhere along the line he had changed clothes. Light glinted on the lenses of his glasses. His hair was rumpled as if he had been running his fingers through it.

"Couldn't sleep, either, huh?" He did not take his attention away from the screen.

"No." She moved into the room. "What are you doing?"

"Thought I'd see if the computer could come up with anything useful."

"Has it?"

"No. Not yet. But there's still hope." He finally looked at her, frowning slightly. "Does that strict company policy of yours allow you to be alone in a small room with an employee of the opposite sex at this time of night?"

"Two thirty in the morning is not a good time to taunt your employer."

"Yes, ma'am."

She ignored his soft sarcasm and sat down on the opposite side of the desk. Belatedly it occurred to her that he had a point about the late hour and the limited confines of the study. The intense intimacy of the situation hit her without warning. A shiver of awareness went through her.

Maybe she should have checked company policy before coming here tonight.

Striving for a little nonchalance, she leaned back in the chair and thrust her hands into the deep pockets of the robe. "I've been thinking about something."

"What's that?"

She hesitated. "If we're right about all of this, if Jonathan Arden is working with someone at Austrey-Post, that inside person doesn't have to be at the top of the organizational chart. He or she could be one of the old furniture experts on the staff. Someone who knows that side of the business.

Someone with the right contacts in Europe."

"Uh-huh."

"You don't sound impressed with my deductions."

He looked up briefly. "I've already run everyone on the staff of Austrey-Post through the database. I got zilch."

"Where did you get a list of the employees?"

"Found it in your aunt's files. Looks like she might have been trying to spot a likely insider, too. But she didn't have the aid of a computer."

"No, but she had been in the business for a very long time. She knew a lot of the players, good guys and bad." Cady sank deeper into her chair. "So much for that brainstorm."

"You don't have to give up on it entirely. I told you, no database is perfect. If this insider hasn't ever been caught or implicated in previous scams, he won't be in my files." Mack paused. "You know, the idea that he's one of the old furniture experts makes a lot of sense."

"It would certainly explain how the pieces could be routinely authenticated before going out onto the gallery floor," she said quickly.

He gave her a wry look. "You mean without involving Randall Post?"

"Well, yes."

"Your scenario also avoids implicating Stanford Felgrove. Why protect him? You said you didn't like him much."

"I don't." She hesitated. "But I don't have any reason to think he'd be guilty of running fakes through his gallery. Neither did Aunt Vesta, apparently."

"Your aunt didn't get very far in her investigations. She had just barely sprung her trap for Jonathan Arden before she died."

"Or was murdered," Cady said.

"Or was murdered," he agreed evenly.

She drummed her fingers on the arm of the chair. "I admit that I'm biased against Stanford because of his history with Randall. But even so, it's hard to see him as a killer. I've known the man for years. We all have. There's never been any reason to think he was capable of violence. Even Randall will tell you that Stanford was never physically abusive."

"Doesn't sound like Randall spent much time in his own home after Stanford arrived on the scene as his stepfather. From what everyone says, the Briggs clan pretty much made him an honorary member of the family."

"Well, that's true. Still, Stanford Felgrove as a killer is hard to envision."

"You probably can't see anyone you know as a killer," Mack said quietly. "Few people can."

"Agreed. It's certainly easier to imagine a stranger like Jonathan Arden in that role." Unable to sit still any longer, she got to her feet and went to the French doors.

She stood looking out at the shadowed terrace. The pool lights were off tonight. The surface of the water was dark and implacable. *Anything could be waiting down there in the depths.*

"Cady?"

She turned quickly. "What?"

"Just wondered what you were thinking." Absently he removed his glasses and set them on the desk. He regarded her with somber consideration. "You all right?"

"Yes, of course." She grasped the lapels of her robe. "I was thinking, that's all. Maybe the time has come to go to the cops."

"Nothing I'd like better, believe me. But what do we give them?"

"We can't prove murder, but we do have strong evidence of a forgery scheme."

He ran his fingers through his hair. "You know better than that. You've been in this business all your life."

She groaned. "You're right. With what we've got now, everyone involved can claim to be innocent. The explanation will be that the experts inside Austrey-Post made some mistakes and failed to spot the forgeries."

"Happens all the time, even at the most prestigious galleries and auction houses and museums. When the fakes are pointed out, you apologize and refund the client's money. That's the end of it. I doubt if we'd even get far trying to pin a scam charge on Arden. The bottom line is that all he really did was help sell a piece of furniture that had been authenticated by a reputable gallery. No crime in that. Just one more screwup by a paid consultant."

"Happens all the time, right?" she offered.

"It happens." He shrugged. "Not all the time."

She decided to let that go. "Maybe we can show a pattern of fraud."

"Very hard to do."

He was right. She knew it. She walked to the corner of the desk and propped one hip on it. "All right, we've got nothing to give to the police. But I think the time has come to tell Sylvia what's going on. She's the CEO of Chatelaine's, after all."

"It's your family and your company.

You're the boss. You make the call."

She swung one leg absently. "We'll tell them we've got evidence that Arden is working a scam through Austrey-Post and that we think he's probably being assisted by someone inside the firm. That's enough for now. There's no point in alarming them with my theory that Aunt Vesta might have been murdered. I doubt if they'd believe me anyway."

"I disagree," Mack said. "If you're going to tell them part of it, my advice is to tell them all of it."

She stopped swinging her foot. "They'll think I'm crazy. Literally."

He shook his head. "They may decide you're being overly suspicious, maybe even a little paranoid, but I doubt that they'll think you're crazy."

"Damn. I wish we had more to go on."

"What we need," Mack said slowly, "is what your aunt was trying to get. Proof."

"How do we do that?"

"I'm thinking about it. I'm the paid consultant here, remember? That's what I do. Think about stuff and then consult."

"Hmm."

"Yeah." Without warning he put his hand on her thigh, just above her knee and squeezed gently. "Hmm."

At the touch of his warm, strong fingers on her bare skin, she stiffened and looked down. She saw that the edge of her robe had parted slightly while she had been swinging her foot, exposing a portion of her leg.

A reasonably modest skirt with a slit would have shown just as much skin, but the fact that it was her robe that was open made the scene unbearably intimate.

He smiled slightly and moved his hand higher, his palm gliding up the inside of her thigh.

"Mack."

He got to his feet and crowded close, very slowly, very deliberately, trapping her on the edge of the desk. He took his palm off her leg but instead of stepping back, he planted both hands on either side of her, caging her. She was suddenly breathless. Not the kind of panicky breathlessness that signaled an attack of acute anxiety; another sort altogether.

"This isn't supposed to happen," she managed. "Not while you're, uh, working for me."

He brushed his mouth against hers, effectively cutting off the small lecture. He raised his head slightly.

"I've been thinking about your company policy against fraternizing with employees."

She swallowed twice. "What about it?"

"I believe that I have come up with a way to circumvent the issues involved."

"How?"

"I quit," he said very softly. "As of now I am no longer working for you. Is that clear?"

"Mack, for heaven's sake —"

"I do not take your orders now." Still bracketing her body with his arms, he leaned in close again and kissed her throat. "Your company policy regarding personal relationships between employer and employee no longer applies."

A shiver of excitement spiraled through her. "I really don't think this is a good idea." That was weak, she thought. Very weak.

"What we find ourselves dealing with here," he whispered into the curve of her neck, "is a scenario in which two people who share a mutual physical attraction happen to be in extremely close proximity in the middle of the night." He nipped the tip of her ear gently, letting her feel his teeth, though. "Furthermore, one of those two individuals is dressed in a nightgown."

"And a robe," she said. "The individual is also wearing a perfectly decent robe."

His response to that was to remove his hands from the desk and untie the sash of the robe.

"The robe," he said, pausing to look down, "is no longer decent."

Heat rose through her, a deep tide of desire that made her shudder. She put her hands on his shoulders, feeling for the hard muscles beneath the black T-shirt.

"What do you think we ought to do now," he asked, "given that we no longer have a company policy to guide us?"

She swallowed again and tightened her hands on his shoulders. "We could always substitute common sense for company policy."

"I don't think that common sense will get us where we want to be."

"Where is that?"

"In bed. Together."

In a single gliding motion he parted her knees and stepped between them. His arms went around her inside the robe. She had only an instant to register the shock of his hard thighs between her legs and then he was leaning into her, capturing her mouth with his own.

The thrills flashed through her in disorienting waves of exquisite sensation. Why was she fighting this? She wondered. It wasn't as if they weren't two mature adults. It wasn't as if she hadn't known somewhere in the back of her mind that this could happen when she walked into the study dressed in a nightgown and robe a short time ago. It wasn't as if she wasn't falling in love with Mack.

It wasn't as if she wasn't already in love with Mack.

Deliberately he deepened the kiss. She felt his hand on her leg again, pushing the nightgown higher on her thighs. Balanced on the desk, her legs apart, there was nothing to shield her from his probing fingers. She sucked in her breath when he stroked her intimately.

Unable to resist, she reached down and found the zipper of his pants. She started to lower it, brushing against the full, firm shape of his erection.

He groaned at her touch and quickly stopped the movement by covering her hand with his own.

"I'd better do that," he muttered.

Carefully he eased the zipper downward. And then he was free, thrusting himself into her waiting hands. She grasped him and tugged gently, savoring the feel of him and the certain knowledge of his desire.

He cupped her buttocks in his hands, pulled her to the very edge of the desk and sank himself slowly into her. She sucked in a deep breath, framed his face between her palms and kissed him back with a sensual ferocity that matched his own.

The feeling of fullness was maddening. The tension inside her reached the breaking point. The world fell away and she tumbled through space.

In that delicious, intense moment when everything was out of control, he was suddenly there with her in the very heart of the sweet, hot chaos.

A long time later he stirred, scooped her off the desk and carried her out of the study.

She nestled comfortably against his chest. "Where are we going?"

"To find a bed."

"Good idea." She munched on his earlobe. "Much more comfortable." She paused when she realized that he had started up the hall stairs. "You're actually going to carry me up those stairs?"

"Or collapse trying."

"Wouldn't want that to happen. I can walk, really I can."

"I believe you. But this is a challenge. You know how guys are when it comes to a challenge."

He was on the third step now, not even breathing hard yet. She could tell that he was moving easily.

She traced the outline of his shoulder with one fingertip. "You're in pretty good shape."

"For a man my age, you mean?" He paused to catch his breath on the landing. "Gee, thanks."

"You're in excellent shape for a man of any age," she murmured in her huskiest tones.

"I appreciate the sentiment." He got her through the bedroom doorway, dropped her onto the bed and fell on top of her with a soft, heartfelt groan. "But having met and overcome the challenge, I may let you walk up the stairs next time."

Next time. She wondered how to take that. A casual, throwaway remark? An indication that he expected this convenient arrangement to last as long as they were working together? Or was he implying the possibility of a long-term affair?

Best not to speculate, she thought, turning her face into his shoulder. Not tonight. She would only drive herself around the bend wondering about the future. She did not want anything to spoil the few remaining hours until dawn.

She could always have a nervous breakdown later.

20

The deep, reverberating chimes of the doorbell brought her awake with an unnerving shot of adrenaline. She sat straight up in bed, blinking, and tried to orient herself. Morning light, filtered by an overcast sky and light rain, streamed in through a window that framed a familiar bay and cityscape.

It was the bedroom that was unfamiliar. Mack's room. Not the one she had been using since arriving at the villa.

The chimes sounded again, seemingly more urgent this time. Beside her, Mack growled a few unintelligible words and shoved aside the covers.

"I'll get it," he said.

He rolled to his feet and reached for his pants. She punched up the pillow and allowed herself to revel in the sight of his nude body. He had a very nice back, she thought. Almost sculptural.

She did not get to enjoy the vision for long. As soon as he stepped into his jeans, he headed for the door, feet and chest still bare. He vanished down the hall.

Cady heard his footsteps on the staircase and then the front door opened.

"Dad." The female voice rose to an anguished wail. "What's going on? Mrs. Thompson told me that there's a realtor coming to look at the house today. How could you do that?"

Mack's daughter. Cady scrambled out from beneath the covers, rose and grabbed the robe that had ended up on the floor beside the bed. When she was ready she hurried out onto the balcony and looked down.

Mack and his daughter were in the front hall.

"What are you doing here, Gabriella?" Mack asked.

"I called Mrs. Thompson. I wanted to ask her to send me a jacket I left behind the last time I was home. She mentioned that she was going to clean today because you had arranged for a realtor to stop by this afternoon. I couldn't believe it."

"How did you get here?" Mack asked calmly.

"I took the bus from Santa Cruz to San Francisco and then caught the ferry —" Gabriella broke off, staring at Cady. "Who are you?"

"Good morning." Cady smiled down at her. Gabriella's eyes were so like Mack's, it was impossible not to smile. "I'm Cady Briggs."

"You're *her*." Anguish and fury etched Gabriella's pretty face. "You're the freelancer who screwed up that job he did for Notch and Dewey. This is all your fault."

"Gabriella," Mack spoke quietly, authority vibrating in his voice. "That's enough. Have a seat in the living room. Cady and I will get dressed. We'll have breakfast somewhere and talk."

Gabriella clenched her fists at her sides. "Why would I want to eat breakfast with your mistress?"

"I said that's enough, Gabriella. Sit down and pull yourself together. You're too old for this kind of tantrum."

Cady winced but said nothing. This was not her daughter, she reminded herself.

"You did it because of her, didn't you?" Tears thickened Gabriella's voice. "You're selling our home because you're having an affair with her. Is this one of those middle-aged crazy things that men go through?"

"Sit down." Mack turned toward the stairs. "I told you, we'll talk later."

"How could you do it, Dad? How could you put our home on the market?"

Mack did not respond. He took the steps two at a time. When he reached the balcony, he brushed past Cady. His jaw was rigid.

"Sorry about this," he muttered in a low voice, pausing at the bedroom doorway. "I always leave word where she can reach me when I'm away from home."

"Of course. Only natural. Don't worry about it."

Down below, Gabriella stomped into the living room and disappeared from view.

"She's a lovely young woman, Mack."

"She's behaving like a teenage brat at the moment."

"It's always a shock to discover that your parents have a sex life."

"This isn't about my sex life. It's about the house."

"Whatever." She started toward her own bedroom. "If you'll excuse me, I'll get dressed, too. But I think I'll let you and Gabriella have breakfast together without me, if you don't mind."

"No. I want you there."

"It will be awkward."

His mouth twisted. "You're right. What the hell was I thinking? It's not fair to ask you to sit through an unpleasant scene with a temperamental kid. I'll deal with Gabriella. She's my daughter, not yours."

Cady hesitated. "Don't be too hard on her, Mack. She's obviously very upset about

334

this. And she's at a difficult age."

"I've got news for you, Cady. Speaking as a parent, I can assure you that all the ages are difficult."

A wistful sensation drifted through her. *Speaking as a parent.* She could not do that. "You're the expert, so I won't argue. All the same, promise me you'll go easy. Speaking as a *woman*, I can tell you that she's genuinely hurt and probably a little afraid of the future."

His expression didn't soften much but some of the bleakness faded from his eyes. "Okay, I'll keep it in mind."

He closed the door.

She went on down the hall toward her room. She had her hand on the doorknob when something made her pause and look out over the balcony again.

Gabriella was watching her from the curved entrance to the living room. Her face was flushed and tight with anger.

On impulse Cady took her hand off the doorknob and went toward the staircase. This was probably not the smart thing to do, she thought. This was not her problem. She and Mack were casual lovers, at best. A couple of ships passing in the night.

She winced. All right, so maybe the sex wasn't exactly casual. But the relationship certainly could not be described as serious. It wasn't as if she was going to have a permanent role in the lives of Mack and Gabriella. Better to stay out of this situation. Let Mack and his daughter work through their issues.

Gabriella did not move when Cady reached the bottom of the stairs. She stood there, glowering resentfully, shoulders hunched, arms tightly folded, cheeks damp.

"Gabriella?" Cady kept her voice low. "Would you like to talk privately with me?"

"Why would I want to talk to you? We don't have anything to discuss."

"I disagree. We seem to have a mutual interest in your father."

"Stay away from him. This is all your fault. I knew something happened on that last job. I *knew* it."

"Why does that worry you?"

Gabriella tensed. "It doesn't worry me. He won't keep you around long. He never gets serious about any of his women."

"Because of you?"

"Because of my *mother.*"

"No," Cady said. "I don't think so."

"He loved her."

"Yes, of course he did."

"How do you know that?"

"It's not hard to tell."

For a moment Gabriella looked bewildered. "Why would he talk to you about my mother? He never talks about her to his one-night stands."

"Maybe he told me about her because I told him a few things about my first marriage." Cady went past her toward the kitchen. "I think the pop-psych people call it 'sharing.' What's all this about a realtor coming to your house today?"

"You know what it's about." With obvious reluctance, Gabriella trailed after her. "He started talking about selling our home after he came back from that job you screwed up."

Cady picked up the kettle and went to the sink to fill it. "Gabriella, you're not tracking here. You just told me that your father never gets serious about any of his female friends. Now you tell me I wield enough power over him to force him to put a house on the market? For the record, I'm not in the real estate business."

"If that's supposed to be funny —"

"Forget it." Cady put the kettle on the stove and switched on the burner. "Want some tea?"

"No."

Cady picked up a package of English muffins. "Want one?"

"No."

337

"Okay." She took one of the muffins out of the package, separated it and dropped both halves into the toaster.

Gabriella watched in ill-concealed irritation. "Dad said we were going to eat breakfast out."

"You and your father can have breakfast together. I'm going to eat here. I'd rather not get involved in your family quarrel."

"Dad and I don't quarrel. We never quarrel." Gabriella's lip trembled. "At least not about important stuff like this."

Cady nodded. "Probably because your father usually goes out of his way to make you happy."

Gabriella shot her a fierce look. "What's that supposed to mean?"

"Nothing much." Cady took some cream cheese out of the refrigerator. "Just out of curiosity, what do you do to make him happy?"

There was a short, shocked silence before Gabriella sputtered back into words.

"Don't make it sound like I manipulate him," she hissed. "That's not how it is."

"It's called guilt-tripping and something tells me you're very, very good at it."

Gabriella paled. "Why do you say that? It's not true. I don't try to make him feel guilty."

"Why do you think he put the house up for sale?"

"I don't *know*," Gabriella sounded anguished now. "Something is happening to him. He's been acting weird for a while and it got a whole lot worse after he hired you to consult on that last project."

"Maybe he's doing the same thing you're doing in college."

Gabriella stared at her. "The same thing? What's that?"

"Getting on with his life."

There was a short, stark silence.

"But why does he have to sell the house to do that?" Gabriella demanded.

"I don't know." The kettle was whistling. Cady picked it up and started to pour boiling water. She had put enough loose tea into the pot to serve two. "But we're a couple of smart females. I'll bet between the two of us we can figure it out."

Mack looked at the man in the mirror above the gleaming white sink and wondered how he was going to explain things to Gabriella. The truth was, he couldn't even explain them to himself. But some part of him had known that this day would come. He just hadn't known when it would arrive.

Life never stood still, no matter how hard you tried to hold onto it. He could only hope that someday Gabriella would understand that.

Meanwhile, things were going to be unpleasant. In the past he had had little trouble keeping his relationships discreetly in the background largely because he'd experienced no compelling need to place them at the center of his life. But Cady was different. He doubted if anyone could ever keep Cady tucked out of sight for long.

He leaned over the sink and splashed cold water on his face.

"He won't marry you, you know." Gabriella stood at the window, gazing fixedly out into the mist. "He never marries any of his women."

Cady carried the two cups of tea to the table and put them down. "This may come as a surprise to you, but I don't consider myself to be one of your father's women."

Gabriella raised one shoulder in a jerky little shrug. "You think you're special?"

"Uh-huh."

Gabriella spun around. "Why?"

Cady went back to the counter to get the English muffins. "Probably because I don't suffer from low self-esteem. Are you sure you won't have some tea? I made enough for both of us."

Gabriella glared at the cup, hesitated and then took two steps to the table. She picked up the tea and went back to her vigil at the window.

"If it's any comfort to you," Cady said, "your father and I have never discussed marriage."

Gabriella flashed her a searching glance and then, apparently somewhat mollified, she went back to the view.

"Let's talk about the house." Cady picked up her own cup. "You go first. What's your theory of why he's going to put it on the market?"

Gabriella gripped the cup very tightly. "I don't know. I just know it has something to do with you."

"I don't think so." Cady watched Gabriella's stiff shoulders. "I think it has something to do with you."

"Me? But I don't want him to sell it."

"What's the house like, Gabriella?"

"What's it like?"

"How many bedrooms? Is the kitchen big or small? Is there a garden?"

Gabriella hesitated. "Four bedrooms. Two baths." Her voice softened. "There's a big, old-fashioned kitchen. Dad and I used to cook dinner together after Mom died. The garden is huge. Lots of shrubs and flowers and a lawn. I had my high school graduation party there."

"Sounds like a nice place."

"It is. It's our home."

"It also sounds like it might be a little empty without you."

Gabriella flinched. Her head came up very fast. "I go home during breaks."

"But the rest of the time your father is there alone?"

Gabriella's very feminine jaw set in a stubborn line that was vaguely reminiscent of Mack. "Dad likes it that way."

"Are you sure about that?"

"He travels more now." Gabriella's voice took on a defensive note. "So he's not home alone all the time, if that's what you're trying to say. And he dates some- times. *Lots* of women. No one person in particular."

"You'll be going back less and less often now, though, won't you? Eventually you'll graduate. Get a job. Craft a life for yourself. You'll probably get married. Start a home of your own. You'll never really live in that nice big house again, will you? That's not how life works."

"You don't understand."

Cady took a slow sip of tea and lowered the cup. "I live alone."

"So?"

"For the most part it's okay. I'm used to it. I've always been alone in my condo, you see." She paused a beat. "There's plenty of room."

"Plenty of room?"

"There aren't any memories around to crowd me. I don't run into an image of a little girl hiding behind the couch every time I walk into the living room. I don't have to share the kitchen with a memory of someone who used to help me cook dinner and clean up afterward. I don't have a garden so I don't go into it and think about how lovely my daughter looked the day she celebrated her graduation from high school there."

Gabriella's teacup froze in midair. She turned, a stricken expression on her face. "Ghosts and memories? You think that's what it's like for Dad?"

Cady looked at her. "Why don't you ask him?"

Some time later Mack got behind the wheel of his car. Gabriella slid into the seat beside him.

"You don't have to drive me all the way

343

back to Santa Cruz," she said. "I can take the bus."

"It's no problem." Mack reversed out of the villa's driveway. "I've got some business with a client who lives in the mountains. We'll stop by his place on the way."

Cady stood at the edge of the drive and waved. He rolled down the window.

"I'll be back in plenty of time for dinner," he said.

"All right," she said. "Drive carefully."

Jeez. Did they sound like a couple that had been married for years and years, or what?

He smiled to himself in spite of the tension vibrating from his daughter and pulled out onto the narrow road.

Gabriella was very intent beside him. She had been unnaturally quiet all through breakfast. He had come downstairs expecting a storm of tears and accusations. Instead he had met only a strained silence. Taking the hint from Cady's expression, he had not launched into a lecture.

"She's different, isn't she?" Gabriella said. "She's not like the others."

"No," Mack said. "She's not like the others."

"Are you going to marry her?"

Something inside him tightened. "We

haven't even come close to the subject of marriage."

"That's what she said."

"It's the truth."

Gabriella bit her lip. "She also said that I should ask you something."

"What?"

Gabriella took a deep breath and seemed to brace herself. "Are you selling the house because it's full of ghosts and memories?"

He said nothing for a while, thinking it through.

"I wouldn't go so far as to say there were ghosts. Plenty of memories, of course. Good ones. But they're not tied to the house. I'll take them with me when I leave."

She shoved her hands deep into the pockets of her sweater jacket and gazed straight ahead through the windshield. "I don't understand. If you don't mind the memories, why do you need to leave?"

"I'm not sure how to explain it. But I'm beginning to think that maybe old memories are like works of art hanging on a museum wall. Sometimes you have to move them around; maybe display them in a different way in fresh surroundings."

"Why?"

"So that you can make room for new ones."

Gabriella looked at him. "Does that mean that you forget the old memories?"

"Never," Mack said. "You don't forget a great work of art."

Gabriella waited while Mack opened the gate and got back into the car. She studied the narrow, rutted path that led up to the A-frame cabin with open curiosity.

"Who lives here?" she asked.

"Guy named Ambrose Vandyke. Collects old armor."

She turned her head. "He's the one who had Dewey's and Notch's helmet, isn't he?"

"Right." Mack shifted into a lower gear. "He's also something of a software genius. Retired last year. I got the impression that he's a little bored these days."

He negotiated the drive with great caution. When he finally halted the car, he saw Ambrose waiting for them in the doorway. Vandyke had his long hair tied back in a ponytail. He was wearing jeans and a sweatshirt decorated with a cartoon picture of a geek on a surfboard with a computer in one hand.

"Hey, Mack." Ambrose bounded down the steps to pump Mack's hand. "Glad you called. Good to see you again."

"Same here." Mack watched Ambrose's

face as Gabriella came around the front of the car. "I'd like you to meet my daughter, Gabriella. She's in school at Santa Cruz."

"No kidding." Ambrose's face lit up. "I get into town a lot. On my way to the beach, y'know?"

"Yeah?" Gabriella smiled for the first time that day.

"Actually, I've been thinkin' about taking some classes at the university. I've been retired for a while now and it's like you can only do so much surfing, y'know?"

"I can see where that would get a little monotonous."

"Yeah, well, hey, come on inside." Ambrose awkwardly herded them through the doorway. "I've got some tea made."

Gabriella went through the opening ahead of Mack. She came to a halt when she caught sight of the heap of old metal stacked in the corner.

"Cool armor," she breathed with reverent appreciation.

Ambrose blushed furiously and actually stammered. "Thanks."

Gabriella turned her glorious smile on him. "I really love old armor."

Ambrose gave her a deer-caught-in-the-headlights stare. "Me, too."

This was getting downright painful, Mack

347

thought. Time to change the subject. "So, Ambrose, what do you think about the offer I made on the phone?"

Ambrose wrenched his gaze away from Gabriella with an obvious effort. Keen interest sparked in his intelligent face. "Hey, man, I told you that night you saved my life that I owed you. I meant it. Besides, this consulting gig sounds interesting. It's not like I've got anything else to do except hit the beach. The only excitement I've had lately was on the night those two dudes tried to steal my armor."

"You're interested, then?"

"Are you kidding? When do I start?"

"Today," Mack said.

Mack had been right about one thing. Stakeouts sucked.

It wasn't just the boredom factor, Cady thought as she started another sketch of the street scene in front of Jonathan Arden's apartment. It was the ever-present worry that someone would come along and demand to know if she was a real artist.

Thus far, two kids had stopped to ask her if she would draw a picture of them, and a senior citizen had inquired about a sketch of her poodle. She had politely declined both commissions, explaining that she was taking a class and the street scene was an assignment.

Two and a half hours of drawing and redrawing the same doorways, rooflines and sidewalks had not improved the overall quality of the picture. In desperation, she had begun working toward a more abstract view but when she examined it objectively, she was forced to admit that it was just a jumble of angles and distorted images.

But then, she had never claimed to be an artist until now. First day on the job, what could you expect?

Across the street the garage door of Arden's small apartment building ground into action. A tiny Ford waited eagerly behind the slowly rising grille. As soon as there was sufficient space, it shot out onto the street. The driver drove away quickly, not waiting to make certain that the gate closed behind him.

The gate did close. Eventually. Leisurely. Allowing plenty of time for someone to walk underneath it into the garage without being seen.

Cady understood how Mack had been able to get into the building without having to resort to breaking-and-entering techniques. She was wondering if it would pay to try the tactic herself. The problem was that getting into the garage would not get her into Arden's apartment. She would not accomplish anything more than Mack had already. Unless she wanted to go through the tenants' garbage again, which seemed pointless.

The longer she sat here on the sidewalk, the more she questioned the impulse to take the ferry into the city after Mack and Gabriella had left. She had not set out with that goal in mind. She had left the house with the aim of taking a walk to assuage some of the restlessness that had hit her when she found herself alone. Her mind had been filled with useless clutter, most of it composed of unanswerable questions. Memories of the night spent in Mack's arms had warred with concerns about his relationship with his daughter and her own uncertainties about the future. Mentally, she had found herself going round and round in smaller and smaller circles until she could feel the early warning signals of anxiety.

It was only after she found herself near the Carnival Night stage that she had looked out across the bay and known how she would spend the day. The only solid information they had in this investigation was the fact that Jonathan Arden was a con man with a lot to protect. Keeping an eye on his apartment made wonderful sense. No telling what she might see.

In hindsight she could only say that it had seemed like a good idea at the time.

She put down the pad and pencil and picked up the last quarter of the tuna-fish sandwich she had purchased earlier at the little take-out place at the foot of the street. She was very thirsty and the salty tuna was not helping the problem, but she hesitated to consume any liquids. One of the big drawbacks to stakeouts, she had discovered, was that there wasn't always a public restroom located conveniently nearby. She had already hiked all the way down to the bottom of the street once today to use the facility in a neighborhood restaurant. The waiter had been gracious but she did not want to draw attention by going back a second time.

The delivery truck pulled up to the curb in front of Arden's apartment house just as she finished the last bite of the sandwich. She watched without much interest as the driver climbed out, collected a small stack of boxes from the back of the van and went up the steps. He leaned on a buzzer. Someone inside the building responded. The door opened and the driver entered.

From her vantage point she watched him make his way to two different doors. The first one was opened by an older woman with curlers in her hair. She seemed eager to chat with the delivery driver. When he finally managed to extricate himself, he went down the open corridor to the far end.

He stopped in front of Jonathan Arden's apartment. There was no response when he pressed the bell. She could have told him that Arden wasn't home, she thought.

After a moment the delivery man checked something on the front of the box. Apparently satisfied that it did not require a signature, he left it on the doorstep.

A package for Jonathan Arden.

Curiosity stirred. She watched the driver leave the building, climb back into the van and pull away from the curb. It was in the hands of fate now, she thought. If Arden returned before anyone else entered the garage, she would never have an opportunity to see what had been left at his door.

But if someone else drove in or out of the garage before he came home, she might be able to get inside long enough to get a glance at the package.

She ambled slowly along the sidewalk, trying to look as if she was searching for a better view for her sketching.

The garage door rumbled just as she walked past. She caught her breath and kept moving. Behind her a vehicle exited the ga-

352

rage, hesitated briefly and then drove away down the street.

The garage door rumbled again. When she glanced back over her shoulder, she saw that there was still enough room to duck under the edge of the descending grille.

If she hurried.

She took a deep breath and sprinted. She managed to slip beneath the edge of the door and came to a halt on the inside of the garage.

No one yelled at her. No dogs barked. No sirens wailed.

The grille closed with a clang against the pavement.

She stood in the shadows for a moment, gathering her nerve. Then she made for the stairs. Just one quick glance, she thought as she went up the concrete steps. That was all she would risk.

She opened the door on the second level, trying to look as if she belonged. There was no one around. The walk to Arden's door at the end of the passageway looked about ten miles long. It felt like a ten-mile hike, too. At every step she was braced for a door to open and the questions that might ensue. By the time she reached her goal, she was tense and a little breathless.

This is no time to have a panic attack, she

thought. Save it for later.

After what felt like an eternity, she reached the door, stopped and looked down at the label on the box. The return address was that of a costume shop in the lively arts-oriented section of the city known as SoMa, the South of Market Street area.

A costume shop?

Curiosity swamped common sense. She leaned down, grabbed the box and hurried back to the relative seclusion of the garage stairwell. She ducked inside and went halfway up the next flight of stairs. She would be able to hear footsteps approaching from either direction.

With great care she loosened the tape on the box and raised the lid. Inside she glimpsed the voluminous folds of a black cloaklike garment. A silver mask designed to cover the entire face rested on top of the cloak.

It was possible that Jonathan Arden planned to attend a costume ball, but what were the odds? Costume balls weren't that common, not even here in San Francisco where the entertainment could border on the outrageous.

But she could think of one very particular venue that would warrant a costume. Carnival Night in Phantom Point.

21

"Where the hell have you been?"

The low throb of controlled anger in Mack's voice stopped her cold in the hall. One hand on the doorknob, she watched him walk deliberately toward her.

She said the only thing that came to mind. "You got home earlier than I expected."

"Yeah, I can see that." He halted a short distance away, as if he was afraid to touch her. "Did you go into the city to see Arden?"

"Take it easy, Mack. You're overreacting here."

He took the last step that closed the distance between them and put both hands on her shoulders. "Did you try to fake your way through an appointment with Jonathan Arden?"

"No. I didn't try to fake my way through an appointment with Jonathan Arden. Satisfied?"

His hands tightened on her. "Did you see him?"

Anger surged. It wasn't as if she hadn't had enough stress already today, she thought.

"No. I didn't see Arden." She jerked away from Mack's grasp and made to stalk past him down the hall. "Good grief, what's the matter with you? You're acting like an irate husband."

"And you're not used to making explanations, are you?"

"No, I am not accustomed to having to explain myself." She dropped her purse on the antique bench and swung around to look at him. "Neither are you. We aren't children, Mack. What's the big deal here?"

"The big deal is that I told you not to go anywhere near Arden."

"I never even saw the man." She spread her hands. "I spent some time watching his apartment building, that's all."

"I knew it." He came toward her once more. "When I got back here and realized that you were gone, I knew you'd done something like that. What the hell's the matter with you? What did you think you could accomplish by taking a damn fool risk like that?"

"I'm not working for you, Mack. I don't take your orders, remember?"

"What did you do?" he asked evenly. "Tell me exactly what you did."

She folded her arms. "I was there when a delivery van left a package at Arden's front door. Arden wasn't home. I went into the building, got the package, took it into the stairwell and opened it."

Mack just stood there looking at her.

"I don't believe it," he finally said, much too softly. "Yes, I do believe it. What the hell — ?"

"There was a costume inside," she said quickly. "Mack, I think he may be planning to attend Carnival Night here in Phantom Point. We've been looking for connections. This is a big one."

"I don't believe this."

"It's another piece of evidence. Think of it that way. Something else we can use to help us put the pieces of the puzzle together. Don't you see? If he's planning to attend Carnival Night, he may be more closely involved with someone here in Phantom Point than we realized."

Mack said nothing.

She raised her chin. "I don't want to argue about this, Mack."

"I'm not arguing. I can't. I'm still in shock."

"Well, in that case, follow me. I'll pour you a drink."

She turned on her heel and walked off toward the other end of the big house.

The kitchen felt cold. He prowled the room while Cady got dinner underway. She

357

had made one or two attempts at a civil discussion but he had rejected them. He was in no mood to make polite conversation. He was pissed.

What really bothered him was that Cady had made it clear that he had no right to be mad.

While she finished making a salad, he poured himself a second glass of wine and went to stand at the window. He told himself that she was right. He was acting like an irate husband. She didn't owe him any answers. He had no real claim on her.

But all the logic in the world wasn't doing much to counter the aftereffects of the fear that had consumed him when he had returned this afternoon and found her gone.

"How did things go between you and Gabriella?" Cady asked.

Another olive branch, he thought. Maybe he'd better grab it. They had to break the impasse sooner or later.

"We talked. It was okay, I think." He turned away from the window. "What did you say to her this morning before I came back downstairs, anyway?"

Cady reached for a knife. "Not much. I just suggested that she ask you why you wanted to sell the house."

He thought about that. "This is the first

time she's ever asked. When I brought up the subject before, she got angry and upset and looked like she was going to burst into tears. But today she actually asked me in a reasonable, adult way." He watched her whisk olive oil and balsamic vinegar together. "I figure that was your doing."

"Did you give her an answer?"

"Tried." He pause to take a sip of wine. "Not sure I was able to explain it very well. I don't think I can explain it fully, not even to myself. But at least she listened today. That's a step forward."

"She's an intelligent young woman and she loves you very much. In the end it will be all right."

"About the mistress crack," he said eventually. "I apologize on Gabriella's behalf."

"Forget it."

"Gabriella knows that I've had relationships in the past. I've usually introduced her to the women I've dated. But I've always kept my private life offstage, if you know what I mean."

"In other words, Gabriella has never walked into a room and found you in bed with a woman."

He frowned. "She didn't find us in bed."

"Close enough."

"She's a big girl. She knows that I've done

more than hold hands with some of the women I've been involved with over the years."

"But you've protected her so that she never had to confront the reality that her father has a sex life, is that it?"

"Some things are supposed to be private. And, yes, I did try to protect her. But the truth is, keeping my relationships on the side was very convenient for me, too."

"Ah. I think I'm getting the picture here." Cady went to the stove.

"Whenever I got involved with a woman, I always made it clear going in that marriage was not on my list of priorities." Why the hell was he trying to explain himself? If she didn't owe him any answers, he sure didn't owe her any, either. "I was very up-front about the fact that I had no intention of trying to force Gabriella to accept a step-mother. I told myself that was only fair to the woman I was seeing."

"But?"

He took another swallow of wine. "But looking back, I think maybe one of the reasons I made a point of making sure my dates understood that the relationships were not going to lead to marriage was because it kept things simple for me."

"Simple."

He hesitated. "You know what I mean. Less distracting."

"In other words, you were protecting yourself as well as Gabriella."

He exhaled slowly. "Maybe. Like I said, it was convenient."

Cady dumped pasta into the boiling water. "So tell me, Mack, what kind of a love life have you had during the past few years?"

"Not great. I got dumped a lot."

Amusement lit up her face. And then she broke into full, unreserved laughter. He listened, bemused, and then he started to grin. The grin became a chuckle and then he, too, was laughing.

The kitchen suddenly felt a whole lot warmer.

Sylvia looked up when Cady sat down at the small sidewalk café table. "I give you fair warning. If you linger here for more than five minutes, you will be forced to have lunch with me and Eleanor Middleton. We're going to discuss my role in the Carnival Night festivities."

Cady looked around quickly, searching for the familiar silver-white pageboy haircut that was Eleanor's trademark. The lunch crowd was still light. She saw no sign of the perennial committee chair.

"Don't worry, I can say what I have to say in four and a half minutes," she assured Sylvia. "Mack and I would like you and Gardner to come to dinner this evening. We want to talk to you."

"Is this the big announcement?" Sylvia asked with a tense tone.

"Big announcement?" Cady thought fast. "Oh, you mean the engagement thing. No, it's not that."

Sylvia relaxed visibly. "We can't make it tonight. We're entertaining one of Gardner's clients. I've got meetings scheduled all day tomorrow, but I think we're both free in the evening."

Cady hesitated, wondering if she should jump straight into the subject of her theories concerning Vesta's death. The knowledge that Sylvia would be seriously shocked stopped her. This was not the time or place. You had to work up to a conversation like this one.

"Tomorrow evening will be fine," she said reluctantly.

"What's the matter?" Sylvia asked with concern. "This sounds serious. Something wrong?"

Eleanor Middleton materialized before Cady could come up with a response. She was dressed in a pair of jaunty navy slacks and a red jacket. A quantity of gold buttons sparkled in the sunlight.

"Cady, dear. So good to see you. You'll be here for this year's Carnival Night, I hope?"

"Uh, yes." Cady stammered. "Yes, I will, Eleanor."

"Excellent. You can assist Sylvia and me with handing out the costume prizes. It will be so nice to have both of you on the stage this year. A lovely tribute to Vesta, don't you think? She was such an institution here in Phantom Point."

Not a beloved institution, Cady thought. Just an institution.

"Glad to help in any way I can," she murmured, struggling for an ounce or two of enthusiasm.

Sylvia gave Cady an amused "gotcha" look that said more clearly than words that escape was no longer possible.

"Wonderful." Eleanor unbuckled a designer briefcase. "The committee has had its hands full this year, I can tell you that. Brooke Langworth was forced to resign a couple of months ago when George took a turn for the worse, you know. We certainly miss her."

"I understand George is very ill now," Sylvia said.

"I'm afraid so." Eleanor shook her head

sadly. "Not expected to last much longer. I must say, Brooke has been very devoted to him in these last few months. Not quite what everyone expected. It was generally assumed that she only married him for his money, you know."

Sylvia looked thoughtful. "Which she will soon have, won't she?"

Cady and Eleanor looked at her. Neither said a word.

Eleanor cleared her throat and hastily pulled some papers out of her briefcase. "Yes, well, Cady, let me give you a copy of the schedule. The prizes will be handed out at nine o'clock in the evening, just before the fireworks."

"Great. I'll be sure to be there. If you'll excuse me, I'll be on my way —"

"Nonsense," Eleanor said briskly. "You must join us for lunch. We have a great deal to discuss. This year's event is going to be the most elaborate Carnival Night ever held in Phantom Point. The committee has authorized me to pull out all the stops."

It was a good forty minutes before Cady managed her escape. She left Sylvia and Eleanor poring over the plans for the presentation of the costume prizes and fled a block to Chatelaine's.

There were only two people in the gallery. Leandra was showing them a Victorian-era painting that featured an Arthurian scene done in the highly romanticized style of Edward Burne-Jones.

She exchanged a nod of greeting with Leandra and then went down the short hall to the little office suite at the rear of the gallery. She paused at the door of the washroom and slipped inside. The small space was empty. She opened her purse and took out a brush.

When she was finished with her repairs, she pressed the button of the liquid soap dispenser several times before she realized that the container was empty.

Bending down, she opened one of the two doors in the cabinet under the counter. There was no spare bottle of liquid soap inside, but she noticed several rolls of tissue and a short stack of small, boxed hand soaps inside. She smiled when she saw the hotel logo on the boxes. Souvenirs of a vacation. She removed one of the little boxes and closed the door.

A few minutes later she emerged from the washroom and went down the hall to the showroom. Leandra's customers had departed. Cady glanced at the picture of the knights in shining armor surrounded by ethereal ladies.

"No sale?"

"Not yet." Leandra looked knowing. "But something tells me they'll be back. What have you been up to?"

"Just had lunch with Sylvia and Eleanor Middleton."

"Talk about fun, hmmm?"

"Stop snickering. I got drafted to help hand out prizes for the best costumes on Carnival Night."

"Duty calls."

"In Eleanor Middleton's case it doesn't just call, it reaches out, grabs you by the throat and sinks in a pair of fangs. By the way, we're out of soap in the washroom."

"The janitorial service comes in tonight. I'll leave a note for them. Did you find my emergency stash under the sink?"

"Sure did. Who went on vacation in Hawaii?"

"Parker took me there a couple of months ago. Ten days of fun in the sun. It was great."

"It sounds wonderful." Cady looked at her. "So, what's wrong?"

Leandra's eyes filled with tears. "Oh, damn."

Cady picked up the box of tissues and offered it to her. "Heard from Dillon again, I take it?"

"He called last night." Leandra blew into the tissue. "I should have hung up on him, but I didn't. Why can't I break this bad habit?"

Cady slowly lowered herself into a chair. "What did he say?"

"Just the usual." Leandra swallowed, tossed the crumpled tissue into a basket and reached for another. "That he's changed. That he wants to try again."

"Leandra, listen closely. Do you think Dillon is dangerous in any way?"

"Dangerous?" Leandra appeared genuinely startled. "Oh, no, he would never hurt me, if that's what you mean."

"You're sure of that?"

"Positive." Leandra tossed the second tissue into the basket. "He's just a bad habit."

"Have you told Parker that Dillon is trying to get back into your life?"

"No. Absolutely not. It would worry him." Leandra slouched dejectedly in her chair. "This is my problem. I want to handle it on my own. I'm a mature, adult woman. I can break the bad-boy habit."

Cady walked into the study and propped herself on the edge of the desk.

"What?" Mack asked, not bothering to look up from the screen full of data.

"I just wondered, now that you've got

Ambrose the wizard on the payroll, do you think he could do a background check on Dillon Spooner?"

He did look up at that. "Probably. Why?"

"Dillon has been calling Leandra a lot since the funeral. Pressing her to give him another chance. Sylvia and I wondered if he might be on the verge of turning into a stalker. I thought maybe you could find out if he has any previous history of that kind of stuff."

"You're really worried about this guy Spooner?"

"I don't know what to think. I don't know him very well. All I can tell you for certain is that no one in the family is very fond of him. They all think he married Leandra so that he could get an entrée into the art world and sponge off Aunt Vesta. He was very dedicated to his art. Too dedicated to be bothered with holding down a real job."

Mack thought about that. "Dedicated or obsessed?"

"I'm not sure," Cady admitted. "That's what's worrying me."

Mack nodded once. "I'll see what Ambrose can find out about him. But even if Spooner doesn't have a history of being a stalker that doesn't mean he might not become one."

★ ★ ★

It didn't take long. Ambrose called with the results less than an hour later.

"Got the three Zs," he said.

"Three Zs?"

"Zero, zip, zilch. Guy's got no record with the cops or the courts. Not even a speeding ticket."

"Anything else of interest show up?"

"Well, his work record is spotty, to put it mildly. Looks like he's held a couple of dozen part-time jobs in the past few years. Same pattern every place he goes. Works for a couple of months and then quits."

"Fired?"

"No. I checked. Spooner's a good employee as long as he feels like working, but when he gets bored, he leaves without much notice."

Mack reached for a pen. "Got a current address?"

"Sure. He lives in San Francisco. At the moment he's working part-time at an art supply store."

Two hours later Dillon Spooner opened the door of his loft apartment. He was a lean man in his late twenties. His head was shaved completely bald, a style which called attention to his high cheekbones. His denim shirt and jeans were spattered with paint. The brush in his hand was stained blood red.

"Who the hell are you?" he asked.

"Mack Easton. I'm a friend of Leandra's."

"Leandra?" Dillon looked as if he'd just been poleaxed. "Is she okay? Did something happen?"

"Take it easy. She's fine, Spooner. I just wanted to talk to you for a few minutes. Mind if I come in?"

"Why?" Dillon asked suspiciously.

"It's about Leandra."

Dillon hesitated. "Okay."

A short time later Dillon handed Mack a paint-stained mug filled with very strong coffee.

"I know her family thinks I tried to sponge off of her," he said. "And I guess it must have looked that way. They would all have been a lot happier if I had gone to work in an office somewhere. Hell, her great-aunt even offered to let me work at Chatelaine's. And I did. For a while."

"What went wrong?"

Dillon frowned. "Nothing went wrong, as far as I was concerned. I worked for a few months, got enough money together to buy more paint and supplies and then quit so that I could concentrate on my art. Got to invest up front in a career, you know? I needed to paint, man."

"But you were married. You had obligations. Bills to pay."

"Did I ever." Dillon's face tightened with outrage. "The damned bills kept piling up, you know? Seemed like every time I turned around there was another one. On top of everything else, Leandra wanted to buy a house. We started to argue a lot. It all fell apart."

"I see." Mack took another swallow of the powerful coffee. It tasted very good. He had been drinking too much tea lately, he thought. "Dillon, I hear you've been calling Leandra."

"So what? That's not against the law, is it?"

"No."

"I'm trying to make her see that things have changed."

"How have they changed?"

"A major gallery here in the city has picked me up. They love me, man. I'm going to have my first really important show in a few months. I'm on my way. I always knew that it was just a matter of time before I got my big break."

"Leandra is seeing someone else now."

Anger leaped in Dillon's eyes. His hand closed into a fist. "That old coot Turner? He could be her father, man."

Mack winced. The old coot, he reflected, was only two or three years older than himself. "I don't think Turner is ready for a nursing home."

"Well, he's too old for Leandra, that's for sure. Can't figure out what the hell she sees in him."

"I'm told he's a nice guy," Mack said.

"I don't give a damn how nice he is. He's got no business hanging around my wife."

"Ex-wife," Mack said gently.

"She's my wife, damn it." Dillon surged to his feet. He grabbed the paint-drenched brush he'd had in his hand when he opened the door and slashed it across an unfinished canvas. *I love her, man.*

Mack looked at the canvas. The brush had left a bright crimson splash of red paint in the center. It looked a lot like blood.

He told her he wanted to take a stroll before dinner. They walked up the hill, following a sidewalk that bordered a narrow curving street. Twilight was bearing down on the bay behind them. Mack wanted to see the house on Via Palatine before the sun disappeared altogether. Houses looked different at different times of the day. Maybe this one wouldn't look quite so right at twilight.

"Well?" Cady asked. "What do you think about Dillon?"

"I'm not sure. He's an artist who's convinced that he's on the brink of being discovered. He's a man who doesn't like the fact that his ex is seeing another man."

"We already knew that much."

"Sometimes it's very hard to pick out the bad guys. A lot of them are very good at blending in with the scenery."

"But do you think he's potentially dangerous?"

Mack thought about the hurled paintbrush and the blood-red splash on the unfinished picture. "Maybe."

Cady came to a sudden halt. "Really?"

"I can't say for sure. I'm not a shrink. We should watch him, though. Let me know if he shows up here in Phantom Point."

She did not appear satisfied but she must have realized there wasn't much else that could be done at that moment. "All right. Thanks for checking on him."

"Sure. I'll just add it to the bill."

She shot him an irritated glance and then turned to survey the street. "Where are we going, anyway?"

"There's a house not far from here.

Thought I'd see what it looked like at this time of day."

Her lips parted on another question but to his surprise, she did not ask it. Instead she walked beside him without a word to the end of the street where the house with the gracefully arched doorways perched on the hillside overlooking the bay.

They came to a halt and watched the last rays of the setting sun turn the walls of the little villa to a mellow gold.

"It's beautiful," Cady whispered.

He had been right, he thought. The house and the woman looked very good together at this time of day. He had been pretty sure they would.

22

Randall's invitation to lunch caught Cady by surprise the following day. He appeared shortly before noon just as she was leaving the little gallery on Via Appia.

"I need to talk to you, Cady."

She sensed the urgency in him and resigned herself to the inevitable. "Leandra, would you please call Mack and tell him that I won't be home for lunch?"

"No problem." Leandra reached for the phone.

Mack wouldn't miss her, Cady thought as she walked into the yacht club restaurant. He had been holed up in the study all morning with his computer and the telephone. She knew that he was working with Ambrose to dig deeper into Jonathan Arden's background.

She slid into a booth across from Randall and glanced casually around. The tables were filled with a trendy crowd. The view of the bay, dotted with colorful sailboats, was spectacular today.

She turned her attention back to Randall,

studying him as he dealt with the waiter. She tried to be objective. He had his faults but it was impossible to think of him as the perpetrator of a major fraud scam that had involved murder. She had *married* the man. Sure, the marriage had ended before the honeymoon was over, but she couldn't have been *that* wrong about him.

Then again, she had not understood the depth of his feelings for Brooke until it was too late, she reminded herself. Maybe there were other things hidden behind the locked doors of his soul that she did not know. Everyone had some secrets.

The problem with men was that they were not nearly so easy to read as a piece of sixteenth-century armor or a two-hundred-year-old ewer.

The waiter vanished with the orders. Randall smiled briefly.

"Like old times," he said. He started to fiddle with his knife.

"Not quite." She looked at him across the table. "What's this all about?"

"I wanted to see you. Alone. Without Easton hovering around like some kind of bodyguard. What's so strange about that?"

"I hadn't noticed him hovering."

Randall's mouth twisted. "The guy's living in the same house with you, for crying out loud. You don't call that hovering?"

She cleared her throat. "Well, we are planning to get engaged."

"So you said. Mind telling me what you see in him?"

"Yes, I do mind. I didn't come here to discuss my relationship with Mack. You said you wanted to talk to me. So, talk."

His jaw tightened. "Your relationship with Easton is one of the things we need to discuss."

"Is that so? Why?"

"Because if you're serious about marrying him, he's going to have a stake in the new Chatelaine-Post, that's why." Randall gripped the knife very tightly. "Cady, are you sure the guy is for real?"

She smiled in spite of her mood. "It doesn't get any more real than Mack Easton."

"Are you certain that he didn't latch onto you because of Chatelaine's?"

"Randall —"

"You've got to admit that this is all kind of sudden. You never mentioned that you were seeing anyone seriously until after the funeral."

"You and I haven't talked that much since the divorce."

"Maybe not, but I keep in close touch

with your family. I talk to Sylvia and Leandra regularly. They didn't know anything about Easton until after the funeral either." Randall put the knife down slowly. "I'm not the only one who's worried about your relationship with him."

"My relationship with Mack Easton is none of your business," she said. But she said it gently. "Look, I know you're concerned about me, but there's no need to worry. I know what I'm doing."

"You're sure of that?"

She shrugged. "As sure as anyone can be. What about you? Seeing anyone?"

He shook his head once. "Too busy with the merger."

"Leandra says you haven't seen anyone seriously since the divorce." Impulsively she reached across the table and briefly touched his hand. "Are you going to put your life on hold forever because of Brooke?"

His expression grew suddenly intent. "Not forever."

"That sounds cryptic."

Randall fixed her with a very steady gaze. "Things will be different after the merger goes through."

"You think so?"

"Yes," Randall said coldly. "They will be very, very different."

A chill whispered down her spine. "Why would things change between you and Brooke if Chatelaine's and Austrey-Post merge?"

"Have you read the merger proposal?"

"I scanned it briefly. I can't say that I've studied it. Sylvia is much better than I am when it comes to analyzing that kind of stuff. Why?"

Randall's face grew taut. "Because the merger reshuffles the cards. After it takes place, it will be a whole new game."

"What do you mean?"

"The board of directors gets restructured under the terms of the agreement. Voting shares will be distributed differently, too. It's complicated." He waved a hand slightly in a dismissing motion. "It would take too long to explain it here. But take my word for it, after the merger, if two or three people who hold large blocks of shares form an alliance, they will be able to control who sits in the CEO's chair."

A shock of comprehension shot through her. "That's why you're so eager for the merger, isn't it? You see it as a way to break Stanford's hold on Austrey-Post."

"You're damn right, I do." Grim anticipation blazed in Randall's eyes. "The sonofabitch will no longer be able to call the shots. Once Stanford realizes that he won't be running things, he'll listen to my offer to buy him out."

"I get the picture."

"Do you? Do you really see what's involved here? This is the first chance I've had to gain control of Austrey-Post since Mom died. I'm not going to let anything stand in the way. You've got to help me."

"What do you want from me?"

He leaned forward and folded his arms on the table. "I want you to promise me that you'll vote for the merger."

He was practically vibrating, she realized. The tension in him set off alarms deep inside her. She held her silence while the waiter put the breadbasket and a small bowl of fragrant olive oil on the table. Then she took a deep breath.

"Okay, I understand why the merger is important to you. Tell me why Stanford wants it."

Randall exhaled, a quick, harsh sound of disgust. "Why do you think he wants it? He sees it as a way to increase his income and his clout. A merger will open up new possibilities for expansion. Higher volumes. It will attract larger, more important consignments."

"But he'll have to contend with a board of

directors that he can't dominate."

Randall nodded, looking satisfied. "He assumes that he will be able to control the new company because he thinks that after the merger I'll continue to take orders from him, the way I always have. And it's true that with our voting shares combined, we would have a lot of power on a Chatelaine-Post board."

"Stanford is going on the assumption that he can control your shares?"

"He's going on the assumption that he can control *me.* And why shouldn't he think that I'll continue to do what he tells me to do after the merger? I've got a long track record of taking his orders, don't I?"

"But things are going to be different in the brave new world of Chatelaine-Post?"

"Oh, yes," Randall said softly. "Very different."

"I see."

"I've been waiting for this opportunity for years. You know that, Cady. You've got to support the merger. This isn't just my chance to get rid of Stanford. *Everything* is riding on the deal."

"Define *everything.*"

Randall glanced around the restaurant and then lowered his voice. "George Langworth is dying. It's no secret that he hasn't got much time left. Brooke has nursed him faithfully. She's done her duty as a wife. But when he's gone, she'll be free. I'm going to ask her to marry me."

Cady sat very still. "What does the merger have to do with your plans to ask Brooke to marry you?"

"George has given her a great deal. She'll be a wealthy woman when he dies. I can't go to her empty-handed. I don't want anyone to say that I'm marrying her for her money."

"Oh, brother. I think I see where this is going —"

"When I get rid of Stanford, I will control his shares. I'm going to give them to Brooke as a wedding gift."

Mack held the phone to one ear while he studied the screen full of data arrayed before him. "Okay, I've got it. Looks like bank account information, all right. You're a genius, Ambrose."

"Nah, I'm a consultant." Ambrose made happy little humming sounds on the other end of the line. "I just sent through the rest of the data. Anything else you want while I'm fooling around with this financial stuff?"

"That will do for now. I'll get back in touch if I need more."

"Anytime. You got a printer on that end?"

"Yes."

"So, like when do you think you might have another job for me?"

"As a matter of fact, I wanted to talk to you about taking an in-depth look at my program. See if you can figure out ways to expand its capabilities and maybe fill in some of the holes in my database. This business with Arden has brought to light some very big gaps. It would be a long-term project. Interested?"

"I'm already on it, boss."

Mack hung up the phone and sent a file of data to the printer. When the machine kicked into action, he leaned back in his chair, put his fingertips together and thought about the next step. He could analyze financial information up to a point, but he was not a trained accountant. He needed an expert to help him decode Arden's bank transactions. Preferably someone who was already tuned into the situation.

Luckily, the ideal candidate for the job was coming to dinner.

Gardner frowned at the stack of printouts. "I'm not a forensic accountant. That's a specialty field."

"If you can't get anything out of these, so

be it," Mack said. "But I'm betting that your inside knowledge of the Chatelaine-Post deal gives you an edge that an outside accountant wouldn't have."

"Maybe." Gardner examined the print-outs warily. "But no guarantees."

"Understood," Mack said.

Cady put one hand on the stack. "Just take a look at them. That's all we're asking."

"I'll do my best. But don't count on any brilliant revelations. I'm a CPA, not Sherlock Holmes."

"I still can't believe that Aunt Vesta was running her own private little sting operation." Sylvia stood up suddenly and began to pace the living room. "But it does explain some of her strange behavior during the last couple of months. Why didn't she tell me what she suspected?"

"As far as we can figure out, she didn't tell anyone except Hattie Woods; and the only reason she confided in Hattie was because she needed her help," Cady said.

"Well, we all know that Vesta was nothing if not secretive and eccentric." Sylvia shot Cady an angry look. "But that's no excuse for you not telling us that you thought something was terribly wrong."

"Maybe not," Cady admitted. "But until we stumbled onto Hattie Woods, I didn't have anything to back up my concerns. I was afraid everyone would conclude that I was off my rocker. I didn't think my theories would be welcome."

"I can't say that this one is particularly welcome," Sylvia muttered. "But given the evidence, we're going to have to deal with it. You're sure that Jonathan Arden is working with someone inside Austrey-Post?"

"We're not positive, but it sure looks like Aunt Vesta was certain of it," Cady said. "In fact, she may have wondered if the problem went all the way to the top. It would explain why she didn't go straight to Stanford Felgrove with her suspicions. It also explains why she postponed the merger vote."

Sylvia frowned. "She thought Felgrove was working with Arden?"

"Or maybe she figured the inside contact was Randall," Gardner offered a little too helpfully. "That would explain why she kept quiet. She always had a blind spot where he was concerned. She would have been very hesitant to implicate him."

Mack winced and shook his head at Gardner in silent warning. But it was too late. Cady and Sylvia had already turned on him.

"I refuse to believe that Randall knows anything about this," Sylvia snapped.

Gardner's expression hardened. "Don't count on good old Uncle Randall being an innocent bystander."

"I'm with Sylvia on this," Cady said quietly. "Randall knows nothing about the forgeries."

"Neither of you can see clearly where Randall Post is concerned. I know it's hard to envision an old childhood friend as a criminal, but that doesn't mean he's not guilty." Gardner looked at Mack for backup.

Mack shrugged. "I don't think we can rule Post out. Not yet, at any rate."

It was his turn to be on the receiving end of two quelling stares.

"Let's try some logic here." Cady stopped beside the desk and tapped the stack of printouts. "Randall is one-hundred-percent focused on the merger. It's very, very important to him. Trust me on this. I honestly don't think he would bother to expend a lot of time and energy on an elaborate forgery scam that would put his plans to link Chatelaine's and Austrey-Post at risk."

"That leaves Stanford," Sylvia snapped. "I can't say I like the man but I have to admit that the same logic applies. Why would he take the risk of running forgeries and frauds through Austrey-Post at a time when we're taking a close look at his books?"

Gardener interrupted. "I can give you one good reason why either Randall or Stanford might have resorted to running frauds through Austrey-Post."

"What reason?" Cady asked instantly.

"To cover up a cash flow problem that might have made us call off the merger," Gardner said.

There was a short, brittle silence. Cady and Sylvia exchanged glances.

"Good point," Sylvia said. She gestured impatiently. "I'm the hot-shot CEO around here. I should have thought of that myself."

"You're a little too emotionally involved with the situation," Gardner said. "Hard to get a clear take on it when you're dealing with everything from Vesta's estate to the possibility that your old friend Randall Post is a crook. Not to mention the merger itself."

"And that kind of insight is why we need you to take a real close look at the information in those printouts, Gardner," Mack said. "You not only have the financial experience to make sense of the data, you've also got a different viewpoint."

Gardner rubbed the back of his neck. "You know, when you think about it, Stanford and Randall might both be involved in running those fakes through their company.

If Austrey-Post is trying to cover up a cash flow problem, they'd both have a vested interest in making the bottom line look good for a potential merger."

"Stanford, maybe," Cady said. "But not Randall."

"Absolutely not Randall," Sylvia echoed.

Gardner raised his eyes to the ceiling and said nothing.

Mack opted for the diplomatic approach. "With any luck, those financial records might give us a clue about what is really going on at Austrey-Post."

Gardner, appearing far more enthusiastic than he had a moment ago, reached for the stack of printouts. "This is going to take awhile but I'll see what I can do."

Sylvia turned to pin Mack with a searching look. "I don't understand where you fit into this picture. You told us you were a business consultant. But you sound more like some sort of private investigator. What's going on here?"

Cady answered before Mack could get his mouth open.

"Mack does a lot of consulting work in the field of lost and stolen art," she said.

Sylvia looked skeptical. "You're a security consultant?"

"Not exactly," he said. "I deal in information. As Cady said, I trace lost, stolen and missing art and antiques."

"And what do you do when you find the missing items?" she asked coldly.

"I attempt to recover them for my clients."

"How?"

"Sometimes it's as simple as arranging a negotiated buy-back or a trade. Sometimes it's a little more complicated."

"What it boils down to is that you're a private investigator," Sylvia snapped.

"I think of myself as more of a go-between."

"Nonsense. You're an investigator." Sylvia turned to Cady. "You brought him here because you knew that something was wrong, didn't you?"

"I didn't know for certain that anything was wrong," Cady said defensively. "I just had a feeling."

"A feeling?" Sylvia groaned. "You sound more like Aunt Vesta every day. What exactly inspired this *feeling* you got?"

Cady cleared her throat and looked at Mack for help. "It's a little hard to explain."

"She thinks your aunt was murdered," Mack said bluntly.

Sylvia and Gardner gazed at him, dumbfounded.

"Sonofagun," Gardner said half under his breath. "Never even considered that possibility."

"*Murdered.*" Sylvia looked at Cady. "What in the world made you think that someone killed her?"

"I don't know." Cady walked stiffly toward the windows.

Mack watched her. "That's not quite true."

She sighed. "Okay, I thought her death was a little too convenient."

"Convenient?" Gardner prompted.

"Because of the merger," Cady said. "She had let it be known that she was thinking of postponing next month's vote of the board. The more I thought about it, the more I wondered if maybe someone didn't like the fact that she might be reconsidering the deal. Aunt Vesta was an unknown quantity. Unpredictable. Eccentric. And she had the power to cancel the merger altogether if she chose to do so."

"Do you realize what you're saying?" Sylvia demanded. "Surely you didn't believe that someone murdered Aunt Vesta just to ensure that the merger went through?"

"Okay, it was a little over the top," Cady muttered. "And as it turns out, I was probably wrong. If she was murdered, it's far more likely that it was because she stumbled onto Jonathan Arden's scam."

Sylvia tried to compose herself. "But the fact that the possibility of murder even occurred to you in the first place —"

"Certainly didn't strike anyone else in the family," Gardner said dryly.

Cady kept her face averted. She started to rub her palms up and down her arms. Understanding knifed through Mack.

He straightened and went to stand behind her. He rested his hands on her shoulders.

"It was because she drowned, wasn't it?" he said. "Because you nearly died the same way that day at the lake when you were fourteen. That was why her death disturbed you so deeply and made you start asking questions."

She hunched her shoulders. "Maybe. But the crucial factor was the timing. I just couldn't convince myself that her death had nothing to do with the merger. I never even considered the possibility of a forgery ring."

"If she had succeeded in exposing the scam, that would certainly have squelched all possibility of a business alliance between Chatelaine's and Austrey-Post." Gardner looked thoughtful. "I doubt if Felgrove could have found any other suitor to take the place of Chatelaine's. Hell, maybe the merger does qualify as a motive."

Sylvia whirled around. "Don't tell me you're buying into Cady's murder conspiracy theory?"

Gardner shrugged. "Money has always been a motive for murder and there's a lot of cash involved in this deal."

Cady turned around to face him. "Thanks for your support. At least, I think that was a show of support."

"What are brothers-in-law for?"

23

The Langworth house was a huge, colonnaded affair perched high on the hillside. It commanded an even more impressive view than the one available from the villa, sweeping from Tiburon to the Golden Gate Bridge. Cady stood in front of the windowed wall of the living room and watched the sun dance on the bay. The light seemed to strike the water and bounce off, never piercing the surface. Or the interior of this big house either, she thought.

The silence behind her grew heavier. The housekeeper who had ushered her into this room a few minutes ago had vanished.

She turned away from the view to examine the vast chamber in which she stood. The looming hulks of a staggering quantity of art and antiques filled every space, seeming to blot up any available light. The brooding shadows locked into the old pieces cast a dark spell on the entire household. Maybe it was the solemn miasma of impending death that jangled her nerves. The stuff pooled like an invisible fog in the room.

She felt jittery. Not a good sign. She glanced at her watch.

"Thank you for coming here on such short notice," Brooke Langworth said from the doorway.

Cady jumped a little at the sound of the soft, throaty voice. She turned quickly. Randall's great love was a tall woman with patrician features. Her honey-colored hair was arranged in a chignon that emphasized her taut, drawn expression. She wore a pale cream silk blouse and a pair of elegantly cut camel trousers. Gold glinted discreetly at her ears and around her throat.

"I got your message," Cady said. "What can I do for you, Mrs. Langworth?"

"Please call me Brooke. Won't you sit down?"

Cady sank cautiously down onto the edge of the sofa. She hoped Brooke had not summoned her here for the purpose of getting a professional appraisal of the collection of old objects that were eating up all the light.

"Would you care for coffee?" Brooke asked.

"No, thank you." Cady made a show of looking at her watch again. "I'm a little pressed for time."

"Yes, of course. I won't keep you long. I

realize this is difficult for you. It's not easy for me, either."

Please don't ask me to put a value on your collection. Your husband isn't even dead yet, and besides, I don't chase consignments from the nearly departed. But if that wasn't why Brooke had called, there could be only one other possible reason.

"Does this have something to do with Randall?" Cady asked cautiously.

"How did you guess?"

"Randall is the only thing that you and I have in common."

"Yes, of course." Brooke continued, "I asked you to come here today because I'm extremely worried about him. I know that in spite of the fiasco of your marriage, he is your friend and you want what's best for him."

"To a point."

"You do realize that he is obsessed with a merger between Austrey-Post and Chatelaine's?"

"I know it's important to him, yes."

"More than just important, I'm afraid. He is consumed by the goal of combining the two firms. I hesitate to say this, but I don't know where else to turn." Brooke paused, as though gathering herself. "I'm afraid of what he might do if the merger doesn't go through."

Cady stilled. "What are you talking about?"

"Randall is convinced that the merger is the only way he can gain control of Austrey-Post and rid himself of his stepfather. He hates Stanford Felgrove. I'm sure you're aware of that. If the merger fails —"

"What exactly are you afraid of, Brooke?"

"Randall has been through a great deal of stress in recent years. The divorce was hard on him."

"It wasn't exactly a piece of cake for me, either."

Brooke flushed. "No, of course not. I realize that it was traumatic for both of you. But it was different in your case."

"Really?"

"We both know that you weren't deeply in love with Randall and it's obvious that there was no one else for you. Your heart was not broken. Granted, the marriage was a mistake, but it was one you could correct easily enough."

"Just one of those annoying little speed bumps on the road of life?"

The evident strain on Brooke's attractive face grew more acute. "I'm not trying to make light of what happened. But you must realize that the marriage and divorce were much harder on Randall than they were on you?"

"Is that so?"

"He was devastated. His sense of guilt weighs so heavily on him. Don't you understand? He blames himself for everything that happened."

"Randall blames himself for the screw-up of our marriage? That's news to me."

Brooke looked first confused and then ruefully apologetic. "I'm sorry. That wasn't quite what I meant."

"Oh, I get it. He feels guilty because by rushing into marriage with me, he screwed up his chance of marrying you."

"I'm the one who must carry the weight of that guilt," Brooke whispered. "I walked away from Randall because I thought he was too obsessed with gaining control of what he viewed as his rightful inheritance. I was afraid that his single-minded determination to loosen Stanford Felgrove's hold on Austrey-Post would destroy any hope of happiness in our personal relationship."

"So you turned to George Langworth."

"George is a wonderful, kind, caring man. But I realized almost at once that marrying him was a terrible mistake. By then, however, it was too late. He had been diagnosed with cancer. I couldn't leave him. Meanwhile, Randall had married you. We were both trapped."

"A couple of star-crossed lovers."

A pained expression flickered across Brooke's face. "Please don't be facetious. I realize that you can't possibly have much sympathy for me, but I know that you care for Randall in your own way."

"My own way?"

Brooke hesitated. "Randall has explained to me that you're a lot like your great-aunt when it comes to strong emotions."

"Meaning I'm cold, controlling, incapable of blazing passions and so forth?"

To Cady's amazement, embarrassment infused Brooke's expression. "Everyone is different when it comes to strong emotions."

"Maybe we ought to get back to the reason you asked me to come here today. Why don't you tell me exactly what you want from me?"

Brooke walked to the nearest chair and sat down. Her voice dropped to a lower, more intense pitch. "I wanted to make certain that you understood just how important it is that this merger go through. It's an excellent opportunity for both firms, of course, but it's vital for Randall's emotional wellbeing."

"Are you telling me that you think he'll go off the rails if the merger falls apart? Maybe sink into clinical depression or something?"

Brooke twisted her hands together very tightly in her lap. "I don't know what he'll do if the merger fails. That's what frightens me."

A man appeared in the opening that separated the living room from the expansive front hall. He was dressed in white trousers, a white shirt and soft-soled white shoes. A stethoscope was slung around his neck.

"I'm sorry to interrupt, Mrs. Langworth."

Brooke turned sharply in her chair, eyes darkening with concern. "What is it, Kevin?"

"You asked to be notified at once if there was any change in Mr. Langworth's condition."

Cady could see from the somber expression on Kevin's face that the change in George Langworth's condition, whatever it was, had not been for the better.

Brooke was already on her feet. "Yes, thank you, Kevin." She was halfway across the room before she seemed to remember Cady's presence. "Will you excuse me? Jill will show you out."

"Don't worry. I can see myself out." Cady rose from the sofa and collected her purse.

Brooke inclined her head once and then disappeared with Kevin.

Cady crossed the huge living room and

went into the front hall. She stepped out into the sunshine and closed the door on the brooding shadows of age and impending death that filled the Langworth villa.

"I think I'm getting somewhere with this financial data on Arden that you gave me," Gardner said on the other end of the phone. "Some patterns are emerging. But I'm going to need more information."

"What kind of information?" Mack asked.

Gardner paused briefly. "We might as well start with the obvious suspects. Can you get me some banking history on Stanford Felgrove and Randall Post?"

Mack thought about how ridiculously easy it had been for Ambrose Vandyke to pull Jonathan Arden's financial records off the internet. "I don't think that will be a problem."

"I won't ask why that is not a problem," Gardner said dryly. "I'd rather not know."

"You and me both. First thing I learned when working with a really good free-lance consultant is not to ask too many questions." Mack heard the doorbell ring at the front of the villa. "I've got company. Anything else you need?"

"Not right now."

"In that case, I'll talk to you later."

The doorbell chimed again. Mack hung up the phone, got to his feet and left the study. He went into the hall and opened the front door.

Stanford Felgrove stood on the front step, smiling his polished smile.

"Thought I'd see if I could interest you in a round of golf, Easton."

"Why not?" Mack said. "Not like I'm doing anything exciting here."

Just trying to pin fraud and maybe a murder rap on you, he added silently. But he could take some time off from that job, he thought. He had some very smart people working the problem. And who knew what he might learn by playing golf with Stanford Felgrove?

He stood on the terrace with Cady discussing Brooke Langworth.

"I think she was genuinely worried about Randall's potential reaction to a failed merger," Cady said. "I got the feeling she thought he might go off the deep end if it didn't go through. She was very intense about it, Mack."

He studied the sunset while he thought about that piece of information. "Maybe she was just trying to push some emotional buttons she thought might encourage you to vote for the merger."

"Maybe. But she seemed sincere, Mack."

"Think she plans to marry Post after her husband dies?"

"I certainly didn't ask her such a tacky question, but I wouldn't be surprised if that's her intention."

"Hmm."

"What does 'hmm' mean?"

"It means that, if you're right, we'd better add Brooke Langworth to your list of murder suspects."

Cady froze. And then turned quickly. "Are you serious?"

"If her feelings for Randall are as deep as you claim, then she had a strong motive for wanting to ensure the success of the merger."

"Love?"

"More likely her motive was to ensure that Randall Post is ultimately in control of the new and improved Chatelaine-Post."

"I don't know, Mack. I can't see Brooke as a killer."

"She married once for money and status. Why wouldn't she want to do it again?"

Cady shook her head. "She may not love George Langworth, but I think she cares about him. I saw her face when the nurse came to tell her that George had taken a turn for the worse. She's committed to caring for him until the end. Don't forget, she could have divorced Langworth after he was diagnosed with cancer but she didn't. She stayed with him."

"She probably stands to inherit a good chunk of his estate. In the end, she will no doubt be a lot better off as Langworth's widow than his divorced wife."

Cady pondered that. "All right, you've got a point. Any word from Gardner?"

"He's still working on the printouts I gave him."

"How did the round of golf go?"

"About how you would expect. Felgrove spent most of the time giving me a sales pitch on the joys of combining Chatelaine's and Austrey-Post. Seemed to think that since I'm planning to marry you, I have a vested interest in making sure that the merger goes through."

She wrinkled her nose. "He believes that you're marrying me because of my connection to Chatelaine's?"

"Uh-huh."

"What a creep. But I can't say that I'm stunned with surprise."

"People tend to assume that whatever motivates them, motivates others," Mack said. "I think it's safe to say that Stanford

Felgrove is strongly motivated by financial considerations."

"I don't doubt that for a second."

"I did learn one other interesting thing about Felgrove today," Mack said.

"What was that?"

"He cheats at golf."

Cady sensed his presence in the doorway of the vault just as she raised the lid of the elaborately gilded and enameled box. She tensed and then glanced over her shoulder.

He stood there, watching her with that curious, searching look that never failed to make her intensely aware of the energy that flowed between them.

"I thought you were busy with your computer," she said.

"I'm taking a break." He moved farther into the chamber. "Looking for the Nun's Chatelaine, I assume?"

"Yes."

"Finding it is important to you, isn't it?"

"Of course it's important. It's extremely valuable."

"But that's not the real reason why you're so anxious to find it."

She sighed. "No." She hesitated, uncertain of how to explain her motivation. It was suddenly vital that he understand. "I have the feeling that when I find it, I'll find answers to some questions I've always had about Vesta."

"What are the questions?"

"People believe that she was cold and unfeeling. Everyone says that the only thing she ever cared about was Chatelaine's."

"Most of the evidence would seem to indicate that the general consensus is correct."

"I know, but —"

"But what?" Mack asked.

She closed the lid of the box very slowly. "I've always believed that something must have happened long ago to make her that way. I don't think she was cold. Not really. Not deep down inside. I think she buried her emotions because she wanted to protect herself."

He shrugged. "If you say so. You knew your aunt. I didn't."

"Yes." She picked up the box and carefully placed it on the display shelf. "I knew her. So did everyone else in the family. They all tell me I'm a lot like her."

"They're all wrong."

"That's what I keep telling myself." She turned quickly back to face him. "I shouldn't have dragged you into this, Mack. It's too personal. Not your problem."

He went toward her. "I can't think of any place I'd rather be."

He caught her face between his hands and kissed her before she could say another word. She made a tiny sound and then her arms went around him. She hugged him with a fierce urgency that had more to do with plain old-fashioned anxiety than sexual desire.

"Mack."

"Yes." He gathered her closer and ran his palm down the length of her spine.

The caress soothed her in a way that no pill or exercise routine could have done. She felt herself soften in his arms. He kissed her again. She touched the nape of his neck with her fingertips and sensed his response.

Hunger and hope unfurled inside her.

Awareness prickled.

Energy sparked.

24

Gardner put the pen down on top of the stack of printouts and absently rubbed the bridge of his nose. "I think we've got two things going on here. One of them is a record of five transfers of some rather hefty sums from Stanford Felgrove's private account into Jonathan Arden's account."

Mack whistled softly.

Cady was suddenly aware of the fact that her hands were tingling. She glanced at Sylvia, who watched Gardner very intently.

"Are you certain?" Mack asked.

Gardner looked at him. "Yes."

"Payoffs or commissions for selling the fakes to his clients?"

"Maybe. The timing on the piece he sold to Hattie Woods certainly fits into that scenario."

Sylvia leaned forward. "No payments from Randall's accounts, though?"

Gardner grimaced. "No. Doesn't mean he isn't involved — right, Mack?"

"Right." Mack removed his glasses from his pocket and put them on in a single motion. "The three could be working together and could have agreed to handle all the payments out of Felgrove's account."

"Wait a minute," Cady said. "Gardner just told us that there is no proof —"

Mack ignored her. He looked at Gardner. "You said there were two things going on. What's the second?"

"There are some other interesting payments out of Felgrove's account," Gardner said. "I can't tell you precisely where the money is going, but I can tell you that, wherever it is, it's offshore."

"Ambrose can probably follow up on those transactions for us," Mack said. "But I'm willing to bet that the payments are going into the account of whoever is manufacturing the fakes."

"There's no telling how much of the income of Austrey-Post is coming from the forgeries," Gardner said. "But under the circumstances, I think it would be prudent to assume that a large chunk of this year's extraordinarily good profits were derived from that source."

"No wonder they're applying so much pressure to get the merger approved as soon as possible," Sylvia muttered. "There's a constant risk that the scam will be exposed. If that happens, the scandal would probably bring down Austrey-Post."

Cady frowned. "The firm might survive if it claims that the fakes were so good that their own in-house experts were fooled and if it refunds its clients' money."

"Refunds on this scale will amount to a considerable sum. Could easily bankrupt the company," Gardner remarked.

"Stanford Felgrove must be the one behind this," Sylvia said. "He has always kept Randall on the outside of the business. If there's something rotten at the firm's core, it is Stanford's responsibility."

"Besides," Cady chimed in swiftly, "Randall would never do anything to destroy Austrey-Post. He considers it his inheritance. His only goal is to take it away from Stanford."

Gardner groaned. "Good old Uncle Randall can do no wrong."

"We *know* him," Cady insisted. "Trust us on this, Gardner."

Mack removed his glasses and turned to Gardner. "I'm inclined to go with them on this. I did some checking. Even if he had wanted to rig the books, Randall hasn't been in a position to do it. Stanford has kept him out of the loop by keeping him on the road chasing consignments and high-end clients."

"Huh." Gardner did not look pleased with that analysis but he did not argue.

Cady breathed a small sigh of relief. "We have to take this information to Randall immediately."

"What can he do about it?" Sylvia asked.

"I don't know." Cady got to her feet. "But it's his family's company. He has every right to know what's going on."

"I'm finished." Randall slammed a fist into the pile of printouts. *"Finished."* He raised anguished eyes to the small group gathered around the desk. "The sonofabitch has destroyed me. The galleries will be ruined when news of the forgeries gets out. I could kill him. Hell, I should have done it long ago."

Cady exchanged an uneasy glance with Sylvia. Maybe taking the information straight to Randall had not been such a great idea after all.

"Randall, listen to me," Sylvia said gently. "We know you had nothing to do with this —"

But Randall was not listening. He erupted from his chair, seized the Art Nouveau bronze paperweight and hurled it across the room. The small missile slammed into the paneled wall and dropped to the floor with a thud.

"Damn him," Randall roared. "After all my planning, the bastard is going to win."

Gardner made a small move toward him. Cady saw Mack shake his head very slightly. Gardner stopped.

"Take it easy, Randall," he said. "We need to talk about this."

Randall paid no attention. He started around the desk with long, seething strides. "I'm going to kill him. If I hadn't been such a damned coward after my mother died, I would have done it then. But I told myself that I would someday get the company out of his hands, instead. I promised myself that I would see him lose everything he had gained by manipulating her. And now —"

"Randall, stop it." Cady leaped to her feet and stepped into his path. "Listen to me. You mustn't do anything stupid. You could end up in jail."

"She's right," Sylvia said. "Randall, calm down and think for a moment."

"Get out of my way." He reached out to push Cady aside.

Mack was suddenly in the way. "Don't touch her, Post."

The order was issued in a savagely neutral tone that got everyone's attention, even Randall's.

"Huh?" Randall seemed confused by the

way Mack had materialized in his path. His hand fell to his side. "What?"

"I said, don't touch her."

"I don't want to hurt Cady." Impatient now, Randall tried to move around Mack. "I want to get Felgrove."

"Sit down," Mack said.

"Leave me alone." Enraged anew at the interference, Randall made a fist with his right hand and swung wildly.

Cady could not believe the degree of fury that was etched in his face.

"*Randall.*"

Sylvia gave a small, shocked cry of dismay. "Oh, my God."

Mack sidestepped the clumsy blow. Randall charged him, intent on getting to the door. Mack grabbed his arm and spun him around.

Off balance, Randall lost his footing and stumbled. He fetched up against the wall.

"Jesus," Gardner muttered.

"Pull yourself together," Mack said to Randall. "Do it now."

Randall stared at him. "What?"

"Sit down." Mack grabbed him by the scruff of the neck and slammed him into the nearest chair. "Killing Stanford isn't going to solve your problems. We need to talk."

"What is there to talk about?" The anger

in his voice melted into despair. He slumped in the chair. "He's ruined everything."

"Maybe not," Mack said.

Cady and the others looked at him.

"What do you mean?" Randall asked, without any sign of hope. "The scandal will destroy the company."

"Austrey-Post isn't the first reputable art and antiques firm to be hit with the problem of frauds and forgeries," Mack said. "You know how it works. You explain that mistakes were made inside the old furniture department. Happens all the time."

"*Mistakes* happen all the time," Randall corrected grimly. "Deliberate fraud perpetrated by the CEO of the company is something else. We're finished."

"Not necessarily," Mack said quietly.

They were all holding their breaths now, Cady thought, waiting for Mack to let the other shoe drop.

"What are you suggesting?" she asked.

"That Austrey-Post follow the usual procedure." He watched Randall. "You apologize to any clients who purchased fakes that were mistakenly authenticated by company experts. You refund money and —"

"And what?" Randall asked.

"And you fire someone," Mack concluded.

Randall snorted in disgust. "You want me to blame some poor expert in the furniture department? I'm sure Stanford will go along with that plan. It won't bother him at all to let someone else take the fall."

"What I'm thinking," Mack said slowly, "was that you fire the CEO."

Cady could almost hear jaws drop around the room.

"I don't understand." Sylvia frowned. "How can you fire Felgrove? He controls the firm. He owns it, for all intents and purposes. You can't get rid of him unless —"

Randall caught on first. A glimmer of anticipation flared in his eyes. "Unless I use the evidence in those printouts to force him to resign. Is that your plan, Easton? Hell, with what I have on him, I might even be able to make him turn over his shares in the company. A major scandal would cost Stanford the only thing he really cares about, his social position. It would kill him to be kicked out of his yacht and golf clubs."

Gardner looked intrigued. "Interesting possibilities there."

Cady nodded. "I'll say."

"I like it," Sylvia said.

Mack looked at Randall. "I do believe that you have the makings of a highly effective CEO."

★ ★ ★

"You're a fool." Stanford finished signing his name at the bottom of the agreement and very slowly set down the expensive fountain pen. "You know that, don't you? You think you've won but you'll screw this up just like you've screwed up everything you've ever touched."

In spite of the harsh words, Felgrove looked even more shell-shocked than Randall had appeared earlier, Mack thought.

The coup had gone without a hitch. Stanford had been taken off guard when Randall and Mack had walked into his house and dropped the bombshell.

Randall's guess about his stepfather's reaction had been dead on target. Faced with the threat of losing everything he valued, Felgrove had signed the papers that transferred his shares to Randall. In exchange, Randall had given him his word that he would not be implicated in the so-called mistakes that had been made with the fake antiques.

"I'll take my chances," Randall said, sliding the agreement back into an envelope.

Post was sounding more confident by the moment, Mack thought. Randall was riding high on the first wave of triumphant euphoria. It would be a while before the reality of what lay ahead hit him full force.

"This is nothing short of blackmail," Stanford whispered hoarsely.

Randall got to his feet. "You've got a hell of a nerve accusing me of blackmail after what you've done to my company. I'm going to have my hands full dealing with this mess and keeping your name out of it. Be grateful you're getting off this lightly."

Stanford's face congealed. "You'll regret this, you stupid bastard. You haven't got what it takes to run the business."

"You're wrong." Randall smiled faintly. "I've got just what I need to run Austrey-Post. Complete control."

The crash came about an hour later. Knowing it was inevitable, Mack took Randall to the bar of a nearby restaurant, settled him at a table and ordered two beers.

Randall drained half the contents of the frosted mug and set it down. He looked at Mack.

"Shit," he said. "I can't believe I did that."

"It's done. But now you've got a lot of work to do."

Randall closed his eyes. "The first thing on the agenda is to contact all the clients who got ripped off."

"Tell them that you became suspicious that something was not right in the furniture department," Mack suggested. "Say you conducted an in-house investigation that exposed the problem and that you now want to refund money to all clients who purchased the reproductions."

Randall raised his brows. "Reproductions?"

"Never use the words 'fake' and 'forgery' if you can avoid it," Mack said.

"Who the hell are you, Easton? How come you know so much about this kind of thing?"

"Long story."

"I've got time to listen." Randall wrapped both hands around the mug. "But the part I want to hear first is the part that involves you and Cady."

"Why don't you ask her to tell you about that part?"

"That's not exactly what you call a direct answer."

"I'm not here to talk about my relationship with Cady," Mack said.

Understanding lit Randall's expression. "Hell, she brought you in to investigate, didn't she? What are you? Some kind of security expert?"

"I'm in the information business."

"Bullshit. She brought you in undercover, didn't she? She must have been suspicious right from the start. Did Vesta tip her off?"

"Not exactly."

"But you said Vesta had figured out that Arden was operating some kind of scam. Did she realize Stanford was also involved?"

"She probably had her suspicions. We'll never know for sure."

"What happens to that phony psychic?"

"I thought I'd drive into the city to see Arden this afternoon," Mack said. "Let him know that his little scam is finished."

Randall's mouth thinned. "I'd give a lot to file charges against him and Stanford both. Bastards."

"Austrey-Post doesn't need the bad press. You've got what you wanted out of this. It's time to cut your losses."

Randall groaned. "Don't remind me of losses. The big question now is how much money will Austrey-Post have to refund?"

An hour and a half later Mack stood in the living room of Jonathan Arden's recently vacated apartment. So much for delivering a warning, he thought. Displaying the preternatural survival instincts of the consummate professional, the con artist had already skipped town.

He walked downstairs into the garage and took another look at the trash bin just in case Arden had tossed anything of interest into it on his way out the door. He rummaged around for a while among the discarded newspapers, beer bottles and empty take-out containers. He saw nothing that could tell him where Arden might have gone.

He dropped the key off at the manager's apartment and walked down the sidewalk to where he had parked his car. He paused in the act of opening the door and tried to pin down the whisper of unpleasant awareness that was stirring the hair on the back of his neck.

It didn't take long to identify the sensation. It was the feeling you got when you knew that someone was watching you from the shadows.

Cady settled deeper into the corner of the sofa. Beside her, Mack stretched out in a thickly upholstered chair and propped his ankles on a hassock. He rested his elbows on the heavily upholstered arms and steepled his fingers in the familiar pose. He had been very quiet since he had walked through the door a short time ago. His mood was making her uneasy.

On the far side of the French doors, night descended on Phantom Point. The process was swift and merciless. Sort of like a vampire greeting a lover, Cady thought.

"The news is out that Stanford has resigned as CEO of Austrey-Post and transferred his shares to Randall," she said in an effort to break through the envelope of silence that enclosed Mack. "Leandra said the people who work in the shop next door were talking about it this afternoon."

"Not surprising. It's a small community."

Well, at least he was talking.

"Stanford is telling everyone he had always intended to turn over the operation of Austrey-Post to Randall when he felt he was ready."

"Anybody buying that story?" Mack asked.

"I don't know. I don't think it matters." She paused. "What matters is that Randall has finally got his hands on the family firm."

"Uh-huh."

"Thanks to you," she added deliberately.

He said nothing.

"You're a hero. Again."

"It was just a job."

Was that really all it had meant to him? *Just a job.* She wasn't feeling depressed, she decided. The sensation flowing through her now could be more accurately described as melancholia.

Which was the old-fashioned word for depression.

"Thought you said you quit."

"Oh, yeah," Mack said. "I did, didn't I? By the way, there's something I've been meaning to mention."

"What?"

"Our cover is getting a little frayed around the edges."

"Cover?" She pulled herself together with an effort and tried to focus on the conversation. "You mean the engagement thing?"

"Yes. The engagement thing."

Silence.

"Well, it served its purpose," Cady said, searching for a neutral tone. "It worked. I suppose it doesn't matter if it's getting thin in terms of believability. We don't need it any longer."

"Guess not," he agreed, in a voice that was even more carefully balanced than her own. "Unless —"

She seized on that. "Unless?"

He looked at her. "Are you satisfied that exposing Felgrove's fraud is the end of the matter? Or do you still believe that your aunt was murdered?"

She tilted her head back against the chair

and contemplated the question. "I think it's possible that Stanford or Jonathan Arden had something to do with the way Aunt Vesta died. They had every reason to want her dead. They must have realized that she was onto the scam when she postponed the vote on the merger."

"You may be right, but it will probably be impossible to prove."

The mists of melancholia grew thicker. "I know."

More silence.

"You want me to keep looking?" Mack asked after a while.

The question took her by surprise. She thought about it for a moment.

"I'd like to know the truth," she said eventually. "Even if we can't prove anything in a court of law, I would very much like to know for sure what happened that night."

"I'll see what I can do."

"You will?"

"If that's what you want," he said.

She glanced at him, trying to read the unreadable expression on his face. "Thank you."

"No guarantees." He tapped his fingertips together once. "But I might be able to check out a few angles."

"Such as?"

"See if I can find out exactly where Felgrove and Arden were on the night your aunt died. Maybe apply some pressure. See how they react if I push them."

She thought about that. "Arden isn't even around to be pushed. You said he pulled a midnight move out of his apartment."

"Doesn't mean I won't be able to determine where he was the night your aunt died. And if he looks like a good candidate, Ambrose may be able to trace him through his financial transactions. Guys like Arden live on credit cards, usually someone else's."

She studied him for a moment. "You don't think Arden's the killer, do you?"

"If," Mack said, "and I emphasize the word *if*, your aunt was murdered, I think Felgrove is the more likely candidate. Not only did he have more to lose, he was less of a pro. That makes him more inclined to have done something desperate, reckless or stupid."

"Unlike Arden."

"Arden is very much a pro. As you can see, when the going got tough, he got going. He knows when to hold 'em and when to fold 'em."

"So the next step is to find out where Stanford Felgrove was on the night Aunt Vesta died?"

"One of the next steps." Mack looked meditative. "Does Felgrove swim?"

"Sure. He's got a pool. Owns a boat that he keeps down at the marina. Why do you ask?"

"It occurred to me that if someone did drown your aunt, he would have had to be reasonably comfortable in the water. From what you've told me, Vesta Briggs was a strong swimmer."

"Yes." A shiver swept through her. "But she was eighty-six years old. And she was a small woman. A man Felgrove's size could easily have held her under until she died."

"But she would have fought?"

"Oh, yes." A flicker of unease went through her. "Aunt Vesta would have fought."

"And maybe screamed for help?"

She hesitated, thinking of the neighbors. "Yes. If she'd had a chance to scream, she probably would have done so."

"The pool terrace is screened by hedges and plants but it's outdoors. No one reported any screams that night?"

"Apparently not."

"There are other ways to get rid of an elderly woman." Mack looked out over his fingertips into the night. "She could have been the victim of a mugging or a burglar or a car accident. Yet the killer, assuming there is one, chose the pool. He accomplished his goal without leaving any marks on the body. No blows to the head, for example. He had to know there would be a struggle because your aunt was at home in the water. Not an easy target, even if she was eighty-six and small."

"I agree that a murderer who wasn't comfortable in the water probably would have chosen another venue. But like I said, Stanford Felgrove can swim."

There was a short pause.

"This habit your aunt had of swimming alone at night. Lot of people know about it?"

"Yes."

"Would Felgrove have known?"

"Yes."

More silence.

"Does he dive?" Mack asked softly.

That stopped her cold. "Dive? As in scuba dive?"

"When you think about it," he said slowly, "the easiest way to drown someone without risking a lot of screaming and a hand-to-hand struggle would be to do it from under the surface."

"Oh, my God." Like a dead man's hand gripping your ankle and hauling you down into the murky darkness.

"A diver with an oxygen tank and a mask could drag his victim under and hold her there as long as necessary," Mack concluded, his expression reflective. "No splashing. No screams. No marks."

It was too much. The image was too vivid. She could no longer hold back the memories. They surged up out of the depths and slammed through her with the force of hammer blows. She was suddenly breathless, drenched in an icy sweat. Her heart pounded. She could almost feel the cold fingers wrapped around her ankle dragging her beneath the surface.

"Cady?"

She ignored him, unable to speak coherently now. She shoved herself up out of the chair, gasping for air. The anxiety attack had struck so hard and fast that there had been no time to fend it off with the usual rituals of deep breathing and calming thoughts.

"What the hell?" Mack was on his feet.

"Just . . . just give me a minute." She went toward the French doors, instinctively seeking to escape the intense claustrophobia that was closing in around her. "Need to get out. Need to move. Stupid panic attack."

She wrenched open the door and stumbled out into the garden. The fresh air

426

helped a little. She forced herself to inhale from the pit of her stomach. It wasn't easy. She started to pace, trying to work off the excess adrenaline that was hurtling through her system.

Mack fell into step beside her. "What can I do?"

"Nothing."

"What about that pill you said you carried in your key chain?"

"Maybe. Not yet." She came to a halt and concentrated on her breathing. "I've been through this before. But it's been a long time. I'd almost forgotten how bad —"

"Take it easy." He stopped behind her and began to massage her shoulders. "You're so tense you feel like you might fracture. Relax."

"Easier said than done." But she was regaining control. The tightness in her chest was starting to ease.

They stood there together in the shadows. Mack continued to work on the rigid muscles of her shoulders, his hands strong and warm and deeply soothing. She ignored the tingling in her hands and focused on her breathing, willing her pulse to slow to a normal pace. She could do this. She had done it before. She knew the techniques.

After a while the worst was over. She still

felt unnaturally alert and painfully aware, but the terrible jittery sensation was fading.

"Never realized panic attacks were so physical." Mack flexed his hands on her shoulders.

"They say it hits you with the same impact as if you'd walked around a corner and came face to face with a tiger. But there is no tiger and you know there is no tiger, but you can't convince your body of that. Your system goes into instant fight-or-flight mode."

"Even though there's nothing to flee or to fight."

"Yes. For me it has always been more like a terrible claustrophobia. Almost a drowning sensation. The way it was at the lake that day."

"Either way, you're left dealing with one hell of a chemical cocktail in your bloodstream."

"It can make you wonder if you're going crazy or having a nervous breakdown," she whispered. "Everyone says that's probably what happened to Aunt Vesta the night she died. They say she must have had an especially acute attack."

"Panicked and drowned."

"Yes."

"But she was a good swimmer so even if she did suffer a panic attack," Mack said, "she probably would have made it to the side of the pool. The same way you managed to get out of the chair, open the doors and walk outside into this garden a few minutes ago."

She swallowed. "After you've had a few panic attacks, you recognize them. You can learn to move through them. It's not easy but it can be done."

"Your aunt was a pro when it came to handling them, right?"

"She'd had a lifetime of experience." Cady glanced at him. The light from the living room cast half of his face into deep shadow. "What are you thinking?"

"That someone, possibly Stanford Felgrove, really did kill your aunt. Now all I have to do is find a way to prove it."

A long time later he woke up, aware that she was not asleep beside him. He put out a hand and found only cooling sheets.

Damn. This was getting to be a habit. At least he knew where to look for her.

He shoved aside the covers, got out of bed and found his pants. He went downstairs to the vault room. As he had expected, the door was open. Light blazed inside the chamber.

Cady was inside. She had climbed the

narrow spiral staircase to the balcony where she was in the process of trying her little gold key in a small chest inlaid with lapis lazuli and gold. Mack watched her for a moment.

"Find anything?" he asked eventually.

She jumped at the sound of his voice.

"Sorry," he said gently. "Didn't mean to startle you."

"I'm all right." She put the chest back on a shelf and closed the glass door. "I couldn't sleep so I thought I'd try a few more locks."

"No luck, I take it?"

"No. But I'm making progress." She descended the spiral stairs slowly. The folds of her robe flowed around her, giving her an ethereal air. "Is something wrong?"

"We never finished the conversation we started earlier. The one about the engagement thing."

"You said you were going to stay on the job. I assumed that meant we'd maintain the cover story."

"A lot of people are starting to have serious questions about the authenticity of our engagement."

"I don't see any problem," she said with astounding nonchalance. "The fact that you deal in information doesn't mean we can't also be engaged, does it?"

He felt the muscles of his belly tighten. "Well, no. When you put it that way, I guess not."

"That's that, then." She reached the bottom of the stairs and smiled coolly. "The engagement thing stands."

25

There was a chill in the air on Carnival Night, but the sky was clear. Cady stood at the rear of the stage and watched Sylvia and Eleanor Middleton bestow a seemingly endless number of awards on an equally endless string of runners-up and winners in the costume contest. As each name was called, her job was to carry the ribbon to the front of the stage and hand it over to Sylvia, who, in turn, presented it to the prizewinner.

They had done six presentations so far and Cady was already bored.

She was not the only one who was losing interest in the proceedings. Midway through the awards ceremony, few in the crowd were paying attention. Those who were curious or personally vested in the results must have found it difficult to hear the announcements over the loudspeaker. The tide of noise and laughter had risen steadily throughout the evening. The music that swirled out of the cafés and bars added to the good-natured din.

At the front of the stage, Sylvia, gowned in

a flowing Renaissance-style cloak, prepared to hand out the next prize as Eleanor made the announcement.

"*. . . and the winner in the junior mask design division is Benjamin Tanner . . .*"

Via Appia and the surrounding streets and lanes were thronged with costumed revelers. The sidewalk cafés were filled. Strings of brightly colored lights and billowing banners marked the entrances to shops, galleries and boutiques that had remained open for the event.

From her position on the colorfully draped stage, Cady had a bird's-eye view of the crowd. She could not see Mack and Gardner, however, although she knew where they were. Earlier, the two had commandeered a table at one of the outdoor cafés. They had vowed to hole up there with the twins and a monster pizza until the awards ceremony was finished.

Undaunted by the fact that she was losing the attention of her audience, Eleanor droned on cheerfully into the microphone.

"*. . . second runner-up in the adult amateur costume design . . .*"

A frisson of awareness passed over Cady. Beneath the heavy folds of her black cloak, she felt tiny goosebumps on her arms. Oh, damn. Not again. Not now. The last thing she needed was another panic attack.

There was a small flash of silver at the edge of her eye. She turned quickly and was just in time to see light glint briefly on a shimmering mask. In the next instant it was gone as the costumed figure vanished back into the throng.

Electricity trickled across the back of her neck, stirring the small hairs there.

Take it easy. Just one more mask in a sea of masks.

But it had been a silver mask. Full face coverage, not just the eyes.

So what? There were dozens of silver masks in the crowd. Eleanor Middleton's mask was silver, for that matter.

She knew what it was that was making her edgy. The mask she had glimpsed a few seconds ago was identical to the one she had found inside the box that had been delivered to Jonathan Arden.

There was no reason to think Arden's mask and costume had been unique. Besides, he had skipped town, according to Mack. Why would he take the chance of showing up here in Phantom Point on Carnival Night? It made no sense.

On the other hand, when you got right down to it, how much risk was actually involved for Arden? Tonight he was just one more masked reveler among many. Talk about being incognito.

". . . and in the category for best professional costume design in the traditional style we have five nominees . . ."

The disturbing restlessness was almost overpowering now. She had to get another look at that mask, Cady thought. She would feel a whole lot better if she could just assure herself that it was not concealing the face of Jonathan Arden.

She glanced toward the front of the stage. It would take Sylvia and Eleanor another twenty minutes to get through their list of nominees and prizewinners.

She stepped behind the heavy red and gold banners that concealed the framework at the rear of the platform and caught the attention of a young woman who was working with the electrical equipment.

"I've got to leave for a while. Can you take charge of the ribbons?"

"Sure." The woman hurried up the steps and disappeared around the banners.

Cady picked her way through the maze of cables and wires that littered the pavement at the foot of the steps.

The stage had been erected at the mouth of a service alley that opened onto Via Appia. The easiest way out was through the narrow passage that connected to a side street. She followed the route, intending to use the next intersection to work her way back to the place where she had spotted Arden. She hoped that he was still in the vicinity. If he had wandered off, she might not be able to find him in the crowd.

She arrived at the end of a short lane and turned the corner to return to Via Appia. The crowd was much thinner here, a block off the waterfront. There were several masked-and-gowned people congregated around tables that had been set out in front of a restaurant, but otherwise she had no difficulty moving quickly.

She was halfway toward her goal when she felt another prickle of awareness. Instinctively, she halted in the shadows of one of the few doorways that had not been decorated with a string of lights.

Arden was walking swiftly toward her down a short cross-street that led to the marina. She held her breath as he went straight past her.

When he reached the cluster of tables that had been set up on the sidewalk, she moved out of the doorway to follow him.

Another chill shot through her. Why would Arden come here tonight? He should have been a thousand miles away.

As she watched, he went quickly past the restaurant and melted back into the shadows. She realized that if he continued in that direction, he would arrive at the marina.

As far as she knew, Arden did not own a boat.

She drifted in his wake, allowing plenty of space between them. The handful of noisy revelers in the area gave her adequate cover until she reached the end of the street.

Ahead of her, Arden was only a shadow moving quickly toward the marina gate. She followed more slowly and came to a halt near the wall of a darkened building. As she watched, he opened the marina gate and went through it. He disappeared among the dozens of boats moored in the shadows.

The large grid of floating platforms was poorly illuminated. Most of the boats were also dark.

She waited for a moment, wondering if Arden would reappear. But nothing happened. The sense of swiftly approaching disaster grew stronger, however. She was tingling from head to toe.

She reached beneath her cloak, pulled out her cell phone and punched in Mack's number.

He answered on the second ring. What

with the voices, music and general din around him, she could barely hear his greeting.

"Easton here."

"Mack, it's me. You won't believe this, but I think I just spotted Jonathan Arden —"

"Where are you?" he cut in swiftly.

"Near the —"

The figure came up behind her so swiftly she never had a chance to turn around. The phone was yanked out of her hand before she could finish the sentence. A gloved finger hit the disconnect. Simultaneously she felt cold metal pressed against the back of her neck.

She could not see the object but every nerve ending she possessed recognized the barrel of a gun.

"I knew that you were going to cause me trouble before this was finished," Stanford Felgrove said, much too pleasantly. "Annoying little bitch. You know, you remind me of your aunt."

"Are you out of your mind, Stanford? What do you think you're doing?"

"Keeping an appointment. Let's go."

He planted a hand between her shoulder blades and pushed her forward. At least the gun no longer touched her skin, she thought.

"Where are we going?" she asked.

"Through the gate. Someone is waiting for us on my boat."

She was scared but not as scared as she should be, she thought vaguely. What was wrong with her? She ought to be in full-blown panic mode. The man was holding a gun on her, after all.

But this was Stanford Felgrove. She had known him since she was a teen. It was hard to believe that he would pull the trigger.

Or maybe she was simply in a fugue state, dazed with the horror of it all. Perhaps her mind had disconnected, just like a cell phone.

With Stanford behind her, she went through the marina gate. The long sweep of her costume cloak caught on a wooden post. She stumbled and jerked the garment to free it.

Ahead, the array of boats loomed in the shadows. She could hear the soft, hungry murmur of the water lapping at the docks. She glanced down between the slats and saw only impenetrable darkness.

For some obscure reason, that was when the real fear kicked in. She froze in midstride, fighting to breathe.

"Keep moving." Stanford shoved her forward again. "You know which boat is mine."

If she did not get control of her nerves, she would have no chance at all. *You can move through the panic. You've done it before. You know how to do this.*

She focused on her breathing and felt it grow more even. Old habits took hold in a crisis, apparently. All those years of regular yoga exercise had not been wasted, she thought. Who said obsession was a bad thing?

She concentrated on walking deeper into the maze. Felgrove's large white-hulled cruiser was moored at the far end of the marina.

"What is this all about, Stanford?"

"It's about salvaging what I can from this mess," Stanford said, still speaking in that unnaturally pleasant voice. "You and that bastard Easton have caused me nothing but trouble. I was so close. So damned close."

"And then my aunt got suspicious."

"Arden described an elderly woman who had called for an appointment and I knew right off that it was Vesta Briggs. I don't know how she figured out what was going on, but when the old bitch postponed the vote on the merger proposal, I realized we had a problem."

The docks were much darker here on the far side of the marina where the larger boats were moored. The low-level illumination was further reduced by massive shadows cast by the looming hulls of bigger vessels.

At the edge of the floating platforms the black waters slapped and slithered and whispered of endless night. Stanford's big cruiser was only a few feet away now.

"Did you kill —"

Cady never finished the question. The explosion of the first round of fireworks interrupted her. Flashes of light sparkled in the night sky above the marina. She sensed Stanford's flinch, heard his muttered oath and realized that he was as wired as she was.

Another boom echoed as the second stage of the fireworks lit up the sky.

"Move." Stanford gave her another urgent push toward the big boat at the end of the dock. "We don't want to keep Arden waiting."

"What is going on here?"

"Arden arranged this meeting. The s.o.b. thinks he can blackmail me. The note I got implied that he would take a payoff to remain silent about my connection to the frauds. But I have other plans. I've worked too hard, too long to lose everything to a small-time, double-crossing con man."

Reality descended with a horrifying rush. "You're going to kill Arden, aren't you?"

"He hasn't left me much choice. Bastard will bleed me dry if I let him do it. That's the way it works. The leeches never let go."

She gripped the edges of her cloak. "What about me?"

"I'm afraid that you have only yourself to blame for what is going to happen tonight, you stupid bitch. You should have stayed out of this."

He was going to kill her, too.

"You think you can get away with murder?" she asked.

"Tomorrow morning the papers will report that you and Arden were killed by an unknown assailant at the height of the Carnival Night activities," Stanford said. "There will probably be some nasty speculation about just what you and a known con artist were doing down here alone on the docks at this hour but I'm afraid that can't be helped."

She had to do something, anything. There was nothing left to lose.

Another burst of fireworks erupted across the night sky. Simultaneously, a cloaked figure appeared at the bow of the white cruiser. The dying lights glinted on a silver mask.

"There's been a change of plan, Arden," Stanford said.

She realized that he had shifted the gun away from her and was pointing it at the masked figure on the boat. More fireworks crashed overhead. Lights flashed and sparkled above the dark mirror of the water. The explosions reverberated. Behind her, Stanford tensed. She knew he planned to use the noise of the fireworks as cover for the shot.

Still gripping the edges of the cloak, she threw her arms wide and spun to the side. The heavy garment flared out, briefly entangling Stanford's gun arm.

"Bitch."

His enraged shout was cut short by the thunder of fireworks. The roar sounded closer this time but she paid no attention. She was too busy diving for the only safety — the water.

Stanford stumbled, lost his balance and slammed into her just as she went over the edge of the dock.

Strange. He was an athletic man. She would have thought he would have been steadier on his feet.

She hit the cold water with a jarring thud. The initial rush of panic was nothing compared to the stunning shock of finding herself ensnared in the heavy cloak.

The thick folds of the costume absorbed water swiftly. The garment was suddenly a massive weight dragging her downward. To make matters worse, Stanford tumbled into the water on top of her.

What was wrong with him? Why wasn't he struggling, just as she was, to get free and get back to the surface? She kicked out wildly. Her foot struck solid flesh and bone, but Felgrove did not push back. He was caught in the folds of her waterlogged costume, but he did not seem to care.

Then she felt the brush of a lifeless hand against her ankle. Old nightmares were suddenly made real. She opened her mouth to scream and got a mouthful of cold salt water.

She understood then that the last explosion she had heard had not been fireworks. It had been a gun. Arden had shot Stanford.

Felgrove was a dead weight dragging her down into the depths.

26

Once you've learned to recognize panic, you can move through it.

Vesta's words of advice coalesced at the heart of the whirlwind of fear unleashed inside her. Cady opened her eyes underwater, trying frantically to orient herself. Light flashed above the surface. More fireworks. Well, at least she knew which way was up. That was a start.

If only she could *breathe.*

The next task was to free herself from the cloak. She found the snaps at her neck and yanked desperately. The fastenings parted. She felt her arms come free of the garment. The lethal fabric fell away into the darkness like some giant manta ray seeking other prey.

Relief swept aside some of the panic, enabling her to focus more intently. Her lungs were burning but the cloak no longer bound her. Somewhere along the line, her feet had come out of her loafers. All that was left were the leggings and the dark T-shirt she had worn under the costume. She was cold but she could kick and she could claw her way back to the surface. It wasn't that far.

Swim toward the bright lights.

She could do this. She had to do it.

She kicked out again and struck Stanford's body a second time. Once more the fear threatened to paralyze her. *Move through it.*

She whipped around frantically, desperately trying to put as much distance as possible between the corpse and herself. She bumped up against the keel of a boat. Another jolt of panic seared her nerve endings.

And then she was at the surface, sucking in fresh air, gasping, filling her lungs with the stuff. *Not so loud, what if he's still here? He'll hear you.* Fireworks burst overhead. Tears blurred her vision. Or maybe that was salt water. She couldn't be certain.

Movement on the docks got her immediate attention. From the shelter of the hull, she watched in fresh horror as a black cloak swirled in the darkness. The silver mask glinted briefly and then turned away.

Arden was still here. He was prowling the floating platforms, gun in hand. She realized that he was looking for his victims. Probably knew he had only hit Stanford, she thought. He wanted to finish her off, too.

But he was searching in the vicinity of where he had seen her and Stanford tumble into the water. She knew then that the only thing that had saved her was the frantic underwater struggle to free herself from the cloak and get away from Felgrove's body. It had resulted in her surfacing some distance from her entry point. The thunder of the fireworks display had concealed her first desperate gasps of air.

Now the boat hull shielded her, and her breathing was not quite so loud. She could only give thanks that Arden did not have a flashlight.

She treaded water in the shadow of the boat, trying not to think about the body that was floating somewhere nearby. She had no choice but to swim toward the marina entrance and pray that Arden would not realize she had escaped him until she was on dry land.

She waited until the masked figure moved to the far end of a long dock. Then she took a deep breath and eased away from the shelter of the boat hull.

At that moment a small group of laughing people appeared at the marina gate. Their voices floated out over the water. Someone said something about a party on board one of the boats.

Yes, please, please, please. Come out onto the docks to party. I'll buy the beer.

One member of the group reminded his companions that the marina was closed for the evening.

Damn. There was always a spoilsport in every crowd.

But the little group was having an effect. At the far end of the dock, Arden froze when he heard the voices. Then he whirled around and started swiftly back toward the gate, his cloak flapping angrily around him. He had apparently concluded that he could not risk hanging around to finish off his second victim of the evening.

She waited as long as she could stand it. When Arden vanished through the marina gate, she hauled herself out of the water and flopped, exhausted, onto one of the floating platforms. She closed her eyes, trying to recover enough energy to get to her feet.

So cold.

She heard the group of would-be partygoers coming toward her, felt their footsteps vibrating on the wooden planks. She opened her eyes and sat up slowly.

Someone screamed.

Another member of the group shouted something unintelligible but unmistakably near hysteria.

"Call 911. Call the cops. Call someone."

Her first thought was that she had inspired the shriek. The reaction was a little over the top, she thought. All right, so her hair was streaming around her face and her T-shirt and leggings clung to her. She didn't look that bad.

She pulled herself to her feet and started toward the group.

Then she realized that no one was staring at her. When she joined them, she saw why they were ignoring her.

They were all too busy freaking out at the sight of Stanford Felgrove's body. It floated close to the surface, where it had become ensnared in a mooring line.

Someone finally turned around and noticed Cady.

Another scream sliced through the night. Cady winced and covered her ears. Maybe she did look that bad.

"Could I please borrow someone's costume?" With an effort, she managed to keep her voice very polite. "I'm cold."

"I think I may be having an anxiety attack," Mack said in a quietly savage voice. He stopped in front of the French doors and stared out into the night. "I can't believe you followed Arden out onto the docks."

"I didn't follow him," Cady said wearily. "It happened just like I told the police. I stopped near the marina office and tried to call you. That's when Stanford Felgrove came up behind me with a gun."

"Damn it to hell." He clenched one hand into a fist and braced it against the nearest door. "You shouldn't have followed him in the first place."

Randall spoke up behind him. "Take it easy, Mack. She's been through an ordeal."

"Yes," Sylvia said loyally. "This is no time to chew her out."

"Sylvia's right," Gardner added. "I know where you're coming from here, Mack, but Cady's had a rough evening. Maybe you'd better save the lectures until tomorrow."

"Yes," Leandra said firmly. "Can it, Easton. Cady's had enough to deal with to-night."

They were right, Mack thought. The last thing he wanted to do was yell at Cady. But it seemed to be the only thing he was good at right now.

"Shit," he muttered.

There was a short, startled silence.

Cady started to giggle.

Mack swung around and glowered at her. She was curled up in the largest of the wingback chairs, wrapped in a fuzzy throw that Sylvia had found in one of the closets. She had showered and changed clothes hours ago before the interview with the police, but she still complained of a chill.

As he watched, her giggles became laughter. But it didn't sound right. There was a disturbing edge to it. Sylvia, Gardner, Leandra and Randall must have noticed the strange tone, too. All of them were gazing at her with worried expressions.

"Are you okay?" Sylvia asked.

"Yes." But the odd, high laughter continued. Cady huddled into herself and buried her face against the fuzzy blanket. Her shoulders shook. The sounds she was making changed to another note.

Randall scowled at Mack. "Now look what you've done."

"Hell, she's crying." Mack started toward her.

"Sorry," Cady gasped into the blanket. "Can't stop."

Leandra sat up swiftly. "It's okay, Cady. I've read that it's good to have a cathartic emotional release after a traumatic incident. Gets rid of a lot of the physical side effects of stress."

Cady sobbed harder.

Mack crossed the room in three long strides and plucked her up out of the chair. He sat down and cradled her fiercely against his chest. She turned her face into his shoulder and sobbed.

No one said a word until it was over. Gardner got to his feet and went to the liquor cabinet. He opened the door and removed a bottle. Mack could see the label from where he was sitting with Cady locked in his arms. It was a very old and very expensive brand of whiskey.

Eventually the tears eased. After a while Cady raised her head, blinking away the last of the moisture. Mack felt her relax against him.

"Sorry about that. I think I'm okay now."

"Delayed reaction," Sylvia said gently. "You couldn't afford to panic earlier so you held on. Your nerves finally got even."

Gardner handed Cady a small glass of whiskey. "Here. Vesta's cure for the common cold and everything else."

"Thanks." She sipped cautiously and looked at Mack over the rim of the glass. Was he going to start yelling at her again, she wondered.

"I'll finish the lecture some other time," he said. "Like tomorrow."

"Thanks, I appreciate that." She took another sip of the whiskey.

She sounded much better, he thought. She looked weary but she no longer seemed so edgy.

Gardner propped one hip on the arm of the sofa on which Sylvia sat. "I didn't get to hear the details you gave the cops, Cady, but I got the impression that Arden and Felgrove had arranged to meet at the marina tonight?"

She nodded. "Stanford said Arden had summoned him there to talk about a black-mail payoff."

"How on earth did you spot Arden?" Sylvia asked.

"I had a good view of the crowds from where I was standing at the back of the stage. I noticed him when he went past on his way to the marina. I recognized the mask and the costume he'd ordered for Carnival Night because I'd seen them the day they were delivered to him."

"Stanford went to the docks intending to kill Arden?" Gardner asked.

"Yes." Cady made no move to get out of Mack's lap. "And Arden obviously went there prepared to defend himself."

"Or because he had intended to kill Stanford all along," Sylvia suggested. "Maybe he wanted to tie up the loose ends of the scam. When you think about it, Felgrove was the only one who could testify against him."

"Maybe." Cady settled deeper against Mack. "But there's no way to know for certain what Arden's intentions were until the cops catch up with him."

"And you got caught in the middle," Mack growled. "Of all the damn fool —"

"Mack, you promised to save the lectures until tomorrow."

"Sorry." He removed the glass from her fingers and took a healthy swallow of the remaining whiskey. "Just slipped out. Couldn't help myself."

Cady turned back to Sylvia and Gardner. "The police think the whole event amounted to a falling out among thieves. Each one wanted to silence the other."

"Looks like Arden was a little faster than Stanford," Gardner mused.

Mack felt the shudder that went through Cady. He tightened his hold on her.

"Felgrove seriously underestimated Jonathan Arden," he said thoughtfully. "Probably assumed Arden was just a two-bit con artist. It never occurred to him that he might be a very dangerous two-bit con artist."

"I would never have dreamed that Stanford was capable of murder, either," Sylvia said. "The man was a full-blown sociopath and none of us suspected it."

"I always knew it," Randall said softly.

They all looked at him.

"Yes," Cady said. "You did."

"I'll never be able to prove that he murdered my mother, but I'll go to my grave believing it." Randall drained his glass. "If nothing else, he pushed her deeper into the bottle."

Sylvia frowned. "I've got to admit, Cady, I'm starting to wonder if there might be something to your theory that he killed Aunt Vesta."

"We'll never know for certain now," Cady whispered.

There was another long silence. Mack wasn't sure what everyone else was thinking, but he knew that he was contemplating the dismal fact that life doesn't always give you answers.

"Wonder how long it will take the cops to find Arden?" Gardner said after a while.

Mack looked at him. "Probably not very long."

"Unless he leaves the country," Leandra volunteered.

"There is that possibility," Mack agreed.

Randall exhaled on a long sigh. "Well, one thing is certain. Austrey-Post is in worse shape now than it ever was. When the news hits the papers tomorrow, there won't be any way to keep the facts about the forgery scam quiet. I'll have to go public and hope for the best."

"You'll get through it," Cady assured him forcefully. "Galleries have survived this kind of thing before. It will all blow over eventually."

But Randall looked unconvinced. "Maybe. If we can hold on long enough. But there's no getting around the fact that we're going to take a huge hit when this gets out. When you add the projected reduction in income to the losses we'll have to sustain in order to make the refunds to the clients who got ripped off, we'll be lucky to survive. And that's without taking into account the damage to our reputation."

Cady studied him for a moment. "You'll find a way to keep the gallery open. That's not the real problem, is it? You're afraid that if the business has to struggle for a few years, Brooke won't stick around."

Randall cupped his whiskey glass in both hands and stared down into the dregs. When he raised his head, his expression was bleak. "She always said that I was too obsessed with getting control of the galleries. Now I've got control but I've got nothing to show for it except a business that's headed for the rocks. I wanted to give her at least some of the same things that George Langworth was able to give her. But there's no chance of that now."

Mack noticed that neither Sylvia nor Gardner rushed to reassure him that everything would turn out all right in the end. Leandra just gave him a pitying glance.

It was Cady who spoke up.

"I think," she said gently, "that you're seriously underestimating Brooke."

"You really believe that she'll marry him when she finds out that his company is in such precarious shape?" Mack asked much later when they were alone.

"Yes." Cady sat on the edge of the bed and yawned widely.

He thought about it while he unbuttoned his shirt. "What makes you so sure?"

She closed her mouth and contemplated the question for a moment. "It's hard to explain. Maybe it was the way she stayed with George Langworth after she learned that he was dying. She could have walked out."

"I told you, that move could easily be interpreted as having been very much in her own financial interests. She will soon be a very wealthy widow."

Cady shook her head slowly. "No, I think she did it because it was the right thing to do."

He was not so sure, but he decided to let it go. "Guess we'll all find out what she's going to do soon enough. The news about the big shootout down at the marina will be in the headlines in another few hours."

Cady said nothing but he could almost feel the shivers going through her.

"You gave me one hell of a scare tonight," he said very neutrally. "You know that, don't you?"

"It wasn't my fault," she said automatically.

He ignored that. "This is the second time in the relatively short period that we have known each other that you have nearly gotten yourself killed. It's an unnerving habit."

"I don't know what to say." She spread her hands wide. "Normally, I live a very boring life. That's why I started taking those free-lance consulting jobs you offered."

"You went to work for me because you were bored?"

"Uh-huh." She braced her hands behind herself on the bed. "I suppose I could have joined the Marine Corps instead but they don't have a lot of openings for experts in European decorative arts."

He tossed the shirt aside. "Nice to know I beat out the Marine Corps recruitment guys."

"It wasn't much of a contest. I didn't like

the thought of wearing a uniform."

Her flippant tone irritated him. She had been through a lot this evening, he reminded himself. He had to make allowances.

Dressed in only his trousers, he walked back across the room and sat down beside her on the edge of the bed.

"Are you okay?" he asked quietly.

"Okay?"

"Do you need anything? A sedative, maybe, to help you get to sleep?"

"No." She stared straight ahead at a small, gracefully shaped vase that sat on the antique washstand. "I'll be fine."

He followed her gaze to the vase. It looked French. Probably early nineteenth century, judging by the design. "You're trying to make it all add up, aren't you?"

"Yes. But it doesn't add up, does it?"

"Not quite," he agreed.

"It all happened so quickly. And I admit I wasn't paying a lot of attention to details. But I don't think Arden was there to negotiate a blackmail deal. He had that gun in his hand when he appeared on the bow of the boat. He came prepared to do murder."

"I suppose it's possible that he brought the gun along to defend himself in case Felgrove tried something violent. But why try to hunt you down later?"

"Because he realized that I could identify him. He has no way of knowing that I recognized his mask and costume, of course, but he certainly knows that I heard Stanford call him by name."

"According to the info that Ambrose dug up on Jonathan Arden, there's nothing to indicate a history of violence."

"People change. You're the one who said that just because Dillon had no record of being a stalker, it didn't mean that he might not become one."

"True."

He fell silent, thinking.

"What is it?" she asked eventually.

"I don't want to add to the confusion, but what makes you so sure that it was Jonathan Arden behind that mask tonight?"

She stilled. "I told you, Stanford called him by name."

"Stanford didn't see his face, either, did he?"

"Well, no."

"Stanford said he got a note? Not a phone call?"

"Yes, I think so."

"But he and Arden had been working together for quite a while. They were partners in the scam. If Arden decided to blackmail

Stanford, why didn't he just pick up the phone and issue the threat verbally? Why send a note?"

Cady's eyes narrowed. "Because Stanford would realize that the voice on the other end of the line was not Jonathan Arden's?"

"When you think about it," Mack said, "Arden would have to be a complete fool to wear a costume that might be noticed and traced to him and to the scene of a murder."

A short time later he sat in front of the computer and contemplated possibilities. He needed to see the pattern more clearly. He could make out some vague outlines but he could not bring the picture into focus. Thoughts of how close he had come to losing Cady kept interfering with his concentration.

After a while he opened the file that contained his notes regarding Jonathan Arden. He studied the contents for a few minutes and then he called up an e-mail form and addressed it.

Cady materialized in the doorway. "Mack? What are you doing?"

"Sending a message to Jonathan Arden."

"You're kidding." She hurried into the room. "Where did you get his e-mail address?"

"Ambrose pulled it off the internet." He did not look up from the screen. "There's no way of knowing whether or not Arden will check his e-mail. He's on the run, after all. But it occurred to me that he might be interested in doing a deal."

"What are you offering?"

He did not reply. Instead, he typed the message and then shifted slightly in the chair so that Cady could read over his shoulder.

Understand you did not kill Felgrove. If you want some help proving it, contact me. You have information that I need. We both have a vested interest in finding the real killer.

Cady straightened. "Think he'll get in touch with you?"

"Don't know." Mack shut down the computer. "But it's worth a try."

27

The following morning he poured freshly brewed green tea into two mugs. It wasn't that he was getting used to the tea, he told himself. It was simply that it was too much work to make a pot of tea and a pot of coffee. Settling for tea was more efficient.

Besides the tea wasn't so bad. Hell, maybe he was getting used to it.

Cady wandered into the kitchen, sat down at the table and picked up the mug he placed in front of her. She said nothing. Just took a long swallow. He studied her closely. The strain around her eyes told him that she had not slept any better than he had.

"Did you do your yoga?" he asked.

"Yes."

"Doesn't look like it did much good."

"Thanks. Good morning to you, too."

He took the seat across from her and helped himself to a slice of toast. "We've got to stop meeting like this."

She blinked owlishly. "Like what?"

"Like this." He moved a hand to indicate the sunlit kitchen. "You. Me. Having cozy little chats after you nearly get killed. It's hard on my nerves."

To his chagrin there was no answering glint of amusement in her eyes.

"You don't have to make it sound like it's a regular habit," she muttered into her tea. "We're only talking two occasions here, that's all. Hardly a routine occurrence."

"You probably won't believe this, but a lot of people go through an entire lifetime without having even one close call with a murderer."

"Is this the start of the lecture? Because if it is, I'd better warn you that I am not in the mood for it."

"No, this is an attempt at breakfast banter. I'm saving the lecture for later."

"I can't wait."

He eased his own mug aside and folded his arms on the table. "Are you all right?"

"Yes. Just a little tired, that's all."

"Any sign of a panic attack?"

"No." She put the mug down very hard on the table. "Look, if you're afraid that I'm going to have a nervous breakdown on you —"

"Take it easy."

"I'm not crazy, you know."

"I know."

"And neither was my aunt." Cady tightened both hands around the mug. "Everyone likes to say that she was flaky and eccentric, and maybe she was. Sylvia talked her into semiretirement, but the bottom line is that she was perfectly capable of running Chatelaine's right up until the day she died. She was not losing it, like everyone believes."

"I never said she was crazy."

"And I'm not going to lose it, either," she continued with dogged determination. "Just because Aunt Vesta and I had some things in common, just because of the tendency toward panic attacks, just because she never married and my marriage was a non-event, and she didn't have kids and it's starting to look like I won't ever have any either, *that doesn't mean that I'm a walking photocopy of Aunt Vesta.*"

"Stop it." He flattened both hands on the table and pushed himself to his feet, suddenly furious. "Not another damn word or I'm the one who's going to lose it. And it won't be a pretty sight."

She looked up at him with the expression of a woman who has been snapped out of a trance. "What?"

"Stop talking about losing it. And don't put words in my mouth. I have never implied that I thought you or your aunt were borderline nutcases."

"Sorry." She looked down into her tea. "Guess I'm still a little stressed out."

"You've got a good reason to be stressed." He moved his shoulders, working out the kinks. "I'm a little tense myself. Maybe it would help to get to work."

She got slowly to her feet, cradling the mug in her hands. "Good idea."

"I've been thinking." He picked up his mug and walked to the door that opened onto the hall. "We've got two sets of facts. One set fits the murder of your aunt to promote the merger. The second set fits the fraudulent furniture scam. There's some overlap. I want to see if that tells us anything new."

He felt her hesitate behind him.

"Mack?"

He stopped at the door and turned. "Yes?"

"You really don't think I'm a wacko?"

"No," he said. "I don't think you're a wacko. Let's go see if we can figure out who murdered your aunt."

Forty minutes later Cady sat back in her chair and surveyed the stacks of printouts that had been sorted into three piles on top of the desk. "I'm pretty good at detecting forgeries but reading runes is not my forte. What does it all mean?"

"For starters, they're credit card receipts, bank statements and financial records, not mysterious runes. I had Ambrose pull information from the accounts of everyone on our list who had something to gain by the merger or the scam. Now we look for overlap."

She shrugged. "The biggest overlapper was Stanford Felgrove. He had a lot to gain from both scam and merger. But he's dead."

"Whoever murdered him must have figured to gain something by it. The more I go over this, the more I'm convinced that Arden didn't shoot him. He had nothing to gain and a lot to lose."

"Maybe he thought Stanford would implicate him in Aunt Vesta's murder."

"I think that's a very remote possibility. If we're right in assuming that Arden wasn't the killer last night, then we need to find someone else who had something to gain."

"Or to lose," Cady said softly.

"Yes," he agreed.

"You're thinking of Brooke Langworth, aren't you?"

"She's on my list, yes. She had a personal investment in the merger because she intends to marry Randall after her husband dies."

"All right, for the sake of argument, let's say she had a motive to murder Aunt Vesta. Where's the connection to the forgery scam?"

"I'll admit I don't see an obvious link, but that doesn't mean I won't find one."

Cady thought about the afternoon she had talked to Brooke in the hushed mansion where impending death had hung in heavy folds. "I just can't see her killing someone in cold blood. If she was the type to do that, she probably would have gotten rid of George by now. It would have been easy enough to push him into the grave. He's a very ill man. There must be a lot of drugs in that house, including some strong opiates."

He hesitated, tapping the tip of the pen against a bank statement. "All right, I'll give you that point. I'm not sure I buy the logic, but you have raised a legitimate issue."

Cady made a face. "Well, there goes our one and only suspect. I sure wish Jonathan Arden would call or e-mail you. Maybe he really does know something we could use."

"Contacting him was a very long shot," Mack warned. "We can't count on help from that quarter."

"So, now what?"

"I'm going to call Gardner." Mack reached for the telephone. "He knows more about the financial aspects of this situation than anyone else, and it all comes down to the money."

Sylvia stood at the window of her living room and peered out into the garden where the twins played with the dogs and their new toys. Cady knew that she was brooding.

"Do you think Gardner can help Mack get to the bottom of the mess?" Sylvia asked.

"I don't know." Cady slouched deeper into her chair and rested her arms along the curved cushions. "I sure hope so. I have to tell you, Sylvia, this whole thing is getting on my nerves."

"It's getting on everyone's nerves." Sylvia folded her arms. "Damn. I thought it was all settled last night. Arden killed Felgrove to avoid being implicated in the fraud scheme. It made perfect sense to me and to the cops, apparently."

"Mack doesn't think it makes sense, and neither do I. We're both sure that Arden is too smart to have worn that costume. He had to know that someone might see it and trace it back to the shop where he purchased it."

"You really do believe that Aunt Vesta was murdered, don't you, Cady?"

"Yes. I've had a bad feeling about the way she died right from the start."

"One of your feelings," Sylvia repeated softly.

"Yeah."

"Tell me, is it the same kind of *feeling* you get that allows you to tell a fraud from the real thing?"

"Sylvia —"

Sylvia turned around. "It's all right. I've always known that when it came to an eye for art and antiques, I would never be as good as you or Aunt Vesta. That's why she left the shares to you, of course. In the end, she just couldn't bear the thought of leaving Chatelaine's entirely in my hands."

"No, that's not true." Cady shoved herself up out of the chair. "That isn't why she did it."

"She wanted someone like herself at the helm. Someone who could look at a piece of furniture or jewelry and see the truth in it. Someone with that special sixth sense."

"That's not why she left me the shares," Cady said very steadily.

"Maybe she was right," Sylvia whispered. "I've got a head for business. I have a vision for the future of Chatelaine's. I can make the company a major force in the art world. I can do a lot of things as the CEO of the firm.

But I'll never have her special talent and she knew that."

"Chatelaine's doesn't need someone with a great eye for art and antiques. It needs someone with great business instincts. You've got those, Sylvia. You can always *hire* the art experts you need. Heck, you can hire me to consult for that matter. But having a good eye doesn't mean I can run a huge business successfully. And it certainly doesn't mean that I want to run one. For the record, I don't."

"What are you saying, Cady?"

"I'm saying that when this is over, I intend to transfer my voting shares to you. I'll retain my nonvoting stock, but I do not want to be actively involved in the day-to-day operations of the firm."

"Do you really mean that?"

"Absolutely. I trust you to do what's best for Chatelaine's. Aunt Vesta trusted you, too. She understood that the firm needed sound business skills at the top. She always meant for you to take over."

"Then why did she leave her shares to you?" Sylvia asked.

"From what I can figure out, she changed her will at the same time that she uncovered the forgery scam. She wanted to be sure that Chatelaine's wouldn't go through with the

471

merger if something happened to her before she could figure out what was going on. She wanted to protect the company. I was her insurance policy."

"You mean she knew that you would sense that something was wrong and push for answers?"

"I think so, yes."

Sylvia groaned. "Why didn't she talk to me and to Randall? Why didn't she discuss her concerns?"

"Because she was going on a hunch and she knew that no one would pay any attention to her if she explained that she had one of her feelings. Also, I think that, deep down, she was afraid that Randall might be involved in the scam. She wanted to be absolutely certain of her facts before she made any move."

"Nonsense," Sylvia said dryly. "She didn't explain herself because she was secretive, obsessive and weird. And getting more so by the day."

Cady exhaled wearily. "That, too."

There was another pause before Sylvia spoke.

"Are you really going to walk away from Chatelaine's again?" she asked.

"Yes."

Sylvia shook her head, bewildered. "I

don't understand how you can give it all up without a second thought."

"I don't like the corporate world," Cady said patiently. "I've never liked it. I much prefer my small consulting business. Aunt Vesta understood that."

"It wouldn't surprise me to know that she had some premonition of her own death," Sylvia said quietly. "She seemed more withdrawn than usual there at the end. I thought she was depressed and suggested she talk to her doctor about medication but she refused."

"Does that mean that you're buying into my theory that she was murdered?"

"At this point, I'm willing to look at all possibilities."

Cady grinned briefly. "The mark of a born CEO."

Sylvia's face relaxed into an answering smile. "Thanks, cousin."

"Hey, Syl?"

"Hmm?"

"Do you think I'm secretive, obsessive and weird? And getting more so by the day?"

"Truth?"

Cady steeled herself. "Yes."

"I think you have definite tendencies in that direction."

"Damn, I was afraid you were going to say that."

"But," Sylvia added very deliberately, "I don't think you'll end up like Aunt Vesta, if that's what's worrying you."

"It is worrying me. What makes you think I won't end up like her?"

"Because you're going to get married one of these days and have a family."

"Having a family will save me?"

"Definitely. A husband and kids of your own are just what you need to keep you from turning inward the way Aunt Vesta did. Our poor aunt never knew how to love anything or anyone except Chatelaine's."

"That's not true." For some reason she felt obliged to leap to Vesta's defense once more. "She loved us, you and me. In her own way."

"She did not *love* us. She was heavily *invested* in us because we represented the future of Chatelaine's. The company was all she cared about."

"Hmm."

"You don't sound convinced."

"Well, it's an interesting psychological theory, but I'm not sure it really explains why Aunt Vesta turned out the way she did."

"Got a better theory?"

Cady wrapped one hand around the

wooden frame of the window. "I think that Aunt Vesta lived alone all of her life because she never found anyone who could understand and accept her."

Sylvia made a small, dismissive sound. "I'll bet she never tried very hard to understand and accept someone else, either. She was the most self-absorbed person I have ever met."

"You don't know that for certain."

"No, but I think it's a safe guess." Sylvia looked at her thoughtfully. "You're in love with Mack Easton, aren't you?"

Cady tightened her grip on the window sill. "I'm not sure. Maybe."

"I expected a little more certainty from you," Sylvia said dryly.

"Hard to be certain when there are so many uncertainties involved."

"I don't understand. What, exactly, is uncertain?"

"He's a widower, Syl. He loved his first wife very much and he's already gone through the kid-raising process. I think he sees that part of his life as finished. Now that his daughter is in college, I believe that he's looking forward to the next stage."

"And the next stage does not include starting over with a new wife and family?"

"He was honest about it. He told me that

he finds it very convenient and comfortable to keep his relationships limited to undemanding affairs. He's in the process of selling his house. Says it's too large for him now that his daughter has left home and he's on his own again. Says he plans to travel more. Expand his consulting business."

"Well." Sylvia tapped one finger on the windowsill. "Either he's trying to be very up-front and straightforward with you so that you don't get the wrong idea, or —"

"Or what?"

"Or you completely misunderstood him."

Cady scowled. "I don't think I misunderstood him."

"One thing is for certain, you can't go on in limbo like this. What are you going to do?"

A twinge of panic lanced across her nerves. Automatically Cady resorted to deep breathing. "There's not much I can do about it except wait and see how things work out."

Sylvia chuckled. "Now, that approach does not sound like the Cady I know."

"You expect me to be more proactive or whatever it is you CEO types call it?"

"Definitely. Proactive is your usual style when it comes to handling just about everything else in life, isn't it?"

Anger flared high, replacing the panic. "Yes, and you can see where it's gotten me. I have a news flash for you, Syl. Proactive women scare men."

"And you don't want to scare off Mack, is that it?"

"I keep telling myself that if I can scare him off, he's not the right one for me, but —" She let the sentence dangle, helpless to complete it.

"You," Sylvia said, "are in love."

"I was afraid of that."

Gardner walked into the study, dropped a folder on the desk and took a chair. "So, what's with you and Cady?"

Mack dragged his attention away from the notes he had been making and tried to pick up the thread of the conversation. "Want to run that by me again?"

"You and Cady. What's going on? Are you serious about her, or are you just fooling around on the side while you work on this investigation for her?"

Mack put down his pen with great care. "Are you by any chance asking me if my intentions are honorable?"

"Yes, I think that's what it amounts to." Gardner helped himself to coffee from the pot Mack had made earlier. "Doesn't seem to be anyone else around to do the job. Her parents are in England and her brother is back East. Sylvia says that leaves me."

"Sylvia gave you your marching orders?"

"More or less." Gardner tried the coffee and grimaced. "How long has this stuff been sitting here?"

"Couple of hours." Mack leaned back and gripped the arms of his chair. "I didn't ask you to drop by so that we could discuss my relationship with Cady."

"I know. That's what I told Sylvia. Also told her that Cady can take care of herself."

"But Sylvia still felt you should brace me?"

"Afraid so." Gardner started to rise. "Mind if I make a fresh pot of coffee?"

"Later. Let's settle this other matter first."

"Thought you'd say that." Reluctantly, Gardner sat down again. "Just give me a yes or no on the Cady issue. I'll report back to Syl and we'll be finished with the problem."

Mack slowly removed his glasses and set them down on the desk. "You mean you will be finished with the problem. I'll still be stuck with it."

Gardner's mouth twitched at the corner. "Sorry about that. But you're the one who got involved with Cady."

"Yes."

"Sylvia and everyone else in the family is afraid that if she doesn't get married and have a normal family life, she might turn out like Vesta."

"Weird?"

"In a word, yes."

"Each to his or her own." Mack adjusted his glasses and looked down at the notepad. "Now, I've made a list —"

"Hang on, I didn't get an answer to Syl's question, and between you and me, I don't dare go back without it."

Mack raised one brow. "Yes."

Gardner frowned in confusion. "Yes, what?"

"Yes, my intentions are honorable. Now, do you mind if we get to work?"

Gardner blinked a few more times and cleared his throat again. "Uh, no. Don't mind at all. What did you need from me?"

"You told me that even though Chatelaine's accountants checked out the merger proposal, you also took a look at it."

"Right. Vesta and Sylvia wanted someone in the family to go over it just as an added precaution." Gardner sighed. "For all the good it did."

"Don't beat yourself up over the fact that you didn't spot the income from the frauds. You couldn't have known about them.

That's not what I wanted to talk to you about."

"What did you want to discuss?"

"Tell me exactly how the shares in the new company would have been distributed if the merger had gone through," Mack said.

"It was kind of complicated," Gardner warned.

"That's what I was afraid of," Mack said. He held the pen poised over the notepad. "Define complicated."

Twenty minutes later Mack put down the pen and studied the notes he had made while Gardner explained the stock distribution plan.

"Well, damn," he said. "I've been looking in the wrong place."

Gardner leaned forward, an uneasy expression on his face. "What do you mean?"

"I've been going on the assumption that the people with the most invested in the merger were all —"

The phone warbled loudly, interrupting him. He scooped it up swiftly. "Easton here."

"This is Jonathan Arden. I got your message."

Mack sat forward quickly. "Where are you?"

"That's not important. I called to ask if you were serious."

"About finding the real killer? I'm very serious. It's in your best interest to get serious about it, too. Looks to me like whoever murdered Stanford Felgrove is trying to tie up loose ends."

On the opposite side of the desk, Gardner watched intently.

"You think I'm a loose end?" Arden asked.

"You've been set up to take the fall for Felgrove's murder. Pretty neat way to tie up a dangling thread, if you ask me."

"How do I know this isn't some kind of trap?" Arden asked.

"I won't ask you to come out into the open. But you've got to give me some information I can use. We're running out of time."

Silence hummed briefly on the line.

"What do you need from me?" Arden asked cautiously.

"Tell me everything you can about the fraud scam."

"How much do you know?" Arden replied.

"Some of it. Not all of it. I'm going on the assumption that there was a third person involved. Yes or no?"

"Yes. Took me a while to figure it out myself." Arden paused a few seconds. "I'm a little new to the art and antiques business. Most of my career has been spent in the financial markets."

"Pyramid schemes."

"I prefer to think of them as investment plans," Arden murmured. "At any rate, the bottom line was that I didn't know the players in the art and antiques business. In the beginning, I just followed Felgrove's instructions. He pointed out the clients and the fraudulent pieces of furniture and I put them together."

"Just a good salesman doing his job?"

"You got it. But after a while, I realized that Felgrove didn't have what it took to know a good forgery from a bad one. I finally tumbled to the fact that there was someone else organizing things."

"Someone who knew the territory?"

"Right. It was the third person who dealt with the Europeans and verified the quality of the products. We had to have very good quality control to make it work, you see. The pieces had to get past at least a cursory inspect by the in-house experts at Austrey-Post. It was my job to make sure they didn't stand around too long on the showroom floor."

Mack cradled the phone against his ear

and went to work on the computer key-board. "In other words, Felgrove used a consultant. An expert in old furniture who could travel on buying trips to Europe without raising suspicions."

"Yes."

"And when it all fell apart, the consultant decided to clean up the loose ends. Felgrove and you."

Arden exhaled heavily. "I have to tell you, Easton, business was a little cleaner in the financial world. Nobody ever got killed in any of my investment plans."

"If its any comfort to you, I think there's more going on here than just a simple forgery scam. I think you got caught in something bigger that went south at the same time that your psychic act ended."

"Actually, that's not much comfort at all," Arden said. "You know, a lot of this is your fault, Easton. Everything started coming apart after you showed up. Who the hell are you?"

"Friend of the family."

"Yeah, right. I tried to get some information on you but I came up with nothing useful. Everything that came back said you were just an innocent business consultant. I figure that was not an accident."

"Were you the one who arranged the

mugging attempt outside the Gallery Chatelaine?"

"That was pure desperation on my part. People who like to keep secrets often keep them close. I thought maybe there would be something in your wallet that would give me a handle on you. Unfortunately, the job of mugging you was farmed out to a bottom feeder."

"You get what you pay for. Talk to me, Arden. What can you tell me about the third person involved here?"

"Not much. Felgrove handled that end of things. My job was limited to dealing with the clients. I'm as much in the dark as you are."

"Give me some dates. Timing is crucial."

Arden talked for a while.

When he was finished, Mack studied the data that was coalescing on his screen. "I think I see a pattern here. Where can I reach you?"

"I'm going to take an extended vacation. The e-mail address will work." Arden hung up the phone without any warning.

Gardner was on his feet, coming around the edge of the desk. "That was Arden?"

"Yes." Mack did not take his attention away from the screen. "He wasn't a lot of help, but he did confirm my hunch that there was a third person involved. Given what you told me about the stock distribution plan and the credit card statement I'm looking at here, I think we've got a qualified candidate for the missing link. Someone who stood to benefit from both the scam and the merger. Someone who knew the territory. Someone who knows how to dive and who rented scuba gear the day of Vesta's death."

"Who the hell meets all that criteria?" Gardner stared, dumbfounded, at the name on the screen. "Damn. You're right. Now what? Call the cops?"

"Not yet." Mack was out of his chair. "We haven't got any proof. Just a set of circumstances that match up." He started for the door.

"Where are you going?"

"To see if I can find something in the way of hard evidence."

"I was afraid of that," Gardner said. "I'd better come with you."

"That's not necessary."

"Yes, it is." Gardner sighed. "Sylvia and Cady will never forgive me if I let you do this alone."

Cady stood in the vault and looked at the next row of boxes. Only a few more to go. She squeezed the little gold key tightly against her palm. Maybe she was wrong about this. Maybe the key did not open any of the glittering works of art.

There was no way to be certain unless she finished the task she had set for herself. She reached for an exquisite little casket that looked as if it had been designed to hold jewelry. The small chest was decorated with tracery, elegantly inlaid and covered with gilt work. Viennese, she thought. Seventeenth century. Property of a lady.

The doorbell chimed from the front hall. She put the casket on a small table and hurried out of the vault.

The bell reverberated again just as she reached the door. Habit made her pause long enough to peer through the peephole. She smiled when she saw who stood on the front step.

She opened the door. "Come in, Gabriella."

Gabriella was dressed in jeans and a sweatshirt decorated with a picture of a bespeckled banana slug reading Plato. The motto "Fiat Slug" formed the backdrop of the illustration.

"I came to see Dad."

"Yes, I figured that much out right away. I'm afraid that he's not here now. He was gone when I got back a little while ago. I don't know where he went but I'm sure he'll return soon."

"I'll wait."

"Did you do the bus to the city and ferry across the bay routine again?"

"Yes."

"You've had a long trip." She closed the door. "This is a weekday. Are you missing some classes?"

"I'll borrow someone's notes."

"Right. Want some tea or a soda?"

"No thanks."

"Okay, then. Maybe you'd like to help me out in the vault while we wait for your father."

Gabriella frowned. "You've got a vault in this place?"

"My aunt had it built to house her collection of antique boxes and jewelry chests." Cady started back down the hall. "A lot of them are extremely valuable."

Reluctantly, Gabriella trailed after her. "What are you doing with them?"

"I think Aunt Vesta may have hidden something important inside one of the boxes. I've got a little key that she sent to me shortly before her death. I'm pretty sure that when I match it up with the right lock on the right box, I'll find whatever it was that she concealed inside."

"No offense, but your aunt sounds like she was a little weird."

"You aren't the first person to make that observation." Cady walked back into the vault.

Gabriella paused briefly in the hall. "Is this a portrait of your aunt?"

"Yes. That was painted when she was in her thirties."

"You look a lot like her."

Cady started back up the spiral staircase to the small balcony. "A lot of people say that."

Gabriella came to a halt in the doorway and gazed around in awe. "This is incredible."

"What you see in here is a collection that was put together over five decades." Cady went along the balcony to the table where the Viennese casket rested. "My aunt loved boxes. Actually, she loved all the decorative arts. She had a great eye for them."

"Dad says you have a very good eye, too."

"That's why he hires me from time to time." She picked up the key.

"Is he going to marry you?" Gabriella blurted.

Cady's hand froze in front of the lock. She felt a familiar, unpleasant twinge. Damn. She did not need another panic attack.

"I told you that we haven't talked about marriage," she said carefully.

"I know." Gabriella took another step into the vault chamber. "I used to think that he would never marry again. But now I'm not so sure."

"I wish you wouldn't talk about marriage. Lately whenever the subject is mentioned, I feel a panic attack coming on. Have to stop and do deep breathing. It's very annoying."

"Oh. Sorry." Gabriella hesitated. "I have a friend whose mother gets panic attacks. She takes some medication when they get bad."

"I have some for emergencies. But for the past few years I've been able to handle them with deep breathing."

"I didn't mean to give you a panic attack. It's just that I've been doing a lot of thinking about what you said the other morning. You know, about Dad needing to move out of the house and get on with the rest of his life. I realize now that maybe he might want to marry again someday."

Cady looked over the balcony railing. "Would that be so bad?"

"It would be sort of strange, at least for a while. But I've been thinking that maybe it wouldn't be a bad thing." Gabriella looked up at her. "Not if the person he married really loved him."

"That would be important." Cady gently eased the key into the lock.

"It would provide him with some companionship."

"In his declining years, do you mean?"

"Yes." Gabriella brightened. "I wouldn't have to worry about him being alone."

"Do you worry about that now?"

"Sometimes. I mean, it's not like he doesn't go out and have friends and stuff. And he's got his work. But lots of times he's just there at the house, all by himself in the evenings. I mean, what if he fell or something?"

"And couldn't get up?"

"Are you making fun of me?"

"No." Cady smiled. "I think it's very nice of you to be concerned about your father. But I wouldn't worry about him too much if I were you. He can take care of himself."

"Well, sure, I know that, but he's getting older and . . ."

Cady sucked in a breath.

"What's wrong?" Gabriella demanded.

"It fits. The key fits."

Gabriella bounded up the twisting stairs and hurried toward Cady.

"Open it," she said.

Cady maneuvered the tiny gold key very gently. She heard a faint click. Cautiously,

490

she raised the lid of the jewelry casket.

A stack of faded letters bound with a ribbon and a photograph lay inside.

Gabriella peered at the old photo. "Looks like you. Except that the hairstyle and the bathing suit are seriously retro."

"About fifty years out of style."

"Your great-aunt, I guess?"

"Yes." Cady picked up the photograph and examined it closely.

It was a picture of Vesta, but not the stern, dour woman she remembered. In this picture her aunt was radiant with happiness. The shot had been taken at a beach. Hawaii, perhaps. There was a grove of palm trees in the background. Next to her aunt stood a good-looking man dressed in a pair of swim trunks. He had his arm around Vesta's waist in a casual embrace that was at once intimate and possessive.

The man looked a lot like Randall.

"Who's the guy?" Gabriella asked.

"I'm not positive, but I think his name is Randall Austrey. If I'm right, he's the grandfather of a good friend of mine."

The shock of what she was looking at hit her in a rush of excitement and dawning comprehension. Randall's grandfather and Vesta? Lovers? She glanced at the faded writing.

"Love letters," she whispered.

"Cool." Gabriella surveyed the interior of the box. "There's something else under the letters. Looks like jewelry."

"Yes." Cady reached inside to pick up the stack of letters.

"This is going to be interesting," Gabriella said. "Mind if I get myself some of that soda you offered a few minutes ago before you open the letters?"

"Help yourself." Cady studied the photo again. "The kitchen's at the end of the hall."

"Thanks. I'll be right back." Gabriella hurried down the twisting steps and vanished through the doorway of the vault.

Cady looked at her aunt's glowing face and smiled sadly. "You never told anyone, did you? He married someone else and broke your heart and you never loved again. But that's why you cared so much about Randall Post. That's why you wanted me to marry him. That's why, in the end, you wanted to do the merger. For the sake of your lover's grandson. What was it like watching him grow up and realizing that he looked more and more like his grandfather every day?"

Vesta smiled back across the years and said nothing.

Cady looked more closely at the photo. Vesta's suit and hair were still wet. She must have walked out of the water only moments before the picture was taken.

"You would never have panicked in the water." Cady looked at the palm trees. There was something about them that made her uneasy.

Then she noticed the snorkeling gear in Randall Austrey's hand.

It took her a few seconds to put it together. But when the truth exploded in her mind, she dropped the photo on the table as if it had burned her fingers.

She rushed down the spiral stairs, grabbed the phone and hit one of the numbers that had been entered into the automatic dialing list.

"So, do you do this kind of thing a lot?" Gardner asked a little too casually as he climbed through the window behind Mack.

"What kind of thing?" Mack surveyed the bedroom in which he stood.

"Break into houses. Worry about running into murderers. That kind of thing."

"Didn't used to do a lot of it, but I've been getting into it more since I got involved with Cady."

Gardner nodded and brushed his gloved hands against each other. "Figures. Never a dull moment."

"Not so far." Mack opened a closet door.

"What exactly are we looking for?"

"I'm not sure." He tried another closet. "I'd give a lot to find a silver mask and a black cloak, but that's probably expecting too much."

"Can't see us getting that lucky. Why don't I try the kitchen?"

"Good idea."

Gardner went down a hallway and disappeared.

A moment later Mack heard a muffled sound from the front of the house. He went quickly along the hall.

"What did you say?" he asked as he walked around the corner.

"I said, shit." Gardner appeared at the other end of the hall. He held a half-eaten apple in his hand. "Someone took a few bites out of this a very short time ago. He's not in San Francisco like we thought. He's here in Phantom Point."

"Damn."

Mack jerked his cell phone out of his pocket as he headed for the door.

The line was busy. Apparently Vesta Briggs had never signed up for call waiting service.

"Damn," he said again. He punched in 911 instead.

He was outside on the street, running now. Gardner was right behind him.

"Hello?"

"Leandra, this is Cady." She paused. "You sound breathless. Everything okay?"

"Sure. I had to run for the phone. I was in the restroom when you called."

"Sorry. Listen, I've got to ask you something. It's going to seem a little strange but just bear with me."

"I can do strange."

"Good." Cady took a breath. "When you and Parker Turner went to Hawaii a couple of months ago, did he do any diving?"

"You're right, that is a strange question." Leandra paused. "As a matter of fact, the answer is yes."

"Dear heaven," Cady said so softly that Leandra didn't hear.

"He told me that he used to dive when he was younger," Leandra went on cheerfully. "Said he hadn't been underwater in years and wanted to get back into the sport. Said that I make him feel thirty again. Isn't that sweet?"

"Dear heaven."

"He wanted me to take some introductory classes but I didn't like the idea of being underwater with all that heavy gear."

"Dear heaven."

495

"Are you okay, Cady?" Leandra's voice sharpened with concern. "You sound a little upset."

"I've got to hang up now, Leandra. I need to call Mack right away. I just hope that he's got his cell phone on."

"Okay, but —"

"Goodbye, Leandra." Cady cut the connection.

The unpleasant shivers were getting stronger. The sense of urgency was almost overpowering.

Something was very, very wrong. It took her a second to realize what it was.

There was no sound coming from the kitchen. Not even the closing of a refrigerator door.

Too quiet.

Cady hung up the phone and went swiftly up the little staircase, trying to make no noise on the wooden treads.

Once on the balcony she opened the door of the nearest display cabinet and picked up the heavy medieval steel chest inside.

The hall was no longer silent. She heard the faint rustle and scrape of shoes on tile. Two sets of footsteps, not one.

A shadow moved in the doorway. Cady looked down from her perch and saw Gabriella walk slowly, hesitantly into the vault. She was unnaturally stiff and awkward in her movements. Fear shimmered in the air around her.

"Come out, Cady," Parker Turner said loudly from the hall. "Or I will shoot her right in front of you."

Cady said nothing. She stood very still at the edge of the balcony, the heavy chest clutched in her hands. People never looked up when they first entered a room, she told herself. Almost never.

"She's not here." Gabriella swung around quickly. "Can't you see that? She must have heard you. She's gone for help. You'd better get out of here."

"Unpredictable bitch. Just like her damned aunt. I know she's here somewhere."

Parker took a step into the vault to check for himself.

Cady hurled the steel chest straight down toward his head.

At the last instant, he must have sensed the movement above him. He jerked backward in time to avoid taking the chest on his skull. The steel box caught him on the shoulder.

He yelled, his voice hoarse with rage and pain. He reeled backward into the hall, reflexively shying away from the source of the assault. The gun clattered loudly on the stone floor, skidded and disappeared partway under a cabinet.

"Get it," Cady shouted. "Get the gun." She threw herself down the staircase.

Gabriella, demonstrating that when it came to a crisis, she was her father's daughter, was already on the floor groping for the weapon.

A sickening thud sounded from the hall. Cady, halfway down the steps, glanced across the room. Through the open door, she caught a flash of khaki.

Gabriella sat up, the gun in a two-handed grip. She had the weapon pointed toward the door.

"Don't shoot, Gabriella. That's your father out there."

"*Dad.*" Gabriella put down the gun and struggled to her feet.

Sirens sounded in the distance.

Gardner peered cautiously around the edge of the door. "Someone got a gun in here?"

"It's okay." Cady leaped to the bottom of the steps. "Where's Mack? Is he all right?"

Gardner glanced to the side along the hall. "He's a little busy at the moment. Looks like he's trying to pound Turner's face into the floor."

28

Two hours later Cady sat with her friends and family in the living room of Vesta's villa amid the remains of the four oversized pizzas that had been delivered a short time earlier.

"Twenty-two years in the business," Sylvia said. "Most of it spent in the old furniture department."

"Aunt Vesta always said he had a great eye for the European pieces," Cady muttered.

"I still can't quite take it all in," Gardner said. "Turner was the brains behind the whole thing. Amazing."

"He got the idea after Leandra's divorce," Mack said. "He knew that Felgrove was greedy enough to go for the fake furniture scam. It was such easy money, after all. Parker made sure that all of the pieces moved through the Austrey-Post galleries so that if the frauds were discovered, Felgrove would be the one left twisting in the wind. Once he had Stanford sucked into the arrangement, he started applying pressure to propose the merger to Chatelaine's.

"He had been close enough to Vesta for a

long time and knew that she cared deeply about Randall and the future of Austrey-Post. He was sure that she would want to protect the firm for Randall's sake. The only way to do that would be to agree to the merger."

"He also thought he had me in the palm of his hand," Leandra spoke dully from the depths of a chair. "So much for my plans for a more mature, adult relationship."

Cady and Sylvia exchanged an uneasy look. They both knew that Leandra was bravely trying for her trademark breeziness but they also knew that she wasn't hitting the right notes. Discovering the truth about Parker Turner had hit her harder than she wanted to admit.

"What would have happened if Leandra had refused to marry him?" Sylvia asked.

Mack shrugged. "The furniture scam was very lucrative. He probably would have continued on with it until it was exposed. Then he would have quietly disappeared and left Stanford Felgrove to take the heat. But Turner decided to go for the brass ring."

"He wanted to marry into the business," Cady said.

"Yes."

Oblivious to the emotional undertow, Gardner sat forward on the edge of the sofa.

He frowned thoughtfully at Mack and then switched his gaze to Cady. "Weird, when you think about it."

"What's weird, dear?" Sylvia asked.

"That both Mack and Cady figured out that Parker was at the bottom of both the scam and Vesta's murder at about the same time today."

"Just another case of psychic interception," Mack said dryly. "No big deal. Happens all the time between two people who are endowed with E.S.P., like Cady and me."

Gabriella looked deeply pained. "Come on, Dad. This is serious."

Mack helped himself to another slice of pizza. "I live to embarrass my daughter."

"There are better hobbies," Cady murmured.

He gave her a disturbingly intimate look. "Yes, indeed there are."

Talk about E.S.P., she thought. She could certainly read his mind. But she decided to ignore the sexy message in his eyes. It was clear that, like Leandra, Mack was still juggling some difficult emotions. Gabriella had been in great danger that afternoon. A father would not soon forget that. He would not forget the reason why his daughter had been put at risk very quickly, either.

A sense of despondency settled over Cady. It was her fault that Gabriella had nearly gotten killed.

Sylvia looked at Mack. "Cady told us that she put two and two together when she saw the photo of Aunt Vesta on a beach and suddenly remembered that Parker and Leandra had gone to Hawaii and that diving is one of the big things to do there. But what was your cue?"

"I talked to Jonathan Arden and confirmed that there was a third person involved in the scam," Mack said. "Someone who knew old furniture and had contacts in Europe. That shortened the list somewhat. At about the same time, Gardner gave me a rundown on how the stock would have been distributed if the merger had been completed."

Gardner picked up a slice of pizza. "I mentioned that under the terms spelled out in the proposal, Randall and Stanford could sell or distribute their shares of stock in whatever manner they wished so long as the recipient was a member of one of the stock-holding families. The definition of a family member included anyone related by blood or —"

"Or marriage," Sylvia concluded grimly.

"As part of the price for putting the fraud

scam together, Parker planned to blackmail Stanford into turning over some of his voting shares in the new Chatelaine-Post."

"In addition, he intended to marry me," Leandra muttered. "Parker figured there would be no problem controlling my shares, too."

"Between the two blocks, he would have wielded a controlling interest in Chatelaine-Post," Mack said.

"Things were going according to schedule," Cady said, "until Aunt Vesta uncovered the first of the frauds. When she realized the scam involved someone inside Austrey-Post, she postponed the vote on the merger."

"Parker knew everything was about to fall apart. He panicked and killed her," Mack added.

Tears leaked from beneath Leandra's eyelashes. "So much for Mr. Nice Guy."

"You're missing the point here," Cady said gently. "Parker wasn't a nice guy."

Early the next morning she sat on the bottom tread of the spiral staircase, the stack of letters in her lap.

Mack came to stand in the doorway.

"Who wrote the letters?" he asked.

"Randall's grandfather. Randall Austrey."

She used the sleeve of her robe to wipe her tears. "Aunt Vesta loved him and the sonofabitch used her."

"How?"

"When she met him, she was a curator at a small museum. He was just about to open Austrey-Post. He needed her eye and her insider's knowledge of the art and antiques business to help him build a reputation. She fell head over heels for him. They had an affair." Cady touched the stack of letters. "I think it must have gone on for some time."

"Your aunt gave Austrey start-up advice?"

"Yes, but even more important, she introduced him to all the right people in the business. One of them was a woman named Meredith Small. She was from a very wealthy, very well-connected family. When Austrey had established himself and no longer needed Vesta, he decided that he wanted to marry Meredith instead."

"Did Randall Austrey and Vesta continue seeing each other?"

"Yes. But not in the way you mean. They moved in a lot of the same circles, so they ran into each other at openings and auctions and such. It must have been very painful for her." She smoothed the letter in her hand and recalled the advice that Vesta had given her in her last phone call. *It's all well and good for a client to find you useful. But don't let yourself be used.* "That bastard had the nerve to try to restart the affair at one point even though he was married. Aunt Vesta refused."

She set aside the letter, got to her feet and went to the gleaming jewelry chest that stood open on the table. She reached inside.

"I found this beneath the bundle of letters," she said.

She opened her palm and showed him the Nun's Chatelaine. It gleamed with the unmistakable patina of old gold and antique gems. Five intricately fashioned gold chains dangled from the medallion, spilling through her fingers. Small gem-studded keys were attached to four of the chains. There was no key hooked to the fifth.

He walked forward to stand on the opposite side of the table. "Impressive. What are you going to do with it?"

"I'm going to give it to Sylvia. She's the one who will have the task of guiding the gallery into the future. She's the true chatelaine of Chatelaine's."

He looked thoughtful. "Well, then."

"Well, what?"

"Now you can go back to your art consulting."

For some reason that observation annoyed her. "Yes."

"I believe you mentioned something about becoming my competition."

Pain lanced through her. She tightened her hand abruptly around the Chatelaine. Her future in the art consulting business was the last thing she wanted to talk about this morning.

"There's room for both of us in the field," she said gruffly.

"Sure. But it occurs to me that if we combined forces we could move into the big time."

She wondered if she'd heard him correctly. "Are you suggesting a merger?"

"I think so, yes."

Anger replaced the pain. She stared at him. "Is this your way of getting rid of the competition?"

"No, it's my way of asking you to marry me."

"Oh." Joy washed away the anger. "Oh, Mack."

"I love you, Cady."

"Oh, *Mack*." She hurled herself toward him.

He opened his arms to catch her. "Is this a yes?" he whispered into her hair.

"Yes," she said. "Yes, yes, yes. I love you, Mack."

"Glad to hear it."

"I mean, I really *do* love you." She heard the wonder in her own voice and almost laughed out loud. Then she noticed the figure standing in the opening.

Gabriella wore her bathrobe and the slightly bewildered expression that went with having been awakened from a sound sleep. She blinked a few times at the sight of Cady in Mack's arms.

"What's going on in here?" she asked.

Mack smiled at her. "I just asked Cady to marry me. She said yes."

"Cool."

Cady searched Gabriella's face for signs of anger or resentment. But there were none.

"I sort of figured that would happen sooner or later," Gabriella added. "Congratulations."

Cady grinned at her. "Just think, your father won't be alone in his declining years after all."

Gabriella laughed.

"Yeah," she said, "and I won't have to worry about him falling down and not being able to get up, either."

"Am I missing something here?" Mack asked.

"Nothing important," Cady assured him.

29

One Year Later . . .

Midway through the party, Mack found Gardner alone near the buffet table.

"I hear Spooner's show was a big success," Mack said.

"So I'm told." Gardner took a large bite of a cracker topped with cream cheese and caviar. "Sold every picture. Looks like he's on his way. Guess the guy just needed some time to get his act together."

"Lot of people getting their acts together lately."

They both looked across the crowded living room to where Dillon Spooner and Leandra stood with Brooke and Randall. There was an aura of quiet happiness around the small group. Gold wedding rings gleamed on the left hands of all four people.

Mack glanced at the light-and-color-drenched canvas hanging on the wall above the buffet. It was a glowing abstract vision of the view from the gardens of the hillside villa on Via Palatine, the same view that Mack saw every morning when he walked out onto the terrace. Dillon had offered to paint the picture as a combination wedding and house-warming gift shortly after Mack and Cady had moved into their new home.

"Glad I got one of Spooner's paintings while I could still afford to invest in him," Mack said.

"Hey, after the way you got that jerk Turner out of Leandra's life, something tells me Dillon would be willing to paint free pictures for you forever."

"It was Cady who brought me into it," Mack reminded him. "If she hadn't been suspicious about the way in which Vesta died, Turner would be a member of the family by now."

"A member of the family with a controlling interest in my wife's company." Gardner's expression hardened. "Every time I think about how close that s.o.b. came to getting his hands on Chatelaine's, I start sweating."

"I know how you feel." Mack helped himself to a slice of cheese. "Still sorry that good old Uncle Randall wasn't the villain?"

Gardner chuckled. "Randall's okay. Between the marriage to Brooke and the job of salvaging Austrey-Post, he doesn't have time to hang around Sylvia and Cady making a pest of himself the way he did in the old days."

"Cady was right about Brooke. She didn't give a damn about Austrey-Post. She was only concerned about Randall."

Gardner used his plastic fork to motion toward Ambrose Vandyke, who stood with Gabriella near the open terrace door. They were deep in conversation with Dewey, Notch and a sparkling Hattie Woods.

"Speaking of marriage," Gardner said, "looks like things might be getting serious between your computer genius friend and your daughter. Does that worry you? They're a little young."

"I know. But falling in love at first sight seems to be an Easton family tradition. What worries me is the fact that I might be getting a son-in-law who can buy and sell me and my entire company several times over."

"And he'd only have to dip into his petty cash account to do it. Still, I can think of worse things than being related to a multi-zillionaire."

"I'll keep that in mind."

"Look on the bright side. He works for you."

Sylvia walked toward them, smiling. The Nun's Chatelaine glittered richly on the belt of her silk trousers. "A lovely party, Mack. Too bad the guest of honor slept through it."

"Yeah, he does that a lot. If you'll excuse

me, I'll go check on him."

Mack picked up one of the cheese-and-caviar-smothered crackers and went into the hall. He walked past the new offices of Lost and Found, with its rooms full of high-tech office equipment and its matching partners' desks. He climbed the stairs to the second floor, walked down the short corridor to the nursery and came to a halt in the doorway.

The cradle was a fanciful Regency piece in the so-called archeological style. It was covered with carved griffins, sphinxes and other mythical creatures. A gift from Hattie Woods.

A colorful, giant-sized plastic replica of the Nun's Chatelaine hung above the cradle. A gift from good old Uncle Randall.

In the corner, a full-size reproduction of a suit of sixteenth-century armor stood guard. A gift from Dewey and Notch.

Cady glided gently in the rocker. She held their infant son to her breast. The happiness in her eyes stole his breath.

"Thought I'd find you up here," he said.

"Did you leave our guests on their own?"

"They can take care of themselves for a while." He could not take his eyes off her and the baby. The wonder of it all never failed to amaze him.

511

"What is it?" Cady asked.

He propped one shoulder against the doorframe and folded his arms. "Just realized I was looking at our future."

"How does it look?"

"Pretty terrific," he said.